what i would do for you

WINTERS

this
love
hurts

W WINTERS

USA Today best-selling author, Willow Winters, brings you an all-consuming and breathtaking romance you won't soon forget.

Some love stories are a slow burn. Others are quick to ignite, scorching and branding your very soul before you've taken that first breath. You're never given a chance to run from it.

That's how I'd describe what happened to us.

Everything around me blurred and all that existed were his lips, his touch…

The chase and the heat between us became addictive.

Our nights together were a distraction, one we craved to the point of letting the world crumble around us.

We should have paid more attention; we should have known that it would come to this.

We both knew it couldn't last, but that didn't change what we desired most.

All we wanted was each other…

Do You Want Me, the prequel of this epic tale of both betrayal and all-consuming love, is included.

"The emotions Willow evokes in this are on another level. This small glimpse into the world of Marcus is thrilling, chilling, a little bit sweet and a whole lot of just wow. You won't want to miss this one."—Ky Reads Romance

dedication

I would be remiss if I didn't mention a group of women who inspire me and keep me moving forward always. I have blatantly taken quotes from these wonderful people regarding the way they talk about my heroes and placed them right in the books.

"I would gladly live in hell with him."

"I need a word that means more than love."

I love you all both for the encouragement you give me and simply for the people you are.

I hope I can give you even a piece of what you've given me.

Lots of love and kisses.

Now, buckle up! I promised you a wild ride with a tempting *tick, tick, tick* all the way up until we fall down this gripping roller coaster.

He who fights with monsters should look to it that he himself does not become a monster. And if you gaze long into an abyss, the abyss also gazes into you.

—Friedrich Nietzsche

part i

do you want me?

prologue

Delilah

H IS GAZE IS SHARP; HE HAS THE MOST PIERCING BLUE eyes I've ever seen. As I freeze where I'm standing in the middle of the aisle, the faint noise of dull music mixed with the sound of carts rolling by fades into the background. It all blurs together in aisle four of the grocery store as my grip on the loaf of bread I'm holding turns so clammy that the plastic slips.

The pitter-patter of my racing heart and my blood rushing in my ears is all I can hear.

Nothing else matters. I can feel his eyes on me. Every time I blink, I see them, surrounded by shadows.

I take my time, placing the items from my cart back on the shelves with trembling fingers. There are only four things seeing as how I just got here, a bag of rice being the first item to go back on the bottom shelf before I slowly and meticulously roll my cart to the end of the only aisle I've been down.

It's chilling, the fear that rolls down my spine knowing he's watching me. Feeling him again. *Is it fear, though?* My heart beats wildly in response to the question, fighting and railing against the decision to act calm. I can't let anyone know. I just need to get out of here… So we can be alone.

My heart isn't afraid, not like my logical side is. When the shadow is just barely seen, tall and foreboding, my stomach drops and my heart flips with recognition. It's an undeniable feeling when you miss someone you know you shouldn't. I try to focus on the sound of wheels squeaking against the linoleum floor and the noisy clang of metal from carts being lined up in order to help ground me.

"Do you need any help?" The question comes from a young man in a red vest that barely hides the nondescript black logo on his white shirt beneath it. I recognize him; I've seen him a number of times in this grocery store. I'm certain he's rung me up a handful of times since I returned here a month ago.

How did I think I could move back, even if the house is on the outskirts in the middle of nowhere, and *he* wouldn't find me? How could I be so foolish to think he wouldn't come for me?

A sinking feeling in my chest moves my hand there, and the paper list in my hand crinkles as I do. I'd forgotten all about it and as I gaze down at the blurred pen lines and wrinkled paper, I do my best to school my expression.

"Oh, no," I say and my throat is too tight as I speak. I close my eyes, forcing a simple smile to my lips and clear my throat. "I just realized something," I answer, finally looking the young man in his deep brown eyes. "I have a call in ten minutes and I'm going to take it in my car then come back," I lie, that smile staying in place although everything in my body wants me to run. Run from here, get far away from other people.

The young man, who looks like he's college age or maybe younger, offers me a friendly smile in return. "Understood," he says with a nod and returns to lining up stacks of carts with the one I've just brought back up front.

Even now, as I take each deliberate step through the glass double doors that slide open automatically as I approach and feel the cool breeze of early spring against my heated face, I try to rid myself of the memories that flash before my eyes.

The bar. The drinks. The feel of a chilled glass of white wine mixed with the scent of whiskey from the man next to me. The court cases and late nights spent getting lost in bed with a man I knew I shouldn't be with. The flirtation, rules being broken.

My heels click as I remember losing my law license, as every dreadful moment returns with the stain of blood. So much blood. Acts of passion that couldn't be taken back. The pain that's already present mingles with so much more.

Wrapping my arms around myself, I attempt to protect my body from the wind but it's useless. The weather isn't what batters me.

The remembrance of his lips on mine and the searing heat of his light touch, force a gasp from me. It's a short one full of longing, knowing those moments are now nothing more than lost ghosts of the person I was. Of the people we were before it all went to hell.

All of the memories are a cocktail that infuses into my conscious thoughts as I listen to my keys clink while I unlock the door to my sedan with a low beep that fills the practically vacant lot. From the time I entered the grocery store to now, a mere fifteen minutes at that, the sun has decided to set, casting a shade of red across the dark tree line of thick forest beyond the store parking lot and stealing the light that was here only a moment ago.

The leather seat groans and the door shuts with a loud thud. All I can do is sit here, my purse now on the console. My keys in my right hand, resting against my lap with the metal digging into my palm since I'm gripping them so tight. My breathing comes in faster and faster although I'm doing everything in my power to stay calm. *He'll be here soon.*

When I hear the click of the back door opening, the one behind my seat, I close my eyes. He didn't make me wait long.

He enters the car accompanied by a chill from the evening wind and the car rocks gently until he's seated behind me and the door is shut. His scent fills my lungs first and as it does, I remember that I've been told that smell is the sense that holds the most memory. Maybe I read it somewhere, but I've never known something to be truer than that fact is now.

When I open my eyes, his chilling gaze is on mine in the rearview mirror and my treacherous heart chokes me in an attempt to escape. It hovers at the base of my throat, pounding viciously in protest.

I did always love him. There wasn't a moment that I didn't love him.

He knows that. He has to know that I still love him; we just simply couldn't be together. We decided. We decided together.

"You said you'd let me go," I whisper, speaking over my strangled breaths.

My gaze never leaves his, even as tears prick my eyes. Not until he answers me.

"I changed my mind."

chapter one

Delilah

Two years before

I'M NOT CRAZY, RIGHT?

My phone buzzes with my sister's text at the same time as another glass of chardonnay hits the small bar-height tabletop in front of me. The round table has a two-foot radius if that; it's meant for two people max but my purse takes up half of it. Making the point quite clear: it's my table.

"Thanks," I say and offer the waitress a smile from where I'm perched on the stool. With a small nod, the all-smiles, petite brunette in a short black dress keeps it moving. She's cute, young, and damn fast on her feet. Plus, Sandy has a good memory. Taking a sip of the chardonnay, I know she told the bartender to make sure he poured my favorite brand. Sandy's table is my go-to every Wednesday. Apps are half-priced so this place is packed on Wednesdays… but it's packed with the right people. I plant my ass in this seat in the far corner of the bar where I can see everyone else, and Sandy keeps the glasses coming.

As I told an old friend from law school once, this waitress is the only hero I need after a long day in court.

The music is easy, the lights dim, and the lemon scent from whatever they use to polish all the dark wood in here is my heaven after spending every fucking day in hell. A.k.a. Judge Malden's courtroom.

I only get a single sip of the smooth wine before my phone buzzes again, vibrating against the menu beneath it that effectively takes up the other half of the table. With most of my light coming from the simple white candle on the table, I read the text, the bright light of my phone's screen hurting my tired eyes for just a moment.

They make me feel like I'm crazy.

Swallowing the harsh truth, that our parents do that to me too sometimes, I answer my sister quickly. My dark red nails fly across the letters on my phone: *It's just the way they handle things. You aren't crazy. It happened. They just want to pretend it didn't.*

Returning to my wine, my gaze flutters from the filled glass to the front entrance as it opens. The two wooden doors with iron handles are wide, worn, and heavy.

This place isn't classy. It's a pub, more or less. But the food is good and the drinks are even better. The latter is why this place is filled in the evenings and everyone comes here after work from a block down around the corner. I've made more deals in this very seat than I can count.

Maybe I'm off the clock, but I never stop working. My job is my life.

When my phone buzzes next, I take a moment to glance around the place before looking at the text message. The white wine slips past my lips, painted the same shade of red as my nails, as my gaze moves from Patterson in his dark gray suit and then to Miller and her subordinate. Patterson's an older man who's been divorced three times now because of his workaholic and alcoholic ways combined. All three of them are lawyers. Well, the third wants to be. I don't know what the hell his name is, but she's taken the young man under her wing. Another way of thinking about it is that she's found someone tall, dark, and handsome, but dumb as rocks to do her filings.

She knows as well as all of us that he's not going to cut it. I'd never trust anyone to come within an inch of my paperwork if they can't pass the bar. A huff of disdain leaves me, but a friendly smile finds its way to my face as I lift my glass to her when her eyes reach mine.

It's short-lived and veiled mutual distaste for one another. She's as cutthroat as I am, but with two decades' more experience. Decades that also taught her she can take shortcuts and bend rules … *bend not break*, as she once said. One day, I'll be one of the bigger names and I won't do it the way she did.

My phone buzzing in my hand is the perfect out to ignore her. Unless I'm trying a case against one of her defendants, there's no reason to engage with Miss Miller. *She's the reason lawyers have a bad rap.* I check my phone again to see a row of messages from Cadence. The summary of it isn't anything I didn't already know: she understands they pretend like it didn't happen and like our childhood was full of white picket fences and tamed rosebushes. Our parents' house may have both of those now, but that's not how we grew up.

Just ignore them, I offer her in a quickly typed message. Her response is even quicker, hitting my phone before I'm able to clutch the thin stem of my wineglass again.

The front doors open, offering some light and distraction in my periphery, but I'm caught in her message.

I love you, but I can't just ignore it like you can.

She's so emotional. My sister is the child counselor at the middle school we both went to when we were kids. Of course she's wound up over this, but this is old news. It's past pain. I take a moment to think about how best to respond, knowing she's hurting. She's sensitive and she needs more support than I ever did in this aspect of life. She doesn't get it though, and I don't know that she wants to. I text her back regardless because she's my sister, and I get it. I completely understand the struggle.

You can't change the past or the way our parents cope. I'm here for you. You aren't crazy. It happened and if you want to talk about it, talk with me, not them.

The exhaustion weighs down my expression, pulling at the corners of my lips. Hurriedly, I hide it all by throwing back the rest of my wine. Spinning the large glass with my pointer and thumb finger on the stem, I take in her messages that she's okay and that she loves me.

That's all that matters, isn't it? That we're all okay now. That's what matters. I wish she could see it like that, but she doesn't. Maybe it's because she sees them more than me. After all, I'm a state away and she only has a neighborhood separating them from her.

As I'm typing out that I love her too, Sandy takes my empty glass and replaces it with another, this one filled nearly to the brim.

"Long days deserve large glasses," she says beneath her breath with a sympathetic tone and a knowing wink. The grin I give her is wider and more genuine than I've given anyone all week. *My girl.*

My fingers toy with the stem absently as I stare at my phone, waiting to see if Cady has anything else to say. I don't know what to tell her. I don't ignore what happened or the fact that my parents pretend like everything's fine. I wouldn't even say that I've moved on. I've just simply moved forward. The past doesn't haunt me anymore. She should let it go too.

"White wine?" A deep voice from my left is followed by the sound of wooden legs grinding against the slate floor as he pulls out a stool and takes a seat. *Agent Cody Walsh.*

I wish I could have contained the jump in my shoulders and

the way my heart beats wildly at the sudden sound of him sneaking up on me.

"Shit, sorry," he says and his tone is light as I laugh, letting my body sway gently as I shake my head, peeking up at him through my thick lashes. I hope my lipstick is still in place. He told me once how the dark red looks good on my light brown skin. I don't wear it just for him, but I can't deny that I like it when he sees me in this particular shade. His gaze drifts to my lips then. That's when the butterflies happen. My thirtieth birthday behind me and I still get butterflies.

Shaking it off is easy for me, but stopping this smile from growing as this handsome man eyes me … well, that's not so easy. Neither is stopping the heat of a blush from creeping up my cheeks all the way to my temple.

"It's fine," I say as I wave him off and seek refuge in my glass of wine. Within seconds I'm in control, relaxed and myself again. I don't know if he saw the heat I felt or if he thought it was just embarrassment, but Cody is a gentleman, so he doesn't say either way.

"I just wanted—" he starts, but Sandy interrupts, dropping a double Jack and Coke in front of him. "Thanks, Sandy," he answers, his tone different. More professional maybe. My stomach doubles over in the best of ways and then that feeling travels lower as I wonder if he talks to me differently than he does to other women.

When I'm consulting with his team, it's men only. I rarely see him out of the office. Especially since they go out of town so much.

There's an obvious masculinity to the strong man in front of me. A hard edge that doesn't seem to matter whenever he flashes me a charming smile. I've spent a number of nights with a toy between my legs, thinking about him. Watching him in interrogation rooms, observing the way he works and the manner in which others look up to him, does something to me. He's only in his late thirties, maybe in his early forties, but the way he does just about everything has an air of authority that's undeniable. Being a member of the FBI will do that to you I suppose.

It's sexy as hell. As he reaches for the glass, palming it with his large hand and takes a swig, I glance at the muscles in his forearms, out to play tonight since he's rolled up his button-down's sleeves. They sure as hell don't hurt his sex god image I've conjured up in my head.

I've been in this town in Pennsylvania since I left New York five years ago. Walsh happened to come here too from Virginia. The same case brought us here and we both stayed. Maybe it's camaraderie from the now cold case or maybe it's the mutual misery we've endured in this gray town riddled with corruption, but every time I see this man, I want to be under him more and more by the end of the night.

"Just wanted to say," he starts again, setting down his glass, the swirling amber liquid more Jack than Coke and he keeps his blue eyes focused on it rather than me for the half second. Reaching my gaze, he tells me, "I'm sorry you went through that hell yesterday."

Confusion hits me first. Then a blip of reality. Right. Of course he's thinking about business and not fucking me into his mattress.

"It was nothing."

"It wasn't nothing. There was no reason for her to bring up that shit." His tone is deathly low although there's nothing but compassion there.

"Her" meaning the reporter, a blonde with perfect hair who goes by Jill and works for the local eleven o'clock news. And "that shit" meaning the case that brought us both here five years ago.

We were both in deep, both devastated when every lead gave us nothing and the one man we could track down ended up dead. There was nothing left that we could do. The murders stopped and the evidence didn't lead to anyone still living.

"It's fine, Walsh," I say, shutting down his anger with a flat tone of my own and reach for my wine again, but I don't drink it. "She's not a lawyer or a detective. She has no idea what she's talking about."

"No," he answers and waits for my gaze to meet his. My chest hollows but somehow feels full just the same when I see his steely blue eyes. "It's not fine." His last statement is almost a murmur. He's the one who breaks our stare to look down into his full glass and then empty in a second when he throws it all back.

I don't look back at him, even though I can feel somebody's eyes on me. Someone else is watching me. There's a prick that travels up the base of my neck, making the small hairs there stand on edge. I can feel it. But not a soul is looking at me when I glance around the room. A shiver rolls down my spine.

The chilling sensation doesn't stop and I have to turn around toward the small window near our table to check there too, but no one's there either.

"I'm sorry, maybe I shouldn't have brought it up." Cody's somber tone forces me to look back at him and I do what I haven't done even once in the years I've known him; I lay my hand on his. The touch is hot, smoldering even, sending a tingle up my arm that jolts me. It's only a fraction of a second before I realize what I've done and I quickly move to pat his hand, but from the look in his eyes I know that he knows a friendly pat wasn't my intention.

"It's really," I say then clear my throat and clasp my hands together in my lap before continuing. "It's fine, I promise you. I can take her criticism when I know I did everything I could."

The first thing I learned in this field is the truest statement: *everyone wants someone to blame.* If Cody doesn't catch the bad guy or if I don't get him convicted … well, then it's one of the two of us who gets blamed.

Cody's gaze drifts to my lips for just a moment; I know it's brought on because I snag my bottom lip between my teeth and maybe he notices the lipstick.

He clears his throat like I did and sits up straighter, the empty glass in his hand staying where it is since the place is busier now and Sandy is nowhere to be seen. With his broad shoulders squared, he looks straight ahead rather than at me when he speaks. "It's not your fault we didn't catch the bastard," he murmurs and for a moment I question if he meant those words for me or himself.

"You want another?" I offer him, not liking this conversation and wanting the easy air between us again.

Tapping the base of the glass on the bar, Cody pauses and then glances up at me, a boyish smirk crossing his face. "Only if you have it with me."

Just like that, all the tension is gone and the smile I had for him when he first sat down comes back.

I tell myself that I'm not like my mother. I don't forget. I don't pretend. I'm aware of my reality.

I'm simply making the best with what I've got.

Right now, that's a tall glass of chardonnay and a handsome man to keep me company. Even if I go home alone to an empty apartment and a too-hard mattress that makes the tight muscles in my back even tighter, I'm doing all right for what I've been through.

chapter two

Delilah

SOME DAYS YOU'RE THE DOG. SOME DAYS YOU'RE THE *hydrant*. My auntie Lindie told me that one when I was young. A student in my freshman high school class pulled my hair. So I pulled hers back. I was the one that the teacher saw and the only one who got in trouble. Both my mother and auntie had things to say about that, but when it came down to what my punishment would be back home, my mom told me to keep my hands to myself unless detention was worth it. My auntie said detention was always worth it and then she gave me that wise line about dogs and hydrants. That day I got in trouble I was the hydrant.

Today, I'm in that bitch of a position again.

"One thing after the other," I whisper into my coffee. The steam flows around my cheeks. The sinful smell of caffeine addiction is the only thing that's been comforting so far today.

My desk chair groans as I lean back in it, staring at the plaque to the left of my door then the framed news article beside it. My

JD and a story about the first case I ever won, which was published in the town's paper. Six years ago I had so much more energy than I do now.

My laptop is closed and I just simply can't find the stamina to open it again. Instead, I find myself wishing I'd just stayed in bed all day and never answered my phone.

As a sigh leaves me, I chance a sip of coffee. It's still too hot, but not scalding like it was when Aaron first brought it in. The shade of brown matches my walnut desk and I find myself smiling over the color of the coffee. I suppose in rough days it helps to be grateful for the little things. And then I catch sight of the bruise on my hand. The same shade as the grain in the desk. *So long, gratitude. See you whenever I find that thing called patience.*

Ignoring the bruise, I turn my attention to the case file laying open on my desk and read the first bit for what's now the fourth time since I first sat in here. The constant ticking of the clock seems so loud today that I stare at it rather than the black and white words and inwardly curse myself.

I never should have gotten out of bed. I never should have answered my phone to deal with my mother. I sure as hell would have made it to the curb on time to move my car so I wouldn't have gotten that ticket. If I hadn't seen the ticket as I was getting into the car, I wouldn't have slammed my hand in the door. And, most importantly, if I wasn't pissed off and in pain, I wouldn't have said what I said to the press when I was walking into the building.

I shouldn't have said it and I shouldn't have gotten out of bed. Tension twists my gut. It's bad; today is a really, really bad day.

Pinching the bridge of my nose, I do everything I can to calm myself down. To pretend like my boss isn't going to walk in here and chew my ass out any minute now.

The parking garage is just across the street. Our building lies between an office complex and small commercial strip. The coffee shop is all the way on the other side, which is a six-minute walk, tried and true. So when I parked with fifteen minutes to spare and a hand that was throbbing just as hard as the headache my mother gave me, I knew I needed coffee.

What I didn't need was the press waiting for anyone from the Assistant Attorney General's department so they could ask questions about a case that slipped through my fingers.

Microphones and camera crews first thing in the morning get my adrenaline going in a way I used to crave. I can even admit that back when I first moved here, I loved the sight of them. The high of knowing information and having a voice that mattered meant so much to me. The fact that I worked on cases that were worthy of press was enough to keep a soft professional smile on my lips and a confident gleam in my eye as I strode along confidently with my simple black leather purse kept tight to my side. I paired a power walk with red lipstick and a skirt suit worth more than my first car.

I thought I had it all back then. This morning though, and lately with the way the press has turned, it was hard enough to keep my lips pressed into a thin red line. Lipstick courage or not, I sure as hell had better things to do with my time than be battered with questions about a conviction that's been overruled.

I barely had a hand in the case. I gave my opinion and that was all.

"Anyone who helps a man do that to children, to little girls who were dead the moment he set their sights on them... a man who helps and does nothing to stop them deserves to rot in hell."

Needless to say, I didn't get my coffee. So I'm stuck here with Aaron's choice of brew. Which is too hot to drink still and every second that passes, the headache gets worse.

My statement plays back in my head followed by the ticking of the incessant clock.

And then suddenly there's a loud bang at my door. The *knock, knock, knock* hardly registers before the door is swung open.

"You said, 'rot in hell.'" Claire Eastings mocks my tone as she swings the door closed behind her with a hard thump from the bottom of one of her flats. She stands taller than me without heels, and that's saying something. Six feet tall and sixty years old, she towers over my desk with a scowl. Another thing Auntie Lindie used to say, *your face will get stuck like that.* ... Yeah, well, Claire's face is in a constant scowl. Despite her resting bitch face and all, she's damn good at what she does. So when she repeats, "rot in hell," drawing out the words with her dark brown eyes wide and full of disbelief, one hand on her wide hip with the other gripping a piece of paper so tight that she's creased and crinkled it, my stomach drops.

My fingers nervously pick at the edge of the case file as I meet her gaze. I have a lot to learn. I'll be the first to admit it. "I'm sorry; I shouldn't have said it."

"No," she agrees then throws her head back and when she does I close my eyes, wishing the ground would swallow me up. I don't react well to being scolded and especially not by someone I admire. Claire paved the way for women in this career, simply by being the best of the best. *Today isn't just a bad day,* I think as I swallow the knot in my throat, *it's an awful day.*

I know what I did. I know I messed up. Just tell me whether or not I'm going to have to sit out on cases and file paperwork as punishment. I have shit to do.

With my jaw clenched tight, I keep the words there at the back of my throat and give Claire's rant the full attention she wants.

Her pencil skirt isn't fitted and it rides up, bunching around her hips as she paces. "Are you kidding me?" she questions, her head tilted and her eyes narrowed at me. When she does that, the wrinkles around her eyes and her pursed lips deepen.

"First the mess that happened two days ago and now this? Are you—" She continues her tyrannical rage and I cut her off.

"What happened two days ago didn't come out of my mouth." Jill earns another dart thrown at her in my imaginary poster of her on the wall in my head. "That was a reporter trying to stay relevant."

"Well, this morning, 'rot in hell' certainly came out of yours."

"I apologize," I say and my sincerity is there when I meet her gaze, refusing to break it even though I'm burning up inside.

"Is it because of what was said? Is it because Jill said you're becoming infamous for serial murder cases going cold? Is that why you had to give your two cents this morning about Ross Brass?"

"You and I both know he did it." As I speak, the emotion that creeps into my voice, cracking it, is something I didn't count on. I know Claire hired me over seasoned lawyers well worth their weight because I'm hard; I keep my emotions in check. That's what she said. I have a hard edge and the emotion rarely gets to me. It's evidence and precedence and getting to the point.

Emotion is a weakness to be exploited and preyed upon in this business. I don't know if it's my family issues or the case from five years ago, but today is hard. I'm struggling to remain unaffected.

"He played a part in four girls dying and he got off on a technicality." I answer her as best I can without letting my voice crack again. It would be easy if all of this really was as simple as dogs and hydrants, but that's not the world I live in. I chose a career with higher stakes and things that truly matter to me.

Sympathy isn't something I anticipated. So when Claire's gaze softens and she takes a seat in the leather wingback across from me, I'm truly surprised.

"Of course he did. But when the evidence is tainted while it's in police custody…" she trails off then inhales slowly and shakes her head, shifting her curly auburn hair around her shoulders. With her hands thrown up in defeat, she adds, "It's on the PD for the way they handled the evidence. Not on us."

Leaning forward, I look my boss in the eye and remind her who she hired and who I am. "It's bullshit that they mishandled evidence and now Brass gets to walk." Taking in a deep breath, I make it known that I have more to say. "He does deserve to rot in hell, but I never should have said that to anyone other than you and our partners. I am sorry," I add emphasis to the last statement, my voice firm and then sit back in my seat. "I shouldn't have said it. Now I know why you say you don't talk to press after six p.m."

"If you aren't on point . . ." she begins and I finish her line for her, ". . . then don't say shit."

Claire's an early riser and gets into the office before everyone else. Claire practically lives at work and handles the press above everyone else, unless it's past 6:00. That's her cutoff. Now I know my limit: No coffee, no talking.

"I think my new rule should be no press before coffee." My muttered statement as I run my hand along the back of my neck forces a small laugh from Claire. If it can even be called a laugh since the sound is just a tad longer than a huff. Her smile lasts though, thank God.

"Are you pulling me off my cases?" I ask her and she shakes her head.

"No, but I will be giving you the cold shoulder in front of Tanner and Shaw. I can't let them think you got off easy." They're new to the prosecution team. Shaw used to handle defense and Tanner is fresh out of law school.

"I was serious when I asked you if Jill bringing up that case got to you," Claire states although it's meant to be a question.

Eating up time by hiding behind a sip of coffee, I deny the stomach drop and the pounding in my veins. "I'm fine," I answer her and then give her a tight smile followed by a distraction. "My mother called this morning, I got a ticket, and I smashed my hand in the door." Holding up my hand as evidence, Claire winces.

"All before coffee?"

With a nod and a click of my tongue, I answer, "Without a single sip."

Within half an hour, she's out the door, my coffee is gone and all of it goes to the back of my mind as I force myself to actually get work done and make today productive at the very least.

Time slips by as I catch up on a case that goes to trial next week. I'll be looking over Tanner's shoulder and he'll be pissed because of it, but it should be an open-and-shut case. The evidence is damning. It would take one hell of a defense or one hell of a fuckup for Tanner to lose this one.

I was so wrapped up in it that I didn't see the missed call from my mother. There's not a chance in hell I'm calling her back until I talk to Cadence. They got into it again.

If Cadence implied that she dates men who hit her because of what we saw when we were children, then my sister crossed a line. And that's exactly what my mother said she told her. I'm not her psychiatrist, but I don't understand why she'd say that. Mom said Cadence was drunk, but I just can't see that and it was hard enough to decipher it all through my mother's tears.

Intent on getting a cup of coffee from Brew House down the block, I head off, checking my phone and noting that my question to her from this morning asking if she's okay has gone unanswered.

I have two more cases to prepare for and one of them is first-degree murder.

This ... tension between my mother and my sister can wait until tonight. That thought is what's on my mind when I'm aware of the familiar prick. The feeling like someone's watching me. The same one I felt last night. A glance over my shoulder proves no one's there as I pass under the awning of a bookstore. That doesn't change my gut feeling though and that fear lingers the entire walk down the block.

I make it there in under four minutes, the insecurity forcing my pace to be fast enough to get my heart racing.

Ordering the flavor of the day with cream and sugar, two of each, I convince myself it's just the case being mentioned. The case from five years ago has never left me.

It should have stayed in the past. It *did* stay in the past. One little blonde reporter with a camera behind her can't bring back ghosts long dead.

I slip the change the barista gives me into the glass jar for tips and listen to it clink as she thanks me and then I make that decision firm—the case is long over with and long gone—and that decision is not to be overturned.

The cold case is dead and there's no one watching me. All the confidence of that statement vanishes about halfway back to the office, when I swear I feel eyes on me again.

chapter three

I KNOW THERE'S A PILE OF LETTERS IN THAT LOCKED FILE cabinet by my feet. Creased from the mail and some crumpled from anger, they stare at me from beyond the thin old metal that keeps them locked away.

What haunts me isn't the past when they were first mailed to me, it's the fact that I got another today. A crisp new letter to join the others.

How long has it been since I last knew *he* existed? Years, I know, but almost five years ago I sent him one after the next and our tenuous relationship became one sided. For a year, we exchanged information. He stopped returning the letters, he stopped giving me hints that started as a taunt and changed into a mutual decision of execution.

Rumors on the street suggested he hadn't died. When the letters stopped, I had nothing left to go on but the fear of kids and a name people spoke of as if they were naming the devil.

A part of me wished it had all ended, but a piece of me that's far too truthful, too primitive and brutal knew one day he'd reach out again.

One day the story we started would pick back up ... I simply don't know how it will end.

The metal goes *thunk* when I kick it, staring at the old dent in the side. The memory flashes in front of my eyes, prompted by the sound. A vision of me kicking the cabinet that held the only pieces of Marcus I had when he didn't respond.

For days. For weeks. Months passed with no word as the case went cold and I lost it. But hadn't I lost everything long before then? Who was I to feel anything at all but relief when Marcus stopped interfering, stopped taunting me, stopped the long-held conversation we had between right and wrong and who was next on the list.

Whiskey licks my lips and the empty glass on my desk suggests that thoughts of the angel of death serial killer will beg me to fill the glass to the brim once again.

I've picked apart the letter, every word and the unique cadence in his writing. I used to think his poetic nature meant he felt highly of himself. But when I realized who he really was, everything made so much more sense.

Knock, knock, knock, the door bangs in time with a friendly rap.

"Yeah?" I question.

"We're going to Bar 44, you coming?" Steve's voice is boisterous. As far as everyone else knows, the case is still cold. They don't know there's been another murder with the same MO.

I can't give them one letter without letting on about the others. And in those, I'm just as guilty as he was. *Not in the beginning. Not until I realized...*

"Be there right behind you. Just wrapping up something," I call through the door. Feeling far too sober than I'd like, but grateful that I haven't reverted back to the raving lunatic I felt like years ago when Marcus left me all alone to dwell on what we'd done.

Steven is off with an "all right, see you soon," and it doesn't take me long to follow. Getting ahold of myself and convincing myself that this letter doesn't change anything.

After all, there are no bodies. No list of names that he's given me.

There isn't even a riddle.

He only gave me a simple message and it's one I agree with. *Ghosts come back and I wish they didn't. He started again.*

Maybe he's gotten as lonely as I have. Maybe he's simply using me again. Although I can't blame my part on him.

A deep inhale then a slow exhale makes my chest rise and fall before I take off my jacket and change shirts to go out to the bar tonight, all while pretending those letters don't exist.

What would they do if they knew?

What would she do? The beautiful woman with deep eyes and a smile she holds just for me, what would she do if she knew I played a part in a case that nearly destroyed her before her career had truly begun?

The thoughts plague me the entire walk to the bar. Even the drum of laughter as I open the heavy doors doesn't stop it.

She wouldn't look at me like she does if she knew. I'm far too aware. Far too stung by the truth that she'd see me as a monster if only the letters were in her hands and not mine.

She'd hate me. I let him get away with his bidding and she would hate me more for it.

The certainty greets me at the same time as she does, with her beautiful smile that makes her high cheekbones appear even more feminine. Her tawny gaze and gentle sway of her delicate shoulders let me know she's more than a few glasses deep.

"Hard day," she says and her excuse comes with an air of ease and flirtation before I can suggest a damn thing. Her smile doesn't falter and the blush in her skin is hot against her sable skin. With the flowing lines of her slim-fitting, cream button-down tucked into her dark blue jeans, no one would deny that she's beautiful.

How someone so soft, so elegant and sweet came into this profession, I'll never know. It's like Marcus sent her to me. The thought makes me close my eyes, lowering and tilting my head in search for the waitress.

Whiskey will be my lover tonight.

"It's been a week since I've seen you." There's an accusation hidden in her tone which is harder now, lacking the flirtation she greeted me with.

"Just busy, promise I'm not cheating on you." The words fly from my mouth without conscious consent as I glance up at her and those wide eyes blink rapidly, her thick lashes fluttering as if surprised, as if maybe she made up what I've just said in her mind.

I'm such a prick for leading her on. But damn do I love to be wanted by her. To be so obviously desired, it makes me feel in ways I've never felt before.

Thankfully Sandy interrupts the moment and I order my go-to Jack and Coke, although I don't actually have to say the words. I simply nod when she asks, "The usual?"

"So," I say and my gaze is drawn to Delilah's slender fingers slipping around the base of her wineglass. The pale wine is fragrant, drifting to me and mixing with the sweet smell of whatever lotion she must use. "A case hit my desk today," she starts and my hackles rise, prepared for whatever case it is to be the ghost that Marcus referred to. "The evidence is unreal, and I'm bored as hell. He's an idiot for not taking the plea."

Delilah's discontent with not being challenged with work always brings a light to my eyes, a fire deep inside of me that blazes hot to tease her, to provoke her in ways I doubt any man has before.

"Is that the case with … what's his name?"

"Tanner. Yes. It's too easy to be fun." She throws back the last bit of her glass and before I can stop her, the waitress stealing my attention for just a moment with the glass hitting the high-top table, she's reaching for the thick red jacket dangling from the back of her chair.

"I've already had enough so I'm going to—"

My hand acts of its own accord, my fingers gripping around her slender wrist. My skin brushing against hers is hot to the touch, singeing and I'm quick to take it back, but Delilah stands there, still and caught in the shadow of what happened for only a split second.

My heart hammers, my pulse quickening although I don't show it like she does. I can hide my desire so easily. I'm a bastard for even thinking about getting lost with her tonight.

I've seen this vulnerable woman standing only inches from me hide everything in the courtroom. I've seen her strong and vibrant but in front of me now, in a room full of people, the lights dimmed but the intention illuminated, she waits for me. She questions everything and I can so clearly see it.

"Right," I say, my own needs protesting against the ease with which I sit back and the calmness in my tone. "Good luck with the trial, don't fall asleep in there." I leave her with a joke that doesn't bring an ounce of humor to her eyes. Even though my gaze lands on the amber liquid as I bring the heavy glass up to my lips for a swig, the corners of her plump lips dropping are clearly seen in my periphery.

I don't know what's gotten into me. For years I've sat with temptation, joked with her and confided in her. The heat between us and the sexual tension is constant, but acting on it with all we've been through together would be wrong on so many levels.

"When are you going to take me home, Cody?" she says as her small hands land on the table. She leans forward, bringing a drift of her perfume and with a single glance, a peek down her blouse, exposing the smooth curves of her chest. The gold necklace she's wearing dangles between her cleavage, swaying until I lift my gaze, staring back at hers that's drowning in need and query.

I part my lips to answer her but she stands up straight, never breaking my gaze as she pulls her red wool coat around her shoulders and slips her black purse gracefully over her shoulder until it lands at her hip. She doesn't back down. She's never been so blatant, never been so clear as to what she wants.

"You want me to take you home?" I question her feigned innocence, but take another drink after. Alcohol and bad decisions taint the air between us.

"I had a really horrible week and I want someone to take me home," she admits to me, teasingly even, taking her eyes from mine only to pretend to glance around the room for a suitable fuck.

Anger simmers with jealousy, but my own need and greed are far more prevalent.

"We've been friends for a while, Agent Walsh. Is that all we are? Just friends?"

The way her strength leaves her, the rawness and slight suffering that are evident in her pinched brow and tightened cords in her neck as she swallows, beg me to tell her the truth.

That I've wanted her from the first time I saw her.

chapter
four

Marcus

IT'S COLDER IN THE EVENING, BITTER COLD. OF ALL THE places we've been, I love this one the most. Lincoln Park is only miles away and I still remember the first time I saw her there. Going over the details of the crime, searching for answers everyone else couldn't find. She doesn't know how close she got and if it's up to me she never will. She doesn't need to be involved.

Cody Walsh though… I think if only she pushed, she'd be able to pull out every dark secret the man has. Just like tonight.

The wind brushes against my neck, leaving a pricking sensation that I tell myself has nothing to do with the way she provocatively leaned into him back at the bar. My gaze moves from the reflection of the moon against the windowpane to the soft curve of her back as she arches. His lips barely leave her skin… not even to breathe.

That's the way I'd do it too.

Cars drive by and I don't bother to look at them. I know they can't see me here, motionless and bathed in the shadows from

Delilah's apartment building. She doesn't know a damn thing about me; maybe she thinks she does, but she doesn't. I know plenty about her, though.

Specifically, that she initially requested a different floor of this apartment building, even though this one was the only one with a vacancy on such short notice. I'm surprised she stayed and didn't transfer apartments as soon as another came available. I waited for that transition, for the challenge of following wherever she went. The workaholic never made herself a priority. Maybe I shouldn't have been so surprised by it all.

But she does that to me more than anyone else. She surprises me.

Her head falls back, her lips parting and her hair laying across her shoulders then over her back as she moves. The repetitive motion is seductive, and Walsh is very much under her spell.

Her gasps aren't heard through the double-paned windows, the gap in the curtain providing my view, but I swear I can hear her still. When her nails run along his back, right before she grips onto his shoulders, I practically feel what it would be like.

Arousal is primitive, obsession demeaning… what she is… is something hypnotizing. It was curiosity at first, then respect, and now… Well, now I'm not certain what she is to me. To us and to what we started so long ago.

With the fire lit behind them, it's the only light I have with the exception of a table lamp that casts beautiful shadows down Delilah's dark skin. Her nipples pebble and just as I'm enjoying them, Walsh takes them for himself. Devouring her flesh as he thrusts into her and forces her to hold on to him.

He's good to her and I recognize that, but it doesn't, not for a single moment, mean that I'll sit back while he plays.

We had an unspoken deal. "Had" being the operative word.

I now have something I truly desire and no reason not to take it.

chapter five

Delilah

AS MY SHOULDERS LOWER WITH A LONG EXHALE, I RUB my right one, still sore from a horrible night of sleep. My gaze never leaves the open case file on my desk. I've been staring at it for hours.

Certain lines on the paper are difficult to read as some cases are, but this one is different. Really, they're difficult to digest.

My mother's denials and my sister's concerns ring in my ears as I read the evidence. Everyone knew what was happening, but no one did anything.

How many times he beat her, where he chose to hit her. It's all documented now, but before last week, neighbors and family all took notice, and that was it. So many neighbors said they knew what was going on. Not a single one called. They didn't think it would go that far. The woman never said anything either.

With a tight throat and a rapid pulse, I swallow and put my pen to the paper, to the exact attempt we should charge him for.

Repeated abuse isn't evidence of malice aforethought. The

choices are first-degree or second-degree murder. I have to make that decision. It's difficult to determine which one we can prove when every paragraph I read is minimized by the memories brought back up so recently. The sound of the slaps and then a cacophony of painful cries that are enough to keep two girls awake in bed together, staring at the door and pretending not to cry because Mom said it was all right.

I lean back in my seat and pinch the bridge of my nose, refusing to let my personal bias affect work. The air has been different this past week and a half. Something inside of me is different and I don't like it.

I'm better than this. I've grown so much and there's no reason I can't take on this case. With a sip of coffee and a deep breath in paired with a longer breath out to calm my sympathetic nervous system—as my counselor sister taught me—I repeat my mantra until I can start from the beginning again. This time I grab a pen and travel along the pages with it to keep track, circling keywords and then scribble on a pad of paper. It's not quite a pros and cons sheet with that sharp black line down the middle of the lined paper. It's a first-degree or second-degree murder charge. Which has enough evidence to thoroughly convince a jury.

I'd focus on something else, anything else, but this needs to be submitted by the end of the day and the only other place my mind takes me is to a few nights ago when I lost myself to Cody Walsh.

Closing my eyes, I can still feel him, the sweet lingering pain of a good fuck even though it's been days. That's all he left me with, though.

I woke up to a slight hangover and an empty bed. If it wasn't for the throbbing between my legs, I'd have thought it was only a dirty dream about a coworker.

Fuck, what did I do?

My attention is so far off from what I need that I shove both the case file and the pad of paper to the left and decide to go for a walk, to clear my head instead.

I haven't seen Cody since that night. I haven't spoken to him either. A deep pain settles inside my chest, digging there and planting seeds of insecurity and doubt.

The insecurity that stands with me as I head to the other side of my office makes me think it's all a childish crush. It was most likely a one-time thing. He may even think it's a mistake. I wouldn't know, since he hasn't spoken to me.

I barely ever dated my entire life. I dated one guy in college for a few months and that shitty experience was enough to convince me to focus on my studies. I had a fuck buddy, though. And then another in law school. It was exactly what I needed. I focused on my work and there was someone around for the release when either of us needed it.

The thought of Cody being just a fuck buddy sends a sharp pain straight through my chest, one I don't expect.

I've always struggled when it comes to men. *I suppose I have my father to thank for that*, I think bitterly as I slip on my red wool coat and cinch it tight around my waist. My sister would argue it's our mother I should blame.

The wool strap digs into my palms as I pull the belt even tighter, staring at one article on the wall and then the next, the light from the large window behind my desk shining against the pristine glass.

Nostalgia lingers for a moment, back to the moment I started hanging the articles. I focused on putting monsters behind bars and got the hell out of our Podunk town in upstate New York.

I was so proud of this office. I thought I'd really made it and it would only get better. I thought *I* would only get better.

The door swings open without an invitation and Claire stares at my desk for a moment, her tall figure draped in a brown twill pantsuit. The expression on her face is foreboding but loses its strength when she takes in an empty desk.

"Right here," I speak up, squaring my shoulders and giving her a questioning look in return to her stricken expression.

"Did you see this?" Her voice is lowered and it's only after she hands me the paper that she turns away from me to shut the door to my office. It's not a loud bang, it's gentle. Nerves prick at the back of my neck as the rolled newspaper crinkles open between my fingers.

Claire Eastings is never gentle.

"Fuck," I mutter as I scan the article.

"'Fuck' is right. They're having a goddamn field day." Claire's comments are accompanied by her pacing back and forth in her short heels, muted from the modern woven carpet until she steps on the hardwood flooring. Then back onto the carpet and so on and so forth.

That rug is the single piece in this room that differs from the rest of the offices. Everyone else has framed photos like me, although mine are articles. Everyone else has the same black leather stationery set on a mahogany desk and an entire wall lined with bookshelves filled with necessary reference texts.

My coat is the only splash of life and color in this place. Disappointment carries to my lips, pulling them down as I refuse to read any more of the article.

"I'm not surprised," Claire comments with her arms crossed as she stands in front of me, her pacing momentarily paused. "You opened the door for criticism."

She's referring to my unfortunate "rot in hell" experience, mentioned in the article … *twice.* "I know," I answer her with a heavy breath and suddenly my rendezvous with Agent Walsh doesn't seem to matter anymore.

"He walked, there's no proof if we can't use the evidence," I say and frustration coats every word. "Ross Brass got off. The press will fade. It's not going to trial. It's done."

"It should have been done. The press can keep it alive and

compare to any other case they want." It surprises me that she's letting it get to her.

"Do you want me to issue a statement?" I offer, feeling that insecurity creep up my spine. "I can't be blamed for the PD's errors."

"No, no …" Unfolding her arms, Claire looks past me and her gaze seems far away. There's no anger, no fire blazing there. Defeat wades in the depths of her irises. It sends a chill down my spine.

Clearing my throat, I question her, "What is it that you want me to do? How are we handling this?" Although my voice is strong and I'm able to stand tall, crossing my arms at my belly and still gripping the paper, I feel anything but when Claire looks me in the eyes again.

"Someone's looking into your background. We were alerted to the files being opened, including cold cases."

Chills flow down my arms and I stand there breathless, expertly maintaining my composure.

"You can't believe the press—" I didn't read it all, but the first line suggests that I'm either incompetent or mishandling cases. I have no doubt that the journalist is good friends with Jill Brown.

"That report is nothing but the product of a wild imagination and a witch hunt," Claire says confidently, cutting me off.

"Exactly." Stress pushes down my shoulders as I respond. "They can just say whatever they want and we … what?"

She nods, continuing before I can make my own guess. "We assume someone is doing an exposé on a member of the Assistant Attorney General's office. A member with an impeccable record, but whatever ghosts you're hiding, I think you should prepare for them to come to light."

"Is there really nothing else they have to write about? Especially given that I've closed how many cases? My reputation is solid and one of the best on this team."

"It's not just work," Claire says then looks behind me at the two picture frames on my desk. "They will turn over every rock."

"I don't have anything to hide." A tingling heat spreads over my skin, denying what I said. But I don't have anything to hide. "I haven't done anything wrong. I've never mishandled anything."

"I know. We can't have that here."

A bitter vein of offense laces my voice when I answer her, "I'm aware of that. They can write whatever article they'd like. They can drag me through the dirt. It'll last for a moment until I win a trial and another. Or until they have something more interesting to write about."

The cords in Claire's thin neck tighten as she swallows. "Is there anything at all that they would find, Delilah? I'm asking as a friend."

Hearing my boss call me by my first name is …. unsettling. The defenses I'd thrown up crumble at the tip-top and my composure slips for just a moment, the tiredness pulling my gaze down and the pain in my back and shoulders creeping to the surface.

"Being the enemy of the press is a vulnerable place to be," she warns and when our gazes meet in the silence of the office, other than the ticking of the clock and my own racing heartbeat, she adds, "I should know."

"There's nothing for them to find. I've had a boring life and I've done everything by the book."

Claire looks away, nodding. "Well then, it will be a boring piece and they won't be able to find anything. Maybe there will be no article."

No article. Please, God, no article.

"Right," I answer and that seems to be when Claire finally notices I'm in my coat. The thick fabric makes me feel that much hotter under her scrutiny.

"Early lunch?" she questions.

"Just need another coffee," I comment and inwardly scold myself for lying. If only she picked up the thin cardboard cup on my desk, she'd know just how full it was.

chapter six

Delilah

"Have a good night then," I say and lift my glass in salute as Aaron leaves the high table in the corner of the bar, giving me a short wave before he slips the leather jacket around his broad shoulders and heads for the door for a smoke.

"You too, Jones," he answers but I barely hear him over the chatter in the packed place. It's busy for a Saturday night and I focus on every face except for his. Every single one, taking them in, watching the way they speak, some of them a little too close as they whisper, some laughing so loud and genuinely that wrinkles form around their eyes.

I take them in like I took in the evidence of the case this morning, distracted and not seeing it at all.

Because Cody Walsh is right there, not even ten feet from me and he's been there all night, but he hasn't spared me a glance.

His phone has eaten up most of his attention and right now he's having what looks to be a very interesting conversation with someone I'm unfamiliar with. He's avoiding me. It's plain as day. He hasn't looked at me once. He doesn't seem to have any intention of doing so either. *What a prick.* Sleeping with him was a mistake. A grave one for my ego but nonetheless, one that's over. We're nothing more than a man and a woman working closely together in a professional setting. Not a damn thing else as far as I'm concerned.

Wine… back to my wine I go because I desperately don't like feeling that twist in my stomach and the tightness at the back of my throat.

Just a sip, and only two glasses tonight. I couldn't focus at the office, so tonight will consist of sitting cross-legged on my bed with paperwork in front of me until I have every piece of evidence in line for the perfect prosecution.

Work is my comfort place and working will get me through whatever these emotions are that I'm warring with inside right now.

Trial is a dance. The steps are all taken carefully and meticulously to get to the twists and turns that wow and convince the room. It's more than a back and forth of questions, there's intention, there's a necessity in every move and every angle. Even the wording of the questions is vital. Being able to focus and pivot is even more important.

I won't sleep tonight until I know the pace and presentation that will be the most alluring and convincing. Some call the courtroom a circus, but that's just a show for entertainment and distraction. I treat every courtroom like a ballet, with a spotlight on the details. Every single detail brought to light with a pirouette given enough time and pause to show the depth of what it means.

With a glimmer of confidence, I take another sip of my wine. Aaron and I went over the basics and in only hours I will figure out exactly how we nail this prick with first-degree murder and nothing else.

"Jones." Patterson's voice startles me, but not so much that I show it. Giving him a professional smile, I offer the experienced man a nod in greeting.

"How are you doing tonight?" he asks, but doesn't give me a moment to respond before adding, "I heard you got a whopper of a case."

A whopper. Patterson's from somewhere in the Midwest, I think. Maybe he wants to know details, I'm not sure. But he should know better than to think I'd give him any. He's a defense attorney and none of his clients have anything to do with any of mine. So this is … peculiar.

"You know how it is," I answer him with a shrug that brings his attention to my blush-colored blouse. But not to my shoulders. His gaze dips lower and the heat of embarrassment creeps up my chest. "When you have a series of plea bargains and boring cases, you get hit with a difficult one to throw you off." Setting my wineglass on the table and pushing it away slightly, I add, "Can't have too many easy ones, can we?"

Patterson looks between the glass, my chest, and my face. The slight sway in his stance and the red in his cheeks betray any air of being sober the man has. He's simply had too much to drink.

"That's true," he comments, pointing at me with the hand he's also using to hold his whiskey. The ice tinks on the glass. My father's a whiskey drinker. Never on the rocks though. He said the ice melts and weakens it.

The thought reminds me that Patterson is old enough to be my father and rich enough to buy him four times over.

Patterson seats himself, occupying the chair Aaron recently left empty. "You know when I worked with your father years ago, he used to say the same thing."

My father was a lawyer decades ago. Pride wore on his face the day I told him I was going to law school. I'll never forget that day. But his career was incredibly short-lived. The lifestyle, he told me, simply didn't suit him and Mom wanted to move back home.

"Is that why he gave it up? It was too easy for him? Or are the stocks just paying better?" Patterson questions me.

I shrug again and this time when Patterson's gaze drops, I lift my glass of wine to block what little of my cleavage could possibly show from that angle.

"My mom wanted to move back home," I answer straight-faced. We never wanted for anything and grew up in a nice enough area. It may have been a small town and not anything like New York City, but we were well-off. Maybe not as well-off as Patterson; I have no idea. "I'm sure he would have stayed had he known what the firm would become," I offer him with a polite smile and a nod of recognition.

There's a murmur of agreement from Patterson and then he takes a swig of his drink. I look away, not wanting to continue the conversation.

Patterson knows far more than I do about my father's departure. I'm not privy to my parents' decisions back then. And I don't like to have conversations involving sensitive topics knowing I'm lacking relevant details on said topic.

"You know I was surprised you came down here of all places." Patterson doesn't quit, leaning back in his seat. "I get it, wanting to stay on the case and transfer…" he pauses and nods, dropping his head. "That's commitment," he comments into his lap and raising his brow, which forms a series of lines on his forehead.

"I was just starting and took it as a sign."

"What's that?" he questions, not following and I don't know if it's because of the whiskey or because, like my mother said, it was crazy that I was moving to stay with a case.

"The firm was a starting point so when the offer came up

and evidence led us here, it seemed like a sign. Like I was meant to get into federal criminal law."

"And what did your father think of that?" Patterson questions. "I'm sure he was able to help you. He has strings to pull. But to help you go into federal criminal law…" he trails off and makes a face just then. One I'd like to punch but instead I simply smile.

My father and him were defense attorneys. "Working for the prosecution shocked him, but my involvement and dedication didn't." I give him the same answer I gave Claire five years ago. And just like her, he nods with understanding.

"You certainly worked your ass off to get here."

The smile on my face is genuine as I say, "And I appreciate the help I got along the way."

His asymmetric smile widens and he lifts his glass to me in cheers, but just after taking my sip, Patterson's smile fades.

Before I can turn to my left to look at whatever's taken his attention, a heavy arm rests across my shoulder and Cody Walsh kisses my cheek.

I barely catch sight of him before his lips brush against my skin.

What the fuck is he thinking? My heart spasms as I smile like it's a joke and push against his muscular chest, which barely moves.

"Do you have a minute?" Cody questions, his brow furrowed as he ignores Patterson. The older man is up from his seat and leaving before I can hiss at Cody, "What the hell are you thinking?"

Adrenaline races through me as I tuck a loose strand of hair behind my ear, the long day wearing on the simple bun I'd styled my hair into this morning, and casually glance around the bar.

Aaron saw what Cody did, that I'm sure of. He has the decency to look away when I catch him staring.

Shit. Shit, shit, shit. It will be the talk of the office. As if I need any more buzz around my personal life and intentions right now.

"I'm sorry I didn't come over sooner; I've been busy." He speaks as if it's a given. Like he was genuinely busy. Does he think I'm a fool? I have eyes and common fucking sense. He was ignoring me and we both know it. I'm not an idiot and I don't like being treated like one.

"What the hell are you doing, Walsh?"

"Saving your ass. He was eyeing you up and you didn't like it. I know damn well you didn't."

"He's my father's age and my father's friend." The excuse doesn't dissipate Cody's scowl; it only makes it deepen. And quite frankly, I second-guess myself at the term "friend."

"Don't lie to me," Cody reprimands me. He has some damn nerve.

I grit my teeth, laying cash down at the bar for the glasses of wine and grab my coat. "You have some fucking nerve to come over here pretending to be a knight in shining armor when you've ignored me for days." The last word is practically spit out of my mouth.

I could choke on emotion right now, but I'm damn good at ignoring it and better yet, at hiding it. I give Cody the cold shoulder and silence as I make my way out of the bar, but the stubborn fool follows me.

Shaking my head and huffing out a sarcastic breath, I turn to look at him as the entrance doors close and a gust of wind blows against my bare neck.

"I don't have time for a man who doesn't know what he wants." My anger is palpable. I don't know what gets to me more. Him ignoring me after sleeping with me, or him affecting the way colleagues see me by implying we have a romantic relationship in the bar.

I don't care to figure it out. Not here in the cold night on the corner of Main and Spruce.

"I'm already up shit creek with the press. I was fine with having something low key. But ignoring me? No, I didn't sleep with you because I thought you'd treat me like I didn't exist after. And

I sure as hell didn't want it out in the open. I get it, you don't want a relationship, but causing a scene isn't my style. I don't need any more prying into my life," I mutter under my breath and push Cody back another step.

"I'm not prying."

"No, you're kissing me in front of everyone after leaving without a word and not speaking to me for days."

"You needed him to back off," Cody says, keeping up his hero mentality and it only pisses me off more. Is he not hearing me?

"Is that what you were really doing? Saving me?" I practically hiss. The weight of the other night lays on my shoulders. I glance around to make sure no one's out here, but even in the empty street, I feel the familiar prick. It's an uneasy sensation, only adding to my annoyance and frustration. "I want to get out of here."

"Because I kissed your cheek?" Cody asks as if it's an insult and I take it as my cue to cross the street. Holding my coat tightly closed and ignoring Cody behind me as I walk as quickly as I can to the garage.

"Don't follow me."

"Don't leave then," Cody responds.

Why does it have to be messy? Why couldn't this have been low key and easy? The same at work as it's always been and if we needed each other, we'd act on it. That's what I thought it would be. Just as I figured Cody would, he follows me as I storm off toward the garage, my irritation growing with every step. Both with myself and more so with Cody.

It's not until I get to the entrance of the garage, standing just before the concrete stairs that will take me to my car that I ask him, "When did I become a damsel in distress? Not once have you walked me home. Not one goddamn time!" The spite in my voice surprises us both. The hurt in my chest lingers and I struggle with what I've just said.

"I would have taken you home if you'd asked."

"I didn't and I'm not now," I answer, turning away from the hurtful look in his pale blue gaze.

"Why are you so pissed?" he asks. "I'm sorry I kissed you in there. I get it. You want this to be low key and—"

"This?" I say, cutting him off, not hiding my shock and irritation. "What is *this*, Cody? Because you slept with me, which I initiated, I take that on, I get that. But then you left without a word and ignored me repeatedly. It would have been fine if it went back to normal. So what exactly is *this*?"

"I don't know," he says and his demeanor changes, like he's struggling between remaining a guarded wall or giving me a look like he's a wounded puppy dog. If he wasn't so handsome, it would be pathetic. But as it stands, the look makes it difficult to stay angry.

"You don't know and I don't know either, but you don't get to make a public statement because I fucked you one time. My career is more important to me. The way they see me in there matters," I say and throw my hand up, pointing at where the bar is down the street. "What the hell were you thinking?"

"I fucked up. I'm sorry."

I don't know how to respond, so I cross my arms, letting his apology sink in. I'm grateful for it, but damn am I hurt and still pissed, even if that emotion is waning.

"I don't know how to do this, but I want to talk."

Now he wants to talk? "Not tonight; I have to work. I had a shit couple of days. I just need to go home."

"Then let me take you home," Cody offers, ever the gentleman and I can at least respect that but I'm not exactly ready to just let it all go. I can't just let it go. Ignoring me, ghosting me, and then getting all touchy-feely with me in the bar? He could have handled this any other way than how he did. I suppose I could have too, but I'm too tired, too overwhelmed, and too pissed off to think about it right now.

"I can take myself. I'm fine." The bitter note in *fine* is the cherry on top of this shitty night. I shake out my hands, trying to let it all go before digging in my purse for my keys.

"I know you're still mad. I'm good at pissing people off."

The confession tumbles out of me before I can stop it. "I wonder if you'd have even come over to me if someone else hadn't hit on me." *Shit.* It hurts to say it out loud. I could have left and he wouldn't have even said hello to me if someone else wasn't scouting out his territory. My hands go clammy. It would have been easier to just ignore him and go about my night. *Why the hell did I let him get to me? Why did I go after him when I knew it wasn't going to work?*

"That's bullshit," he says and his conviction makes me doubt myself.

Lifting the strap to my purse higher up on my shoulder, the keys still not found, I question him, "How would I know? You didn't message me. You couldn't even look at me. Was it really that bad?" I'm proud that my voice doesn't break out loud like it does in my head. "No one likes to be ignored. Especially not by a man I just slept with this past weekend."

"Don't do that," he says. Cody's voice is comforting but I don't fall for it.

"I'm not your problem, so I can do anything I want, Agent Walsh." I'm close to turning away from him when he takes my elbow in his grasp and before I can object, places something in my hand.

"I was texting you this," he says and closes his hand around mine, forcing me to take his phone. "Just read it. All right?"

"I don't want to read a text when you could have sent it and didn't." My annoyance does nothing but fuel him to stare me down until I let out a frustrated sigh.

"Just read it."

Finally, I look down at the phone, if for no other reason than to appease him enough to let me leave. The bright screen lights up and I see he's brought up his messages between the two of us. It's a long message that he's referring to, one left unsent. I have to scroll up and when I do, I accidentally hit send. Shit. I guess it doesn't matter if I'm reading it anyway. Letting out a slow breath and ignoring the squeal of tires from someone leaving on the opposite side of the mostly vacant garage, I start to read the message Cody thinks is going to change my mind.

I enjoyed last night.

That's the first line and I don't get much farther. "It wasn't last night," I comment, letting my head fall to the side and seeing for the very first time in years, a vulnerable Cody Walsh.

With the lights from the parking garage illuminating his face, he looks younger than I've seen him before and my breath slips out easier as I remember his hard body over mine, his muscles flexing as he took me, pressing my back against the sofa and rocking himself into me ever so slowly but deeply to bring me closer to my own release before he found his.

"I didn't start writing it today," he admits, scratching the back of his neck. His five o'clock shadow combined with that boyish smirk makes me warm to him.

Dropping his phone back in his hand, I don't read the rest of the message.

"I enjoyed it. I like you. I just don't know how to not fuck it up."

"Going caveman isn't something I'm interested in," I offer him.

"You want this to be discreet?" he asks and I simply nod.

"Read the rest," he presses, pushing the phone toward me but I reject it. Only the phone; I don't reject him. My heels click on the pavement as I close the space between us and tell him, "I sent it to myself so I'll read it when I get home." With a nod and a simper, I add, "Maybe I'll text you back before the week is up."

It's only a lighthearted joke and it does exactly what I want it to. Cody relaxes his arms around me, letting his hands fall to the small of my back. I'm tall in my heels, but he's still an inch or two taller than me so he has to lower his head to whisper against my lips, "Don't be mad at me." His plea isn't lost, but neither is my frustration.

"Don't ignore me … and don't kiss me in public," I say and the statement isn't spoken harshly. Maybe there's even a small plea hidden in the gentleness with which I spoke it.

As I close my eyes, I know I shouldn't be doing this. I should end it between us. My life is complicated enough. It felt so good though and I've wanted him for far too long to throw it away. Even when all the warning signs are flashing bright red lights in front of my face.

He pulls back just slightly, his inhale making his chest rise and I find my fingers itching to slip up his jacket and lay right there against his white t-shirt that's taut against his skin.

"Is this public?" he questions, his voice laced with desire and his pale blue eyes simmering when I lift mine to his.

As I part my lips to answer him, he captures them in his, stealing my response and my breath just the same.

Tilting my head and rising up just slightly on my heels, I meet his need with my own. His hands play against my back, keeping me to him and my own reach around his neck, loving the skin-on-skin contact and wanting more of it. Needing more of it.

As his tongue melds with mine, the heat of our embrace enveloping around the two of us, I wish I could get lost in his touch tonight.

But I can't. My eyes open before his and I pull away, breathlessly and with a heat rolling through my body. Cody stays perfectly still a second longer than me and takes his time opening them. His steely blues stare me down with the look of a hunter. A look that makes me feel so very much as though I'm his prey.

"Not tonight, Agent Walsh," I tell him with my heels steady on the ground and he grins at me before stepping forward and planting the smallest of kisses on my jaw, his strong fingers brushing against my neck and hardening my nipples with the simple touch.

He catches that my eyes close when he kisses me. I know he does from the look of triumph on his handsome face.

"Drive safe, Delilah."

It's not until I get home that I read his text.

I enjoyed last night. I enjoyed you.

I don't do flings and I don't do girlfriends.

I don't fuck around with coworkers or people I see day to day.

You know I don't have time for a relationship. I've failed at every one of them I've ever had. I'm going to fuck this up. If this is even a thing. If this is something that you want to do again.

That doesn't change that I want you. I've wanted you for a long damn time and even after last night, I want you still. I can't offer you commitment and I'm not good at much of anything other than my job.

That's where his message stopped and I'm quick to respond before I think too much about anything he said in this text and focus only on that kiss under the lights in the parking garage.

Don't think about it, just take me home tomorrow night.

chapter seven

Delilah

EVEN WITH THE CURTAINS CLOSED, THE SUN CREEPS IN, waking me from a much-needed deep sleep. My eyes are heavy at first, but my body is so relaxed and at ease. The blush comforter, two shades lighter than the matching curtains, slips down my body as I sit up, stretching and note that the side of my bed Cody slept on last night is empty. I can't help but to touch it and when I do I find it's cold.

He left already.

He's good at that. We leave separately from the bar, and meet back here. At least we have the last two weeks. Thus the relaxed muscles and deep sleeps. A good fuck is a miracle worker for the tired mind and sore body.

Letting out an ungodly long yawn, I stare down the paper-work that litters the top of my dresser. I worked magic in this apartment to give it a mature, fresh and feminine feel. A place I could hide away and forget all the bullshit and hardness of my day job. Who was I kidding? Every surface of the bright white furniture is covered with evidence of what I do. The fact is, I bring my job home. Always. It's not about being a workaholic; it's simply that I can't let go of things that matter.

There's a memory for every inch of this room. Moments when haunting evidence seemed to unveil a truth to me in the late hours when I couldn't sleep.

I can make this room as pretty as a page out of a home décor magazine and it still wouldn't matter.

The silk sheets rustle as I get up and that's when I see the note on the bedside table between the alarm clock blinking 12:00 in bright red. In other words, someone in the unit tripped the fuse again. With a frustrated exhale, I check my cell phone for the time and fix the clock before reading the note Cody scribbled out for me.

Going to New York for a case. I'll miss you.

Two sentences are all he wrote, but the last one leaves a smile on my face.

Opening the drawer, I slip it inside with the two others he left me.

The first:

I'm sorry about the last few days, but not about the part in your bed. Call me whenever you want. Or text. I'll be waiting and I'll try not to kiss you whenever some prick eye fucks you at the bar. And yes... I meant it when I said you look sexy with that silk scarf in your hair.

The second one he left is inconsequential, like this one, but I keep it anyway because it makes me smile. Nothing has changed at work between us and there haven't been any other incidents. If Aaron or anyone else suspects we're seeing each other, they keep it out of the gossiped conversations in the break room. Or at least they haven't had the nerve to confront me.

My bare feet pad on the floor and I wrap the belt to my thin cotton peach robe with cream lace tight around my waist as I make my way to the kitchen. Today's my first day off in … Lord knows how long. Coffee and then I promised myself I'd relax. Truly take a moment and read or maybe I could take my sister out to get our nails done. It'll be a little over an hour drive for each of us, there's a shopping mall halfway between us. It's perfect for our get-togethers. She's barely spoken to me since our last call. We've had our ups and downs but of everyone in this world she's my rock. Only a year and four days apart, we've gone through life together. Everything that's happened, every milestone and pitfall.

We fought like cats and dogs in high school and I even have a faint scar on my face from one spat where she scratched me. College came and we drifted apart for a moment; the photos on my fridge are proof of the distance. So many pictures of when we were children, then nothing of us together until I was a junior in college and her a sophomore. I went for a law degree, following my father's path. My sister went for psychology. We studied together, partied together. We were each other's wingwoman in every way. My mother always said we'd be best of friends and that we needed to rely on each other. It's odd for her to say that considering her falling-out with our aunt, but she was right.

Ever since college, we don't go long without a call between us. It's been nearly two weeks, the longest that I can remember, and the realization makes my empty stomach sink. I've been too preoccupied with Cody and work.

Pressing the brew button and listening to the water heat up in the coffee machine, I write out a quick text to her:

Off today and tomorrow. When are you free to meet up?

After I press send, a deep crease finds itself in the center of my forehead. I have twelve unread messages and two missed calls. Both of them from Claire. No voicemail left.

Swallowing thickly, I go through each of the messages.

I'm so sorry.

They're such assholes.

Are you okay?

You need to call me.

The texts vary from coworkers to family members. I'm confused about most of them, not writing back a response until I know what the hell is going on.

A text from Aaron includes a link to an article. Written by Jill Brown's associate. The opening paragraph makes my jaw drop and it's then that the coffee machine sputters, announcing the hot cup of coffee is ready.

As if a cup of coffee could fix this.

I wondered what they'd write about and of course I'd give these assholes ammunition to keep the negative press running.

With my fingers going numb, I read the entire article in record time, feeling the anger rage inside of me. They bring up my father and his old cases, which is infuriating. His career has nothing to do with mine.

Worse, they bring up my relationship with Agent Walsh. Questioning if either of us were fit for the case given our romantic relationship. As if we were in one back then.

Can Miss Jones's judgment be clear while pursuing a romantic relationship on the field? The first case that went cold was with him and since then a series of murder investigations have led to no arrests. Those cases are worked by both the woman in question and Cody Walsh of the FBI.

I feel fucking sick to my stomach. Dropping the phone to the counter, both of my elbows hit the granite and I bury my head in my hands.

My father's integrity as a lawyer has never been questioned. Oddly enough, Patterson isn't mentioned and I wonder if he had a heads-up on the story. If maybe he even leaked the information about Cody and me.

Rubbing what little sleep remains from my eyes, I process everything again, breaking it down bit by bit in between swigs of coffee. Claire is going to be pissed. She's going to be furious.

But the facts remain the same: they're running a story because

I've been notable recently, even if in the past there were a number of cases that ended up going cold. A pissed-off criminal lawyer, fairly inexperienced and working for the Assistant Attorney General… they were given one comment I made on the street and they ran with it, letting imagination get in the way of facts.

Internally, I prepare my response to Claire.

I didn't make the press by losing cases. The media has focused on the fact that so many of my cases don't have enough evidence to even go to trial. Cases that they plaster everywhere and then demand justice. They want someone behind bars. All the cases are murder investigations. At least the ones mentioned in the article are and those are the ones that require me to work with Walsh. Mostly against crime organizations that are established and difficult to penetrate.

They aren't the only cases that matter, but they bring in the most headlines, and higher ratings on the news.

They want someone to pay, and they thought going after my family's history in murder trials and my romantic relationship would paint me as a villain. As someone incapable of performing her job. Worse still, they question my intentions for this position. The last lines of the article imply I have ulterior motives. That I don't want the cases to go to trial because like my father, I'm protecting murderers, the mob, and serial killers.

With shaking hands, I reach for my phone, desperate to get in touch with Walsh. This is bullshit. I've never been so angry in my life.

I worked tirelessly to get here. I've dedicated every waking hour to pursuing the same assholes they want to see locked up. It's one thing to not be good enough, it's another to have your intentions questioned.

As I hit the call button, two things happen at once.

I get an email from Claire that I read while I place the call on speaker, listening to the ringing:

We're issuing this statement in response to the article and you have a mandatory one-week paid leave while we investigate. Lay low, and stay out of the press.

See the attached document.

Investigation? Really? I don't expect to feel betrayal, but I do. The attached document is a defense for me but it's short. I don't know what else I could expect. The statement is merely them covering their ass.

The second thing that happens at that same time is that my sister texts me.

As I read the text, Walsh's voicemail greets me when he doesn't answer and I don't have the presence of mind to hang up. I'm lost in what my sister wrote more than any of this bullshit. Dread sinks down to the soles of my feet and anchors me there in that moment.

Mom's in the ER. You need to come home.

chapter eight

J*UST LET IT PASS.* C*ODY'S TEXT IS A SINGLE LINE.* H*IS ANSWER TO* my extremely long voicemail is a single line.

Hours go by before he texts again, hours of driving through the mountains of Pennsylvania and up to the Podunk town in New York where I grew up.

I'm at a gas station before he messages again: *This break will be good for you. Your mom needs you and by the time you get back, all of this political bullshit will have passed.*

My stomach stirs with the faint smell of gas and the whirl of cars driving down the worn asphalt road beside the gas station. Staring up at the faded sign, I do what I've always done—I breathe through it all, not letting it get to me.

My mom's arm is broken. She's not sick or dying. I won't be here for long and then I'm going home to look into that journalist. With my message sent, I slip the phone into the cup holder and finish up at the gas station.

Regarding the article, I'm pissed, Cody seemingly couldn't care less.

When my phone rings at the swinging red light to get back on the interstate, I nearly answer it until I see it's my sister. I'm pissed at her too. My heart fucking stopped when I saw her message about our mother.

I didn't even know it was only her arm until I was halfway here.

She wouldn't answer; neither would Dad.

Anger swarms inside of me. Coupled with disappointment and resentment. Could anything else go wrong this week?

Some days are harder than others in the career I've chosen and it took me a long time to realize it's like that with family too. Some days … some days I just wish they would be honest. I still would have come. I know Cadence would argue that I wouldn't have, but I had the time off and I didn't need to be manipulated into coming back home.

That's exactly what it feels like and my discontent with my sister is why I drive the rest of the way, nearly two hours, without the radio on and my phone on silent. I didn't even realize it until I parked in the hospital lot that I hadn't turned the volume back up. Sometimes a person just needs quiet.

A few hours of quiet to clear my head and let Cody's suggestion sink in: *Just let it pass.*

I can do that, I think as I climb out of the car, my purse hanging from the crook of my arm and the light jacket I threw on before leaving not doing a damn bit of good up here where it's colder. At least I can try, but I can't stop caring.

Absently, I nudge the door shut with my hip, cradling the bouquet of flowers I picked up for my mother in my arms. As I walk into the small hospital, I can't recollect what I even packed. It was a furious effort to gather up my luggage and leave immediately.

I asked my sister what happened. She said she didn't know.

It's a difficult task not to set my jaw into a straight line when

I see her as the glass double doors open and the visitor section to the left of the desk is visible. *Mom could've been dead. I thought she was dying. How could she let me think the worst and not answer me when I demanded to know more?* The words pile on top of each other in the back of my throat when I see my sister, but she doesn't see. She doesn't see any of the resentment, any of my anger through her blurred vision.

I nearly tumble back when my sister, slightly taller than me, skinnier and frailer in every way, wraps her arms around me and sobs in the crook of my neck.

I'd hold her back but I can't move my arms; she's gripping me so tight and my hands are full.

The anxiousness and fear sink back into my blood, slowly coursing through me.

"It's just her arm," I whisper to my sister in a dual effort to comfort her and also remind myself. "It's just her arm, isn't it?"

Cadence is slow to unwrap her delicate self from my body. She should've been a model, I swear. As she does, I take in the scene behind her. Auntie Susan is in the waiting area too. My God, I barely even recognized her. I don't see Dad anywhere. The only other people in here include the woman working behind the desk and a man with his son in the opposite corner of the waiting area. There are only two rows of seats on the right side of the entrance. But we have our own corner it appears, judging by the two coats spilling over one chair and where Auntie has her purse on the coffee table next to two cups of what I know is tea. None of the women in my family drink coffee but me.

My gaze is brought back to Cadence when she sniffs and wipes her eyes, apologizing with that hint of shame for breaking down. Steadying her with a grip on her forearm, I ask her, "Where's Dad?" The rustling of the plastic around the flowers is all I get in response because Cadence breaks down again, silently crying and walking off to gather a tissue.

Hitching my purse up my shoulder and straightening my coat, I take my time making my way to my auntie.

I set the flowers and my purse down on the end of the coffee table and take off my coat, laying it on the third seat from the end. My auntie in the corner, then my sister, then me.

"Hi Auntie," I greet her, stepping in front of my sister to lean down and give my auntie a hug. I expect it to be brief but she holds on to me tight, whispering that she's glad I'm here before she releases me.

Her tone is tense and that's what keeps me from asking the question again: *it's just her arm, isn't it?* Dread is a difficult thing to swallow; even more difficult to talk through.

"Dad's talking to the police." My sister speaks up before the silence passes too long. Her slender fingers run under her eyes gracefully before wiping the mascara that mars the tip of her fingers on her black skinny jeans. I know my sister very well, and she simply threw on those clothes. Yet, she still looks beautiful. Her hair in curls, her face fresh and bright eyed. She's wearing a chunky cream knit sweater that hangs just low enough to show her chest and the cream against her light brown skin complements her perfectly.

Even with tears in her eyes, she's beautiful. And she looks just like Mom. Everyone used to say it growing up; her skin is lighter than Mom's, but that's the only difference between them. She got our mother's femininity, and I got our father's intellect and ruthlessness.

"Why?" I question, crossing my ankles and observing, taking everything in. "What happened that he has to talk to the police?"

My auntie looks off in the distance, staring at the worn mural on the far wall. It's nothing special, a mundane piece of art displaying trees and a sunrise made of tiny mosaic tiles. Something to comfort people and do nothing more. My auntie stares blankly at it while my sister stares at me, her hand landing on my forearm.

"She broke her arm; she said she fell. But the other bruises are older and she has a number of fractures." My sister whispers the last sentence, swallowing harshly as she lets the implication hang in the air.

My first thought is that it's been a long time since they've fought. We were children back then and he never touched her like that after. How awful is it, that I know even as my chest goes tight and my fingers cold, that he's hit her before and yet I don't want to believe the accusation.

"Did he hit her?" I ask outright. How the question comes out evenly, I don't know. I can feel them both staring at me, their eyes boring holes into the side of my face as I stare at the steel elevator doors, wishing a doctor would come down and say I could see my mother, so I can ask her, rather than sitting here with people who don't know. They don't know. Mom would tell me. She'd tell me the truth. They had their problems early on, but they're over. She broke her arm, that's all.

Dad wouldn't do that; he wouldn't hit her. My mother is a strong woman. She wouldn't let him. This is all a mistake. Isn't it? It's just a misunderstanding.

Fuck, I think as I drop my head and close my tired eyes. My mind's playing tricks on me and my emotions are storming inside of me, whipping me around until I can't think straight.

"Did he hit her?" I repeat myself, louder this time when neither of them answers. Auntie doesn't say a damn thing, but she doesn't stay silent either. She's deliberate when she grabs one of the two cups off the table in front of us and makes her way around the other side of it, saying she'll give us space.

It took me a long time to realize the reason for the tension between my auntie and my father.

He came from money, had a white-collar job. He was powerful, older and white, marrying a younger black woman from a poorer neighborhood. "Trophy wife" was a term used a lot when we were younger.

My mother once screamed at her family that they couldn't be happy for her. That they hated him because he wasn't like the rest of them.

I thought she was right because my grandmother, her mother, never did seem to like him. But then again, my father's mother never seemed to like my mother. It went both ways. All of my grandparents died before I was ten and I hardly remember them but I do remember the way they looked at their child's spouse. Like they didn't belong together in any way.

I thought my auntie had the same ideas as my grandmother.

Until Mom left him one day, taking us to Auntie Susan's and both of her sisters told her she needed to leave him. I was too young to realize what was going on. Cadence knew before I did. She's younger, but she remembers far more than I do. That was the one and only time, though.

"I wouldn't be surprised if he did," my sister finally speaks, her voice lowered and careful. "They haven't been getting along recently."

"Well, what did Mom say?" I question her, feeling my pulse strike harder. I struggle with the way my sister sees my father. I know they had fights, they had bad moments, but there were so many good ones. So many times they kissed each other in front of us. So many happy memories and occasions that were pure joy. What they went through before was a rough patch. That's what my mom said, it's what she called it, a *rough patch*.

"I want to know what really happened," I comment and as I do, I feel warm tears at the corners of my eyes.

"I think I started it," Cadence whispers in a choked voice then reaches for her tea. She holds on to it like it'll protect her, her shoulders hunched inward. "I called Mom because… that guy I was with. He was rough the other night and I don't know why, I called her and I blamed her." Her voice cracks as she slumps back into her seat.

"What?" Disbelief runs rampant through me. Unpacking everything takes time, but the first reaction I have is to protect her, to defend her from whatever fucker she's referring to. "What do you mean he was rough with you?"

"He just pushed me against the wall. I told him to leave when we got into a fight over something stupid. I don't even remember."

"Who is he?" I ask and my voice is deathly low.

"No one now. I'm done with him. I blocked him and he's not interested in me anymore anyway. Not after what I said to him."

I can only nod once before waiting for her to continue.

"I was upset and I called Mom and told her and she was so… so judgmental." The hurt is there in her voice, but so is guilt. It's riddled with it between each quickly taken breath. "So uppity about him and what happened and all I could think is that it happened to her and she stayed with him.

"And I went off on her… I said some things I shouldn't have."

"You think she got into it with Dad afterward?"

"I don't know for sure, but … I just …"

With one arm wrapped around my sister's shoulders, I pull her into me and let her rest there as her face contorts and she cries again.

"Have you talked to Mom?" I ask her and she shakes her head. "It's been hours," I remark.

It takes my sister a long moment to respond, "She was unconscious."

There are four nurses in the corner of the hospital cafeteria. And then there's my auntie with a plate she hasn't touched, and myself. I move the mac and cheese around with my fork, in the same situation as my auntie. Not wanting to eat, but not ready to leave just yet.

My mother seemed fine, apart from her arm wrapped in a cast.

She smiled, she gave me a kiss. She said it got stuck in the railing when she tripped. She was trying to hold on to it and instead she only made it worse.

If it wasn't for the look on my father's face, I'd believe her. He got her two vases of daisies, her favorite flower. The smell of them in the hospital room haunts that moment for me. Three vases total, one bouquet from me, lining the room and bearing witness to that conversation.

I can't be in the room with them. I don't know how my sister's doing it. How she can sit there with speculation but not say anything.

"How's the city life?" Auntie Susan asks me and I bring my amber gaze up to meet hers. It falls quickly to her gray sweatshirt with the block letters from my uncle's alma mater. He passed a few years ago, a car accident caused by black ice.

"It's not like New York City."

There's a hum of understanding as she stirs a pack of sugar into a steaming cup of tea. Her dark eyes watch the swizzle stick as she asks, "You like it better down there? I bet it's warmer."

"It is. It's ten degrees colder here every time I come up."

The small talk doesn't do anything to help the hollow feeling in my chest. Or the numb prick along my arms. I want to talk to someone, but words fail me. That and shame. I don't want it to be true, but my gut is hardly ever wrong.

"You know what I told your mama?" my auntie Susan speaks up, and the bluntness of it forces me to meet her gaze. "I told her when she went back to him, that I was always there for her. If she wanted to come stay, if she needed money. I told her if she wanted a family dinner, I'd sit next to him but not in his house. I would never step foot in that man's house."

Hate seeps into her words, her disgust showing through and

the first crack in her armor showing. My auntie's frame is larger, not at all delicate like my mother's. She shifts her weight and corrects her expression before continuing, hardening her disposition.

"We make choices, and your mother made hers. Your father made his. I make my own too. I'm not leaving her, but you can't make sense of it with your mother."

I don't speak. Not to her. Not to my sister. Not even to my mother.

I'm silent as I take it all in. Collecting the bits of evidence and forming my own conclusion. I feel dead inside. There's this pit in my stomach that's cold and unforgiving.

My mother says it was an accident and that's all there is to it as far everyone else outside this room is concerned.

I leave before everyone else and without telling them. The last thing I want is to be alone with my father. I don't want him to look me in the eyes and lie to me. Worse, I don't want to believe him when I feel so certain that he assaulted my mother and should be behind bars right now.

Flowers are waiting for me at the hotel desk when I check in. I wish they made me smile, but they're so much more beautiful than daisies. That's all I can think.

They're the first thing I see and that smell… the smell fills the entire room. Tossing the keys onto the dresser and letting my purse and the luggage bag sit at the front of the room, I make my way to them.

My fingertips trail down the deep red petals, the smell of the roses covering up the memory of the daisies. A dozen deep red roses.

After washing my face and changing into sweats, I text Cody: *You didn't have to send flowers. But they're beautiful.*

His first text hits me like an ice bath washing down my bare skin. *I miss you and I've been thinking of you, but I didn't get you flowers.*

A follow-up text from him does nothing to help: *Now I wish I had.*

He's the only one who knew I was staying in this hotel. I only told Cody because he asked if I was staying with my parents and I told him, I always stay here.

My limbs are shaky as I move to the window of the hotel room. I'm on the second floor so there's no reason I should see anyone there, but still, I look over every inch and then do a search in the room, checking in the closet, in the bathroom. I search every inch and then lock the door before heading back to the roses. There's no note. No indication of who they're from and the clerk at the desk said she didn't know. They were simply left here specifically for me when I checked in.

A dozen red roses that keep me up most of the night until I slip into a light sleep, filled with brutal memories.

chapter nine

Delilah

THREE DAYS IN MY HOMETOWN IS PLENTY.

Add in two family dinners with forced smiles and my mother doing her best to tell us she's fine and everything's all right, and I couldn't wait to leave. I spent every moment I could in the hotel providing lies about how much I was needed at work.

There was only one moment I was alone with my father and he called me out on that lie subtly. All he mentioned was the article and he told me the same thing that everyone else did: it'll pass.

He didn't say a word about Mom. He didn't let on that it was obvious there was tension between us. He knows I think he hit her. He knows everyone thinks it.

But in that moment at the restaurant when everyone left and I had to go back for the to-go box of leftovers I'd forgotten, he didn't mention a damn thing but the article when I ran into him scribbling on the receipt at the table.

Three days of feeling insignificant and like I'm only playing a part in a poorly written film. Four times I tried to reason with my mother, coaxing her to tell me the truth when we were alone. All four times she denied anything had happened other than her being careless. Even when I stared at the other bruises. I've never seen a sad smile on my mother's face until I said I was leaving. I'm just not sure what she's most sorry about.

I need to see you. My text to Cody remains unsent even though he's back in town and so am I. But we haven't seen each other. I spent two days at home before forcing my way back into the office at work.

Claire only agreed because I promised I had no intention of doing anything but paperwork.

There's always plenty of that to do, was her answer.

It wasn't a yes and it wasn't a no. So here I stand, in my office staring between the piles of cases that need to be sorted and filed electronically and my empty cup of coffee. Aaron is technically in charge of these tasks, but I'm grateful to simply be doing something and he's grateful for the help.

If I told a younger version of myself who thrived on working in the field that I'd be hiding behind files in a silent office for days on end because of PR pressure … I would have snorted the most disbelieving laugh followed by a quick, "Fucking hell I will."

Reality is a bitter pill to swallow sometimes.

The rap of a quick knock at the door is a pleasant distraction. "It's open."

Claire's gaze moves from me to the stack of folders over a foot high and the open cardboard filing box. "You busy?" As she asks, her smile quirks up and her left brow raises comically.

"I think I need another coffee before I dive into the next stack," I comment offhandedly. "You have something for me?"

At my question, she makes her way into my office, closing the door behind her with a soft click.

"Just checking on you."

With my head down, moving several folders from one pile to the next, I peek up at her and her dark gray skirt suit before answering. "I don't need checking on."

"Of course you do." My motion pauses in the air, a manila folder in my clutches before she adds, "We all do."

I've been an honor roll student, salutatorian, and been given every kind of overachiever trophy a person can be awarded. I don't like the idea of being someone who needs to be "checked up on."

"I'm good. Almost through with this stack and then it'll be ready for Aaron to put in the system and be digital." My statement is practically robotic if not for the dismissive tone.

Crossing her arms, Claire leans back, one heel up and braced against the closed door. "Shaw is clumsy and Tanner struggles to read the jury."

The huff that comes from my lips brings a smirk with it when she adds, "They're too green and I want a string of cases to go our way. I might've managed an article with the *Journal* but it's on hold until we have a series of verdicts go our way."

"Running defense?" I question her, hating that she spent any time at all to combat the article that ran last week.

"I'm doing what has to be done. We need you in there."

Silence weighs heavy on my shoulders. I can't remember the last time I went this long without preparing to go before a judge. I haven't even gone to Bar 44 or seen anyone other than Aaron and Claire since the article hit.

"Everyone goes through it," Claire speaks up as if reading my mind. "Shake it off and meet me in the boardroom. I'm not giving this case to one of them to fuck up. Nail it and we'll ring it out for all it's worth. As far as I'm concerned, the investigation has been conducted and we found nothing."

"What are we looking at? Case wise?"

"Double homicide," she says. Her answer is spoken easily

enough and with the glimmer of a challenge in her eyes, a fire lights inside of me.

This is why I do what I do. I put the bad men behind bars. Some people claim we're only here to show the evidence. That there's no desire or intention to punish.

Fuck that.

"You need this," Claire claims and I nod.

"I need it more than you know." I let the truth slip out firmer than I would have liked.

"How's your mother?" Her question comes with an assumption that I need the case as a distraction. She's not wrong.

"She'll be all right. Just tumbled down the stairs and hurt herself pretty bad." Even to my own ears, the statement is spoken without any emotion. Inside, turmoil spreads, disgust even because I don't tell her what I really think. Sucking in a breath and letting it out in one go, I stare down at my boss in her typical professional attire and tell her I'll be there, abruptly ending the conversation.

I'm busy making sure I put the files back in the correct boxes and email an update to those who need it when Cody messages me.

I need you tonight.

That's when I see the message I never sent him, still waiting: *I need to see you.*

I change it to: *I want to see you too, but I have a lot of work and probably won't go to Bar 44.*

Even though the three moving bubbles make me aware that he's writing something in response, I quickly add: *But I need you too.* There's a vulnerability I don't like in my words, so I lighten it by adding a joke: *Come to my place? Make it a quickie?*

I can't explain why I feel sick to my stomach over it. Or why unease spreads through me until he responds, *It's a date.*

chapter ten

Delilah

"I HEARD YOU MIGHT BE LEAVING TOWN FOR A WHILE." My voice carries a purr to it as the bottle of beer hits the high-top table. It's nearly 2:00 a.m. and the bar's clearing out.

A week of normalcy does wonders. No one's brought up the article and as far as I'm concerned, it never existed.

"Bad news travels fast, doesn't it?" Cody's formerly charming expression dims under the bar lights. Office, trial, Bar 44, and bed with Cody. Every day on repeat.

"I thought you were going home?"

"I am," he answers, tipping back his drink.

"Going home is bad for you?" The disbelief in my voice makes me feel like a hypocrite and Cody's amused expression displays the sentiment.

"I don't really have a home anymore. And I never liked that town to begin with."

There's something sobering I didn't know about Cody. It's

easy to get along with the man, easier to get in bed with him. But getting information out of him is something far more difficult. I consult my wineglass, giving him a moment before questioning more. "Your parents?"

"They passed when I was younger. I went to live with my uncle who never wanted kids and he has dementia now." He shrugs, but nothing he said is casual in the least.

"Sorry to hear that," I respond apologetically and brush my thigh against his, leaning closer to him even though I know the bar is hardly packed.

"I hate his dementia. Hate going to see him even if I love the man. He was more like a friend than a father. And now…"

"He doesn't remember you?" The question tumbles out of me with pain and it's relieved when he shakes his head and answers, "He remembers me. He knows who I am most of the time.

"It's just … he asks about things that happened before. He forgets about my parents passing. He thinks I'm my father sometimes. And then others he remembers. It's hard to tell what reality he's in and what I'm going to get when I visit him."

It's quiet for a moment and I want to tell him I'm sorry again but it seems not good enough. They're just words and I struggle to find something more than just an apology.

"He used to ask about cases. I liked that better."

"Yeah, it's easy to talk about work," I'm quick to agree with him, nodding my head even and offering a gentle smile. "If you need to vent about anything, I'm always here."

His mood shifts back to easy when he smiles and tells me, "I'm not leaving for a week, though."

The way he raises his brow makes me huff a short laugh and say, "I guess I'll just have to put up with you for a little while more then."

As I joke with him, he brushes the back of his knuckles against mine and the heat unfolds inside of me.

There's not a lot that makes me melt, but I swear he does.

"It's easy to hide in work. Even easier to hide under the sheets and get lost, forgetting who we are and what we do," Cody admits, speaking lowly, like it's a secret.

"Why do we do this?" I don't know why the question leaves me. It's not with conscious consent. I suppose it's the thought that neither of us likes to go home. We don't like to talk about anything but work. Why do we put ourselves through this? Why do we prefer to meddle in lives that are long gone and stay buried there when there's so much more to life than this?

Walsh's gaze slips lower than it should, landing between my breasts as he questions, "Do what?" The edge of the bottle rests against his bottom lip for a moment too long, forcing me to pay too much attention to his expert lips.

"Do this job," I answer firmly and holding an edge that doesn't last. With my teeth sinking into my bottom lip, I return his hungry eyes with a heat in my own.

We should stop this conversation in public. I should stop leaning so close to him.

We've gotten too comfortable and even when I glance around the place, noting that no one's watching and no one cares, I know damn well we shouldn't be reckless. Especially after that article and the insinuation made. Even if I've nailed four trials in a row, I don't need the judgment affecting my job.

"Why do we do what we do..." Cody's intonation lowers, becoming more serious as he stares at my nearly empty glass of white.

"That's what I was wondering?" My question doesn't bring his gaze back; he's lost in something reflected in the glass.

"I know I do this because of my brother." Every muscle in my body tenses. Carefully, feigning a casualness that I'm all too aware is absent from this conversation, I pick up the glass and sip the white wine after commenting, "The one who passed?"

We spent over a year working together before anyone mentioned the fact that Cody Walsh had a brother. It's one of the very few things I knew about him.

"Yeah, he's the only brother I had. He was just a kid."

"You were too, weren't you?" I question, my memory betraying me. I'm almost certain his brother was seven or eight and Cody was only ten.

"Maybe I should stop. It's been a long day and I've had too much."

I shrug nonchalantly and say, "Whatever works for you. I do love getting to know you, though."

I always knew Cody had demons. Something dark and twisted that kept him quiet and guarded whenever his personal information was in question.

The second his guard would start to crumble when I first met him, another would go up behind it, thicker and even more impenetrable. There's not much about the man's past that I know.

He's a workaholic like me. He cusses under his breath when he's pissed and likes beer on easy days. Jack and Coke when he wants to think about something that's bothering him. He always says it's a case. He lives for his job with the FBI and I get it.

My first real job was with the FBI, although not as an agent. I was only a lawyer working the cases with them. Cody was the knight in shining armor, willing to do whatever it took. Last one to call it a night and the first one to gather us in the morning.

Brutal tasks require brutal men. To this day I don't know what makes Cody the man he is, only that I want to know his secrets. I want him to trust me enough to do so.

"You don't have to stop. I want to know." Laying my forearms on the table and leaning forward so I'm closer to him, I add, "You can tell me." I'm vaguely aware of a couple nearby gathering their things and leaving. The sound of clinking from glasses being collected fades as I fall into Cody's light blue gaze.

It swirls with an intensity, but deep inside the shades of silver and cobalt are secrets locked away, rattling behind the bars where he holds them hostage.

"What happened to him? You never did tell me the story. All I know is that you two were split up and he passed a little while later."

"It was years, not a little while. I went with my uncle; he went to my aunt when our parents died." When he told me the two of them were split up, I assumed his mother and father had split. I didn't know they split after.

"That's rough," I barely speak, feeling a tingle of unease run through me. "It must be difficult to be separated like that… especially after losing your parents," I offer even though my voice is tight.

"We were never close." Cody's response isn't spoken coldly, but it strikes me still. "He was years younger than me. He was only a kid," he repeats the last statement in a whisper, finding refuge in his beer and I get the impression that the conversation has come to a halt until he speaks again, surprising me.

"It was a group of three men. They kidnapped and murdered those kids. Fed their remains to the dogs. The one who lived told the cops they had to watch it all. They saw everything happen to the kid before them. One at a time as they huddled together in the cell and were forced to watch."

"That's sadistic," I respond and I don't know how I'm able to even speak.

"They got off on scaring them," he responds and his tone is harsh.

"They got them though, right?" *Please tell me they got the bastards.*

"You could say that. They're all dead. It never went to a trial."

How did they die? The question is right there, but that's not the one I ask. "You were how old?"

"I was twelve. My brother was eight. We were split three years before."

"I'm sorry."

"One of the kids they abducted when they took my brother survived. The one who lived said my brother died only hours before the police got there."

My heart pounds in agony. "So that's why you do this?"

"Yeah," he says and pretends like he's tired, and that's why he rubs his face down with one masculine hand before looking away.

"You want to tell me your sob story now?" Cody asks and he makes fun of himself, trying to downplay it all, but I see right through him and I love what I see there.

I answer his question with one of my own, "You want to get out of here?"

chapter eleven

Marcus

I WAS CORRECT IN MY ASSUMPTION THAT DELILAH WOULD call the front desk and then call the local floral shop when she received the roses. Both of which would give her nothing. I was right about her not telling Walsh as well, beyond asking if they came from him.

With the pad of my thumb running down the stubble along my jaw, I wonder if she would have told him had she not been in the position she was in. If the stress of that article and her family dynamic didn't make her so tense and she was more clearheaded.

I can practically hear her laugh as the waitress gives her another glass of white wine. I'm not sure what Sandy told my Delilah, but it brings a glimmer to her gaze that's been missing for days.

It still surprises me how easily she hides so much pain behind that gorgeous smile. I lean my head back against the leather headrest, listening to the police scanner and diverting my gaze to the front of the bar as opposed to the window I can so easily see her through. For a moment I wonder if I should have sent her wine instead of roses. The smile slips across my face, the feeling unusual as I imagine her uncorking it just to dump the bottle down the drain, not knowing who it'd come from.

She would have enjoyed the smell of it, though. I've seen her inhale deeply so many times when that cork is popped from her go-to bottle of *Valley Pines* Pinot.

The leather seat groans under me as a familiar operator announces a disturbance four blocks from here. Nodding, I recognize the address and continue to hear the flow of conversations, but I'm not listening as intently as I should. Instead, my gaze moves back to Delilah as she talks to her coworker, Aaron Curtis. She doesn't know how he watches her.

She doesn't see but I do. As does Walsh.

At least the young man knows she's out of his league. He doesn't have the balls to admit he wants her. There's a small bit of gratitude I offer him from a distance. It's one thing to know Walsh takes care of that need for her. It'd be different if the man fucking her was … so inferior.

As if it's his cue, Cody comes into view, sidling up beside her at the bar-height table. She stiffens, becoming far more serious than she's been all night. A voice alerts me that the scanner is still on, the shrill white noise of it filling the cabin of the car before I lean forward to turn it off, silencing it to keep any more interruptions from disturbing this moment. The days have turned to weeks of this. Him approaching her, the two of them pretending there's nothing between them.

The act may have fooled most of them, but Aaron knows just like I do. He saw it months ago, when they started to drift together.

Unlike Aaron, it only makes me watch more closely. I want to know what Cody says that convinces her to leave when he does, to let him meet her at her house and let him through the door.

I want to know what she whispers in his ear when he enters her late at night when they think they've gotten away with it all. When they think that no one knows that he comforts her at night.

He must know that I know. How could he not? *We had a deal.* Maybe I hadn't made myself clear enough.

Rage simmers inside of me, but it's easily subdued.

Cody Walsh had to know what he was doing by bringing her into this mess. The article was his warning. I know he read it and received the message loud and clear. Perhaps he doesn't care and he's going for her, giving in to the temptation regardless.

I'll bring up the past, then I'll bury him in the present. Even worse, I'll start the chase all over again and lure little Miss Delilah back to me.

I was so close to having her before. I wonder if she remembers.

She's still the same, even if years have passed. Still the same vivacious woman with a heat in her eyes and yet there's an innocence about her.

The vision of her is only obscured for a moment by Cody walking around her to speak to someone else. I watch her watch him.

Her lips part slightly before she forces herself to look away.

The ache is indescribable. She could look at me that way. If things had been different, she could look at me the way she does him.

I've never wanted anything or anyone like I want her and the sick part of me knows it's because Cody pursued her. It's a jealousy I haven't been able to kick.

Still, I wanted her first. There's no way he doesn't know.

He knew I cared for her and he stayed close to her.

He knew I was watching and he fucked her.

He knew what it would do to me. Cody Walsh knows me far too well to be unaware.

Even worse, he ignored my latest letter.

Do you ever regret it? Letting that evidence slip through your fingers so you could ensure I executed a different plan of yours?

There was an unspoken deal, a bit of camaraderie between us. I'm not the one who changed things. What happens next is his fault, his doing. Not mine.

part ii

this love hurts...

chapter twelve

Delilah

"I'D LIKE TO REMIND YOU THAT YOU'RE UNDER OATH, Miss Parks." I'm aware my voice is harsh, demeaning even, as I look across the courtroom at Missy Parks' flushed expression. The sheen across her forehead and upper lip only adds to my suspicion. I think she drove the car. We don't have proof. Not a shred of evidence, so I don't hint at it; I didn't charge her with a damn thing because I wasn't certain I had enough to convince a jury. My red heels click on the shiny obsidian marble floor in Judge Partings' courtroom. I may not be able to tie her to the robbery, but her testimony is crucial to ensuring her boyfriend goes down for his part.

After all, he's the one who killed the eleven people inside the bank that night. My hunch that she was driving the car is only that, an inkling based off of years of experience. My gut instinct tells me she didn't know he was going to shoot anyone. Thus the sweat along her brow and how frequently her voice shakes, requiring her to repeatedly clear her throat.

She's an accomplice to murder and she knows it. I wonder if the guilt eats her alive at night.

"I'll ask you again, did you expect your boyfriend at the time, the defendant, Mr. Wilson, to meet you at your home that Friday evening?"

"No, I mean," she says as she shakes her head, her gaze on the floor to my right. She can't even look me in the eye and knowing that, I walk with a set pace toward her, forcing her to look at the harsh sound of my heels clacking. "He—he…"

The pencil skirt of my suit is tight as my gait widens. It's custom tailored, as is my jacket. In contrast, Missy is wearing a shirt far too large for her frame and the same could be said for her jeans. Her attire reinforces her mousy demeanor, making her appear that much more minuscule as she raises her widened eyes to me from the stand. The poor girl looks like she hasn't eaten in days and her hair pulled back in a ponytail so tight it makes my own scalp hurt, only makes her appearance look worse.

"We've gone through your whereabouts and text messages surrounding the time of the crime, Miss Parks. The defendant saw you every Friday evening." I make sure I point to him, forcing her to look back at him. *Look at him. Look at the man who you know committed murder.* I pray the jury sees how her expression displays horror just glancing at him.

"Six weekends in a row he met you at your house and stayed the duration of the weekend. After the previous Sunday, he was out of town so you wouldn't have been able to meet in person and according to your phone records there were no calls between the two of you." My voice is tight in a ruthless manner as I stare into her eyes now glossed over with unshed tears. I'm conscientious about keeping my body language nonthreatening. My tone and the way our gazes meet may be strict and unrelenting, but the jury needs to relate to me. They need to want to ask the same questions that I'm asking. I lower my voice just slightly and knit my brow as if I'm confused. "So please, enlighten me as to why you wouldn't have expected him to be at your house that evening. Because every shred of evidence points to the fact that your boyfriend should have been with you that evening."

Her bottom lip trembles as she shoves both of her hands into her lap. With her shoulders hunched she appears defeated. It would be a dream come true for her to just admit it. To admit she drove to pick him up. That they spent six weeks together planning a robbery and she's the one who drove. If only she would admit they were together… but that would be a fool's errand.

Wiping under her eyes, Missy sucks in a deep breath, her shoulders shaking as she holds back a sob. I'm quick to grab the square box of tissues and hold them up to her.

"I realize this is a difficult time, Miss Parks." She nods, greedily accepting the tissues and playing the part of a mourning woman. Someone shocked by the actions of her on-again, off-again boyfriend. But the twenty-four-year-old won't get much sympathy from this jury. It's filled with married women much older than her and the evidence of the defendant's past led to one very obvious question: why was she still with him? And the manner in which it's presented points to a conclusion: she was the one who had control over him and bailed him out, but then left him to rot when she couldn't handle it. She called the shots, at least in her relationship.

"So why wasn't he with you on the night of August fourteenth? Why didn't you expect him to be there?"

"I lied," the young woman blurts out, blinking rapidly as she looks me in the eye, tears still clinging to her lashes. Hope blooms that maybe she'll confess. She speaks clearly, "I did expect him." She nods quickly and repetitively and then speaks to the jury, not to me. "I don't know why he didn't show up and I was expecting him."

"Why lie and say you weren't?"

"I just… I didn't want to hurt his case anymore."

Anymore.

The word lingers and I allow a space of time to pass. I let it hit the jurors one by one. In my periphery I see the juror in the back row on the left, a man in an old brown suit, tilt his head, the question marring his forehead with a deep crease.

I could ask how she'd already hurt his case; I could push her more. But this dance is delicate. I have to play my part as well.

With a soft nod, one of sympathy, I announce that I have no further questions.

Let the jury think I'm inadequate by not pushing for more. After all, my gender and race already do that for some of these men and women. Let them be angry that I didn't interrogate her. That I didn't ask the obvious question. Because the implication is already there. The defendant's girlfriend knows he's guilty.

I know it. They know it. And that's what I needed from her.

Glancing at the defendant, I catch sight of his anger and more importantly the betrayal in his eyes as he stares at her, his ill-fitting black suit sagging on his slight frame. *Now he'll talk.* I'm not the only one who knows she drove. Nothing in this world is more spiteful than a scorned lover.

I make a mental note, as the nineteen-year-old holds his girlfriend's gaze for as long as he can while she exits the stand, to offer him the deal again. To give up the getaway driver in exchange for a lighter sentence.

Tapping my pen to the untouched legal pad on the table in front of me, I think, *I'm damn good at my job. If nothing else, at least I'm damn good at this.*

A familiar prick at the back of my neck follows me all the way back to my office. I offer tight smiles to everyone I pass as I make my way to the elevator, both hands on the handle of my twill briefcase. Chills flow down my shoulders, the kind that make your insides churn. Glancing over my shoulder when I feel eyes on me again, I know there's no one there, but I can't help it. I half expected to see Missy. Maybe to give me damning evidence, maybe to tell me the truth and offer to make a deal since she has to know he's going to throw her under the bus now that she's given up defending him. Goosebumps run down my arms when there isn't a soul in sight. I stare a moment longer, looking past the empty hall and toward the large bay windows.

People pass quickly, walking on their own or in pairs beyond the glass. Not a soul sits still. There's no one.

Ding. The elevator arrives, snapping me back to the here and now.

Shaking off the nerves, I keep my head in the game. Sometimes this happens. The brutality of what I deal with gets to me sometimes. The doors shut and in privacy I snag a mint from the pocket of my tailored jacket. Sucking on candy or mints helps at times. I read an article about how breathing affects the nervous system and sucking on candy is one of the ways to control breathing. I chose mints after learning about that little trick.

With the small mint on the center of my tongue, I suck, pressing it against the roof of my mouth as the doors open, once again announced with a *ding*. It's all very mundane and repetitive. Day in and day out, I do the same thing. To the office, to the courtroom and then home; or to the bar first and then home. Day in and day out. It's the way it goes and the sight before me is one I've seen time and time again. The emotions though, the charge of energy, the relief at times and the disappointment at others… there's nothing mundane about that.

Alone in my office, I quickly busy myself with writing up the proposal to present to the higher-ups regarding Winston's case. Missy's boyfriend has to know by now that the writing is on the wall. When the phone rings, I've nearly finished, but it doesn't matter.

It's Carl, Winston's lawyer. He already handed over his girl-friend and confessed everything. "Get the testimony and I'll sign off on everything then present it to the judge tomorrow."

The asymmetric smile on my lips grows to a full-on grin. I'll take my win however I can get it.

Hanging up the phone and relaxing into my chair, I check my cell phone. I've never wanted to share my victories before. Not even with my sister. She doesn't like to hear the details and it's impossible for me not to give them. But right now, I want to tell Cody. I know he'd get it. He'd understand the high of nailing both of them—that's real justice. But he'd also get the draining feeling after the adrenaline dissipates. When it all comes down and the next case hits my desk.

Dropping the phone to my desk on a stack of folders, I opt for a glass of wine from the mini fridge of my office. The small door opens and reveals there's not a damn thing in it but a half-eaten sandwich that I should probably throw out and a nearly empty bottle. I can't believe I left that small of an amount in it. It's maybe a quarter of a glass, if that.

Well damn, I think with pursed lips and kick the door to the fridge shut with a gentle nudge, the bottle in hand.

I pour it all out into a clean mug from my desk that's supposed to be used for coffee and boasts some company's logo on it. The sip is sweet and I savor it. Letting my eyes close for a minute, the moment they open I stare at my phone.

I can put away murderers and pit lovers against each other… but I can't text a man I'm sleeping with. A ridiculous huff forces me to shake my head and I down the last bit of wine; it's practically a shot.

I check our messages.

There are no new texts from him. We last spoke when he called two days ago and it was a quick conversation, but still, he called. He made that move. He showed he was interested. My inner voice tsks that I'm trying to make a pros and cons list in my head rather than having the balls to just message the man.

I could text him. I could tell him how proud I am that I got a conviction without having to rely on a fickle jury for a guilty verdict.

Still, I hesitate for one reason. I've never leaned on anyone before, simply because I don't want to. I don't want to get in the habit of having someone there, only for them to leave one day.

I'm already a little too close. A little too eager.

A knock at my door shuts down my thoughts and I set my phone aside once and for all, facedown before slipping my heels back on and answering it.

It's late now; most of the people in the office should be gone. Nearly everyone left at 6:00 for a celebratory drink I turned down to work on this plea deal. The door opens with a click as I ask, "yes?"

To no one.

No one is there and as I lean out of my office, checking left and then right down the empty hall, the chill comes back, that prickling along my neck which then flows down my arms.

It's as I'm closing the door that I see the note.

At least I think it's a note. I'm quick to pick it up and even quicker to close the door and then lock it. The freezing cold runs through me and it's followed by confusion as I turn over the thick rectangular white paper, finding it to be blank.

What?

Swallowing thickly, my throat dry and a nervous heat coursing through me, I stare at the closed door, wondering what the hell is going on and finding myself more anxious or nervous or possibly even scared than I'd like to be.

"It's only a piece of paper," I chide myself out loud and move to toss it in the trash can along with the empty bottle of wine, but as I slip my fingers down it to throw it away, I feel a groove in the paper, an etching along the crisp page.

It takes me a moment of standing there alone in my office as the sun sets deep and low, stealing the lighter colors of the evening sunset with it, before I reach into my desk for the only pencil I have. I'm careful as I angle the tip along the one groove I feel. I follow it along the paper, listening to the ticking clock seemingly slowing down as my heartbeat picks up and I read what it says.

Breathe. I force myself to steady my breathing and double-check that the door is locked.

It wasn't a random piece of paper that was dropped, and I didn't imagine the knock I heard. I don't hesitate to call security, slamming down the buttons as I stare at the door and then below it, to the strip of light that shines through unobstructed, letting me know there's no one there. I'm still not moving from this office without security.

They answer on the first ring. "Security."

"I need an escort."

"Ma'am, are you all right?"

"No. Someone is on floor three or was a moment ago. They left a threat at my door and I need an escort as soon as possible, please." I'm vaguely aware of how calm my voice is even though inside chaos ensues.

I'm not crazy. Someone was watching me today. Someone wants me dead and I think I know who.

The man on the line tells me to stay with him and asks what the threat was. I read the note aloud. "If they rot, you rot with them."

"We have the footage from the security cameras," the detail informs me. "We'll find whoever it was." He doesn't tell me anything

I don't already know, but still I nod in understanding and thank him.

The man's voice is deep but professional. It's soothing too. When he rapped his knuckles on my door and called out my name… I'm ashamed at the immediate relief I felt. I have a gun I carry too. Still, there's a lot to be said about having a trained professional by your side.

"We'll know who did this within the hour."

"I know," I say again. I've hardly spoken and I know I'm poor company at the moment. "I just want to go home right now." *And get the hell out of here.*

With his black hat on and heavy beard, I barely get a good look at Steve. He has broad shoulders though and his uniform doesn't hide that. The other one, who's waiting outside the garage, is less impressive in size. I'm far more familiar with him, though. His name's Taylor and he's been here for years.

Steve must be new; I haven't met him before. "I prefer the stairwell if—"

"I do too," I say, cutting off the newcomer, already knowing protocol. This isn't the first time I've been threatened. Although this feels different. If someone's waiting for me, the last thing I need is to have a set of doors open and reveal a gun pointed at me. Stairs all the way, my thighs be damned.

Pressing the side button, I check my phone again to see if Cody's called back as we walk up the flight of concrete stairs to the second floor where my car is parked. The sounds of the city traffic behind us reverberates in the lot as I see I have no missed calls or messages.

My throat is dry and tight with that new information. I called him the second the two men in uniform came to my door to escort me to my car, relieving the security guard who was on the phone with me.

With a deep breath in and an even deeper one out, I tell

myself he must not have his phone on him. That's more comforting than the more likely scenario: he saw and judged my call to be less important than what he was already doing.

"You all right?" the man to my right asks me as I pull out my keys. There's a note of something in his voice that throws me off. It's probably only concern, but it sounds more intimate with his voice low the way it is.

A breeze whips around me and I hold my purse closer to my side, my keys in my hand. I hit the button to unlock my car, noting that it's just the two of us now; the man I trust is a floor below. The beep resonates in the garage, bouncing off the concrete walls.

"Just shaken up," I admit and try to get another look at his face, but he lowers his head as I do, so it's only his sharp blue eyes that I get a glimpse of. Only a glimpse.

For a second, I think it's Cody. A split second, but I know that's only because I want it to be him. That disappointment only adds to my discomfort.

Slipping his hands into his pockets and nodding at the ground, he answers, "Yeah, I can imagine." There's an air about him that I'm drawn to. He's intentionally keeping his distance, but there's something else. I can't put my finger on it.

Before unease can come over me fully, he turns his shoulder to me, effectively dismissing the moment, and tells me to drive safe. Taking it as my cue, I ready myself to get the hell out of here and go home. I miss my bed and the safety of those four walls.

The click to my door opening is met with the screech of wheels from someone on the street below and I glance up to see the security guard has already walked away and is standing at attention in front of the elevator. He stands with his back to it and I know that means he's waiting until I drive down to leave.

My engine turns over and I put the car into drive before I can secure my seatbelt. I want to get the hell out of here.

I don't expect Steve to step forward as my car rolls by him. With a racing heart, I slow and again I'm surprised when he offers me a folded piece of lined paper on my way down. My window's rolled up and he didn't block my way.

A part of me knows I don't have to stop. I could keep going. If I wasn't curious or I didn't want to get a better look at the man, I would have done just that. I would have kept going and gone on my way guilt free.

I don't put the car in park, but I do stop and roll down my window. I'm very much aware of the gun in my glove compartment.

"Delilah." He calls me by my first name and a pang in my chest alerts me to it. "If you need me," he says, slipping the paper through my window. With my fingers wrapped around it, he doesn't let go. His eyes are sharp with slight wrinkles around them, showing his age. Mid-forties maybe. There's a darkness that lies in the depths of his irises, and a severity in the way he looks at me. That's not what has me sucking in a sharp breath; it's the heat of his fingers as they press against mine until he lets go of the paper.

The contact is so hot, so unexpected, that I rip my gaze away from his to glance at the note in my hand. By the time I look back up, his back is to me and he takes his spot again at the elevator, not giving me a chance to respond.

Lifting my foot off the brake, I continue down to the ground floor of the garage and I don't stop until I get to the exit. My head is a whirlwind and I'm so messed up right now, that by the time I reach for my pass to slip into the meter, I've convinced myself I'm making things up in my head. The note scared me more than I'd ever admit to anyone and I just wish the man were Cody. I miss him… worse… I feel like I need him.

The arm to the gate lifts and my eyes shift from the gate to the lined paper hurriedly tossed in an empty cup holder.

Taylor nods for me to leave but I don't. I reach for the note and it crinkles as I unwrap it to read a phone number and then a name. A name that drains the blood from my face.

The biting frost drenches me from head to toe as I read: *Sincerely, Marcus.*

Slamming the car into park and listening to the *ping, ping, ping* as I grab my gun, leaving the glove compartment open, I then leave the driver door wide open too. I run to Taylor, screaming for him to call backup. At the sight of my gun, panic flashes in his eyes.

"Backup," he says into the radio on his chest as he reaches for his gun, turning in all directions, searching for whatever's spooked me.

With my breathing coming in hard, I position myself with my back to the wall and alternate looking between the elevator and the paved road that would lead Marcus down to us.

I'm all too aware that he could escape down a stairwell on the other side of the garage. He could already be gone and more than likely is. Hiding, stalking… he's probably watching me right at this very moment.

My heart pounds as Taylor screams at me, his gun now pointed at the stairwell next to the elevator, very much catching on that someone's here.

Sirens wail in the background and I know we'll be surrounded soon.

And the man I've heard called a ghost, the grim reaper… the angel of death… he'll be long gone but he'll know my reaction.

With my throat tightening and my lungs screeching to a halt like the tires outside, I can barely breathe.

This is what true terror feels like.

Marcus is here.

He touched me.

Taylor relays the events through his walkie-talkie and several cop cars make their way past us, not stopping and heading to the next floor, searching the darkened place with flashlights.

"How well do you know that man?" I question.

"Who? Steve?"

"Yes!" I say, practically screaming like a crazy woman and feeling a burn at the back of my eyes. "Steve is a wanted suspect. He's a murderer."

"You requested him."

"What?" Disbelief colors the single syllable.

"He met me as I walked up. You requested him!"

He's the man who was never caught. The cold cases that are turning up again.

We thought he died or moved on when the evidence ran dry and the murders stopped.

Every crime scene I've been on flashes before my eyes. The blood, the faces. Vomit threatens to come up as I try to answer Taylor.

"He's a murder suspect." I barely manage to say the words as three cop cars park just outside of the exit with their lights flashing blue and red in ominous patterns.

My arms fall to my side and my knees feel like buckling as I brace myself against the wall, my defenses down.

As the doors open and close and more men stream out, their guns drawn, Taylor continues to question me. His voice berates every sense I have.

"He's the one who left the note…. he's—" *Oh my God.* I can barely breathe. He threatened me.

"No. No, they caught the kid who did it. There's footage." Blinking back the very real fears wrapping their arms around me, I take in what Taylor tells me. They found the kid, they have him in custody.

"So there are two men out for me?"

"Did Marcus threaten you? What did he do? Tell me everything."

Taylor's gaze sinks deep into mine, pleading with me and the numbness inside takes over as I clear my throat and relay everything. The odd feeling between us, the note. The signature.

"I'm going to need that, Miss Jones," states an officer I hadn't even realized was beside us, reaching for the note.

"Of course," I answer but don't hand it over just yet. "Let me take a picture first," I add. I don't wait for his response and the objection is thwarted by Taylor; he knows me too well.

With my back to the two of them and the building surrounded by men in uniform, I photograph the note and a chill comes over me. My fingers slip over the words and I note the lack of indentation, the smooth writing, the curves of each letter.

"We found something," a voice calls out from the stairwell, coming into view with the slapping of his shoes against the concrete. Staring at him, I wait with bated breath and note there's something in his hand… he carries it over to where we're standing, the red and blue lights still flashing across our faces and the stone wall behind us.

"Is it possible he was wearing this?" the cop questions. I've seen him before.

It's short, it's dark and as I close my eyes and picture Marcus, his sharp blue eyes scold me, forcing my eyes to bolt open. He was wearing a fake beard and that's what's in the cop's hands.

"I didn't get a good look at him," I answer with my arms wrapping tighter around myself, "but yes. I think he was."

The night continues, the sounds and the flashing lights and the speculation consuming every moment but all I can think about, all I can see and feel are those pale blues and the singeing touch.

If he's not the one who left the note, how did he know to insert himself so seamlessly the way he did? Questions pile up and not a single answer comes to light.

"You need to go home. I'm taking you home." Taylor's

statement comes with a hand on my shoulder that startles me back to the present.

With muted voices on his speaker and then white noise, Taylor presses the push-to-talk button and answers, "Copy that," before moving his hand to the small of my back.

"Let me drive. Andrews will follow and I'll ride back with him." With a nod and a thank you, I don't protest. I can barely think straight. I can barely even see what is directly in front of me. Instead I recall the cases. The first time I met Cody and the FBI team that was assigned when the bodies started compounding on one another.

His signature was the letters. His script matches the note. The entire quiet drive home I glance between the photo on my phone and Taylor, who does his best to comfort me, but the kindest thing he does is turn on the radio.

If he wants me dead… I'd be dead.

What the hell does Marcus want from me?

chapter thirteen

Cody

THE MESSAGES COME THROUGH ONE AFTER THE OTHER. Reception out here in this part of Virginia is a bitch and as I sit in the back of the van, I listen to each of them get worse. It's the makings of a horrific nightmare.

In the first one, Delilah disguises her fear with a sense of indignation. Knowing she's scared, my blood instantly runs cold. *Where are you?* But she ended the call with a softer, *I need you.*

She can't hide the fear in that statement.

Which makes the second and third messages harder to listen to.

Marcus.

My reaction to hearing his name on her lips is visceral. *Bastard!* Anger tears through me that he went to her, that he dared to make contact with her.

I'll kill him. If he touches her, I'll cut his fucking throat open.

Attempting to play off the emotions that roll through me while surrounded by my team in the back of the van, I can barely respond.

"Right, Walsh?" Evan jokes, shoving his shoulder against mine as we head down the highway.

"Right," I say as I nod in agreement and then lean forward, gripping the back of Parker's headrest. "Hey, I need to stop up here for a minute," I call up to the driver, Bradley. The van has always seemed small with the six of us spread out in the eight-seat vehicle. Two in each row and the black cases in the back stacked up just behind me.

I do all right playing it off even though I feel sick to my stomach, and my hand's wrapped around my phone with a viselike grip.

They all know about Marcus, but they don't know the truth. The details are where the betrayal lies and they wouldn't understand that.

I don't rush out of the van when we stop. If I did, they'd know something's up. They probably already do. I don't want them involved any more than they'll insert themselves without being told shit. They only need to know what they already know about me and Delilah, which isn't a damn thing.

She's for me to take care of and unless I really need them, I'm keeping them in the dark. That's the way it has to be. The rest stop is typical. They're always the same. Gas station on one side for passenger vehicles, with diesel pumps on the other for trucks and other commercial transport. The smell of gasoline is strong as I make my way past the pumps. There's a convenience store with an entrance on the outside and then inside contains a food court and restrooms. The brisk night air is the only comfort against my hot skin.

Evan, a man taller than me and with more years in the bureau too, climbs out behind me and yells for me to wait up. The walk with him is silent and I know he's catching on to the tension but he gives me my space. Lord knows Evan has his own secrets and if the man is good at anything, it's respecting boundaries.

This time of night, there are fewer families in the rest stops than during the day, but this particular one has never been empty any time we've stopped here.

The interior is littered with cheap tables that are half-filled and the smell of burgers and fried food lingers in the air. There's only one corner relatively vacant and I pick that one, ignoring Evan's questioning look as he heads for the restroom and I don't.

The legs of the chair grind against the speckled linoleum and I take a moment to compose myself before I call Delilah. The tips of my fingers are numb as fear and anger stir inside of me.

If he threatened her, I'll kill him. I'll find him and kill him. If anyone has a clue as to where Marcus hangs out, it's me.

I don't know where he lives or what he looks like, but with the information I've got, my team will find him. I'll come clean, for her. I'll confess everything.

If it wasn't him who left the note and he knows who's after her… then we have an even bigger problem on our hands.

Her number's on speed dial and without thinking twice I hit number 8, my lucky number, swallowing thickly as I stare straight ahead, mindlessly watching two kids pull on their father's jacket, begging for a cookie that's larger than the size of their small hands. They're all the way across the food court, but everyone in here can hear their pleas.

The phone rings and rings and just when I think it's going to voicemail, Delilah answers.

"Cody," she says and the longing and relief contained in the single-word answer does something to me. My heart sinks but in a way that's difficult to describe.

"I'm sorry I wasn't there," I tell her first, dropping my gaze to the gray lacquered tabletop. *Fuck, I'm sorry for so much.* The truth goes unspoken.

"It's okay. I'm okay," she answers quickly. "They found the kid, he works for a pizzeria and he's the one who left the note. He said a woman asked him to drop it off for me. She told him she was my friend and it was an inside joke. He had no idea."

A kid and a woman? The man I knew years ago as Marcus would never have involved children in his work. Never. Maybe she was right in the last message she sent. Two different situations, both colliding. My instincts tell me Marcus, at the very least, knew she'd be threatened. He has a hand in every sin that occurs in our city and I don't believe he just happened to be there. If the last decade has taught me anything, it's that there's no such thing as coincidence.

"And Marcus?" Anger flares in my tone and I have to close my eyes to keep it at bay. When I open them, Evan is across the court, watching me but remaining at a distance. I wave a hand in the air to let him know I'm all right, but he stays where he is, diligently keeping an eye on the surroundings.

I'll have to tell him something. I'll think of some excuse. A partial truth maybe. Something happened to a woman I'm seeing. She's shaken up and I need to get the hell home so I can help her. That'll do it. Only Evan, though. The entire team doesn't need to get wind of this.

When one of us is down, all of us pull together. But this? They can't go digging into this.

Delilah's inhale is easily heard on my end of the line before she says, "I only think the man who walked me to my car was Marcus because of the note he gave me. The number is untraceable, probably a burner and when they called no one answered. They tried to track it and they got nothing."

Of course he didn't answer. There's no way he wasn't watching her every move. He knows she told the cops what she suspects. I should feel terror at the realization because Marcus isn't known for having mercy, but he told me how he felt about her once.

He wouldn't touch her. He made that clear.

He better fucking not.

"You saw his face?" I question her, my hand forming a white-knuckled fist at my side. He's a sick fuck and a ruthless murderer. It doesn't make sense that I'm this calm. That I can hold back this much of what I'm feeling. Except for one little truth. One small detail I've never told anyone.

"Only his eyes. Caucasian male with blue eyes."

No one's ever seen his face but me; and back then, it was only a glimpse. The details of who Marcus is choke me as I force my body to relax in my seat. It's only to put Evan at ease. What is reflected on the outside is nothing at all like the turmoil that rages inside of me.

"Is someone with you?" I ask her, praying the security team had enough sense to take this seriously. If everything she's told me is true, all they have is a note from a man who said he was Marcus. On paper it's not a threat, but in reality, she should be terrified.

"They put four men on me and they have two teams on the case. One for the note and one for Marcus."

I can only nod, words refusing to slip through my tight throat. She says his name so easily. Marcus. If only she knew.

Biting back a bitter taste, I tell her I'm sorry again and that I'm coming home. "You'll stay with me."

"You don't have to do that. I'm having security—"

"You will go to my place and stay there until I'm home. Your apartment's not safe until you get a security system. I'll do the installation myself." There's no margin for negotiation in my tone and as I lean forward, my jaw clenched and lungs still, I know that's not the tone Delilah typically appreciates. Her silence at the demand confirms my suspicions.

"Do it for me," I plead with her, lowering my voice as I do. "You don't have a security system, you're in an apartment with neighbors everywhere. My place is on its own; there's no risk and I spent a fortune on the security system." The reasons line up in my head. It's a mistake for her to stay in that building. Marcus could be just one floor up and there isn't a damn thing we can do about it. "Please," I add for good measure.

"Text me your address." Her tone is reluctant.

"The security code is eight seven four three. Got it?" I ask her and rub the back of my neck.

"I got it. When will you be home?"

"We're driving back now. Just twelve hours to go. I promise I'll be there soon."

There's a shift between us. It's been happening for weeks now. It's easy to deny what's between us when we both go along with it. But there's no question that she means something to me and that I mean something to her.

What that is… we don't have the time to delve into it right now. I just want to feel her, to hold her and know she's safe.

"I'll protect you. I promise."

We end the call as if nothing's changed between us, but I know it has.

I'll see you soon doesn't capture the meaning of what I want to tell her.

With the call over, I watch Evan motion to someone outside. The guys are ready to go. Irritation consumes me. I need a fucking moment to figure out all this shit and get a grip. Years of history come back to me. The details of a man I said goodbye to and thought I'd never hear from again.

I motion to the bathroom to Evan and he tilts his chin in acknowledgment.

When I'm enclosed within a stall, I text a certain number knowing full well if this blows up, the evidence will be damning. It's the only number I have of his, though. And I'm unwilling to not reach out and tell him I know what he did and that he crossed a line.

You went to her? He sees the message almost immediately but doesn't answer and it pisses me off. Someone enters the restroom as another person leaves. I need to wrap this up. *You weren't sup-posed to go near her.*

The responding text is immediate: *Neither were you.*

The sounds of a faucet being turned on, a distant cough and footsteps in the men's restroom turn to white noise as Marcus continues in a series of messages that drain the blood from my face, even as it heats to an unbearable degree.

Where are you now, when she needs you?

Don't answer that.

It doesn't matter.

I'll take it from here.

chapter fourteen

Delilah

STILL STARING OUTSIDE THE WINDOW, I END THE CALL with Cody. The phone is heavy in my hand and I find myself gripping it tighter than I should. With my left hand holding open the curtains, I let my eyes adjust to the dark night and take count of the men outside.

I invited them in, but that's against protocol. Fine. They can stay out there all night. I don't care what anyone else does at this point. I just want to be able to sleep.

Exhaustion and disbelief weigh me down as I pull my robe tighter around me. A hot shower didn't do a damn thing to calm my nerves. I'm so tired, I feel as if I could lie down and fall asleep in only seconds. But I know better. With the way my mind is reeling, I'll be lucky if I can keep my eyes closed when my head finally lands against the pillow.

Reluctantly, I grab an overnight bag and begin packing. I only take enough for one night. Cody said he'd be back tomorrow and that'll give him hours to install a security system up here. It's plenty of time and I'm not staying at his place for more than just tonight. Especially when it's only so that one of the two of us can have less to worry about.

We're... we're not boyfriend and girlfriend. We aren't anything but friends who wind up in bed together. I barely even know a personal thing about the man. Much less the state of his place. I don't even know if it's an apartment or a ranch house or... whatever it is. Hope is nonexistent but I'm praying for it. The truth? The real truth? Even with the men outside, I'm so fucking scared. I've never been this terrified in my entire life.

It comes with the territory. The nature of my business is to be met with threats and stare them down while demanding justice. But from what I know, Marcus has his own version of justice and I don't know where I fall in his eyes.

My breathing hitches remembering his steely gaze, but I keep moving, grabbing my earplugs, sleep bonnet, and lip moisturizer from the nightstand and tossing them into the small travel bag then zipping it up.

I pretend I'm not falling apart with every step. I keep moving, grabbing a sweater aimlessly and then two blouses for underneath. It's when I'm folding them, the note coming back into my mind and the knock at the door of my office playing back in my head, that I nearly lose all control. Marcus is one beast and the threat is another.

The half-full bag sags on my bed as I cover my face with my hands and just breathe. I finally get dressed, and just breathe. *Just breathe.* It's only once I calm myself down that I realize my hands are shaking.

Hugging myself, I sit on the edge of the bed, rocking slowly and pulling myself together. I let myself slip off the side, falling to the floor and leaning my head back against the mattress.

I could call my sister, but it would frighten her more than anything. What good would that do? I could call my father and he would overreact. He would make demands and attempt to take over… not unlike the man I just ended my last call with, but at least I can go along with Cody's decisions.

I wish he were here. I need him and I don't want to need him like I do, but my God I do.

Is it so wrong to want to be held and protected? It goes against everything in my nature, everything I've worked for, but right now I desperately need it. A little human contact that reminds me I'm safe and okay and nothing bad is going to happen.

Because every time I close my eyes, all I see are the photographs from various crime scenes. But instead of the victim lying there, it's me. It's my eyes that are wide open, staring aimlessly and my body that's broken and lifeless.

Without thinking about it, I reach for my phone and text Cody as quickly as I can: *Please drive fast.* When it's sent, I can't take it back.

After wiping my eyes with a tissue and a handful of water splashed on my face, I give myself a cursory pass and pretend like none of that happened.

I take my time, reorganizing the bag and thinking about everything other than what happened tonight, grabbing some sleeping pills for safe measure before leaving my bedroom. I'm damn sure going to need them tonight.

Letting time pass, I go over everything I need and then do it again, making sure I didn't miss anything before zipping up the bag with a sound of finality echoing in the room. I saved a pair of gray sweats and a comfortable olive hoodie to wear tonight. I certainly don't look like a damsel in distress; I've never been a fan of that.

Taking deep breaths in and deep breaths out, I put on light makeup before making my way out of my bedroom, ready to relocate as per Cody's not so gentle request. The security detail will just have to follow me to Cody's place. I don't know what they'll think about it or if it goes against protocol, but I don't have the energy to fight and they can't make me stay here, so… it's up to them if they come or not. The last thing I'm going to do right now is fight with the only person I can confide in.

I don't want to be alone either, though.

With the straps digging into my shoulder, I carry the heavy bag past the kitchen and the bright bloom of gorgeous red petals catch my eye.

Roses. Dozens of roses.

The heavy duffle bag slips from its place and plops onto the wood floors. I'm still in bare feet and my soles pad on the floor as I make my way over. My first reaction is to touch the petals. They're velvety soft and the flowers are fragrant. There are at least two dozen roses in a simple vase.

Knock, knock, knock, there's a knock at my front door. The loud bangs startle me, forcing my fingers to pull back, not unlike Belle when the Beast came up from behind her, but I make haste getting to the front door, and see Taylor in the peephole. I could laugh at the reference to a fairytale; oh, what a poor excuse for a princess I would make.

I don't have to wonder why Taylor's here from the look in his eyes. Before I've finished opening the door, he's already started talking.

"I got a call from Agent Walsh about a relocation?" he questions. The quizzical look is paired with a knowing one. Swallowing a bit of embarrassment, I nod and then look him in the eye before I say, "He insisted."

There's a pause, and for a moment I imagine Taylor is going to question further, but he doesn't. "All right then. We're ready when you are."

"I just need five minutes," I tell him. Before he can fully turn his back to me to walk back down my front yard path the way he came, I ask, "Who brought the roses?"

"What?" he says and a cold chill flows over my neck and down further. Fear threatens to derail my composure. *How could he not know about the roses?* "What roses?" he asks when I don't say anything.

Opening the door wider, I ask him to come inside with me. "Is everything all right?" Taylor questions as he reaches for his gun.

I don't know. An awful sickness washes through me. It's not possible that someone came in here while the men were watching the place. It's not possible. My imagination goes a step further, questioning if the roses were here all along. They must have been. I was so out of it that I had to have missed them. Right?

Sensing how off I am, Taylor uses his transmitter to update the men that he's going inside and to do a sweep of the interior. I'm numb as I watch Taylor search through my apartment and then he checks each lock. Only the sounds of Taylor moving quietly and quickly from room to room accompany this horrible feeling that grips me like a vise. I only break away when he says there's no one else here. Searching the flowers for the card from earlier, I find nothing. *Where did it go?*

Holstering his gun, Taylor questions lowly, calmly but with authority, "Were they here when we got here earlier?"

"They couldn't have been," I answer in a whisper, but my head shakes subconsciously. Maybe it's disagreeing with me. "I don't know."

I've never felt so helpless and foolish all at once. "It's been a long day." Taylor's comment is meant to be consoling but it only adds to my humiliation.

With one last look at the roses, I let Taylor take my bag and follow him out to an unmarked black sedan, sliding in the back of it. My hands are still shaking, so I hold them tight and shove them between my knees the entire way to Cody's place. That's why I wasn't holding my phone; it's why I didn't see I had a new text until I was safely tucked away in Cody's home.

It's from a new number, one not in my contacts and I nearly drop the phone when I read the series of messages he sent me.

I didn't mean to startle you with the roses.
I meant it when I said I'd protect you.
No one will hurt you, my Delilah.

I had to change my number. Don't give this one away like you did the last.

chapter fifteen

Cody

I'M A HELPLESS PRICK. THAT'S ALL I COULD THINK THE entire ride. Sitting in the back of a van, not able to do a damn thing but think.

I offered to drive, to do something rather than sit here being useless, but Bradley wouldn't let me. Evan hasn't pried, but I notice how he keeps glancing at me. If I noticed, so did everyone else.

Maybe that's why it's so fucking quiet.

Pretending that I'm on my phone only works for so long before the guys pick up on the air around me. Then I pull out some paperwork. Even as the vehicle jostles over potholes, I stare down at the black words on stark white pages and give my best effort to appear that I give a shit about what's in the files. It doesn't throw them off, but the message comes across loud and clear: don't fucking ask.

I can't think of anything else but her. Delilah.

Her and the man I've strategically aligned myself with. It

happened so slowly, so carefully that I didn't realize what I'd done and how deep down the hole I'd gone until it was too late. There's no going back from the things that I've done.

I remember the first time I met the man who calls himself Marcus. Met… isn't the right word. It was the first time I came into contact with him. That's a better way of putting it.

Memories of the stench of that back alley behind an old strip joint on the east side come back to me as the van moves over yet another pothole and I'm tempted to cover my nose with the inside of my elbow like I did back then. It hit me hard, the smell of rotten garbage overflowing in the alley where the body was found. The steel cans were missing their lids and the ruined cobblestone streets the city refused to pay to fix were the highlights of that part of the city five years ago. I heard they cleaned it up some now, but back then, it was a hellish place to live.

If you found yourself that far toward the bay, it was best to go any other direction but east as quickly as you could. It was my third year on this job and my patience had worn thin on a series of murders we all knew were hits from a local mafia organization.

Everyone knew, but no one talked. Cuffed and placed in holding, all anyone said was that they wanted their lawyer if they were being charged. And if they weren't being charged, they didn't have a damn thing to say and wanted to be released. Being in holding for forty-eight hours didn't break down a single man. In a city like that, where everyone's down on their luck and the one place to find a hot meal is funded by a man who runs the streets… well, it was impossible to get anyone to turn on them. They all asked for the same lawyer, the mob's lawyer.

So when this body showed up, and no one saw anything and no one had anything to say but *get off my porch*, it wasn't surprising.

The body had been there for at least three days and when the trash bag that covered it was removed, the stench only got worse.

I remember how my partner at the time had heaved, nearly puking right there on the body. That would have been damn awful for evidence.

My partner was much older than me and constantly bitched about wanting to retire and stop living a waking nightmare day in and day out. He was offered retirement last year, but from what I heard, he turned it down. I remember thinking back then, there's no way out of this. The work will stay with you long after the badge hits the bottom of a drawer.

I sent the old man away when we got to the scene and he gagged; we didn't need two of us back in the alley while we waited for backup and transport for the body. Sirens were a constant, and one bellowed behind us as he headed toward the street. The sun was setting. I watched it fall for a moment and did my best to avoid making eye contact with an older woman who peeked out of her curtains three stories up in the worn brick apartments across the street. She wouldn't talk, I knew that much. I also knew everyone fed information to the mob. If a person breathed in that town, they did the dirty work of Romano. Whether out of fear or a need to survive, I didn't know and I still don't.

I had an evidence bag in my hand, ready to pick up a necklace that looked like it'd been ripped from the woman. A thin red gash colored her neck and the silver chain was dull with dried blood as the streetlights flickered on.

"Shame, isn't it?" I heard Marcus before I saw him. He's good at sneaking around and hiding in shadows. Monsters like him all do the same.

With a hand on my holster, I heard the familiar sound of a bullet being chambered in a Glock. He tsked me as I stood there, painfully still, with my blood rushing in my ears.

"Don't do anything stupid."

I could try to pull out my weapon, and probably get shot. I could call out for my partner and probably get us both killed.

Instead, I stared down at the woman's face and held my breath waiting for his next move. I didn't know where he was. Somewhere above me and to the left judging by how his voice carried. The alley sat between buildings with shops on street level and apartments five stories up. Back then I assumed he was watching from a window in one of those apartments. He had the upper hand and the cold sweat on the back of my neck made me all too aware that I knew he was the one in control.

He told me not to turn around, right before I heard the thud of a man jump and land behind me. The sun may have been setting but there was enough daylight to see him if I dared to disobey.

"Who are you?" I questioned, although I had an inkling. We'd been keeping tabs on the local mafia for a while; we knew the real names of their members, had files on their whereabouts and aliases. There was one name that was only whispered. A rumor, a ghost. A single name and no other information save a list of bodies the people around here credited to him. We thought he was an assassin but as the truth unfolded over the years, I learned he was more than that. He was an angel of death. A murderer who killed based on his own morals and judgment. The chills flowing down my arms and the way he spoke made the name resonate in my mind before he spoke. When I first started, I thought the man didn't exist, but years in that town made one thing very clear. Monsters are real and the one named Marcus was the worst of them.

Marcus, he answered me and I knew the man behind me was a wanted serial killer who caused fear to run down the spines of even the hardest men from the mob that we'd interviewed. They called him the grim reaper, the monster under your bed. They called him a lot of things, but they only ever whispered his name in a single hiss.

He didn't stop to ask my name; he didn't ask me anything at all, merely made a comment about the dead woman followed by a sucking sound of discontent. And how it wasn't supposed to be her.

"What do you mean it wasn't supposed to be her?" I downplayed my interest as best I could, all while trying to conceal the nerves that rattled me and the fear that forced me to stare down the alley the way my partner had gone. I was alone with a man I couldn't see who held a gun at my back.

It was quiet for a long moment. Too many seconds passed for my liking. "I don't know that I can trust you yet."

"Are you going to kill me?" I didn't give myself conscious permission to ask, yet I did. I didn't want to die. Sure as hell not in some dirty alley with a gunshot to the back of the head.

"Why would I kill you? You want what I want."

I didn't answer and I didn't need to. All Marcus did was direct my next steps.

"Go down this alley and make a left at the corner store. You'll see it if you're looking for it."

"Looking for what?"

"For the weapon that ties Romano's predecessor to the crime scene."

Adrenaline spiked in my blood and I nearly turned to face him but the tsk and reminder of the gun he held kept me firmly placed where I was. I didn't trust him and I can't say that's changed much, even with everything I've learned.

I asked the obvious question, my eyes narrowing although they still looked at nothing in particular. "Why are you helping me?"

"I told you." As I stared at the crumbling brick wall in front of me, I heard him start to walk away as he spoke to my back. "We both want the same thing. It's hard to admit, but in this instance… I need you. And you don't have to admit it, but I know damn well that you need me."

Those were his parting words to me.

My partner strolled back not a minute after, two detectives in tow.

"You look like shit," he commented and the other two laughed.

Coldness surrounded every inch of me. It happened so quickly, I nearly thought I'd lost it. I could have told them what happened, but I didn't. Instead, when one suggested it was the odor that made me look so pale, I told them I needed a walk. I followed Marcus's advice and we nailed the son of a bitch who killed that woman and tied four other murders to him. We couldn't get Romano but Marcus told me later he had a plan and Romano was useful for it. Instead, he offered me a list. Letters came and kept coming. And I kept responding as the bodies piled up at my feet.

chapter sixteen

Delilah

CODY'S COFFEE MAKER SPEWS AS IT SPITS OUT THE LAST bit of coffee to fill the plain white cup. It's this high-pitched sound and I'm all too aware of it as I stare at the sputtering machine flicking droplets of brown liquid against the upper sides of the bistro mug.

It's damn good coffee though, strong but not bitter, and even the smell of it helps me to wake up just a bit more.

As I set the mug against the gray, speckled counter and reach for the sugar, I try to remember if this is my third or fourth cup. My conclusion as I pour far too much sugar into the mug, is that I haven't got a clue.

After stirring in a bit of creamer, the spoon clinks against the mug and I leave it on the napkin I put down this morning that's already stained with a round ring of chestnut coloring.

With my back to the counter, I blow across the hot cup and take in the expansive kitchen. It's just like the rest of Cody's single-floor ranch home: modern, monochromatic with all blacks, grays and whites, and hardly any personalization whatsoever.

Everything is updated and top of the line. The simple lights that hang down are sleek and look expensive. But there's not a single item on the counter, except for a toaster that looks brand new, the coffee maker, and now a stained napkin and spoon. This place is barren. It's too empty to even serve as a model home.

I breathe in the delicious fragrance and then take a short sip. It's comforting and tastes like home so I indulge in a longer sip next.

All night, I thought about every case I ever worked on where Marcus's name was mentioned. It's more than a few dozen of them. At least one hundred. A hundred times his name was implicated in some way or another. I used to think of him as the boogeyman. Some made-up horror story that criminals blamed when really, he didn't exist.

A number of times last night, my mind drifted to the roses he gifted me, which are now where I left them at home. But the red quickly bled into crime scene photos. Pools of blood and then their eyes, followed by his sharp blue gaze. I didn't tell anyone. I can't write it down or speak the reality. He was there in my most private of spaces. And what's worse is that he saw my reaction. I'll tell Cody when he's here, but for now, the confession is stuck with disbelief at the back of my throat.

There's one other reason… one I'm ashamed to admit, as to why I didn't tell a soul he'd messaged. *I have a lead.* I couldn't breathe, I couldn't speak; all I knew was I had a lead and sharing it with anyone else would ruin it. How fucking reckless is that? It's buried at the back of my mind, but the reasoning is very much there. Marcus is a wanted man… and I have a lead.

A lead and a vase of flowers.

The sight of roses turning into blood is the image that snapped my eyes open each time I tried to rest. It was like Marcus was watching me. I've convinced myself the pale blue of his eyes must be due to contacts. They're simply far too blue, far too beautiful.

Ping.

My phone dings on the counter. Setting my mug down I click on the screen to see it's another message from my sister. As if fate couldn't be any bigger of a bitch.

I've gotten three messages already today.

My mother left my father. She's an emotional wreck and my sister is in shambles even though for years she's been saying they aren't good for each other. Of course they need me now. Of all times, my sister wants me to come home *right now.*

She's practically demanding it and holding the fact that all I do is work over my head.

Hell… if she only knew.

The first time my phone went off this morning, I was making my first cup of coffee and I stared at my phone on the other end of the island where I'd decided to work. It couldn't have been any later than 6:00 a.m. My initial thought when the chime went off was: it's Marcus.

There was a hiss in the back of my mind, one provoked by the memory of his fingers against mine in the parking garage. One that taunted me. One that claimed I didn't tell anyone because it was my secret to keep. No one else was allowed to have it.

I'm only faintly aware of that voice. It can so easily be blamed on the lack of sleep and the loneliness that crept up on me in Cody's large, cold bed covered with black cotton sheets and a white and slate striped comforter.

The only bit of personality in that room was due to the full shelf of books. They're classics and their spines worn down. The one that made me smile was *The Hound of the Baskervilles.* It figures that Cody would like Sherlock Holmes.

I tossed and turned in that empty bed, doing everything I

could to rid the day from the deepest, darkest places of my conscience. I even took four of those sleeping pills I packed, but they didn't do a damn thing.

I crawled out of bed and was met with that text from my sister, then one from Claire telling me to work from home today.

They don't want me back in the office until they have more information on who is really responsible for the note left at my door, a.k.a. a lead.

It was easy enough to agree and keep my feet planted in Cody's place. Not that I can focus enough to actually work. All I can think about is the phone number, each digit burning into my memory.

I haven't messaged Marcus; I haven't told anyone about it. Those four sentences feel like a ticking time bomb, and I don't know how to find the wires, let alone cut them to prevent inevitable ruin.

My sister's constant texts are the cherry on top of this shit sundae. At that very thought, another comes in:

I mean it, Dee. She won't stop crying. She's hysterical.

My sinking heart drags every cord down as it drops, stretching out the agony of it all.

Sometimes we see things we shouldn't. We go through moments that take ahold of us. That's the only way I can explain how I've felt since last night. It's not detached, it's overwhelmed. There was a time, when I first started, that I had to watch video evidence of a woman being beaten to death. It was only minutes and in this field, it wasn't the most gruesome thing I'd ever seen. But there was a child present, and he couldn't have been more than three years old. He was screaming and crying. He hit the man who was beating the woman. He wasn't even her son.

I wasn't right for a while. Days, maybe a week or two. I heard what people said to me but it took a moment too long to process, because all I could hear were the cries of a child wanting the bad man to go away. I understood how I felt, but the way my body responded and the way my thoughts weren't keeping up, I just wasn't right. My mind was stuck on the sound of a small boy crying out in time with the crunch of the woman's skull hitting the concrete pavement.

I can take a lot. I like to believe I'm a strong woman, but I'm slipping just like I did then, only now it's so much worse and seemingly slower. I'm slowly falling into a place I don't want to be and I don't know how to stop it. There's no side of a well to cling to… I'm simply falling into an abyss.

My phone pings again; it's my sister guilting me into taking time off since I hardly ever come home anymore.

I wish that I could. I wish I could just pause all of this shit like I did that video in the back office when I first started crying. Freeze it in time and let it turn stale while I go back home as if nothing's wrong. As if there isn't a security detail on my ass and a serial killer telling me he'll protect me. Calling me his. *His Delilah.*

A shiver snakes its way down my back, leaving a chill in its wake that even the hot coffee can't undo. Maybe I could leave and all of this would simply pause. Maybe Cody could come with me up to my sister's. He should be back now any minute. He could stay by my side and protect me from all the warring thoughts in my head. Maybe he'd even call me his. *Now I know I'm dreaming.*

With a roll of my tired eyes, I shake it all off. The self-pity and delusions combined.

I type back a message and then delete it: *I wish I could.*

I will talk to my boss and find a way. That's the response I settle on. Cadence thanks me, says she loves me. All the while I know I'm a liar. I could confess it all and tell her there's no way I'd risk bringing the mess I'm in to her doorstep, adding to her madness, or I can stay the workaholic sister who's trying but failing, and never comes home. I choose the latter.

The thud of my phone hitting the counter comes just before a creak of a wooden floorboard. It's a sound that freezes everything inside of me. With my body still, my eyes locked on the doorway it came from, I can barely breathe.

Someone's in the house. I can just barely make out their shadow.

The shadow shifts along the stark white wall in the hallway and before I can move, I hear his voice. The voice that haunted me last night says, "I already took your gun."

My back heel had pivoted, the desperate need for a defense already decided, but with a harsh swallow, I stand firm where I am, attempting to calm myself.

"You said you wouldn't hurt me," I manage to speak, my voice tighter than I'd like, but it comes out loud enough.

My gaze flickers to the butcher block. I could at the very least, arm myself with a steak knife. He called me his, he left me flowers, but this man is deranged.

"Never." His answer is spoken with conviction and I'm once again pulled to the shadow that's stopped in the hallway just beyond the kitchen. The bright daylight has dimmed, but there's plenty shining through the window, enough to see the outline of a tall man with broad shoulders.

I remember the security guard, his sheer size and the balls he had to have to walk beside me.

Swallowing thickly, I question him, "Then why take my gun?" I even shrug, as if I wouldn't use it. As if I believe him for one second when he says he won't hurt me.

His chuckle is unexpected because it comes out so easily. A second passes and my heart hammers wildly, not at all enjoying his amusement. "You know why, Delilah. Let's not play games; our time is limited."

"What do you want?"

Tick, tock, thump, thump; my heartbeat races as I wait for the man to do something or say something. Time goes by far too slowly.

Roses. Red. Blood. Roses. Red. Blood.

Again I'm bombarded by images and confronted with the gruesome reality, unable to pretend I'm not terrified. "Please don't hurt me," I say, and my plea is joined by a half-backward step of my bare feet on the floor.

I've never wanted to run so much in my life.

"Nothing I want to do to you involves pain." Marcus's answer calms the fight-or-flight instinct just barely.

"What do you want?" I repeat the question, attempting to numb myself as I trace the outline of his shadow with my eyes and inwardly curse Cody. *How could he have gotten in here? How utterly useless is this protective detail?*

"The note, it came from the desk of a man called Herman." Marcus seems to huff a laugh at the name.

"Herman threatened me?" I ask quietly and calmly, although every inch of my skin pricks with fear. With my head tilted, and my voice sounding subservient more than anything, I brace myself with a hand on the counter and it takes every fiber of my being to listen. I settle on telling him the truth.

"Herman. I don't know a Herman."

I sound ridiculous to my own ears. I like to think of myself as a good actress under pressure, but my abilities seem to be failing me.

"He was hired to protect them. He paid off the cops who tampered with the evidence of your case that was just dismissed."

"The case against Ross Brass?" I question, little pieces of the puzzle falling into place. My tired mind catching up on details. Ross Brass was let go after evidence was handled improperly. "Ross paid this man to get him off and to threaten me?"

"Yes."

"Why threaten me? Why—" Before I can practically fall into

the familiar steps of conducting an interrogation to uncover motive, Marcus answers simply. As he speaks, his shadow shifts, and the floor creaking drags my gaze back to him.

"Because you mocked him. You bruised his sensitive ego. Apparently he doesn't like the notion of rotting in hell." His words sink in, my mind finally filled in and crisper than it was ten minutes ago. I'm not certain I believe Marcus. To threaten someone under the DEA… after he got off scot-free? He'd have to be an idiot to do it.

"How do you know that?"

"Because I do."

"How can I prove that?"

His answer comes just as quickly as my question. A tit for tat, a back-and-forth. Although I don't care for his conclusion. "You can't."

The revelation sits between us, the air thickening. My initial thought was that the threat was from Ross in some way, but not directly. A fan or an accomplice. *If they rot, you rot with them.*

"You didn't sleep and I thought the information would give you some peace." Marcus's comment brings me back to the present. To the other monster taking control of my life.

"That's why you're here?"

"That and to tell you those men outside are unreliable and can't be trusted."

"If they knew you were here—"

"They wouldn't do anything because Taylor's right-hand man works for Brass. He's in his pocket."

"No—"

He cuts me off, saying, "Taylor you can trust, but I wouldn't count on the others."

He's met with silence as the heat kicks on and I'm suddenly very aware of how the lowered temperature has wrapped itself around me.

"I'll protect you."

"Why?" The single word leaves me breathless as I stare at the unmoving shadow. *Why me? Why does he care?* I have to ask and fear settles inside of me, knowing that wasn't the right move. For some mysterious reason, this man feels a connection between us; I'm only safe because of that. With a cold sweat lingering on my skin, I know I've messed up.

Marcus doesn't answer. Instead he says something entirely unexpected.

"I know you're going to want to tell him. You trust Cody more than me. I'm all right with that. I accept it and he'll be able to pull strings I can't. Tell him."

There's a pain etched in his voice and I hate that I feel sympathy. I shouldn't feel anything for this man.

The shadow moves, an arm raising as he adds, "I'm going to leave a USB flash drive with some files for you."

"Why are you helping me?" I question him further, needing an answer. *Tell me the truth, Marcus,* a voice pleads in the back of my head.

He ignores me, taking a small step forward as he says, "I want you to close your eyes and when you do, I'm going to come near you."

My heart pounds and my throat tightens.

"You won't open your eyes."

It takes great effort not to step backward as Marcus moves forward again, only a single step.

"Keep them closed," Marcus commands and I can only nod, fear stealing my voice.

He takes another step forward, blue jeans coming into view and my eyes close. With my hands fisted, I grip my cotton tank top to keep from moving.

"Stay still and keep them closed." This time when he speaks, his voice is clearer and his steps easy to place. There's a clink on the counter; I imagine he's set the flash drive down there but then he takes another step forward.

"I give you something, and I'd like something, Delilah." His soft voice is comforting, a soothing balm although it barely penetrates the nerves.

I can only nod.

Another step, and then another. I count them in my head until I can feel the heat of his body and the presence of his shadow over me, blocking the light, wrapping me in darkness.

"I'm going to cover your eyes with my hand," he tells me and then adds, "And then I'm going to kiss you."

My fists tighten and my lips part just slightly, maybe to object, I don't know but it all happens too fast.

My feet move backward, his steps just as fast as mine, until my back hits the fridge. His hand presses against my eyes and his other at my hip, pinning me there as his lips meet mine.

Soft, yet demanding. It's all too hot and overwhelming. His body pressed against me sends a bolt of longing through me as he molds his lips to mine and groans deep and low in his chest. The vibrations only add to the flick of desire that comes with the flames of danger.

With his hand still firmly over my eyes, my back against the unforgivingly hard appliance and Marcus's grip digging into my hip, I stand there breathless, nearly shaking.

His teeth rake down the side of my neck and a gasp escapes me. True want and need roll through my body.

Shocked and breathless, attempting to cope with my own reaction, I stand there helpless just as I am, listening to him leave with haste and without a single word. I can still feel every inch of him: his heat, his demanding touch, and the all-consuming kiss.

It was only a kiss. If I tell myself that enough, one day I may believe it.

chapter
seventeen

Delilah

I WASN'T IN MY RIGHT MIND. I HAVEN'T BEEN. THE HAZE OF whatever came over me, the sleeplessness and the reckless, wild thoughts, all vanish once my skin chills and the reality slams into me like a car without brakes.

I wasn't in my right mind. I couldn't have been.

It's all I can think as my hands shake at my sides. I've been staring at the cup of coffee on the counter as if it's the coffee's fault. Maybe it was drugged or poisoned. Because there's no way in hell that I just kissed a serial killer and felt anything other than disgust.

My mind is playing tricks on me.

The thought has my trembling fingers barely brushing along my bottom lip, where the kiss still sears my skin.

The creak of the front door opening forces a silent gasp from me as my wide eyes stare at the kitchen threshold. My body's so stiff, I can't do a damn thing but stare with bated breath. I only exhale when I hear my name called out by a familiar voice.

"Delilah." Cody says my name and as it echoes, I grip my

right hand with my left to keep it from shaking as much as it is. Eyes closed and head down, I tell myself over and over: It's just Cody. Cody's here.

Oh thank God.

"Here," I say. My own voice contains tremors and I clear my throat. "I'm in here," I try to speak loud enough for him to hear me, but my voice falls, and my gaze turns toward the back of the house, in the direction Marcus left. I heard the door close. He's gone. I know he's gone. But how the fuck did he get in?

With confusion swirling in my mind, the tension and the disbelief still at war inside of me, I don't know what to do or say. The front door closes with a resounding click and heavy footsteps come fast toward me, getting louder until I can see Cody's foreboding figure in my periphery, the shadow of a man who I've desperately missed. His scent wraps around me in a comforting way, but it can't penetrate the strong feeling that engulfs every thought and emotion that rampage inside of me, wanting to scream, to do something!

Marcus was here. He kissed me. A serial killer was just here and I let him walk away.

"Gun, gun," I sputter out the word and keep staring down the long hall. "Marcus was here," I say although I don't know how I get the words out. "He was just here." With my trembling hand I reach out to Cody, but it's useless. It's his strong back that greets me, pinning me against the counter. The marble digs into my lower back as I try to breathe, to get a grip on the here and now.

The sight of Marcus shrouded in darkness in the corner, my name on his lips…

"He's gone." I push out the words. "I heard the door shut and he said he was leaving. He's gone but he was just here."

"Which way did he go?" Cody questions with his back still facing me.

"He's gone," is all I can say and again I reach out, my fingernails digging into Cody's strong frame and my cheek slowly resting against the black leather of his jacket. I take in his warmth, his broad shoulders, his height and I try to cling to all of it. I try to reach normalcy again. The mindset I had before Marcus broke in and shattered my sanity.

Cody tries to move, to do something, presumably sweep the place, but I don't care what. I need him here. I need him close to me. "Stay. Please, please." I have to swallow the harsh ball that lingers at the back of my tongue. "Please don't move." My plea is a whisper and I feel myself losing it. He can't move. I just… I just need a moment.

"What did he do to you?" The question holds an air of its own darkness, a threat of what Cody would do to him. Cody turns ever so slightly to face me but still his eyes keep hold of the back hallway.

"Nothing," I lie in a quickly hissed answer. Why did I lie? Why hide the truth? Shame runs down my spine with a chill that rolls down my body and I find myself pulling away. My arms cross over my chest as I slip backward.

"What did he say to you?"

"Nothing," I repeat, feeling the spiked ball grow in an attempt to suffocate me. "Wait, no, no, he left information. He left it." My own story confuses me and I can imagine what it does to Cody. He doesn't answer for a moment, a long moment and I finally come back down from wherever I was, grounding myself and getting ahold of what happened. My eyes open slowly and I rest my head on Cody's chest. My lashes brush against the jacket while I'm staring at nothing, but seeing everything.

"Did you see him?"

Shaking my head against Cody's chest doesn't give him a quick enough answer. He turns fully, granting me his full attention as his arms wrap around my waist.

He kisses my hair and his body heat lingers, warming me slowly. Yes, this is what I need.

"Did you see him?" he repeats his question and I finally pull back, crossing my arms in front of me, the ghost of this reality still very much present.

"No," I say and shake my head again. "But I know it was him. It sounded like him and he knew things."

"What kind of things?" Cody's tone shifts. It's no longer comforting and it seems his interrogation is starting.

With his gaze narrowed and on me, I remember what happened. "He said he knew who left the note. A hired man from Brass. And he left the proof. He also said one of Taylor's men is in Brass's pocket."

"Shit," Cody sneers the curse, apparently believing Marcus instantly. "Taylor's crew is gone," he says and nods at his own decision, shifting his weight as his hand rubs the back of his neck. It's his tell when he knows shit has gone south and we have to pivot tactics. He truly does believe Marcus. With his eyes pinned on me, he repeats, "Taylor's crew is gone and I'll hire a new one. I know the firm. Consider it done."

It's hard to swallow, seeing the devotion and commitment Cody so obviously has to keeping me safe. My heart refuses to stay where it's supposed to, beating wildly. I don't have long before the moment is over, Cody hell-bent on taking control and quite honestly, I easily give it to him. With a nod, Cody seems to right himself, the man I know from work shifting back to the man I know from the bar and my bed.

"He *left* information?"

The single question stirs between us and I nod in the direction I heard the clink. Sure enough, a small metal USB flash drive lays there on the counter. "He said it would all be on it."

"Are you okay? All he did was come in here and deliver information?"

"That's all he did," I say then swallow harshly at the lie, doubling down on it and then I look into Cody's eyes, the shades of blue staring back at me with regret, remorse, but something more than that, something deeper. "He didn't hurt me. But it scared the shit out of me, Cody. I didn't have my gun and I thought I was safe here."

I ask the obvious question when silence sets in. "How did he get in here?"

Cody's gaze moves to the back hall once again and his jaw sets firmly in place. "Do you know how he got in? Window or door?"

"I don't know." I repeat myself as he stares down at me, "I don't know." In the back of my mind I think it shouldn't matter, the security locks were engaged. The alarm should have gone off either way. Unless he knew the code.

It doesn't seem possible, but somehow Cody's large frame gets closer to me as his hands grip my shoulders. "You need to give me something about how he got in," he tells me, his sharp blue eyes begging me even though his statement is barely spoken, it's a dark whisper.

With one hand shoving his right hand off of me, I step away from him, regaining myself.

"I was standing right there," I say and point over by the coffee maker. "And I heard him before anything. He knew my name. He broke into my house yesterday." The sudden exposure, voicing out loud the lack of boundaries that man has, leaves me feeling numb all over.

"I know," he says and Cody's voice is gentle, consoling even. "I know he did that. He left roses. But that was yesterday and that was your apartment, not here…" his voice trails off and then he adds that Taylor told him. Taylor didn't know what to think, but Taylor hasn't worked against someone like Marcus before.

"You're sure you never saw him? He came close to you into this kitchen and you never saw him?"

It takes me a moment to realize he's questioning if I really saw what I saw. Is that what he's doing?

Spitefulness lingers in my tone. "He was standing right there," I practically yell, pointing to the corner. I'm quick to point out the evidence. The physical proof he was here. "He left this," I say and snatch the flash drive off the counter then shove it into Cody's chest. "He has the name of the man who left the threat in my office. He said he wants to help me."

My throat is raw from the indignation of my statements. The evidence lining up. "He was here, Cody! He came into your house and he could have hurt me, but he didn't." I keep from screaming only by forcing the words through clenched teeth. The tremors return, the anxiousness from knowing everything that could have happened.

When I look back up at Cody, resting my elbows on the counter in an attempt to steady myself, regret lays in his expression. It takes a moment before Cody's brow morphs into a straight line, leaving a deep crease in the center of his forehead. The anger that brews there for the man named Marcus only makes Agent Walsh look more protective.

"He came in here and left this for you? And that's all he did?" he questions again. And again I lie.

I nod yes, although it's a short-lived motion. "Yes, and then he left and you came. You came in right after. He just left. He was just here." My sentences tumble out at once and again I cross my arms in front of me protectively. Glancing from the corner where Marcus was and then back up to Cody.

"Are you okay?" he asks yet again and I watch the cords around his throat tighten as he swallows. I respond weakly, "Yes." I am okay. It's difficult for me to grasp. The grim reaper himself kissed me. The man who everyone fears *wanted* to kiss me.

"He didn't hurt you or threaten you?"

"No, he didn't. It was the opposite. He said he would help me. He promised to protect me. How did he get in here, Cody?" I ask the more pertinent question.

"I don't know." His answer is cold. "We need to get out of here and do a sweep."

"No, no, don't tell anyone." I'm quick to cut him off and then reach for his forearm when his shock and hesitancy are evident. "He has proof; he wants to work with… with us." I include Cody, praying he'll listen while a tingling sensation spreads through me that feels an awful lot like desperation. If Marcus knows who's after me… I would rather work with one devil, than die by the hand of another.

"Hire new guys and have them do a sweep for precaution. Hopefully figure out how the hell he got in. But don't tell them." I peer into his questioning gaze as I plead with him. "Please. I want to catch this guy as much as you, but if he knows who's after me…" I let my plea hang in the air, most of it unsaid as my heart bows in agony in my chest. *What am I doing? What am I even asking?*

"You need—"

With my hand on his, I leave only an inch between us, praying that he'll listen to me. "I know what I need. I know the look on your face. The look that you know better and that I'm not all right." I tilt my head up to meet his gaze and prove I'm all right, keeping my spine stiff and my shoulders squared.

"You want to make a deal with him? A deal with a murderer?" Cody doesn't hide the slight disgust, which adds another layer to my shame, but there's also a hint of hope. Because he didn't say no.

"There was no deal…" I whisper the lie, finding it hard to keep eye contact with the man in front of me. A man who came back here to help me. A man I lie in bed with. A man who right now, looks at me as if I've lost my mind.

After a moment of quiet, he questions, "Are you sure about this?"

I don't hesitate to answer yes. Swallowing thickly, I remember all of Brass's case. I remember it all and vengeance spurs inside of me. "If we could get Brass—"

Cody cuts me off, changing the dialogue between us as he says, "If we could get Marcus, it would be the end to three open cases and a string of murders."

"I know. I know."

"You're shaken up right now." Cody's strong hand lands on my shoulder, pulling me in closer and I pull away just slightly, hating that he's placating me.

"Come here, Delilah. As me and you. For the love of God, let me hold you."

"I don't want to tell." I offer up my end of the bargain and that's exactly what this is.

"Let me hold you." Cody repeats his, his brow lifting and his arms opening.

With my feet planted I tell him, "We aren't telling anyone anything and we need to see what's on that flash drive."

After a short pause of consideration, Cody agrees and pulls me in, telling me he's sorry he wasn't here. Murmuring all the right things and it's in his arms that I feel right again. My mind right and sound. But he can't hold me forever.

chapter eighteen

Cody

"I saw your APB. Figured you'd want to come see this." Officer Brady nods his head as I walk carefully across the street while avoiding piles of litter and head to the back of the convenience store.

"Just put it in last night," I call out over the loud drone of traffic behind us. The APB for Herman Jackson went out the second I got his name from the flash drive Marcus sent. The fucker was as good as dead. Apparently someone else thought the same.

The city is bright and lively against the stark yellow tape I know so well, draping the crime scene and bringing in onlookers.

Brady lifts the tape and the two of us duck under. With my watch telling me it's 9:00 a.m., I know it's been an hour since the body was found. It took that long for me to get through morning traffic so I could see it for myself.

Someone offed Herman Jackson before I could. The rage that boils inside of me, knowing I can't question him, isn't unexpected.

"You sure it's him?" I question, keeping my pace with his as we avoid the trash bags and stand over the body. With his dark beard, height, and evidence of a long-ago broken nose, I know this is him. Herman's dead on the street in front of me.

Fuck. I stare to my right, hands on my hips as Brady pulls out the victim's wallet from an evidence bag to check for ID. The crowd doesn't try to hide their curiosity, but from this angle, I know they can't see a damn thing.

After I hired Evan's crew, we did a full sweep, we checked the camera footage. Bastard must've had Delilah's phone tapped when I told her the code. He was there before she even got there, turning off the cameras. I won't make that mistake again.

She's not allowed to be by herself. Whether she likes it or not. Dread eats me alive at the thought of Delilah and him being left alone together. She knows damn well what he's capable of; we both do.

It's not going to happen. It can't happen.

"Yeah well, judging by the body, he was already dead, probably forty-eight hours at most." Brady's voice brings me back to now. Back to the fact that this fucker was dead before Marcus even told Delilah about him.

I give Brady a nod, short and to the point. "You have any idea who did it?" Brady questions. He's a street cop who I've seen a handful of times. Enough that I know his name. I know he has a wife and kids, two, I think. Running a hand over the back of his head he adds, "If you've got any leads, I'll take them. Unless the FBI is taking this case from me?"

Clicking the side button to my phone with irritation, I note Marcus hasn't written back.

My own message to him sits there. *You crossed a line going to her. If you touch her, I'll kill you. I won't think twice about it.*

"This one's yours. He was only wanted for questioning. I put it out for a friend," I answer Brady, feeling a tightness linger in my chest.

"All right," he concedes, and another cop calls him over, back to the street side, her hand covering a phone and telling him someone needs him.

"You good here?" he asks me and I nod, patting his back for good measure. "Thanks, Brady."

Again I drift back to the texts, hating that he's one step ahead of me. Pain lingers in the message. Acts done in fear are harmful and lack intelligence. He told me that once and it stuck with me, because it's so fucking true. I never should have sent it. I gave him the edge. I can't deny that his willingness to approach Delilah scares me. What Marcus is capable of, terrifies me. Even if I feel pity for him. Even if I brought all this on…

"Walsh, you hear me?" Officer Brady questions, staring up at me from where he's now crouched on the ground next to the body.

"No, what's that?"

"There's a note if you want to take a look at it. Just in case it has to do with your case."

A note? Goosebumps spread in an instant, taking me back to the first case that I ever worked on where Marcus was involved.

Already tucked away in a ziplock plastic bag, Brady passes me the note.

It's not in his handwriting, it's in the font of a phone message. Same size too.

That motherfucker. It takes everything in me not to react when I read it. To stay calm and pretend to rack my brain for what it could mean when I know damn well it's from Marcus.

I'll be her hero this time.
The hero gets the kiss.

The coroner and another cop come up alongside us, distracting Brady for a moment as he watches them. With fire in my blood, I hand the note back to him, clearing my throat to get his attention. "Sorry man, I have no idea, but I'd get that to processing."

I'll be damn sure to keep an eye on the forensics for this case, but I already know it's a dead end.

There won't be any evidence. Marcus doesn't leave anything behind. He's too careful. All this was intended as a show for me.

"If you could keep me updated with the case, I'd appreciate it," I say then tilt my head to stare down at the body and add, "I want to know all of his connections."

"What is it you think he did?" Brady questions, standing up and wrinkling his nose from the stench.

I keep my tone as casual as I can. "He threatened a lawyer I know, trying to cover up a case she was working on."

"How do you know it was him?"

"A kid IDed him." That was the first call I got. This was the second.

And there's not a damn thing I can do now, but question Ross Brass without a warrant. I already know how that will end.

chapter nineteen

With the suspect Herman dead, Claire didn't fight me when I said I wanted to get back to work. She did say I had to see the department psychologist first though. Luckily, he cleared me.

He doesn't know about Marcus and Claire doesn't either. That is, nothing apart from the incident in the parking garage and the suspicion that it may have been Marcus. The leading theory now is that it was someone hired by Herman. At least that's one of several.

Cody's on board to keep quiet about what happened between Marcus and me, plus the flash drive. It's not like we could use it in court anyway. It's inadmissible evidence because of how it was acquired. The kid IDing Herman we can use, though. Now it's just a matter of tying Herman to Brass.

The terminology "rot" is all I've got to work with and that's not enough for a warrant. I don't need a warrant to know that Herman worked closely with a man named Harrold Reynolds. He owns a dry cleaning business on Thirty-fourth Street. He was never a suspect in any case, but he was brought in countless times for questioning. His lawyer is familiar to our firm. He represents the mob.

It doesn't make sense. Or least it wouldn't without the bank accounts and proof of laundering. His former secretary is one of the women I suspected was murdered by Ross Brass, although I never did know why.

And there's the connection, if only I can find new evidence that wasn't tampered with that would lead Ross back to the secretary's murder, which connects him to Reynolds who is already connected to Herman. It could be my way in. My mind spins, going through everything just as it has all morning and afternoon well into the evening. Glancing at the clock in the upper right corner, it's already 8:00 p.m. It's time to go.

But the case doesn't quit.

Ross Brass committed a series of murders and got off on evidence tampering. The man whose release got me so worked up that I fell into a PR nightmare. I know he killed those girls… the laundering part is new, though.

Maybe Ross was the first man for hire. He isn't the starting point, so we'll have to look back further. I'm not sure, but the evidence on the flash drive files isn't enough. There are deposits to a number of bank accounts, but none can firmly be traced. Not without a warrant and I don't have evidence I can submit to get that warrant.

The theory: The mob hired Ross to launder. Ross used the money and Harrold Reynolds to commit other crimes, eventually leading to murders. When he got caught, he hired Harrold's buddy, Herman, to get him off. It worked, but I pissed off Ross with my comment and Herman was hired again. Maybe I would have been murder number five. Maybe I still will be.

It's only a theory with weak connections. Still, it's a theory. My tired eyes stare at the white computer screen. There are so many pieces, so many crimes and only so much information I have that can go toward motive.

I click my phone on, wondering if I asked Marcus, would he tell me? Does he already know? Staring at his phone number listed under just the letter *M*, it feels like I have a direct line to the devil. It's unused. Not a message has been sent back to him since the first text two nights ago… But I have it. I could use it. I could nail that son of a bitch if only I had more to go on. If I could get my hands on something definitive that no judge can dismiss.

A ping from my phone catches me off guard, my anger waning at the sound.

Are you doing all right?

The text from Cody stares back at me.

Am I all right? No.

Cody can tell I'm not and I hope he thinks I'm off because I came in close contact with Marcus. He's got a hired man outside my door and it's… at best, distracting. At worst it's causing rumors and could be a potential lawsuit. *"If the DEA allowed someone to come back to work while under protection…"* Claire's warning from earlier today echoes in my head. Telling her my boyfriend is just being protective earned a laugh and then a stern, *"That better be all this is."*

Better than this morning, I message him back.

I don't know what to think or really, what I was thinking when it all happened.

The shrink this morning told me to "jot it all down." As if it's that easy. As if there are no repercussions. If I do, it's evidence. If I don't, I'm opening myself up to committing obstruction of justice. So, I haven't written a damn thing.

I text Cody again, even as I stare at the bottle of expensive white wine that was waiting for me when I got in here. *I'm fine. Not getting much work done, but I'm fine.*

It's a lie. When did I become such a liar? Every other sentence out of my mouth today has been a lie.

When Cody asked me if I was all right being alone. When Claire questioned if I was stable enough to come in. Not to mention the lying I did in the shrink's office.

Just thinking about that session has me eyeing the bottle of *Valley Pines* Pinot, my favorite wine, wanting to uncork it and have a long, slow sip of the sweet addiction. Hide away in a bottle and pretend like this past week never happened.

How can a small series of events over such a short period of time drastically affect me like this? They make me question who I am.

For instance, the wine. I know who it came from… and yet it remains where it is and I have every intention of drinking it. Maybe I felt unsafe at first.

I did what any normal person would do, what the previous version of myself would do.

I asked who brought it to my office. The bottle of red came in a pretty bag with a bow—and a note. *I thought you might need this.*

First roses, and now wine. It's another gift from Marcus. I know his handwriting now.

He watches me; he must. How else would he know that I keep wine in the office and more importantly, that I was out, confiding in the psychologist just so I could get back in here. It was the perfect opportunity for a delivery man to bring in a package and no one would object or question in broad daylight. No one was here who would have thought it was suspect. It's clearly a gift from a friend who heard what happened. I'm certain that's what they all thought. Bought and paid for by John Smith according to Greg, the delivery man who signed in and left the wine with security.

Instead of telling anyone, I added it to my growing pile of secrets.

Marcus gets into places he shouldn't be able to. He hides his identity with disguises and multiple aliases. Marcus is truly like a ghost. Coming and going as he pleases with no obligation to the laws the rest of us abide by.

So when I heard Herman was dead, naturally my mind put two and two together and I stared at the bottle of wine, willing it to spill more secrets like Marcus had.

I should be grateful that the man who worked to help threaten me is dead. A piece of me is. A small, ragged piece that broke off right about where I'm standing now while my fingers grazed over the threat that was embedded in that note.

But another piece of me feels… sick. And responsible. I can't help but to feel complicit in his murder. Not just because I wanted him to pay for what he did to me, but because I know things that no one else does.

No one but Cody… and Marcus.

The soft knock on my door is welcome, stealing me away from these thoughts and the trails my mind is leading me down. At first I think it's the security detail, wanting to know if I have an ETA for when we'll be home. Evan's already asked twice. It's not, though. It's Claire.

"What's going on with you?" Claire asks as she shuts the door, her black silk blouse reflecting the yellow light as she does. "Still shaken about the threat?" she asks with the soft click of the door shutting. A friend is what I need now. Thank God for Claire checking in on me before I lose it all.

Shaking my head no, which oddly enough is true, I answer, "Just focusing on Brass."

"The four murders?" she questions, touching on the cases he walked on.

"And the note. The threat I got."

"You really think Herman and Brass are connected? That Brass was behind it all?"

Yes. I do. Only because of Marcus. If I tell her I do… well, a good lawyer wouldn't jump to conclusions. "It's a hunch. I just want it solved."

"Understandable. Threats shouldn't be taken lightly," Claire answers easily as she gracefully takes the seat across from me. She adds, "A man like him doesn't stay out of trouble… so we'll nail him one day. Speaking of, did you hear Herman was found dead this morning?"

"Yeah, Walsh told me."

I don't miss the way her head tilts slightly and her arms cross against her chest when I admit that Walsh told me. It strikes me as odd. Why wouldn't he tell me?

She questions, "You think Brass did it?"

No. I think Marcus did. I think he did it for me. It's only a hunch, but I feel it deep in the marrow of my bones. Every time his name comes up, Marcus, a deep need runs over me to close my eyes. To remember the way his scent and his heat wrapped around me. If I'm not thinking about the details of the case… I'm thinking about him or pleading with Cody to keep me occupied.

I'm desperate to know how Marcus became the man he is. Did he really do everything everyone claimed he did? The questions bombard me once again and with them screaming in my head, I look back up at Claire and try to remember her question.

I'm fairly certain Marcus killed Herman. That's not what I answer, of course, and another lie slips out. "I think so. I think Brass knew the kid would ID him and he wanted to make sure Herman couldn't rat."

Claire nods. Her eyes are discerning though when she says, "It's a decent theory."

I can hear the questions she'd typically rattle off. Questions to get me thinking. They all start with the other man from that night. The man with the blue eyes who called himself Marcus. Ross Brass doesn't have blue eyes or fit the physical description.

She doesn't ask a single question, though. Not one and that knowledge makes my skin heat with the sense that she knows I'm hiding something.

Or maybe that's just guilt.

I pause, leaning back in my chair, wishing I could tie Brass to Herman's death. It would be so easy. It would be justified. "The only thing we have is the ID of a kid," I tell her, breathing in deep and racking my brain for some evidence from the secretary's murder that would tie Herman and Brass together more closely. That's all I need and we can bring Brass in.

"And the dead body," Claire comments.

"Right, and a dead body."

"What about the note at the scene? Did Walsh tell you about that?" Her questions come back-to-back, berating me. I understand she's a bit overbearing given everything that happened. But she can back off of whatever trail she's on. She's dead wrong.

"No. He didn't. What note?" She doesn't answer me; instead she searches my eyes for something and whatever it is she's looking for, I don't think she finds it.

"To be frank, the only thing keeping you from being a suspect in his murder is your alibi with Taylor."

What? My eyes widen with both contempt and disbelief. "I know you wouldn't do something like that. But the fact that it came up at all as a theory… That's a little too close for my liking. Especially given it was only a month ago that the article came out and the animosity there. We don't need any more heat. You," she says while she points directly at me and I want to snap her finger off, "you don't need any more heat."

"I don't have anything to say to that." It's all I can respond, ignoring her and the pissed-off feelings seeping through me.

"You're too close to this case." Claire's voice is gentle and I understand why, but it doesn't matter. She can't take me off this one. I know it better than anyone else here.

A huff of a laugh leaves me as I close my laptop, rubbing my eyes and knowing that's far too true. This case is everything.

"You need to take time off, see your sister or your mother." Claire's advice strikes a nerve with me for a number of reasons, but more than that, more guilt. Guilt on top of guilt.

Shit. Shit shit shit. That's exactly what I feel like right now. I never texted her back. In all the hours I stayed awake last night, refusing to close my eyes because every time I did, I could feel Marcus's hand pressed against them, I didn't once think about my sister.

I bet she hates me right now. I haven't even spoken to my mom. My heart swells with a pain I know too well.

"You can't focus." Claire interrupts my train of thought. "You aren't going to be productive here." Numbness crawls across my skin. I have to be here. I have access to everything here.

"All I have is my work." I tell her a single truth that she knows just as much as I do.

"Well, right now, you don't have that."

"What?" My blink is slow as my brow creases.

"I told you to go in for evaluation," she says and Claire's tone is accusatory.

"And I did," I answer pointedly. Where the hell is she going with this?

"And he said you aren't ready." Claire's arms cross, wrinkling her black blouse as it shifts from where it's tucked into her gray pencil skirt. "In his particular phrasing, 'her grip on reality is loose.'"

What does that mean? What the hell? That's not at all what he told me. "He signed off on me returning to work," I say and disbelief coats my response.

"Are you depressed? Anx—" Anger waging against any sense of reason, this time I cut her off.

"Depressed? Do I look depressed to you?" I question, truly taken aback. There's not an ounce of me that's depressed. I know I'm not with it, but depressed? Fuck that.

"Well, what is it then? You aren't yourself." The statement Claire gives comes complete with a flash of a man, only his shadow. My heartbeat slows and chills flow down my shoulders, but every other piece of me is hot as I attempt to breathe.

"I'm shaken up is all," I confess to Claire, to give her something that would change her mind. "Don't take this from me, please."

"How many times have you asked me that in the past few months?" Claire responds and it stings. "This Brass case has worked its way into your head, and I can't have it here. You need to go home."

"I was cleared—"

"You didn't tell him everything," Claire cuts me off, stern and to the point. Silence fills the space and my gaze drops to the bottle of wine. "So you aren't cleared."

My voice would shake if I were to speak right now, so I don't.

"It's just temporary. Go home, see your family." Claire's gaze burns into me but I don't return it. Not even when her tone morphs to something more consoling as she adds, "Just take care of yourself."

Cody wants me at his place, which is cold and the only heat I feel there when Cody's absent is from the memory of a man I should be terrified of.

How am I supposed to get better? How do I get through this if I'm not allowed to work on the case that's fucked me over?

The one-word answer is all I give her in response. "Fine." My tone denotes everything I'm feeling. Finality, betrayal. That fucking shrink cleared me.

I don't hesitate to put on my coat. There's no use in fighting and I'm not at all in the right mindset to argue. The last thing I want is to lose my job. That's something I would never recover from. With a tight throat and tension throughout my entire body, I ask, "How long?" My fingers are numb as I button my jacket. I can barely focus enough to do it although my back is turned to Claire, so the silver lining is that she can't see how unnerved I am. Even as I grab the bottle of wine, intent on drinking every last drop of it tonight, I hide everything I'm feeling.

"Come in next week for another psych evaluation."

Evaluation, my ass. If they really knew what was going on in my head...

I can only nod and as I go to leave, Claire calls out my name. "Delilah." My feet stay planted as I stop where I am but I don't turn back around when she tells me, "I'm doing this for your own good. You'll see that."

The words I want to reply tumble over each other at the back of my throat. Suffocating me as I leave the building, Evan following in tow, asking questions that I don't answer.

chapter twenty

Delilah

To LOVE IS NEVER WRONG.

That's a phrase my mother told my grandmother years ago after an angry conversation that was taken to the kitchen.

I was only a little girl, but I remember it well. It's one of my first memories in fact.

Her voice shook when I peeked in the doorway to find her face-to-face with my grandmother whom I loved so much. I could tell she'd been crying and she told my grandmother, "To love is never wrong."

After recent events, I have some thoughts on that memory. But still, the words ring clear in my head. To love is never wrong.

Yet here I am, with feelings stirring for one man, one I should certainly not be attracted to, let alone love… while sitting in the living room of another man.

It's not love. Not for either of them. I know it's not, but the longer I stay here, the more I can feel myself slipping.

Every sip of wine, in this empty place, only leads me to think of Marcus. And oh my Lord, my mother would eat her words if she knew what I was thinking. It would be sickening if I really did feel anything toward him. But I can't stop thinking about that searing kiss. I can't stop questioning, why me? And remembering all the notes from years ago. The closed cases that all led to one elusive man.

I don't know if it's shock or if it's PTSD but I've been in a daze since Marcus showed up and approached me.

Maybe even before then. When his fingers brushed against mine in the parking garage, when he left me flowers and then the kiss.

With a whirl of my wrist, the pale yellow wine swirls in the glass. It's my third and the bottle will be empty by the fourth.

I'd be ashamed if I gave a fuck. I can't go to work, so I've chosen not to go home and to stay at Cody's place instead. I'm out of my element, losing all control and therefore my mind.

There's a constant security detail present and every time I go outside they stand at attention, not speaking, just waiting. I feel like a prisoner more than anything.

Evan is nice enough, but he's gone, and I can't even remember the names of the two men out front. I decided tomorrow would be a better time to get acquainted more thoroughly. Tonight, the only interest I have is finding sleep at the bottom of this bottle.

So, sitting on my ass in the middle of the rug in Cody's living room and staring at the large modern art piece on the stark white wall is what I settled on when 10:00 p.m. rolled around and Cody said he had a lead and would be out later than he said he would. The black splotches that fade to gray don't say a damn thing. It's pretty. That's all it is. Monochrome and pretty to look at.

I down another sip, letting the sweet liquid pool on my tongue before slowly sucking it down. Another large gulp empties the glass and I stand up, stretching out my back and listening to the background noise of some cooking competition show that's on the large flat-screen TV behind me.

My head feels lighter, the tension in my shoulders nearly gone.

Nothing matters as I stare at the corner of the room where I first saw Marcus. Willing him back so I can question him the way they all question me.

So I can ask him why… why kiss me? Why help me?

More than that, what does he know about Cody Walsh? There's something there. I know there is. I can feel it. Like a gut instinct.

Of course, he would deny it. But didn't I deny it too? The dim light from the fridge gives a bit of warmth to the spartan kitchen as I grab the now nearly empty bottle and set it down on the marble counter with a loud clink. A softer clink follows with my wineglass.

I pour the last bit of wine and stare back up at the corner, trying to remember the silhouette of his body. With the memory, my eyes close and he touches me again. His hand wraps around my waist and—*Stop!*

Wrapping my fingers around the stem of the glass I hold it tightly as I sway where I stand.

I wish Cody were here. I wish I'd let him touch me and kiss me rather than pushing him away, which is exactly what I did last night. I need to wash the memories of Marcus off of me.

With a deep inhale, I take a look in the pantry, needing something of substance to help absorb the alcohol. Without something in my stomach, the thought of anything at all sounds scrumptious.

Three bags of tortilla chips and a loaf of bread are all that's there. Checking the fridge, I find similarly disappointing choices. And no salsa for the chips.

His pantry is evidence of one thing: Cody's never here, so it shouldn't surprise me.

Yet it does. I open a bag of chips and take it with me as I go, walking slowly and taking in every detail of Cody's place. It's sparsely furnished, one could argue it's a deliberately minimalistic style choice, but it's almost like the place is staged. Like no one really lives here.

There's a guest room with a bed and dresser. The bed is pristine, the sheets neatly tucked in as if housekeeping from a hotel had made it. I hesitate, eating a chip and staring at the black varnish before pulling out a drawer. Empty.

I toss the bag of chips on the bed and pull out another drawer and then another until I've looked through all of them. They're all empty.

The closet drawers are the next to be opened. Again, there's nothing but a folded spare blanket.

It is the guest room, after all. I doubt Cody has many guests. His uncle isn't well and doesn't like to travel. I can't even remember a single time Cody's spoken about someone coming to visit or stay with him. It's only ever him going back home.

The closet doors shut easily enough and I continue my exploration. When I put the half-empty bag of chips back in the pantry and glance at the red digital clock on the oven to find it's nearly 1:00 a.m., I'm empty-handed on any new information at all about Cody. There's nothing personal. Not even in his bedroom.

My tired eyes beg me to sleep. My mostly unsatisfied appetite begs me to eat. And my conscience begs for more wine.

Shutting the still-barren pantry door again, with the same amount of disappointment as before, leaves me staring down the hall at the half bath and the small closet just beside it. It's the last place to look and with nothing better to do and thoughts of Marcus still lingering and threatening to take over, I head to the narrow door.

The wooden shelves boast few toiletries and spare washcloths. His place is so bare, it's… uncanny. I've nearly closed the door when

I realize there's a box on the very top shelf. It's unlike anything else in this place because it's a cardboard storage file box. Everything else seems luxurious, even if it's bare and minimal. But the box on the top shelf is dusty from years of sitting still. I can't reach it even though I try to and in my drunken state combined with boredom and… curiosity, I'm quick to grab the ottoman from the living room, drag it down the hall and get my hands on the box.

It's heavy, so heavy and the sharp edges force me to wince when they dig into my forearms. I nearly drop the thing and I'm glad I don't, because it's filled with papers but also a thin, hollow tin horse. It looks like it was once a piggy bank, but its detail makes it look like a trinket one would give to a newborn baby.

It's old and dingy, but I imagine once it was a beautiful gift at a baby shower. What the hell is it doing in a box that looks like crime scene evidence?

With the box on the ottoman, I sit beside it, cross-legged in my sweats and lift one of the straps to my tank top back into place. Confusion etches a deep line into the center of my forehead when I read adoption papers from almost forty years ago. Until I read the last name—Walsh.

First name: Christopher.

It must be a box of his brother's things. It looks like Cody's aunt legally adopted his brother after their parents died. Quickly I go through paper after paper, finding legal records, the criminal reports of his brother's abduction and an autopsy. My hands tremble and it's hard to read when my eyes water at the description of what was done to him. I can't imagine reading all of this and knowing your younger brother… Swallowing back the tears, I push through, needing to know more and understanding why Cody would hide this box away.

It's heartbreaking to the point that I almost miss the other names. The other boys who were abducted, including one named Marcus.

A sharp, frigid cold pricks down my spine and the lights seem darker as I read the black printed text on off-white paper, aged from sitting in a box, buried in a stack of articles that have yellowed.

Marcus Henry. The reports say he died but his body was never found. Only teeth and bones, which the police took as evidence of his passing.

Only one child made it out alive. I knew that; Cody told me.

I can't shake the name of the smallest and youngest child, or his photo from evidence, barely a photo with how difficult it is to see his face, staring back at me in black and white. He's a little boy in an oversized baseball jersey, holding a bat. I can barely make out any details of him. But the writing is easily read. Only eight years old when the picture was taken, according to the script on the back of the photo. And next to his age, his name: Marcus. It can't be *him*. He's dead and it's just a name.

Rubbing both of my hands down my face I try to pull myself together. I wish I hadn't drunk the wine. I wish I could get the hell out of my own head. I can't breathe, I can barely see straight.

What the fuck am I doing? I shouldn't be going through Cody's things. This is a box of what he has left of his brother, I inwardly scold myself. Hating all of this.

He's protecting me and I'm violating his privacy. Oh my God, what came over me?

What the hell is wrong with me? As I frantically pile the papers in the stack they were in and place them back in the box, a small picture slips out, in black and white.

Two boys, with the tallest maybe ten years old, and the other a few years younger. Cody. Cody and his brother, Christopher, both the spitting image of the man behind them. Maybe their uncle.

The sight of the two of them together only heightens the guilt I have of betraying Cody's trust and rummaging through his things. What right do I have to go through his personal belongings?

Jesus Christ, what has gotten into me?

He lost his brother and these poor boys were murdered, yet here I am concocting some sort of connection with a man who broke in and kissed me in Cody's kitchen. I'm disgusted with myself. I've truly lost it. It's all I can think as I shake my head and brush away the tears from under my eyes.

I have to move the ottoman before I can shut the closet door. I'm halfway through the hallway, dragging the heavy thing back to the living room when I hear the front door open.

"Delilah?" Cody's voice is hesitant.

I don't call out, "In here," until the ottoman is back where it should be. My heart races and I know it looks like I've been crying when Cody steps into the doorframe, looking all sorts of the handsome man I fell for years ago. With grocery bags in both hands and shadows under his eyes, gratitude and unworthiness wrap themselves around me.

"Baby," he says and his voice drowns in agony as he drops the bags where he stands and eats up the distance between us before I can even take in a staggering breath. All I see in his face is his brother. "Why are you crying?"

I don't want to lie. I can't lie anymore, but I don't tell him the truth either, I simply shake my head, burying it into his chest and attempting to calm myself down.

This is what rock bottom must feel like.

I cry for him and for this craziness that's taken me over, but mostly I cry for his brother and the other little boys.

"I'm sorry," I finally answer and wipe away the tears. I don't need to be even more of a mess than I already am. "I'm sorry, I just I couldn't sleep and I got to drinking." That's when I realize I didn't tell him about the wine. I didn't tell anyone.

With both palms pressed to my eyes, I pray for sanity. For all of this to end.

"Don't be sorry," Cody says then kisses my hair, and I rest my head against his shoulder as he rocks me, comforting me. And I know damn well I don't deserve it.

With that thought comes the nagging prick again. The one that tells me Cody knows more about Marcus than he's let on over the years. The pictures flash in my mind. And the realization dawns on me. *Why weren't there pictures of the other boys? Why was it all about Marcus and his brother?*

The nagging prick comes back as I stand there, feeling the chill of the air before the click of the heater comes on. I know Cody knows something. I know he does. I knew it the second I mentioned Marcus came to me. It's what's gotten into me.

Cody remains calm and comforting as the feeling of deceit takes over once again. This is what's making me crazy.

"I need to ask you something." My heart races as I give voice to words a part of me knows I shouldn't, not daring to look up. "I don't want you to lie to me, though." I pray I'm not wrong. If he doesn't know something for sure, he at least thinks it. He has a theory. I know he must. I can *feel* it.

"I won't," Cody swears, trying to look down at me but I cling to him, refusing to look up. "What do you know about Marcus that I don't?"

but i need you

W Winters

USA Today best-selling author, Willow Winters, brings you an all-consuming, sizzling romance featuring an epic antihero you won't soon forget.

Some love stories are a slow burn. Others are quick to ignite, scorching and branding your very soul before you've taken that first breath. You're never given a chance to run from it.

That's how I'd describe what happened to us.

Everything around me blurred and all that existed were his lips, his touch …

The chase and the heat between us became addictive.

Our nights together were a distraction, one we craved to the point of letting the world crumble around us.

We should have paid more attention; we should have known that it would come to this.

We both knew it couldn't last, but that didn't change what we desired most.

All we wanted was each other …

dedication

To my husband.
My hero and my love.

"It's so much darker when a light goes out than it would have been if it had never shone."

—John Steinbeck

prologue

Marcus

Twenty-one years ago

IT'S WARMER IN THE BARN. HERE IN THE CORNER, NESTLED IN the hay, it's far warmer than it is outside. More importantly, in this back corner, there's not a place for the brutal wind to slip in. The tips of my fingers could just as well be pieces of ice tucked under my chin as I hunker down in the hay. It smells like dirt and pigs, but the warmth is more comforting than anything I've felt in days. By the looks of it, there hasn't been a soul here in quite some time.

I spent the past three nights outside. Last night I dug into the ground to try to hide from the vicious wind that whipped through my tattered clothes. The hard earth was like a brick of clay and it took far too much energy to dig deep enough. It helped, but my throat is sore, my body is weak and I don't know that I'll ever get my hands warm again. There's only one thing I'm certain of: I can't keep going on like this. Something has to give.

Late fall in the northeast turns frigid sooner than most cities.

My teacher used to refer to all the backwoods towns off the highway outside of New York City as Podunk. So that's what I've been calling them all, the Podunk towns. I don't even know where I am other than somewhere deep in the woods but to the left of the farms. It's open fields out there, wide open with nowhere to hide.

This barn looks abandoned, a lonely decrepit place, and perfect for one night. Just one night to close my eyes and get the strength to keep moving. I don't know how far I'll run, but he told me his home was past the Podunk towns and that's where mine used to be ... if only I can find it.

When I close my eyes and ignore the smells, all I can hear is his voice. I try to forget the worst parts and only think about the stories he told me. He had so many good ones about his mother and how she was going to find us and save us. I remember how sure he was whenever he said we were safe. It was the only way I could sleep although I would have never admitted that to him. I was the one who was supposed to be protecting him, not the other way around. Safety surrounds me for a moment; a long enough moment that my eyes feel heavy and my body sags against the barn wood, begging me to give in to much-needed sleep.

Every muscle still burns from running. Even worse so because I ran up the mountain and into the thick, dense forest when I heard the cars coming. I won't let them get me too. I'll never be caught again. Each little cut stings and seems to sear the memories into my skin with every small movement, but I focus on the stories ... the good ones he told. The ones that almost made us smile, the ones that made us forget where we were.

Sleep nearly takes me ... almost there.

Until a sudden creak forces my tired eyes wide open and my heart races, listening to a man pry open the doors of the barn.

chapter one

Delilah

MY FATHER ALWAYS TOLD ME TO TRUST MY GUT. HE also said when someone shows you who they are, believe them. It's always made sense to me, as has most of my father's wisdom, and from the day he gave me that piece of advice until now, I've lived by that motto.

Right now, though, as I stare into Cody's eyes, listening to him reassure me that I know everything he does about the cold cases and about Marcus, I doubt myself. I thought I knew him. I thought wrong. The man I know Cody Walsh to be is nowhere around and a stranger stares back at me.

I find myself in his home feeling anything but secure. He's lying to me. It's the only thing I'm certain of and I can't even begin to process how much it hurts. Of everyone I've worked with to solve these cases, I trusted him the most. I've leaned on him for years and right now, I question everything.

Men have secrets, my mother used to whisper. Back then I thought she was the crazy one. Now I'm wondering if I inherited that trait as well.

"I'm telling you," Cody says, starting up again, bringing my gaze back to his. "You're worked up and I don't blame you, but there's nothing I know that you don't." His voice is calm and comforting, but his eyes are flat and devoid of commitment. It's like they want me to know he doesn't mean a damn word he's saying.

My tired body begs me to give in to Cody, to just believe him and shake off the horrible gut-wrenching feelings that seep from the marrow of my bones. Every time I close my eyes, though, I see the picture of the boy. The statements. The death certificate.

"I don't think you believe me," Cody says when I don't answer him. The sizzle of the thick slice of ham he places in the frying pan brings me back to the present. It's pitch black outside, but still the streetlights filter in through the curtains in Cody's dining room.

With my arms crossed, I lean my hip against the counter and I have to clear my tight throat before telling him again, "It's just that I feel like there's more to it." Shame washes over me. I should tell him I went through his things. I should confess that much and maybe he'd confess too.

"Because the cases haven't been solved. Every case I've ever had that went cold … I've felt like that," he says, speaking to the stove instead of me, flipping the ham and then scooping potatoes from the back pan onto the two simple white plates beside the stove.

Even with my sanity stretched far too thin, somewhere in the back of my exhausted mind I'm fully aware that I should be grateful for Cody and that, as far as I know, he doesn't have any reason at all to lie to me. I can't shake this feeling, though. My gut instinct is that he's lying … it also whispers that I should keep what I know hidden from him just the same. One old case file I opened while I was snooping has shifted everything.

He continues, "Because there *is* more to it. To all of those cases we didn't close. You and I both know that." He adds under his breath, so low I almost don't hear, "There's more to all those cases."

With a deep thump in my chest that ricochets a pain that can't possibly compare to his, a flash of the photo I found comes to mind. The black and white photo of Cody and his brother standing with an older man, maybe their uncle since they resembled him closely. The image is followed with more thoughts of the case that was never fully closed. At least not for him.

The silverware clinks against the porcelain as he places a plate in front of me, not missing a beat of his explanation. "Of course you feel like there's more. There is more; I just don't know that we'll ever know the truth."

My gaze flies to his, but he isn't looking at me. He's focused on spearing the ham and eating, like I should do. Lord knows I've had more to drink than I needed tonight.

With every swallow, questions beg to be spoken.

I barely taste the meal, although the heavy scent of butter and pork makes me believe it should be delicious.

"We may never know the truth, but we did everything we could." Cody's statement carries a note of finality. As if it's the end of the conversation.

A sadness washes over me. I'm sure that's what he thinks about his brother's case and it tears me up inside to imagine him as a young boy, being handed paperwork and most likely, told little lies to lessen the blow of what happened to his younger brother.

We did everything we could. I've heard it so many times. Everything isn't always good enough though, is it?

"Eat something." Cody's command sounds more like a plea. He even wears a half smile, as if smiling would make the thoughts in my mind disappear.

The atmosphere changes when his gaze softens. "Delilah, baby," he says, dropping his fork and striding toward me to pin me between him and the counter. A hand rests on either side of me, but he doesn't touch me. "You haven't slept, I'm guessing?" he says and he guesses right. "I know you haven't eaten."

The way he cares for me, obviously trying to console me, destroys that nagging bit inside that believes he's being deceitful.

"You need sleep." With a single kiss on my forehead, suddenly my mother's warning fades and I remember what my father told me. I trust my instincts from years ago, when I first met and fell for this man. My gut back then said that I could love him. And the part about secrets? Well, just like I told my mother back then, we all have them.

I share one of them right now. "I'll have nightmares," I say, whispering the confession, feeling a flurry of fear run through me.

Cody's eyes flash with shock and then he rests a hand on my chin. "Is that why you aren't sleeping?" With both of my hands I pull his away, kissing his knuckles and nodding against his chest.

Leaning into him, it's easy to close my eyes.

He's gentle as he holds me, rubbing soothing circles on my back and the fight … or whatever that was a moment ago seems to vanish. Disappearing like it never happened.

He plants small kisses along the crown of my head and tells me, "You're going through hell. You're stressed and it's killing you."

My eyes slowly open and I stare at the curtains as the panel on the right sways gently from the air exiting the floor vent beneath it.

"I know," I say and it's all I admit. It feels like I'm drowning, but there isn't an ounce of water to baptize my sinful soul in.

There's a rumble in Cody's chest, deep and masculine when I lift up my lips and kiss his throat, right against his Adam's apple. The stubble there tickles the tip of my nose.

A contented sigh leaves him and so I do it again.

I let him feel the hint of my smile against his hot skin when the growing erection he has becomes more than obvious.

"Look at what you do to me," he groans, as if it's an apology or perhaps like I'm torturing him.

"How about you fuck me to sleep," I suggest, wanting nothing more than just that. "Make me forget it all." My murmur pleads with him and in an instant, a yelp is ripped from me as he lifts me by my ass and sets me on the kitchen counter.

The sudden movement has my heart racing but the heat is all from the longing look in his steely blue gaze.

"Now that I can handle," he says before capturing my lips with his. His touch is strong, unrelenting and easy to get lost in. With his right hand steady on my hip, his left roams up my shirt and lingers over the curve of my waist. I wrap my legs around his hips and press my feet against his ass so I can feel his hard length against my core.

I'm shameless as I grind against him. I only break the kiss to take a breath of cool air, but Cody doesn't take the moment to pause. He continues his relentless touches, trailing his warm lips down my neck and kissing along every inch. My nipples pebble as a moan slips from my lips.

"Please," I beg him. And that single word is his undoing.

"Not here," he says as he lifts me into his arms and I cling to his broad frame while he takes me to his bed.

When he's done with me, after fucking me until I scream his name and forcing my release from me, I thought he'd done exactly what I'd asked: to fuck me to sleep and make me forget it all. I thought he had, but he didn't. Sleep eludes me and all I can see are the palest of blue eyes watching me from a memory in the dark night, judging and waiting.

Cody's eyes close faster than mine and even though my lungs beg me to breathe in time with him, the sound of his inhales and exhales so soothing, I can't fall asleep.

I can still feel him inside of me as I slip out of his bed. Leaving the warm sheets behind, I let out a small hum of satisfaction at the hint of pain and pleasure that lingers.

I'm quiet as I slip out, gathering a chair from the dining room and bringing it to the hall closet so I can have just one more look. Sitting cross-legged in the early morning on a hallway floor, plagued by insomnia, digging through a box of a lover's darkest moments … that's certainly not anything I ever thought I'd be striving toward. Yet here I am, obsessing over doing exactly that.

As I reach up to the box, my shirt lifting, I'm only vaguely aware of the floor creaking behind me. With my mind focused on the little boy in the photo labeled with the names of two brothers with their uncle, and what exactly each of those papers tells me about him and maybe little hints of what made Cody the man he is, it doesn't register.

My subconscious is aware that someone is behind me, but my desire for the truth is greedy and requires answers.

"Those aren't yours." The single sentence is chilling. With my heart slamming into my throat, I whip around to face Cody, nearly falling off the chair. Caught red-handed.

What makes matters worse is that his eyes look how mine feel. Exhausted and spent. The remainder of his expression, though, is hard and lacking forgiveness.

Swallowing thickly, I tell him, "I'm sorry."

"I mean it, Delilah." Cody's pale blue eyes hold a warning as he adds, "Everyone has their boundaries."

chapter two

Marcus

THE MAJORITY OF PEOPLE IN DELILAH'S HOMETOWN, A staggering ninety-two percent, are born in the hospital that's thirty miles from her home. It's where she was born and her sister too. We're far away at the moment, but I think of that hospital oh so often.

Nostalgia, perhaps.

When I looked up her birth records years ago, I noted her mother was also born in that hospital, delivered by the same doctor. A woman named Meredith was proud to be the lucky doctor who brought them both into the world. Isn't it a beautiful thing, bringing a new, innocent life into this chaos?

Staring at the monitors while Delilah stares at Cody, I think back on those days, the earliest ones of my life. There's not much before the barn that I remember. Only the immediate events leading to it. I consider those events my conception. After all, had they never happened, I wouldn't be who I am.

She was born in the hospital and I was born in that barn.

"I appreciate it, Cody, really I do … but I can't stay here." With her arms crossed, Mr. Walsh should know he's not winning this one. It's his controlling nature, his arrogance even, in thinking his home is better suited than Delilah's.

Turning my head to face the window, I can make out their silhouettes through the curtains. From my vantage point, and given their positions, it's easy to tell they're having a heated argument. Having the monitors, though, is far more helpful. I should feel guilty that a system I put in place years ago is now being exploited. I should feel many things … and I am, just not the correct emotions.

My phone buzzes with a message, but it's not one from either of them and I'm far too interested in this development.

Their argument is unfortunate. Not because I wish them pleasantness, or because either of the two are making a better case than the other. It's unfortunate simply because the raised voices and harsh tones are so very reminiscent of a lovers' quarrel.

Memories swirl and I lean back against the roof tiles. With the moon setting just beneath the tree line, it's dark enough that no shadows can survive. They'll never see me, but I can see them just fine.

And with the monitor in my hand, I can hear them just as clearly.

The tears that streak down Delilah's face remind me of the first time I went to the hospital that carries so much weight on my conscience this morning.

It was that little girl, with the same tears, who changed my decision. She was there and I didn't expect it. Had the events been different, and her father been the only one brought in with the unconscious woman losing her breath, I'd have told them all. I would have relied on what a former version of me was told to do, before this new one was conceived.

I could have spent hours mourning over every vision and letting it all spill out, but I kept it all in, swallowed it down and watched her being held in the arms of a monster. And she clung to him. Her head was tucked so carefully under his chin while the woman was whisked away on a gurney.

I remember standing there, thinking this very thought: this is where people are born. The stark white walls and the yells of nurses blurred with the wide eyes of a little girl who was scared. I wonder if she would remember. I doubt she does. I remember it all, though.

The thing about that unit is that most of the people I surrounded myself with were born there. I wasn't. I was so far gone from my hometown because I ran north when I should have run south. I know that now, but back then I didn't. I wasn't born in my hometown either, though.

I was birthed in that barn.

With the stench of pigs, and old dirt that felt like clay. The child who ran away, somehow escaping certain death, thought that structure would be a place to heal. But that's all he was, a child who should have died. A child who deserved to die for what he'd done.

So I let him. I let that boy suffer, I forced him to watch and accept what he allowed to happen. I didn't tell anyone what had really occurred and I knew that woman would die.

But the monster was comforting his little girl. How I could I, of all people, take someone's parent away?

The biggest difference between my birth and so many others, is that they came into this world innocent, being held dearly, if screaming wildly. Well … most of them. The lucky ones.

I became the person I am when I was seeking shelter in that barn from monsters and watching a man who I knew nothing about commit unspeakable acts of horror that haunted every night of that sanctuary.

I suppose it doesn't matter where or how you're born, though … much less so than where and how you die.

"I'm leaving, Cody." Delilah's voice is raised and it wavers at the end of her statement. The pain she's feeling is etched into his name. *Let her go.* She doesn't need a damn soul comforting her. Least of all his.

"How can you protect me better than anyone else if there's nothing you know that I don't?" the lawyer in her whips at him and a slow grin crawls into place on my face. She knows he knows, and she can't let it go. That knowledge brings me more peace than it should as I breathe in the crisp fall air.

"Please," he says, pleading with her and his tone is genuinely desperate. I catch the small details of her expression shift. The thin creases around her downturned lips and the way her gaze softens.

Holding my breath, I watch him touch her as if she belongs to him. As if he can hold her and comfort her and make everything all right.

That's not the way it works. He can't make it better. What's worse is that he *knows* he can't.

She's a strong woman, but not strong enough. That's obvious from the way she says his name, like it's the only word she knows.

We all know better. As he leans in and kisses her, her arms wrapping around his shoulders, all I can think is that we all know better.

My phone buzzes again and his messages can't wait any longer. I could stay here and listen to her sweet moans all night … but then he'd be the one kissing her.

Personal conflicts aside, I'll have to leave this ending to be a surprise.

If people knew the story of how I grew up, they would feel so badly for me. Most of them would. If, however, I started that tale with the barn … a sarcastic huff leaves me as I picture women securing their arms around their children and slowly backing away.

The metal stairs to the fire escape creak and groan as I climb down until my boots hit the pavement.

The streetlights shine down on me and that's just fine. With the jacket that's tight across my shoulders sporting an electric company logo and the nondescript black bag in my hand, I'm merely out on the job. Fixing a broken cable box or whatever the hell will do the trick to get bystanders feeling comfortable.

I went from being a boy abducted from his shitty hometown with crime rates that rivaled the most dangerous cities, to becoming an onlooker in a sleepy suburb, hiding in an abandoned barn while I observed the most heinous of crimes. I spent my days watching a man who defended both the innocent and guilty for a living, a man everyone seemed to look up to.

It wasn't often he came to the barn with his victims. But my birth was a long one and I learned who I was, what I wanted, and more importantly, how and why I should kill.

I was the lucky one who escaped one hell, only to be birthed into another.

chapter three

Delilah

IT'S FAR TOO QUIET IN THIS APARTMENT NOW THAT I'M alone. It's late and the residents above me, the Whitmores, must have gone to bed early or left for vacation. I haven't heard a thing through the floorboards. It would offer me peace any other time to know the obnoxious pacing and thuds of heavy footsteps are silenced for whatever reason, but not tonight.

I can't help but to focus on the fact that last time I showered here, Marcus brought roses to my kitchen. He broke in and not a soul knew while I was in this very bathroom. I check my bedroom the moment I step out of the shower, wrapped in nothing but a towel, although I hold on to my gun with a tight grip. The light-weight Beretta hasn't left my side since I've come home.

I take careful steps into every room and I truly wish there were some sign of someone else, even if it's only Mrs. and Mr. Whitmore arguing over the television channel and what to watch next.

No one's here. Not a sound can be heard except for my own

nervous heartbeat. My apartment is empty, the security system up and running. A click on the keypad to my laptop, open on my kitchen counter, would show any movement at all surrounding the apartment. Of course I see various people coming and going, mostly neighbors and their friends flowing through the locked front door as they're buzzed in.

With the pads of my feet still damp, I vacate the empty kitchen. The perfectly cleaned island counter, lacking anything at all on it, stays in my mind.

Back in the bedroom, I recheck all the windows. It's the back bedroom window that I'm certain Marcus came in through before. I don't have any proof but it would only make sense. It backs up to brush, so it'd be difficult, but it's quiet along that street with hardly anyone there to witness a break-in.

With a prick climbing up my spine, I stare at the window, the gun slipping against my palms until I breathe out a frustrated sigh.

This is necessary. Getting used to being home alone after a break-in is something that simply has to happen. I'm not the only one who goes through this anxiety. There's a break-in nearly every thirteen seconds, adding up to over two and a half million a year. So many people go through this. Still, as I set the gun down on the counter, remove my shower cap and stare at my reflection, I loathe that fear is leading my actions. I suppose the comparison isn't quite the same. Two and a half million people don't encounter serial killers … or get gifted flowers and forbidden kisses during their break-ins.

My gaze drops to my lips and I let my fingertips drift there. It's not like I'd use the gun, I remind myself as I set it down and go about my routine.

I have questions and Marcus has answers. Answers Cody supposedly doesn't have. Taking my time with my moisturizer and normal nightly routine, I let the accusations toward both Cody and Marcus build up in my mind. Right before shutting them all down again.

My bed creaks when I sit on the edge of it, spreading a sweet-smelling lavender lotion down my thighs and calves. The oversized sleep shirt I'm wearing is a soft cotton and I let myself breathe for a moment. Auntie Susan used to tell me, *You have to give yourself grace; no one else will.*

I can't help the small whisper in response at the back of my mind: *Cody would. Cody would grant me grace.* Hell, letting out my frustration in a huff, I place the amber glass bottle of lotion on my dresser and know that he gave me more grace than he should have this past weekend. I don't deserve it, and he knows that now. Yet he still wanted me and I can't fathom why.

My mind is still a whirlwind of everything that's happened in the past few weeks.

Pretending as if I'll sleep at all tonight, I take the lightweight gun with me to the kitchen for a glass of water to bring to bed. This gun is coming with me everywhere. I have my firearms license and there's not a chance in hell Cody would have let me walk out his door without it. The kitchen light is still on and the front door boasts a blinking red light, signifying the alarms are all set. If anyone were to try to join me tonight in this place, the alarms will sound and Cody will know instantly too.

I'm not blind to the fact that he's circled the building multiple times. In fact, it warms something inside of me.

If anyone had told me years ago that he would look out for me like he has, I'd have told them to fuck off and stop filling my brain with white knight fantasies.

I didn't get to where I am in life by relying on anyone else. Taking another sip of my water, I lean against the farmhouse sink.

This morning, naked in Cody's bed, I came to a simple conclusion. I want to be in my own home and alone. No security detail, no prince in shining armor with a sad backstory. No nothing. I need to be on my own. How am I going to get better if I rely on Cody? I can't and I won't. Given this past weekend, I've obviously lost it.

Half a day on my own has already been good for me and clearing my head. The first half was spent arguing with Cody … again. The water rushes out of the faucet and I fill my glass before heading back to my mostly cleaned bedroom.

I spent the rest of the day unpacking and cleaning up the piles of paperwork, all while talking to my sister. We spent nearly three hours on the phone. First, I let her unload and then I did some unloading of my own, keeping out some small details. Like every piece about Marcus. Somehow, he's become my secret and I don't know what will happen if I tell anyone. Really I'm afraid of what will happen if I tell. I'll lose him and quite possibly ostracize myself, lose my job … forfeit my sanity. No one knows I kissed him, and I'd like to keep it that way.

My phone buzzes on my nightstand, so I trade it for the glass of water and plop down cross-legged on the bed.

Mom is doing better.

I answer my sister quickly enough to hopefully put her anxious mind at ease: *Good. I knew she would.*

I'm still worried. Something's just not right.

I hesitate, not knowing what to tell Cadence until I settle on: *You're a worrier. Mom is fine and she knows she can come to us if she needs anything.*

My fingers reach up to the collar of my throat, to that dip where a thin chain would rest if I was wearing a necklace. It's a nervous habit, but instead of touching metal it's only skin brushing against skin as I assure myself, yes, she would. *Mom would tell us if she needed us. She'd tell us if anything was wrong.*

My message to my sister goes unanswered even though I'm aware she's read it and so I start to doubt myself. Without waiting any longer for her to reply, I promise her I'll be home this weekend and we can have a girls' night. *Just the three of us.*

Her joke about me having time off over a reporter and bad press makes me roll my eyes, but more than that, I'm grateful for the distraction. I shake my head at the thought that all that's wrong right now in my life is just bad press. What a pretty little lie.

The truth will come out and you'll be back to your workaholic self. It's the last text she sends before I plug in my cell and decide I really need to sleep. I've barely slept to the point where now my eyes are raw and dry. I got in a half hour catnap earlier but woke up with my heart beating out of my chest. If I can sleep tonight without waking up in a panic, I'll count it as a win.

No sleeping pills, though; I want to stay alert. No, I think as I sigh heavily, I *need* to stay alert.

The moment I lay down, a satin wrap around my hair and the blanket tucked all the way up to my chin, my phone pings but it's not my sister like I expect.

I'm only a phone call away. Cody's message elicits a guilt that barricades my throat. I have to swallow it down before telling him I know and I'm here if he needs anything.

I add in a *thank you*, although it doesn't offer me any peace. I shouldn't be thanking him for my independence.

It's not like we're more than fuck buddies and I almost tell him that, but my wretched heart hurts daring to think the words, let alone say them. I don't want anything more, and neither does he that I'm aware of. So all of this … the protection he's given me … it's just him being kind and doing what he knows how to do. I appreciate that.

I appreciate you, I write to him because that's all I know how to say right now. It doesn't explain why the back of my eyes prick with unshed tears and I suddenly feel so alone.

Lying on my back and staring at the spinning ceiling fan, I come to the only conclusion my exhausted mind has to offer: I think I'm falling for him and that's terrifying. In all of this mess and turmoil, my heart is apparently in chaos too. Last night, I slipped deeper into his arms than I ever have before.

He's only a phone call away and he's texted me that twice already tonight. That's good enough for now.

I swear I try to sleep. I forced my eyes closed, my bed is warm and cozy … I even got up around 2:00 a.m. for a drink of chamomile tea that I sucked down as quickly as I could so I didn't have to have my eyes open for too long. All the effort to sleep doesn't work; sleep evades me.

The alarm clock reads nearly 4:00 a.m. as I sit in my bed, reading through a folder of evidence. If I can't sleep, I can at least work.

Ross Brass is the one case I chose. Even if his charges were dropped, he's a suspect in another case. There are more murders with his signature and now an APB is out. But he's in the wind.

It's the case that makes the most sense for me to look into. With nothing but time on my hands and a stain on my reputation, both because of him, I want this bastard behind bars for more than one reason. It's not a vendetta, though, it's simply my fucking job.

It's not the case that's opened on my laptop laying only a foot from me on the bed. The dim light of it calls to me to come back to it even though I've read through it a dozen times already. There's not much there, to be honest. Twenty years ago, detective work wasn't what it is now. The lack of forensics and technology and protocols … it all adds up to incomplete files, scanned papers that are more incoherent thoughts and assumptions that aren't backed up than anything else.

What is known is that there were three men, at least, who kidnapped, assaulted and sexually abused a number of boys ranging from six years to ten years old. Two men were found dead at the scene, where the remains of the missing boys were found buried along with evidence that they were fed to the dogs roaming around the property. The third man was badly injured by the dogs; with his throat ripped out, he died in the hospital hours after discovery. One boy was alive when police arrived, only to die shortly after in the care of medical professionals who simply couldn't treat all his injuries.

The case is a horror story and a tragedy that kept mothers awake at night. It destroyed a small town in northeastern New York and I can't even imagine what their families went through.

Including Cody, given that Christopher was only identified by teeth buried in the black dirt and the little boy who survived said he was alive only days before. A week would have made a difference in a life. A single week. The lead detective on the case retired shortly after and one note I haven't forgotten is in the files. A note stating that he suspected one of the men nearly a year before they were caught, but nothing came of the home search.

A photograph stares back at me as I drag the device into my lap and lean against the headboard.

Christopher Walsh was one of the sixteen boys over the course of four years.

There's no one to question now, only ghosts.

Yet questions pile up in my mind, refusing to let it go, because deep down inside I'm vaguely aware there's something here that I'm supposed to know.

The creak of the floor is synonymous with a number of things. The first being a striking fear that runs through me, followed by a chill that rolls down my spine. The second and most obvious is an unsolicited exhale and the memory of the last time I saw Marcus.

His mouth on mine, his body so close I can still feel the heat of him. The detailed reminder that comes with a whisper of his kiss against my lips washes away so much of everything else in this very moment.

Still, my gaze shifts from the darkened corner where a man obviously stands, to my gun, very much in clear sight on my nightstand.

With my pulse both heating and racing, I struggle to move. Another creak of the floorboards shifts the shadow and I stare into the darkness.

"It's only me," he speaks, breaking the silence.

My question is merely a murmur. "Should I close my eyes?" I don't know how I'm able to breathe, let alone whisper the words.

I can't see a damn thing but I swear I know he's smiling when he answers me, his voice gruff as if he hasn't spoken in a long, long time. "It depends on two things."

The thumping in my chest is harder and my body hotter in every way possible, to the point that I desperately need to move out from under the covers, but my body is far too paralyzed to do   so.

"What two things?"

"Can you see me?"

A hesitant exhale accompanies the headshake I offer as an answer.

"Good."

"And the second thing?"

"Is that gun for me?"

Lie to him, my inner voice hisses, but the truth comes out instead as I say, "Yes. You or anyone else who broke in … but I figured it'd be you. How did you get in?"

There's a hint of something in my voice I can't quite place. My gaze follows the slight shift along the dark shadow.

"Because you're scared?" he asks and ignores my questions. A hardness as well as curiosity are present in his tone.

"Yes," I say, offering the word but I'm not sure he heard it so I nod and with it, my arms finally move. Even that small a change seems too much and I do everything I can to be as still as possible.

It feels as if my body is trembling, but when I peer down, I'm still as a statue.

"Don't be afraid. I don't have any desire to hurt you." The recognition of his voice, of the event that transpired in Cody's kitchen loosens my coiled muscles. Again I peer at the gun before turning back to the darkness in the corner. He must be leaning against the wall.

"Does that mean I don't have to close my eyes?" I ask him.

"You really should."

My throat is tight as I swallow and the sound it makes is audible and wretched.

Marcus only chuckles, and then tsk-tsks me. "I said don't be afraid, Delilah."

"How long have you been here?" I ask him, focusing on my alarm clock that now blinks 12:12 in a harsh red, mocking me. My phone never alerted me that the power went out.

"Maybe a half hour… That seems about right." Gesturing to the blinking clock, the man I believe is dressed in all black, or at least dark colors, only responds, "It had to be fast not to set off the alarm. Don't blame yourself for not noticing right away. You were so caught up in … a case? I presume?"

I still can't make out his features, but I know he has a hood above his head. Something that could easily block his face if he wished. His outline is defined with broad shoulders and the height of a tall man. Every other detail, though, is hidden from view.

So I keep my eyes open and ask again, "How did you get in?"

"The same as before. Does it matter?" he asks and I shake my head although it feels deceitful. Of course it matters. Every detail matters.

"I have a question for you," I say and the words come out unbidden.

"I have some for you too, want to trade?" Amusement laces his response and I can't ignore the stir in the pit of my belly.

There's a touch of menace in his question but I gather my strength and my sanity, refusing to fall deeper into the hole I've found myself in.

"How did you get in before? The power didn't go out then." Although the second statement is firm with resolve, the moment it slips from my lips I question its truthfulness.

His tone reflects boredom and that strikes a chord inside of me as he turns his back against the wall, no longer looking at me. Instead he stares at my door and all I'm offered is a silhouette. "I know your security code; I know the brother of a man who was on your security detail who was preoccupied with … a more pressing matter. Another was busy with a broken light in the parking lot. Distractions. I get in with distractions and contacts and information that's easily traded."

With his tired and clearly disappointed response, he inhales deeply and I ask another question, some mundane part of me still stuck on the *how* or possibly not yet willing to dare ask about the *why*.

"Who told you the code?"

With another tsk he reprimands me, much more seemingly entertained. It's then that I find I've repositioned myself to face him squarely. With his head still firm against the far wall of my bedroom, he turns to look at me and for a moment, I see an outline of his face.

The way he turned and a hint of light from a passing car down the back alley behind my apartment aid me in the moment.

There are details of plump lips and a sharp jawline. Not the hideous face of a killer I once placed on him years ago. I dare to think that he's handsome even. But just as quickly as the light fell on his face, it's gone.

"I have a question for you first." A hum of what could be laughter is caught between his lips as he straightens to ask me, "Why didn't you tell him?"

"Tell who?"

"I don't want to play games, Delilah. The kiss." The singular word is hissed although there's no anger that lingers. Not even a threat lays on the word, yet it sounds worse than sinful. "You didn't tell Cody about our … moment."

"I—" It's a struggle to identify why, caught in his gaze I can't decipher. The moment after between Cody and I … I should have, but I lied. "I didn't want to upset him."

"It's not because you're ashamed?" he asks.

"Maybe partly," I say and the heat of anxiety dances along my skin with the admission. It doesn't escape me that this man could do awful things to me if only he wanted, and yet again, I find myself glancing at the gun. I'm dealing with a sociopath; at least that's what his profile determined years ago. I'm well aware of the risks. A smidgen of fear trickles down my spine at the thought of disappointing him … but I imagine it would be much worse if I lied. Something in my gut refuses to let go of that hunch.

It's Marcus's sudden movement that prevents me from lingering on the horrid possibilities. With an easy stride he takes up residence by my vanity in a tufted chair that's far too small for him. It's almost like a throne he's outgrown.

"It's been a long day and I'm sure you have more … interesting questions than the last one you asked?"

His statement lingers in the warm night air as the heater kicks on and I can't remember what I asked him last, only that my first question bored him. "I'll give you one more question. Only one. Do you still want to know how I knew the code? Or is there something else burning inside you'd rather have answered?"

His posture isn't expectant as he waits for me, but it's in this moment I decide to take advantage of the opportunity to ask him what pricks at the farthest spot of my consciousness. The article about Cody's brother and the other boys that would still light up on my laptop screen if only I brought it to life will haunt me if I don't ask.

"Do you know about …" Hesitation wraps itself around me and I have to clear my throat before continuing, "What do you know about Christopher Walsh or the other boy who died … the one named Marcus?"

"Hearing that name …" His tone is dampened with sadness. "I know everything about it. More than any one person should. I know the men didn't suffer enough. They never do, though? Do they? It's not about them suffering." He adds the last bit almost as if it's a reminder for himself. "It's about ending what they're capable of."

"You were there?" All the questions I want answered could fill a vault and I edge against the warmth of the comforter, closer to his now hunched figure. But all that anticipation is quickly put out like the flame of an extinguished candle.

"That's another question."

"Please," I beg him out of instinct, my fingers gripping the comforter tightly with the single word. Marcus's head rises ever so slowly and a pale, pale blue stares back at me. The case matters. I knew it did. Other questions scream in my mind. *What about Cody? How much does he know?* They line up one by one, held back only by biting the inside of my cheek.

He's my witness, my ghost. But this isn't a courtroom, a cell or an interrogation. I don't have an ounce of power here and I'm left at his mercy.

The small voice that's been reckless and foolish reminds me of the kiss we shared and my gaze drops to his lips. It reminds me that he came to me. There's a small bit of power in my grasp, but just like every other fact I've uncovered, I don't know why. "I just …" It takes great effort to lean back in my bed and its groan of protest doesn't stop me from a plan that's more than likely foolish. "How do you know Cody? You know him, don't you?"

"He thinks I'm someone I'm not. He wants me to be that person." Marcus's swallow and exhale reveal the cues of a man struggling. But also a man who's dying to confess. I can be his priest, his doctor, his executioner … whatever he wants, so long as I'm given that confession. I want it more than I've wanted anything else in a long damn time.

"I'm not that person, but he keeps my secrets and pretends. And together, we've done so well. We both lost someone at the same time in our lives. I think it's really the bonding that binds us together more than anything. It's the loss."

The cryptic words don't tell me everything, but they tell me enough to know Cody lied. He lied to me. He's keeping Marcus's secrets … or at least that's what this man believes. "What about—"

"Stop," he commands with an authority that's frightening. One not to be denied. "Shhh." He's quick to add the gentleness to his voice when he shushes me, but it's far too late to prevent fear from pressing my back firm against the headboard. "I gave you another question because I have one of my own."

"Yes?"

"Did you like it when I kissed you?" he asks, repositioning himself in the chair, leaning forward so his forearms rest on his thighs as he stares at me through the dark.

The rush of my blood in my ears nearly drowns out every other sense.

Logically, I should tell him yes to appease his ego, his need for control. I've been trained on how to deal with personalities such as his. Although, this is much, much different from any scenario I've confronted in the past. The reality, the truth of his question … it's still a yes. Even as scared as I am, there's a spark that crackles between us. Knowing what he's capable of and yet how soft he has been with me draws me to him for reasons I can't explain.

"Yes," I say and take a deep breath.

"Another trade?" he asks me and before I can stop myself, I

answer yes. More than any other reason, it's because I don't want him to leave without knowing more. *I need to know what happened.*

"A touch for a touch?" he says and my eyes widen at the offer. "I didn't let you last time and that seems … selfish of me."

I can't help the innate fear I feel. The idea of him getting closer to me, close enough to touch, to kiss, all while I stay buried in my bedsheets is both erotic and terrifying.

I know he must see it; I'd be a fool to think I could hide it. Hell, my heart beats so hard, he'd have to be deaf not to hear it staggering with dread. "I'll sweeten the deal. I'll tell you how I know your code. I'll tell you now, if you want."

My gaze peers deeper into his, and I find myself wishing for more light. His desperation is … not understood. He shouldn't want me, but he does. I can sense it; his desire caresses every inch of me, preparing me for him.

Marcus wants me and I'm ashamed to admit what that knowledge does to me.

Met with silence for too long, Marcus continues. "I have small cameras on the outside of your building. I can watch who comes and goes and more importantly, I can see you put in the code, Delilah. And anyone else I want."

"That's not true. I searched the place down myself."

With a huff of laughter, he leans back in the chair and responds, "They look like nailheads, so small, and everywhere I want them to be." The arrogance doesn't go unnoticed.

"How long?"

"How long have I been watching you? You have so many questions that you already know the answers to, don't you?"

His taunt prompts me to remember the first week I moved in when there was a day when the power went out. There wasn't an ounce of me that suspected anything. That was years ago … Years. The answer sends goosebumps down my shoulders that don't stop until a shiver takes over.

"I have unusual ways, invasive, I know. But I tried to stay away and let you be. This is how I managed. And then ... you kissed him. You fucked him. It ... it's taking a lot of effort to not be jealous. He's been there for you and you've seen what he's done for you. It makes sense. You haven't seen what I've done for you, though."

I can barely breathe listening to him.

His jealousy is a shock. And given all this new information, my body trembles. "You told me not to be scared, but I am." I admit the truth out loud because it's too much. It's far too real.

"You're a good girl for telling me." *Good girl.* From anyone else, I would snap at those words. There's a trigger inside of me wound tight and it would spring free. But from him ...

He adds, "We're going to have to work on that. Lie down and let me help you."

"What do you want?" I ask and my voice shakes.

"Again ... You already know the answer."

He's not wrong. I know what he wants; even my body is aware as my nipples harden against the soft cotton of my sleep shirt.

As if he's read my mind, his nearly silver gaze drops to my chest. "Fear is a funny thing, isn't it?" he comments but remains where he is. "I bet you're hot too, aren't you?"

All I can think about is Cody. Marcus may know things, but Cody may not. And whatever I do here, could come back on a man who has done nothing but protect me.

"Marcus ... I'm with—"

"I know. I saw it all. I saw you kiss him again yesterday. Really kiss him like you love him. You do, don't you?" There's not an ounce of anger in his voice, only knowing.

"Marcus—"

"I'm not mad. You don't have to be afraid. But I deserve a chance. I don't regret much in life, but I regret not taking you when I had the chance."

"When was that?" I ask only to allow more time to pass. To give space to the moment so I can think.

"Questions. So many questions, my Delilah." Sitting straighter, his fingers wrap around the arms of the chair as if he's holding himself back. "I answered you, I gave you more information than I should."

"You told me not to be scared, but—"

"If you'd like, I can make it easier on you."

I can only nod.

"Lie down, Delilah." With trembling limbs I slowly do as he says, lifting the covers for a moment, glancing at the gun that's still within reach and knowing it was never going to protect me against Marcus. He takes his time giving me orders, and all the while I listen obediently.

"Close your eyes," he whispers and they're the most seductive words I've ever heard. If only sinning with your eyes closed saved your soul from the devil.

Every little hair stands on edge when I hear the telltale creak of him rising from the chair. My chest rises and falls chaotically, every fight-or-flight instinct within me screaming with pure adrenaline.

"Don't turn around," he commands and I'm certain his steps are deliberately loud as he rounds the bed, walking behind me. Ever so slowly, the weight of him is felt when the cool air from a raised comforter kisses my skin.

With my eyes closed tight, he climbs in behind me and I have to part my lips to inhale. It's a shaky breath that's suffocated in his heat as he gets closer, inch by inch, until his hard chest is nearly against my back. With every breath, I barely graze him. With one more adjustment, his erection presses against my ass. A whimper leaves me and it's then I feel his shadow weighing down on me. His fingers slip a strand of loose hair down my shoulder and he whispers along the curve of my neck.

"He likes to kiss you here … I understand the desire."

chapter four

Marcus

I'M EVER SO CAREFUL WITH MY LITTLE MOUSE. THE CORNERS of my lips tug up at the nickname that's been buried so long in my conscious. It's been a lifetime since I thought of her like that. Which is quite different from what I imagine she's thinking right now.

Her shyness and timidness are … more appealing than I ever dreamed. Although my illicit fantasies that included playing games didn't hold an ounce of wavering. Not on her part and certainly not on mine.

"Touch for a touch, little mouse," I whisper and let the promise … or threat … linger before I add, "I go first this time."

The hitch in her breath is accompanied by her eyes shutting tight. The light lays there on the delicate hollow at her throat and unlike what I planned, I graze my teeth along her slender neck, noting how her back arches and her heartbeat pounds. My bottom lip tips just slightly before lifting away, leaving a small bit of moisture just beneath the tender side of her ear.

I can't resist blowing ever so slightly and my reward is a sudden, sharp intake of breath.

"Your turn," I tell her, but she's still for far too long. Doesn't she know what she does to me? How everything twists with her around. Black and white bleed together and all that remains are gray blurs, bringing only her into sharp focus.

"Whatever you want," I say, practically pleading with her as I drop my lips to the shell of her ear. "Take it, ask it, do as you please." Everything about her threatens to make me lose control.

"A question," she says and the words rush out of her. "A touch for a question."

Disappointment is a heavy weight, but I should know better than to push her too soon. My scared little mouse.

"My touch, your question," I respond although I don't agree.

"What do you want after?" she asks and I smirk, my lips grazing her ear as I admonish her, saying, "So expectant."

Goosebumps flow down her caramel skin and I'm eager to touch, lick, and cover them in every way I've dreamt. "After what?" I practically dare her to say it.

Her bottom lip quivers ever so slightly and those long lashes stay down, covering her gaze I'm desperate to see.

She doesn't answer even though her lips part. I have mercy on her. She deserves that at the very least.

"Don't be afraid. No matter how much I want to fuck you, I won't until you beg me."

I hate how her body relaxes even if she doesn't do it purposefully. It's a tangible sense of relief and that tells me many things. For one, she thought I would take from her. Pressing my hand against her lower belly, my fingers would play along the seams of her panties if the shirt wasn't in my way. I push her back to my front and make sure she feels how hard I am for her before telling her, "Your body may want me now, but you'll be begging me to fuck you, Delilah. You will feel deprived without me inside of you."

A huff of amusement leaves me as the sound slipping from her lips mimics both a moan of pleasure and tortured agony.

"Another question?" I ask her. "My next touch will be lower."

With my warning lingering, she surprises me. Lifting her arm slowly and whispering, so low it's almost not audible, "A touch." Although her eyes stay closed and her body remains as it is, her arm moves behind her head and then behind mine.

Closing my eyes, I let her press her palm against my neck, certain the rough stubble will grate along her soft skin. Her fingers linger there, feeling every inch of the back of my neck and then move higher, up my jaw. When she trails them to my lips, I can't resist the urge to nip them.

Shock ignites within her and she rips her hand away, her eyes opening for just a moment. A moment where perhaps she felt the danger once again.

She'll learn, she'll grow to be at ease around me. I'll make sure of that.

With her breathing erratic still, she forces her eyes closed and I make my next move obvious. Slipping my left hand under the thin fabric of her sleep shirt, I slide all the way up to where it was just a moment ago and then lower, lower still, slipping beneath the elastic of her panties until her pubic hair rests against my fingertips. She's hot, every inch of her, but I'm more than aware that just a bit lower will greet me with a warmth that already has my cock leaking precum.

"Another move on your end?" I whisper softly, daringly. "Question?" I whisper against her hair. "Or touch?" I let the tip of my nose touch her, acutely aware that it breaks the rules, but not giving enough of a damn to stop myself.

It takes every ounce of effort not to turn her onto her belly and take her how she wants to be taken. The way I imagine it is raw and deep. Far too tempting for my lack of patience right now. I allow myself the small nudge of my nose against her neck.

Her swallow is slow, her words even slower. "If I ask you for a time and place, would you agree to only seeing me then?" she asks and what a waste of a question it is.

"No." I answer her with honesty as I slip my fingers lower, drifting them to her slit and bringing her arousal to her swollen nub to rub gentle circles. Her back presses against my chest and her neck arches, bringing her chin closer to my lips when I admit, "I'll see you whenever the fuck I want."

I don't stop the heavy petting, loving her ass pressed back against my sweatpants. Just the feel of her writhing against me forces an aching need to override my senses. Her body tightens and I still, not wanting to send her over the edge just yet. "Another question?" I dare to ask and I do something I haven't in a long damn time. I pray. I pray she has one more so I can press my fingers deep inside her cunt and feel just how tight and hot she is.

"If I message you to come to me, can I see you whenever the fuck I want?"

I hope she can feel my smile against her heated skin as I whisper something I've heard her say a thousand times when she's well aware the answer is no. "We'll see." I wish I could. I wish it were that easy.

With the rest of my answer unspoken, I thrust two fingers inside of her heat, curling them and stroking along the front wall of her pussy while my thumb still presses against her clit. I'm meticulous, drawing it out and memorizing every detail of how her body reacts to the pleasure. Her fingers dig into the covers while her plump lips part and as much as I want to take them with my own, rules are rules. One touch is all she gets.

"Marcus," she says, mewling my name. That's how she comes undone. With me inside of her and my name on her lips.

My last commands to her, which she willingly obeyed: *Stay very still. Close your eyes now. And sleep.*

chapter five

Marcus

THE BAD MEN ALWAYS LOSE.

The boy told me that. I truly believed him back then. I can even remember nodding my head in agreement.

They will lose. They always lose. I look back on it now and know it was the heroes that led us to believe that. Comic drawings depicting superpowers and cartoon shows that came on every morning on the weekends. Even if it was naïve, it's still true. I'll be damned to admit anything else.

The bad men will always lose.

His large eyes stared back at me from across the cell. He said it like it was a question; after all, I was older by almost a year than him and taller too.

"Yeah," I told him, my voice scratchy from lack of water. "They always lose." I think the entire time we were there together, I barely spoke. Those may have been the first words I uttered out loud besides my name. Because he needed to hear it, and deep down inside I needed to hear it too.

He was the one who did the talking. All his stories kept us going.

The boy said that first night, sometimes they win, and that's what makes them bad guys. Everyone has bad thoughts, but they have to act on them … for someone to truly be bad. He went on and on, but I didn't respond or agree with that ideology. The boy weaved a story, while I sat against the cold broken stone of reality and let him.

It was only months later when I decided the man who came into the barn every so often with a victim of his own was a bad man. He didn't prey on little boys like the ones in the cell did, but those women were victims nonetheless.

The first time in the barn, my safe haven and escape, I was shocked and sat in horror because it couldn't possibly be happening. Not again. The second time, I crawled out and tried to wake the woman the moment the barn closed with that eerie creak from rusted old hinges. I shook her, I did everything I could to get her to move. That's when I realized I was too late.

What a weak being I was, to shy away until it was too late. Yet that was who I was at my core. It's what defined me. Both the boy and the woman showed me that. Her blond hair was matted with dirty blood when I realized how lacking I was in morality. Hiding to protect myself while allowing others to perish disgusted me, but that's what I did.

I didn't know if the woman was innocent, but the boy was and that's when I heard his voice again: The bad men always lose. Wasn't it bad that I didn't do the right thing? That I wasn't the hero he'd told stories about. I was nothing like the person he thought I was.

And so I waited and I watched because I wanted the bad man to fall. I thought maybe it would make it right. It would make sense, all of the tragedy would, if only I aided in this man's demise.

So I waited, I followed, I watched and planned a way to help the good guys bring him down … because back then, I thought there were heroes who wanted to take down men like him. I thought they would listen and they'd bring the monsters to justice.

It didn't take long before I realized no one would come. They came after me instead. They wouldn't listen to what I was saying. I was a dirty, lost kid and all they wanted to know was my name. They didn't listen to me. And I couldn't bring myself to say my name. They couldn't take me away. Not when I had so much work to do to make up for the bad things I'd allowed to happen.

I decided I had to be the one. I'd be the reason that bad man would lose.

It would be justice for the boy. All of the bad men need to pay and it started with him.

I hadn't counted on her sneaking in, her hair in wild curls and the smile on her face so pure and full of hope. It had been so long since I'd seen a smile like that. Shock held me in place as the screwdriver in my hand, the longest one I could find in the abandoned place, slipped to the floor. He would have heard; she would have been my undoing if not for her shriek of laughter hiding the dull bang.

What was that sound doing in this place? It didn't belong here. She didn't belong here either.

She called him Daddy and ran to him while he cleaned his hands with the same towel that had blood on it not too long ago.

Through the broken wood slat I watched, the weapon at my feet in the hay that I was certain now smelled more like me than I reeked of it.

Conflict took ahold of me for the first time in a long time. I wasn't sure what to do and the boy's voice was quiet. I think he would have liked her too.

The man was a monster, but I watched him hold her hand.

I followed from a distance, safe enough to see it all.

The man was bad, that I knew. And he would lose; I knew that too.

My small child's mind was uncertain where she fit in and where I fit in. Until I came up with another plan, one the boy loved even more.

He can teach me how to kill. He does it so well.

I'll let the one bad man live for a while. After all, I needed some-one to teach me. Who best to learn from than the monster himself? And I couldn't be the reason the girl stopped smiling. I couldn't take her father away, not when I knew how much pain it would cause.

Sitting back in the worn leather seat of the marked van, I watch the series of text messages on my laptop. They're not to me, but they certainly hold my interest.

Everything about her holds my interest these days. I've been watching and waiting, not so differently than what I've done for years, but for far different reasons.

The dim light of the evening approaches and I'm aware that the residents of this friendly neighborhood will find their way back to their two-story homes on this quiet street. I'll wave and smile as they pass by in their large SUVs and family vans with lit-tle stick figures of their children on the back windows. And they'll do the same, smiling and waving back. I've been told I should have been a dentist because of my smile. Not the electrician I'm pretending to be.

Another message pings on my screen and a shred of jeal-ousy seeps into my blood. I don't recall experiencing the feeling as much as I have recently. Even back then, when she loved the monster and didn't even know I existed.

Years passed and there was never a time that I was jealous. Even as I played with the strings bringing Delilah and Cody closer together. I couldn't be with her, not when I had so much work to do to make up for the mess I allowed as I learned. I had so much to make amends for. But then he kissed her.

And she kissed him back.

I know she wanted him to for a long while. She wanted his lips on hers. She wanted more than that.

I imagine tonight he'll lean in for a kiss but I'm uncertain if she'll allow it. Since I kissed her last. I wonder which kiss she enjoys more.

Honk, honk, the man I saw just a moment ago waves me down from the other side of the street. He's heading the other direction now, the front end of his car parallel to mine and his window rolled down.

With jet-black hair speckled white and wrinkles lining his eyes, he narrows his gaze at me, a harsh crease in his forehead emphasizing his wrinkles.

A smirk is my response as he motions for me to roll down my window. I do and immediately ask him, "You lost?"

"No, no, I thought you might be?" he says with a half grin but skepticism still lingering in his gaze. I've dealt with many men like him, so not an ounce of nervousness trickles through. They're all the same.

I imagine he's retired, the grandfather of one of the youths who play in these fenced-in backyards. I wonder if he thinks he knows everyone on this street. Maybe he does.

"Not lost," I say as I shake my head and switch the tab on my screen to the work order scheduled at 47 Lewisville Drive. "I'm just waiting on the Jenkinses for their appointment."

The Jenkins family has an appointment, but not with me. Before they arrive, I'll be gone. I'm not interested in their home in the least. This street, however, is one of my favorites for the view I needed tonight. From this exact spot, I can easily see through the back windows of the Italian restaurant a mile down the road, using the camera in my dashboard. Technology has made what I do substantially easier to keep tabs on certain men.

This man is right to be suspicious, but this street will never be harmed. It's far too valuable to me.

"I'm hoping they'll be home soon although I'm early. I got done with my last appointment a little early and …" I don't finish the statement; instead I hold up a half-eaten sandwich.

"Right, right," he says and the grin on his face widens, acknowledging my lies with understanding. He seems to be a good man. One who'd fill me in if ever I needed to know anything about this street. I wouldn't even have to pry for him to confide in me. Men like him are proud to keep an eye out and protect the neighborhood. They're the ones who take it the hardest when something … unfortunate occurs.

I call men like him the birds. They watch, they swoop down to be heroes, but they are so limited when it comes to putting down the dogs.

It's only once the man, who told me his name is Dave, has driven off do I click over to my tabs on the laptop. First checking the cameras and waiting for Ross Brass to make his entrance. He's a no-show at the moment, but given who he's meeting, I'm certain he'll arrive any moment now.

In the meantime, I read the texts between Cody and Delilah.

I need to see you. Cody's been relentless. I can't blame him. He's worried and for good reason. I haven't responded to the messages he's sent me. I'm sure that's caused some unfortunate thoughts to enter his mind.

I never thought I'd hear you say that. I can practically hear her voice hum the somewhat flirtatious response.

Please, tonight.

It must be more than jealousy that I feel when she gives in. Perhaps … it's obsession. Although from what I know of that shortcoming, it often comes with anger. And there's not a bit of it at the thought of her loving Cody. She has such a big heart. I've seen her love a monster before. She could love me too. I know she can. But it would be so much easier to love Cody.

The faint sounds of chairs scraping and men with thick accents greeting each other force me to click over to the other screen. It's already recording but still, I watch and wait. These strings are more important to pull than the ones of lovers.

chapter six

Delilah

I'T'S EASIER TO PRETEND LIKE IT DIDN'T HAPPEN THAN TO face the reality. Every other minute, those piercing blue eyes penetrate my every thought and remind me that I saw him again, kissed him again, and was dying for it like I had before. Not only that, but so much more transpired.

And I enjoyed it. I wanted more.

I could lie like an expert witness on the stand and tell myself it was for answers, but the crackle I felt between us, the dose of lust and shot of heat can't be ignored. There's something fucked up in my head. It's wrong and I'm aware, but I can't change it, no matter how much I lie to myself.

Shutting off the blinker puts an end to the clicking as I park my car in the parking lot. My motions are automatic as I reach for both the umbrella and my purse before stepping out onto the wet asphalt. There's only a bit of rain spitting from the skies, but with my hair newly done, I'm not risking a drop landing anywhere near me.

The whoosh and click of the umbrella opening amid the staccato of my heels is followed by my car door shutting as I search for Cody's car.

A coffee date with my FBI agent lover two days after I came apart in my bed at the hands of a serial killer, I would imagine, is unique for the patrons of this diner.

It's a cute place with cozy seating, located at the corner of a quaint street on the far end of town. Even the pastel blue sign that reads Pick Me Ups in a flowing script is adorable. It doesn't fit the man I'm meeting or the relationship we have. Coffee is coffee, though, and this is far more casual than the dinner date he preferred and I turned down.

The second I spot Cody's car, I know I should quicken my pace to get to him. I already told him I was running late, and I hate to keep him waiting. My limbs betrays me, though, and the thumping in my chest refuses to support my body's need to move.

It's almost like this moment is the same as the other night. I'm participating, but not really here. There's space between and I'm merely observing.

The flesh and bones of my body are present and yet I'm only the shadow. Oh how easy it would be, if one could slink away and hide from reality that easily. But as I approach the black glass front doors and shake out the umbrella on the thick black welcome mat out front, I know all too well that I did what I did.

I just don't know what Cody's done, what he knows, or what I'm willing to tell him.

There's more than what he's willing to tell. Between coffee and small talk about scandal and murderers threatening me, I have to decide where Cody fits into all of this with far too limited information.

The door swings open and warmth hits my face while the delectable scent of coffee and citrus pastries swarms my lungs.

Black and white checkered floors, subway tiles and a long

coffee bar with black leather stools give the place charm and a '50s flair.

I didn't even want to see his handsome face. I didn't want those steely blue eyes to see right through me, but in this moment, when Cody's gaze locks onto mine from a booth in the back corner, I feel weak. Drawn to him and eager to tell him everything. Literally, I'm desperate to tell him everything.

To expose every little detail. The desire passes as quickly as it came.

"Would you like me to take that for you?" a waitress with coral pink lipstick asks and smiles at me. As I hand over the umbrella and my coat, my pulse quickens. Cody's gaze is still on me, but I can't look back at him.

I'm second-guessing everything. Every move. Every piece of the puzzle. With a heavy exhale I take the seat across from Cody and offer him a simper.

"Still in one piece," he comments and with it I broaden my smile, which makes him smile in return. It's always struck me as such a charming smile. "You had me worried," he says.

Although I part my lips as if I have an easy response to give him, which I don't, I'm saved by the waitress. The same one who took my coat in her poofy dress with puffed sleeves and a black apron tied at her waist.

"A hot cup of coffee is exactly what I need, please."

"Flavor of the day is blueberry."

"Just regular, please." She nods and turns to Cody.

"Black for me." The waitress blushes at Cody's response, as if he's just hit on her by ordering coffee.

"Not sleeping well?" he asks when she slips off.

I shake my head no, although that's not quite true. I'm sleeping better now than I was at his place. It seems unnecessary to tell him that, though.

"You could always come back," Cody says and the guilt weighs down on me at the offer. When did the tables turn between us? With him pining for me while I keep my distance?

The truth nearly slips out from between my lips as my heart aches inside my chest, moaning something to my lungs about how much we need him. I wouldn't be able to forgive myself if something happened to him. That's the one truth that hasn't faltered. That and the fact that I'm certain something bad is going to happen.

When you play with fire, you're bound to be burned. I refuse to let him be a bystander in the wreckage I'm headed toward. Thankfully I don't have to answer, since the waitress is back in no time with our coffee.

We're quiet, neither of us speaking until she asks us if there's anything we'd like to eat.

"Cinnamon buns," we answer simultaneously. The smile I wear on my face at that is a sad one and Cody sees it.

"So … about my place versus yours?"

Swallowing thickly, I carefully pick up the simple mug of coffee and take a sip before giving him an answer he should accept.

"I'm not sure if you remember, but I wasn't sleeping well at your place either and I like being on my own."

Images blur together in my mind. The memory of Cody's broad chest above mine as he thrust himself inside of me, mixes with the sharp intake I took as Marcus pressed himself against me.

The sudden onslaught of detailed debauchery has me nearly dropping the white ceramic mug on the saucer. It clanks in protest and with trembling hands, I cover my eyes. Vaguely, Cody's apology is little more than white noise.

"Sorry," he says but I'm quick to object to it.

"No, I'm sorry. You don't need to apologize."

"Are you sure you're okay?" he asks and all I can think of saying in response is a lie.

"I told you. I'm tired." I'm not, though. I cling to my coffee cup. This is how cheaters must feel. This wretched twisting in my gut roils and churns. We didn't have a label, we didn't have rules or boundaries. Nevertheless, we have secrets.

It was odd before, between us. But caught in Cody's gaze, it's almost torturous now. I sit across from a man whose only personal possessions are those of a boy he lost long ago. And I know Marcus knew his brother. What I don't know is if Cody knows it too.

Without trust, the tension is palpable as I pick up the bun the waitress sets down, the one I'm certain I won't be able to stomach.

"Thank you for coming. I know after the other night ..." he doesn't finish his trailing thought.

"I'm sorry." The apologies don't quit and for once, I don't mind it. Because I am so damn sorry. Truly to the pit of my stomach. Every definition of the word.

"You don't need to be sorry; I just need to know what's going on," he says, emphasizing the last bit.

"What do you mean?

"It's been days, Delilah."

"Very uneventful days," I say but stare at the pastry. "You aren't my keeper, Cody. You don't have any responsibility to protect me."

"What if I want to?" he asks.

With a slow inhale, I stare back at him and note the darkness under his eyes and the way his right hand rests palm up on the table. As if it's waiting to be held.

"Any more letters?" he asks and I shake my head easily.

"No letters." I decide to give him all of the truth from yesterday, but none from the night before. "I kept the monitor and the gun right beside me all day and didn't leave my place."

"And nothing?" he questions further, his brow knitting.

"My ass is flat and sore from the way I sat in bed, but no, nothing to report." I hate the way the lie comes so easily.

"Do you remember the letter from the cases we were on in the beginning?" I ask him, treading into the murky waters with so many unanswered questions. "The ones the article mentioned from that bitch reporter who first got me suspended?"

Cody's posture changes instantly. He remembers. We both know he does and unlike what I've been doing, he doesn't lie to me. "Yeah. I remember."

"One of the last FBI task force meetings … do you remember how I had to walk away for a moment?"

"The crime scene photos were awful," he says and I nod, remembering how the graphic pictures of the victims nearly made me vomit on the spot and I walked off to be alone.

"Right, but it wasn't because I got sick … I was crying. It was too much, the way the bodies …"

I can't even begin to think of how he'd left them like that. Cody agrees, "It was brutal."

"I swore I felt someone watching me back there when I stepped outside to get away from it all." I dare to confess something I haven't before when I add, "I thought it was you. I thought you followed me out … but now I wonder if it was him."

An anonymous tip was left at the station later that night. "He said he'd stop and he did."

"Yeah." Cody nods in agreement and remembrance. "They couldn't find anything on the note. No prints or residue. But they matched the handwriting."

"After that the case went cold."

"I remember. It was like he vanished. We knew he hadn't, though."

"So many cases went cold," I say, recalling them all. All the faces of the deceased. It helps that Jill Tucker from the local eleven o'clock news happened to list them all not too long ago.

"We didn't have the evidence we needed." Cody gives the same excuse the DA gave. Evidence. It doesn't matter what happened. All that matters is what we can prove.

"We knew, though," he says.

"Yeah … we knew."

When did he start keeping secrets for Marcus? The question echoes in my mind. I wonder if it was then. I swear I felt someone watching me then. It had to have been Marcus.

"I know I asked you before …" I trail off as nerves creep up, weakening my voice and I wish I could take it back, but I can't. Instead I clear my throat and reach for the dewy glass for a quick sip of water instead of coffee. The cold beads of condensation on the side of the glass make it slip in my unsteady grasp.

"I asked you if there was anything you knew about Marcus that I didn't," I remind him and my nails press into the pads of my fingers as I anxiously fidget under the table. Marcus said Cody keeps his secrets. What secrets would he keep from me? Are they about the case? Cases that may get me disbarred if that reporter has her way. Or is it all about his brother. "If there was anything at all that you knew."

"You did," he says and I can see there's more on the tip of his tongue but he swallows it. It wouldn't have been a revelation. Judging by the look of condemnation on his face, it was an accusation. Probably something to the effect of, *after you searched through a box of my dead brother's belongings.* He wouldn't do that to me, though. He wouldn't throw it in my face. That's not the kind of man Cody is.

I wish he would. I wish he'd give me a reason to throw the truth at him just the same.

"You'd tell me, wouldn't you?" I ask him cautiously, reminding myself of the history we have together and the grace and protection he's given me. "Even if you had secrets with Marcus?" My words are barely audible.

They hang in the space between us, joined by the flashes of memories that dance with shadows and illicit thoughts you're only ever supposed to dream about, not live.

The waitress comes by with a smile but it vanishes when she pauses at our table, the tension palpable. "I'll leave you to it," she murmurs and taps the table. "If there's anything you need, you just let me know."

With nods from each of us, she's gone.

"Even if you had secrets with Marcus, you'd tell me, wouldn't you?" I question him again, unwilling to give it up, and his response determines my next move.

"Of course I would," he answers and then sips his coffee, but his voice is flat and so is the thud in my chest.

Like it's given up.

It's wrong, so wrong. Something is badly fucked up in my head knowing that I trust a beast like Marcus over Cody Walsh.

"I'm going to see my sister this weekend," I say to change the subject. "And my mother."

Cody only nods and the silence prolongs itself. There's only the chatter of other patrons and a ding at the door when someone leaves.

"Did something change?" Cody asks with a hint of pain in his tone.

"It does feel different, doesn't it?" I respond with my own question, my walls up and solid as stone.

"I don't know," he says then shakes his head and huffs, his thumb tapping on the side of the mug in front of him. "I don't know if you'd even let me kiss you right now."

Tink, tink, it's the sound of a lifeline. The moment slowing between us and I'm so very aware that I'm the one left to make the deciding factor.

There's one reason why I lean in and kiss the man who I'm certain is lying right to my face, as I'm doing to him.

It's because I want to, because I love him. And more than anything I want him to know that he is loved. Even if we are lying to each other.

I want to pretend it's only the shadow of a kiss, and that it will stay there on the black and white penny tile of a coffee shop, where our story can change with every new couple who sits in these seats. But it's not. It's the bittersweet, sad kind of kiss, the one where you don't want to move away because it feels so final if you do move.

His lips are soft and his hand cups the side of my head, holding me there. I'm grateful for that, for all of it.

Everything up to this moment has felt like a lie, everything but this kiss and the next words spoke.

With his forehead resting against mine, he inhales in relief but exhales slower.

"You know I'll keep you safe. You know I care about you, don't you?" With his question spoken, his eyes peer into mine and he pulls back.

He pulls back in that way that makes me want to move closer to him.

"I do." *I really, really do.* "You know I'd do the same, right?" I ask him.

"You don't have to, though."

It's a sad smile that plays quietly on my lips. That's the only response I can give him.

chapter seven

Delilah

THE NUMBERS ON THE DIGITAL DISPLAY CLIMB AND climb while the smell of gasoline lingers. The wet spots on the cracked asphalt prove whoever was at pump three before me left droplets right where I'm standing.

Leaning against my car, I glance up at the lone vehicle that drives down the small-town road this gas station resides on and then check my phone again. It's an old town and just across the street are houses long overdue for renovations. I couldn't imagine living there. Maybe a long time ago it wasn't like it is now. Some other time a lifetime ago.

With a deep inhale, I turn my attention back to my own problems and my own life. Or rather my cell phone.

Two messages. Two different numbers. Two very different men.

Marcus: *You haven't told Cody about it. But you also haven't messaged me.*

For a woman with such a curious mind ... I expected you would message me.

Cody: *Call me when you get there. I need you to keep me updated.*

Both men have expectations. Yet I have no idea what I can truly expect from either of them. Cody swears he has a lead on a case that'll put him only twenty minutes from the hotel I stay at when I visit home. He lies. He lies to me shamelessly and now that I know that, I see him so differently.

Marcus sent a small bouquet of pink roses before I left. I thought of bringing them along to give to my sister or mother, just to get them out of the house. There was no note, no name, just a small bouquet of the palest pink roses. Their stems were cut down to only six inches or so and the half dozen sat in a square glass vase. I left them there, though, on the kitchen island where the last bouquet sat.

Two men. Twice as many expectations.

I leave both messages alone, not texting either of them back.

After less than a minute passes, my phone buzzes with another text. The nervous butterflies in my stomach settle when I glance down and see it's only my sister, telling me to drive to our mom's instead of her place and that she'll be there a bit later. She had an emergency session come up.

It's easy to respond to her. Although if my life were any semblance of normal, maybe I'd feel the anxiety of my previous visit.

The memories of the bruises flash back, complete with my mother's smile. The accusations. The uncomfortable moment with my father. Mom said my father won't be here, though; he's headed out of town for a convention tonight.

I'll add that to a list of things to be grateful for. At the very least I don't have to look into my father's eyes and wonder if he hits my mother.

With a clunk, the gas pump halts and the wind blows a colder air from the roaming hills and mountains off the highway. Goosebumps travel down my blouse and my gaze instantly moves to the back seat where my luggage rests and my coat remains draped over it. The cream sweater wrapped around my shoulders is made from crocheted yarn and the bitter air easily moves through the holes.

It's fine, I tell myself, ignoring this nagging feeling in my gut. Everything is fine for now.

It's only when I'm seated back in my car, with the *ding, ding, ding* from my keys resting in the ignition driving my irritation higher, that I read the texts again.

I turn on the car if for no other reason than to stop the incessant dinging. Both messages came within two minutes of each other, both as I veered off of the highway and onto these less traveled but somehow more worn paths. It must've been an hour after I left. Cody's first and then Marcus's.

To Cody I respond: *Just stopped for gas; I'll be there in two hours and text you then.*

A text, not a call. I realize there's a difference, but given that I'm going straight to my mother's and not the hotel, he can deal. Even if things hadn't changed between us, I still wouldn't call him when I got to my mother's. Calls are for emergencies and a text will do just fine. A churning in my gut refutes that statement, knowing I'd be pushing Cody away and not liking it in the least.

To Marcus, I fail to come up with a suitable response. He fed me information and all it did was prompt me to rattle off more questions. So I ask him, *If I had more questions, would you answer?*

Both men respond in the same way the initial messages arrived, one after the other, Cody's being first.

I'll talk to you soon. The response from Cody is exactly what I expected.

The exact same response from Marcus does nothing but give me chills: *I'll talk to you soon.*

With a shiver running down the length of my neck and trailing over my shoulders, I turn up the heat and head back onto the road.

Somewhere in the back of my mind, I know this is only a distraction and things are going to get worse. I'm only hiding.

I'm grateful to be hiding, though, and with every mile I get closer to my mother's, I find myself watching the clock and wishing I were home.

For the first time, it's not my mother and sister who need me, I realize, it's me who needs them.

With hours to pass on my way up to my hometown and the radio playing, but my unwilling mind not listening, tiny memories come back to me. They seemed so insignificant, these little blips that didn't really matter when I was younger. But as I sit in the car, turning the heater on and off nearly as much as I shift in my seat, my critical eye taints the sweet memories.

One in particular never made sense.

Mom was sobbing when we got home from a trip that she didn't come on with us.

I can still hear her wretched cry of relief when we walked into the living room.

"Mom? What's wrong?" Cadence asked as I stood there in shock, a small doll hanging from my right hand. The floral backpack Cady wore had the gifts we brought back for Mommy. We were so excited to give them to her. All three of us, Daddy included.

Never in my little mind did I expect to come home to my mother crying on the floor of the living room.

"My babies," my mother cried out and swept Cady into a tight hug. I stayed back watching her sway; I'm sure my expression mirrored Cadence's shock. "Where were you?" She heaved in a breath at the same time the question ran away from her.

"We were good, so Daddy took us on a trip."

"A trip?"

"Of course, Mommy." My father's voice was far too upbeat at the sight of my mother crying and distraught. Didn't he see she was scared? He stood behind me in the kitchen, his large hands resting on my shoulders. "Silly Mommy," he joked. "We're home," he said and beamed with a bright smile. It was odd, everything about the moment. Maybe that's why I remember it so well.

"I got you taffy, Mommy," I offered and my mother gripped me in the tightest hug, holding on to me and squeezing too tight. I didn't understand what was wrong with her. Our father said she was just being silly. Back then I felt awful, though, since she'd obviously wanted to come with us. That's what I thought.

"Of course we came back. We'd never leave you." I think those were the words from my father. *"Family doesn't ever leave."*

At the time, I was so happy to see my mother smile, wiping under her tired eyes and clinging to me and my sister. We made her happy, although it didn't make sense that she was upset at all. We'd been good, our grades and our behavior both, so it was wonderful to be rewarded with a trip to the amusement park for the weekend. How could Mom not have known?

The realization never clicked. The pieces didn't add up and the questions stayed buried at the back of my memory where childish things that didn't matter went to die.

The crickets are already out and chirping noisily when I pull into the driveway. It's dark for only being seven but the fall brings early sunsets in this part of the country, especially in these Podunk towns in the mountains of northeastern New York.

The old fence in the backyard has been patched with newer

pickets that stand out even in the dim illumination provided by the streetlights. They're a bright white among the dingy, worn paint of the others. The grass needs to be cut too. I imagine that's what my father would be doing this weekend if he weren't headed out for a conference. Vaguely I wonder what conference it is. If I was earlier in my career, I'd have already texted him and would have preferred to spend my weekend at the conference rather than the dinner and movie plans my sister concocted. That seems like a lifetime ago too.

Sitting back in my car I stare up at the two-story family home with dark red brick and cream shutters. So many memories are carved into the walls of this house. Good ones and bad ones both, but right now, all I can envision are the times I smiled along with my sister.

As our mother did our hair at the kitchen sink and all the games of hide-and-seek that drove my father crazy. All the good times do little to settle the sadness that lingers in my chest. It's a weight that won't move and maybe that's because back then, there was so much hope. So much innocence.

All I can think is that little girl I used to be would be horrified by who I've become.

My eyes burn with the sting of exhaustion and something else. I grab my purse, leaving my luggage and coat where they are even though I'm certain it's bitter cold out there. It's always ten degrees colder up here than it is down in Pennsylvania.

There's an ominous feeling that greets me as I approach. After the large front door creaks open and shuts just as easily, there's only silence in the large old house. I can't remember a single time when it was this dark and quiet. "Hello?" I call out and expect my mother to shout down from upstairs. Maybe she's still getting ready.

The lights being out in the foyer don't help that strange feeling, so I flick them on as I call out for my mother, "Mom?"

A torn sob echoes from somewhere to the left, beyond the kitchen. I think it came from the living room.

"Mom?" I repeat, crying out as dread spreads through me and I pick up my pace. My keys rattle in my hands and my purse nearly slips as I get to the threshold.

My mother's there, on her knees on the floor and she doesn't stop crying as I approach. It's like she can't hear me.

"Mom, what's wrong?" The moment the question is asked, my heart stops. There's blood. So much blood. But it's not touching her. I follow the pool and find it leads to my father. My purse drops along with my keys as my knees hit the stone floor hard.

My hands shake and I make my way toward him, inching myself along with my hands in the air as if to reach for him but they're held back.

There's so much blood and the smear of it in front of me, a smear from his leg being dragged through it is dried. With my right hand trembling, I place my palm on his back.

My mother's sobs still haven't stopped. My name is incoherent in her last cry as she rocks back and forth.

Breathe. He doesn't.

Tears flow freely down my face, stinging my eyes.

"Dad," I call out and then with the back of my hand, I press my fingers to his cheek. The second that skin touches skin, I pull back and push myself away.

His skin is cold as ice.

Thud, thud, my heart pounds and attempts to race, but it's like it's caught in free fall. It can't speed up or slow down, it simply is what it is.

"Mom … what happened?" My question's strength is nonexistent. It's faint and full of the same fear that courses through my body.

Until I see the glint of metal next to my mother. A gun.

"You shot him?" I don't know how I'm even able to question

her. It's not real. Of course she didn't. She wouldn't kill him. She can't kill anyone. It's my mother.

Before I can apologize, my mom speaks.

"I had to, baby girl," my mother cries, tears streaming down her face, dragging the remains of mascara with it. With a sniff and a harsh wipe across her face, my mother's dark brown gaze stares down at my father's body. He lies on his stomach, blood soaking through his shirt and creating a halo of darkness around his face. It bleeds into his cheek, staining his skin.

There's no movement of his chest. No breathing, no blinking, no signs of life at all and vomit rises up my throat as my trembling fingers cover my mouth.

My entire body shakes, glancing between my dead father and my mother who just admitted she murdered him.

"I had to, Delilah …" she whispers. "I had to."

"No," I say, denying it, shaking my head and crawling backward until my back hits the cabinets.

"You don't understand. I'm sorry. I'm so sorry."

"Mom, no," I whisper. The realization grips my shoulders the way I wish I could grip my mother and shake her. Shake her and demand she tell me the truth because this can't be real. She didn't do it.

With her bottom lip quivering and my mother's expression worn and full of pain, she looks me in the eye and tells me, "I'm sorry I didn't do it sooner."

Evidence convicts. Confessions can lead to convictions too, but as I drive exactly fifty-five miles per hour with my mother laying down in the back seat of my car, careful not to go over the speed limit, I refuse to let her confess to anything to anyone.

It doesn't make any sense. Not what my mother did and not what I did. I dragged her out of there as she pushed against me, fought me even. I pulled her away and I'll be damned if I'm going back there.

She's not going down for murder.

I won't let it happen.

"Lilah, baby," my mother pleads with me between the sobs.

"Shhh, Mom," I whisper and lick my bottom lip, tasting my own salty tears. "I just need time to think. I'll fix this. I promise," I tell her. I can't believe she did it. She didn't. My mind's at war with itself.

There's something missing, something wrong and I can't let anyone know until I know what really happened.

The convenience store sign is lit, but half of it is out when I pull into the Gas & Stop. I've been to this place countless times. It's stood here since I was a little girl. Around the corner there's a pay phone. I've waited for years for it to vanish like the rest of them have, but somehow it's remained.

I stop here every time I visit. And I've always thought the pay phone was only there for criminals and cheaters. As I park and release a breath I didn't know I was holding, telling my mother to just stay in the car for a moment, I realize this time I'm the criminal.

Fleeing the scene of a crime.

Aiding and abetting a criminal.

The charges whisper in the back of my mind as I dial one of the only numbers I know by heart.

The images flash through my mind as it rings and my hand slams against the booth as I brace myself.

She didn't do it. I lie to myself until my sister's voice is heard. "Hello?"

"Is anyone around you?" I ask her without telling her it's me. She'll know. She'll know it's me.

"What are you—"

"Answer me," I say and my tone is deathly low and I'm aware it must make my sister nervous.

"Of course," she answers and her breathing is heavier on the line now. "Yes," she says, strengthening her tone as she continues, "there is." There's someone around her. Someone who could watch her take this call and testify. Evidence. It's all about evidence right now.

"You're not talking to me, you're talking to a patient and everything is fine."

"What's going on?" Her voice is barely even but she makes an effort to hide her fear. My own creeps up my arm like tiny spiders racing across my flesh. I can't believe I'm doing this. My expression crumples and pain runs through me as the memory of my mother on the floor flashes before my eyes. The blood. My father.

I struggle to speak, but heave in a breath, knowing I need to do this. "You're going to go to Mom's," I tell her and my voice gets tight. "And you're going to call the cops when you get there."

"Why … why would I do that?" She corrects her tone, keeping it sounding light, but if someone's paying attention, this call is going to be suspicious.

"Remember," I say then swallow and brush under my eyes as I breathe out. "Someone could be watching you. You need to make it appear that this call is normal."

It takes a handful of breaths before my sister says, "Right, right. I know that. It's fine." I can just picture her standing there with her arms crossed and leaning casually against the wall. I hate that I have to tell her this way. *Forgive me. Lord, forgive me.*

"I cleaned up the evidence." My throat is tight and I find myself gripping the pay phone handset harder, both hands clinging to it as I stare at my car. I can't see her, but I know my mother lays in the back seat. When I parked, she was silently crying.

"Of what?" My sister's swallow is more audible than her question.

"I'll explain it all to you after. But when you get home, we won't be there. You're going to call the cops and the last you heard from me were the texts we had earlier."

"Is it Mom?" my sister practically cries and I hush her, reminding her that she's talking to a patient.

"They're gone. They just left," my sister says in a breathy voice on the other end of the line, and it takes me a moment to realize she's referring to whoever was in the room with her. She heaves in a shuddering breath as if she's strangling on her words. "Did Mom kill herself?"

"What?" I ask and my heart races.

"I confronted her."

With a pounding in my pulse, I watch as a cop car rolls up to the red light outside the convenience store. I'm quick to turn my back so he can't see me. But that also means turning away from my car and my mother. Who's obviously in shock among every other reeling emotion that's taken her over.

"You confronted her about what?"

My sister begins to answer but I cut her off, not having the time. "Mom's okay." *Dad isn't...* The words are right there waiting to be spoken aloud but they don't come.

"And Dad?" she blurts out and I can't answer. "No, no ..." My sister's tone is wretched. "I should've kept my mouth shut," she says weakly. Even over the phone I can feel her breaking down.

"When you get home ... I need you to tell them I was supposed to be there with Mom and that we're missing. I'm going to try to clean it up."

"Dad?" my sister cries, and the back of my eyes prick. "They were fighting. I heard them."

"No!" I'm quick to shut her down and breathe out slowly. "No, you didn't. You didn't confront Mom about anything. Dad was supposed to be at a conference and we were having a girls' weekend. That is all you know," I say and I'm firm with her.

"You need to act normal but I wanted you to be prepared. I'm going to protect her. I promise," I tell my sister although the pieces of how exactly I'm going to do just that still haven't come together in my mind. The sound of traffic moving along allows me to peek over my shoulder, finding the cop car gone and my own sitting there, waiting for me. "I'm going to protect her from this."

"She killed him, didn't she?" My sister guesses the truth and all I can tell her is that I love her and to take care of what I asked her to do.

It's a sickening feeling as I get back to my car. Like the world is crumbling around me and there's nothing I can do to hold it up.

chapter eight

Delilah

"Y**OU'RE MY BABY GIRL**," MY FATHER TELLS ME IN THAT *singsong way that lets me know he's in a good mood. "No one's ever going to hurt you."*

"I'll protect you too, Daddy," I'm happy to tell him back. "That's what I'm going to do. I'm going to protect people."

"Oh yeah?"

"I'm going to grow up and be just like you."

"You think so?" he asks me and I nod my head in response to his raised brow.

"That's what we decided last night."

"We?" he asks. As we walk down Main Street to the post office, I hold his hand and he swings it to and fro. When we get to the block before the post office, I skip over all the dark lines of the cracked pavement.

"Cady is going to be like Mom and I'm going to be like you."

Don't step on a crack or you'll break your mother's back. *The children's rhyme plays in my head.*

"All right then. That sounds like your mother and I are doing a good job then, huh?" Daddy's smile is bright and the sky behind him the prettiest shades of blue. There's not a cloud in sight. "I'd say so," I answer him. My father. My hero.

I must've been around five in my earliest memories of my father. His handsome face barely resembles the man on the floor of my parents' living room, the man with the face lined with worry and aged from the passage of time.

With sweaty palms, I have to grip the wheel tighter before wiping off the moisture on my pants and getting a grip.

He's dead. My father's dead. The prickly harshness in the back of my throat is a precursor to crying but I hold it back. Not yet. I can't lose both my parents. I can't lose them both.

"Where are we going?" My mother's voice wavers as she rises up, her reddened eyes peering into mine in the rearview mirror. The hand over her mouth quivers slightly. Maybe the reality is sinking in.

"Somewhere for us to hide for a moment, get you cleaned up—"

"You need to turn back." She's firmer than when she voiced her initial question, but altogether her tone lacks strength. I imagine doing what she did took it all away from her.

"No, Mom." I swallow thickly and speak to her as if what I'm saying is fact; there's not an ounce of negotiation in my tone. "We're twenty minutes from the hotel."

I've got cash in my purse, cash that's meant for my sister to pay her back for the last salon visit.

"Turn back now." Her hardened voice used to scare me when I was a child. Even into my teen years. My mother hardly ever yelled. That's what our father was there for. All the discipline. Hearing it now, though … she just sounds desperate.

The *tick, tick, tick* of the turn signal follows us down Asher

Lane. I recognize the street and know the hotel is only one block down. It's in a quiet area, small and close to the off-ramp to the highway. It's an old building and used to be some kind of chain. Everything about it screams dated but I guess the owner sold the place rather than updating it.

"Gunshot residue doesn't lie and you need somewhere to wash it all off, plus a change of clothes."

"I shouldn't have done this," she says and my mother's statement is a plea. As if she wishes she could go back. I've heard that cadence so many times. "Just take me back."

"I'm not taking you back until I make sure you're all right."

"Did you see what I did?" she says and her voice cracks. With a shuddering breath she croaks out, "You shouldn't have to deal with me. I'm so sorry. I'm so sorry, my baby girl."

"No talking now. Please, just wait." It's always a struggle when a child watches their parent break down. But right now? It feels like that bullet went straight through my heart.

"Let me get you inside."

"Don't help me. I don't deserve it." She begs me as I pull into the parking lot.

"I don't know, but …" I trail off as I struggle to justify anything I've done.

"You don't know what he did." Pain lingers in each of her words. "I couldn't … I didn't know it all. I just thought … Oh God …" My mother's sobs wrack through her and she rocks back and forth. A shivering chill flows over me as I slam the car into park.

Something's been broken for a very long time. More broken than the cracks I skipped over as my father held my hand down Main Street.

How did I ignore it? Waves of heat and anxiety crash within me. Suddenly I need the cold air outside just to breathe.

The lot is mostly vacant. Which is expected. It's not like this town gets a lot of tourism.

There are a few cars, all of which are much older models than my own.

I turn back to look at my mother, wanting to calm her down or at least make sure she knows to stay here for just a moment. The seat groans loud and heavy as my mother sways with a hand over her heart, her face tilted up to the roof of the car. Like she's praying.

"I want you to tell me everything."

"Don't risk—"

I smack the passenger seat to get her attention. Her eyes whip up at me.

"I've already abandoned the scene of a crime. I'm going in that office right there, getting a room and then I need you to tell me everything." I spoke it all too quickly. But I got it out at least. Licking my cracked bottom lip, I wait for her to say something, anything.

The nod of my mother's head is subtle, but she agrees. "I'll stay here."

I'm firmer this time, like I am with the defendants. "I'm going to need you to tell me everything."

My mother hesitates but again, she gives me that small nod of agreement. Not wasting another second, I get out of the car and the cold air is nothing but brutal and refreshing at once.

Sniffing and wiping under my eyes, I brace myself to face the first person I have to encounter, a potential witness.

The check-in area isn't any larger than six by six feet. A counter spans the length of the room and behind it there's a plain white door that I imagine leads to a back hall or closet.

As I place my hand on the sign-in sheet, wanting to tap it instead of the bell, attempting to get the attention of the man laying back in the chair, his feet up on the counter and a hat over his face, I see under my sleeve of the cream sweater.

There's just a spot of blood on it.

My father's blood. My own runs cold as I pull my arm back just in time for the old man to lift the hat from his head.

"Didn't hear you come in." He speaks while rubbing his eyes with just one hand and then pinching the bridge of his nose. "Allergies always get me this time of year. Excuse me," he says and then blinks away whatever sleep he was attempting to get.

"A room for tonight. Maybe the weekend?" I ask and even to my own ears I sound out of breath.

My tone gets the man's attention. He glances away from me to look past me.

"Just you?" he asks and I nod. It's a lie, but better that than the truth. Why the hell would I get a motel room for me and my mother when she lives in town?

"How much?" I ask, already prying out my wallet and counting the bills.

I've stayed here plenty of times. It's only sixty-five dollars for the night. He tells me one hundred and I hand it over in a single bill. He eyes it for a second too long before taking it.

It's only then I can breathe. "Thank you."

"You all right?" he asks, his lips in a thin line.

I let out a sigh and close my eyes before telling him, "It's been one hell of a drive and it's way too cold for September."

The clerk huffs a laugh while the register clangs open. "It's only going to get colder this weekend."

With everything that happened, I didn't realize my mother was wearing a dress. The top part is a solid navy blue, which complements the bottom portion that's a dark blue paisley. I also didn't realize she wasn't wearing shoes. She ran out in her slippers and I didn't pay attention to that either.

I'm sure there's plenty I missed. I got the part where she shot my father and laid there for hours sobbing next to him, though. *Hours.* She sat there next to him for hours. The prosecutor in me would have a field day with that fact alone.

Unbuttoning the top button of her dress, I wonder if she planned on a girls' night out to a nice restaurant downtown when she put it on. I bet she thought today was going to be a good day. It was one worth dressing up for.

She didn't get to her hair or makeup, though. Or else it all came undone when the altercation happened. I can't ask the first question that's begging to be brought to life. *Did he hit you, Mom? Did he threaten you?* I don't want to bring it up, just as much as she doesn't want to talk about it.

The navy cotton fabric slips down her arms easily as I help her out of it. She hasn't said a word, but her eyes are drenched in worry and tragedy and unspoken questions.

I don't think I've ever seen my mother scared. Not like this.

"There you go," I barely get out as the fabric falls to the floor and I wonder if my father saw her like this. Is that wretched look what she wore when she pulled the trigger?

The steam in the shower builds, fogging the top of the mirror's edge and the warmth is positively suffocating. I busy myself rubbing my sore shoulder and barely watch her from my periphery in the foggy mirror as she slips down the rest of her dress and climbs into the tub.

The clothes will have gunshot residue on them too.

The hot water splashes and with it is the sound of my luggage unzipping as I pull out the toiletries I packed.

The goal is simple enough: get rid of the residue, calm my mother down, and come up with a plausible defense.

A nagging voice in the back of my mind whispers to ask her why. Swallowing thickly, I ignore it. But when I close my eyes, every little moment I ignored before flashes before me.

I pray this hot water can cleanse away these sins.

"You ran to find the killer." I speak as I set a bottle on the edge of the tub. With the curtain pulled back, I can't see her and she can't see me.

"You were distraught at your husband's death and how it happened so fast, there was nothing you could do."

My body sways, my breath stolen for a moment as I envision a different reality. "But you saw the man." With a heavy exhale I place a second bottle next to the first and tell her to wash her hair. My mother hasn't moved, hasn't spoken.

"I went into the foyer but no one was there and then I saw you running out the back. I saw something or someone else first but I didn't get a good look, but I saw you and ran out, wondering what the hell you were doing. I chased after you and when I finally got to you, you were trying to hurt yourself, sobbing uncontrollably."

"Trying to hurt myself?"

"It lays a claim that you weren't in your right mind."

"Though in your version," she starts and my mother's words are spoken both slowly and lowly, "I was after the real killer?" I glance up at her as tears streak down her face.

"You were, you were running after him after you found Daddy dead, but he got away and you couldn't take it."

"As if they'd believe I could run faster than you." My mom offers her doubt. "I could just tell them the truth."

Ignoring her comments, I continue. "You were too scared to go back inside. I thought you were having an episode. I was going to take you to the hospital, not having seen anything inside, until you begged me not to. You just wanted to leave, to get away so I did that. I made that happen, not understanding what had happened."

"That's what you've got, baby girl?" My mother's question is nothing but melancholy.

"You fell asleep, then in the morning you told me everything."

"I don't want you to lie for me," my mother says and it's then I see she still hasn't touched the shampoo.

When I don't respond and instead grab the shampoo and force it into her hands, she speaks. "I thought he cheated on me," my mother says, her voice tight with the confession. "I swear, back then I thought he was cheating and I didn't know."

"Didn't know what, Mom?" I'm too scared to ask and when I do, she looks down at me, the steam flowing around her.

With a wobbly smile that doesn't reach her eyes, she shakes her head and says, "Nothing, baby."

"Mom, what happened?" I ask and tears stream from my eyes just as they do from hers.

"He did it for the last time. I had to."

"He hit you?" I say my guess in a whisper and my mother's weak smile broadens with sympathy. "Yeah, baby, he hit me."

"I'm sorry." I barely get out the words, bracing myself against the cheap cabinet of the sink.

"When you and your sister were little," my mother interjects, "you two were as thick as thieves and I remember praying you'd stay close like I wish me and my sisters were."

I can't even think of Cadence right now and what she's about to walk in on. My heart breaks today for so many reasons; I don't know how it still beats.

"You remember that time you ate all the candy from the canister? I found it empty and called you two in."

"You knew it was me the whole time?" I ask her, knowing just how this story plays out.

My mother nods her head. "Cadence was so quick to take the fall for you. And that time she stained the back seat of your auntie's Buick, you took the blame for that one."

The past events play out before me. We were just two sisters getting into normal trouble.

"You two were always looking out for each other."

"Mom, what's this have to do with Dad?" I ask and she only shakes her head, finally opening the bottle of shampoo. "Nothing, baby girl. I just want you to know I love you. I love you both so much and you can't stop loving each other. Even if you stop loving me."

Using a wad of toilet paper, I stop the tears from flowing but stay in the bathroom, the shower curtain closed so I can't see behind it.

It's quiet a long time, other than bottles opening and silent tears being swept away.

"You're throwing your career away doing this," my mother warns and a piece of me is all too aware of that possibility.

"You better get good at lying then. And holding on to that story, Mom. Because I don't want to lose my job, but I'll be damned if I lose you."

With a harsh swallow I repeat what I just came up with as if it just happened. "I came home and no one was there but someone caught my eye as they ran out to the backyard. And then I saw you running into the woods. I was going to take you to the hospital because you wouldn't stop crying and tried to hurt yourself." I add in that last detail. "And I almost took you in, but you begged me not to."

Rising to my feet, my body aches and my bones crack. Carefully, I pull back the shower curtain and pour out more than enough conditioning treatment as my mother's head hangs in shame, and I lather it. I make sure to get it all, refusing to let any residue stay behind.

"I didn't do it, I didn't bring you in, because of what happened last month," I whisper and my mother's composure cracks. "They're going to know about it, Mom, and it's motive so it's best we bring it up and control the narrative."

She's silent as I work the conditioner through her hair and then comb it through. "It needs to sit," I tell my mother and she nods. The water's still hot and the steam smothers me.

"Ask for a lawyer, speak as little as possible. I have the story and I'll make sure it'll stick. You just have to be quiet as much as you can and stick with the story I gave you."

It's quiet for the rest of the time, the hot water splashing onto my arms and chest when I rinse out her hair. It soaks into my sleeve where the blood resided and I watch the pink droplets fall into the tub. I'll throw away the clothes. All of them and buy new ones for my mother in the morning.

Over and over in my head, I rehearse our story and hope it's our way out of this.

My mother's only silent or crying, nothing more than that until she tries to confide in me, "I wish …"

My motions stop, the lather on my hands a stark pure white and smelling sweetly of lavender.

This time when I ignore her, when I don't press for more, I know why I'm doing it. I'm not strong enough to handle any more than this tonight. "There won't be a damn shred of evidence to tie you to this when you go in for questioning. Don't give them any. Don't give them a damn thing."

"What'd you do with the gun?"

"It's wiped down, and it's Dad's, isn't it?" I know it is. It doesn't make sense to hide it when there are no fingerprints and they'll know the gun that killed him matches the one he has registered.

"You will not go to prison for this. I swear by it." Holding back the emotions I'm feeling, and relying on the ruthless lawyer inside of me, I step away and tell her to comb the leave-in conditioner through, as if she doesn't know.

"I'll leave these sweats for you." My mother's a bit larger than I am, but they'll fit. My pajamas are always baggy and loose. She'll be fine tonight in them.

Leaving them on the sink, I leave the bathroom, worn and damaged in a way that hits me the moment the cool air batters my skin. With the click of the door behind me, I lean my head back as shuddering breaths leave me.

My father's dead. My mother's a murderer.

And my mind can't wrap itself around those facts. Fresh tears threaten as my phone sounds out. Sniffling, I pull myself together.

Cody's called. Multiple times.

My sister's called but she didn't leave a voicemail.

No one else. So I don't think she's gotten home yet. She hasn't made the discovery or called the cops. In the mindset of supporting my story, I should turn off my phone. And so that's what I do right now. I hold down the button on the side until the screen turns black, shutting out the world and hiding. Just for one night.

And what about tomorrow? It's Cody's voice that questions me. The guilt of it squeezes like a vise around my chest.

I can't tell him anything. Not any part of the truth. I can lie to the police all day, I can turn an interrogation into a children's story. But Cody? He'll see through it all, and I can't confess to him.

The one person I want to talk to is the one who's gotten away with murder—the one I need to make sure I don't lose my mom too.

I help my mother brush her hair when she's finally out of the bathroom and lying down on the bed. I brush her hair like she used to do for me.

When her chest falls and rises steadily, and I know she's sleeping, I stand on weak legs. I clean it all up, tossing the clothes at the bottom of the tub, and rinsing them down.

I let them soak before tossing them out. There's no reason to keep them, but if somehow they're found, they'll at least be clean of residue.

When I get back into the room, well after midnight with new clothes from the 24/7 Walmart two towns over, there's a faint knock on the wall.

Knock, knock, knock knock knock … knock, knock.

Like a child. Like I used to do with my sister in the house and my father when he went up to the old barn.

As I get closer to it, the sequence comes again.

Knock, knock, knock knock knock …

I hesitantly reach out my hand and respond: *knock, knock.*

chapter nine

Marcus

I WOKE UP TO THE SOFT CRIES OF THE BOY WHO WAS HUDDLED in the corner opposite of mine in the cell.

I know what that means and I swallow the jagged rock lodged in my throat that seems to block my voice.

It took a long time for either of us to speak. We've been here for … at least a week together, but he was here longer. I don't know how long and I don't want to ask. I don't want to remind him of the first time.

I can trace every outline of my ribs. It tickles slightly when I do it and yesterday I did it so much the skin on my right side feels raw and still tingles when anything brushes against it. Sleep takes up most of the day and night. It's easier to sleep now than it was before. The first few days I was terrified they'd come if I closed my eyes, but now I know they barely come at all. Unless we do something against the rules, they stay upstairs and forget about us. That's what I pray for, for them to forget about us, even if that means we don't eat for days.

The soft sound of his throat clearing comes with a hollow look. There's a darkness around his eyes; I'm certain mine must mirror his.

"Do you think they're gone?" he whispers and I nod although I don't make the nod too obvious. They have cameras to keep an eye on us and they don't like us talking. They let the dogs in if we talk. I don't want to see the dogs. He knows that. I'm certain he does.

It's so quiet that I can hear when his head thuds against the wall. Looking in his direction, his eyes are closed and he looks as tired as I feel. But more than that, he's terrified.

"How did you get here?" I ask just to say something to distract him from his own mind, but I hate the unspoken follow-up question that begs to be asked.

"I was walking home from school," he says and as he answers his pointer finger draws on the cement. From the other side of the cell, I can't see what he's tracing.

"Where do you go to school?"

"I don't know the name but my teacher is Miss Harrow. She teaches the kindergarteners."

He's younger than me. I almost ask him how old he is and what his name is, but the door to the upstairs suddenly opens. My first thought is that they're sending down the dogs but it's not. It's worse. Much worse.

My shoulders slam against the brick wall as I hear a loud clang of a gate followed by a grunt. They're back. Terrified eyes pierce into mine and with a quick and rushed movement, I gesture for the boy to come over to my side of the cell. His bare feet leave a sound I wish was the only sound I could hear, a pattering of small feet on the damp ground.

But the heavy boots outweigh the pitter-patter and even more so a muffled cry. A small voice that begs for help. The boy trembles next to me, smaller, weighing less and wearing less too. He's cold, so cold but the shaking is from the same fear that works its way through my bones. My right arm wraps around his small body and I try to stay strong for him, forcing my eyes to stay open as we huddle in the corner farthest away from the iron gate. I watch because he doesn't, he closes his eyes tight. One of us has to watch. This time it's me.

"Shhh." I hush him as his whimpers get louder. They're almost here. The two men I know in my nightmares. There's oil on their hands. I think it's oil; it's all I can smell when they come. They smell like the garage used to when my father's car broke down.

The one on the right, the tall one and older one heaves the cell gate opposite ours open. The shorter one who's heavier tosses the bag into the cell and a vicious crack sounds out followed by a shriek of pain.

Hot tears leak down my face, but I don't look away. I have to make sure they stay over there, in that cell and not ours. And they do. The gate closes, locking with a click that will haunt me forever, and I watch because someone has to and the boy can't.

The screams don't stop for hours.

chapter ten

MY MOTHER KILLED MY FATHER. THE STATEMENT IS FIT for a tragedy, maybe one of Shakespeare's plays. I hated English Lit in college. I only took the class because I had to. All the while I remember tapping my pencil against the textbook as I did the assigned readings, thinking how unrealistic it was. How outdated and far too dramatic the stories were as they unfolded.

As my mother lies on the edge of the queen bed, I can't help but to be brought back to that moment, and suddenly I feel foolish. *How did this happen?*

With trembling hands, I close my eyes and pretend like it's only a story. I don't know if it's the adrenaline that kept me from thinking about the reality … but my mother killed my father.

And I'm helping her get away with it.

Knock, knock, knock knock knock … The pattern of five faint knocks on the door to the hotel room draws my eye to the dull white door. A shadow is vaguely seen creeping from under the locked door.

My heart slams against my rib cage as a slip of paper slides under the crack.

Even from where I sit, huddled with my knees pulled into my chest and my eyes burning from lack of sleep and the prick of former tears, I can see the dark scribbles of handwriting.

The second the paper lands on the worn, thin carpet, the shadow disappears and it's quiet again with the exception of heavy footsteps outside, followed by the creak of the next room's door opening. I sit there, very much aware that it has to be Marcus who's next door. It must be him. And more importantly … he must know what happened or that something has happened. How else would he have found me?

How much does he know? The question lingers as my body stays frozen.

Knock, knock. The last two taps of the game I remember from my childhood come through the wall only feet from me.

A shudder runs through me and I can only look back at my mother, still sleeping. Unaware of the fear that keeps me crippled in this chair.

A second passes and then another before the realization sinks in that I'd rather go to him than have him come here. I don't know how I'm able to move my horrified limbs, but I do, bending down to read the slip of paper with the simple command on it.

Come over.

With a deep breath in I slip on my flats, once again staring at my mother's sleeping form. Even in her rest, there's a crease etched in the center of her forehead and her brow is pinched. Even in her sleep, she's plagued by what's happened. There's no escape from it.

As I creep out of the room, all I can think is that she really did it. This is happening and I'm caught in the middle of it all.

Hesitation overwhelms me as I stand on the outdoor walkway

in front of the room next door. The small peephole is a black pupil that stares back at me as the chill of the fall night air wraps itself around my shoulders.

With the back of my hand, I barely form a fist and rap: *Knock, knock. Knock knock knock* … I don't have to finish. On the last knock, and with an eerie creak, the door opens. Not enough for me to go through, but enough to see the bathroom light is on inside. No other light, just the one and it barely bathes the room in the dim yellow glow.

"Hello?" I call out, my voice raspy and not at all sounding like myself. Clearing my throat, I gently push the door open wider. My heart races until I hear his voice.

"Come in. I've been waiting."

Thump, thump, it all slows when I hear how calm and expectant he is. The deep baritone comes from the far left of the room. His room's the same as mine, only mirrored. So his bed touches the wall where mine is placed. It's only inches from where my mother sleeps.

That knowledge sends goosebumps down my back.

"Didn't mean to keep you," I tell him although I'm unsure where the response comes from. All of it is surreal and I find myself praying to just wake up.

"You were busy with your mother, that's understandable."

Thump, thump. The tips of my fingers go numb as I make my way to the chair seated in front of a simple desk. The other would be more comfortable, but it's closer to him.

At the thought, my gaze lifts and I see more of him than I did before. For a moment, only a split second, I think he's Cody, not Marcus.

With his dirty blond hair, just a bit too long to be Cody Walsh, and the width of his shoulders, he looks so much like him.

My head spins and I lean forward in the chair, unable to hide my reaction. Maybe I just wish Cody were here. I wish it were him sitting there.

"I look like him, don't I?" he asks and there's a pain present in his tone. Undoubtedly so.

"You do," I say and a shudder runs through me at the admission.

"They used to say, never to us but to each other, the boy and I could be brothers."

My heart pangs in my chest and I swallow thickly as I look up at him. "The boy?" I ask but Marcus only shakes his head.

"I'm sorry. I shouldn't have brought it up. You must have so much on your mind."

The words jumble at the back of my throat and my gaze shifts to the light from his bathroom. The door is open and I can clearly see the shower curtain pulled back. I bathed her to get rid of evidence. I'm an accomplice to murder.

My father's murder.

My head hangs lower and I have to part my lips to take in a shaky breath.

"You don't want to talk about it?" Marcus asks.

My hands tremble as I pull my knees up and sit so damn uncomfortably on the small chair. My back leans against the wooden slats and my shoulders rest on the barely padded back of it.

"Do you know what happened?" I whisper, although I already know the answer.

"I do," Marcus says. He stretches his legs out on the bed, still sitting up against the headrest. He's taller and leaner than Cody. I take it all in. Some awful, devious voice whispers in the back of my mind that I could leverage what's known about Marcus and his crimes. I could save my mother that way.

And myself.

With a quick shake of my head and a gut-churning sickness, I cover my eyes and drown that thought.

If I tried that, I'd be dead. Although as it stands, I may be dead already. The rabbit hole Alice fell down and the ridiculous plays they made us read in school … none of it was as fucked up and unreal as this.

"Have you come up with a plan?" Marcus asks and I tell him.

I spit out the story I told my mother three times tonight and I'll tell her again tomorrow.

Marcus's response is merely a murmured *hmm*. Prolonged and drawn out, lacking in either approval or disapproval.

"Why are you here?" The venom in my tone is shocking and judging by the tilt of Marcus's head, giving more light to the left side of his face although it's still dark from where he lies, it shocks him as well. I hold on to the strength. I ask, "Am I collateral? Is this blackmail?"

The dim light gives a sheen to his teeth as he smirks with a huff. Readjusting against the headboard, the bed groans before he answers, "To see if you were all right."

The sick feeling from earlier drops into the pit of my stomach as my gaze lowers to the foot of the bed. Then I dare to look back up at him as he readjusts once more.

"And to give you an out. I could help with your mother." The world stops for a moment, my lungs stilling completely as I watch him reach to the nightstand to hold up a pad of paper. "I left a note behind. Thought you should know." The thud of the pad hitting the end table is followed by Marcus's comment. "I'm not sure your sister is expecting it, but given how bad of a liar she is, it'll only help your mother."

"You didn't implicate my sister—" My words are rushed as I scoot closer to the edge of the chair, desperation overwhelming me.

Marcus's tsk cuts me off. "I'm here to help, little mouse. Be careful, be quiet … and what I've set into motion will be good enough."

"What does it say?" I ask. When he doesn't immediately answer, I add to clarify, "The note. What did you leave?"

"It's of no concern to you. It would lead to more questions because you're missing so much of the story."

"Tell me then," I plead with him, my throat going dry.

"More questions for questions?" Marcus asks and the sibilant sound of each *S* lingers like the hiss of a snake. Goosebumps rake down my body, the memories of the other night more than eager to replace the fear that lays over every inch of me.

"It seems like you have more answers than I do." The thudding in my chest beats faster, but this time for a different reason. The small room is suddenly suffocating and there's not enough room to separate us. It's one sided and so very obvious.

Ignoring my comment completely, Marcus says, "Cody's a bit hung up but he had a feeling. He's perceptive like that."

My eyes close as I sit back, letting the low blow make me feel even lower. I have no words although I wish I could respond. I love him. I love the man and I know I do. But he's a liar and I don't trust him.

"He blames himself, if that helps. And he'll fight for you." Lifting my eyes to Marcus's pale blue gaze, I keep my questions to myself.

"Maybe a smoke would help?" he says. He's toying with me. That's what this is to him, a cat and mouse game. That must be where he gets that nickname for me from. Anger would normally be my response. It should be. But it's entirely absent from my reaction to the slight. The wash of sadness is just as unexpected and only adds salt to the wound.

I watch as Marcus opens the drawer to the nightstand and lights a blunt.

With a puff of smoke, he offers it to me, but I shake my head. "I don't smoke."

He takes his time inhaling deeply before gesturing to the small fridge. "Wine it is then," he tells me. I'm frozen in the small chair, watching this powerful man let out a cloud of smoke from between his teeth, the white and black playing among the shadows.

"Don't be shy. I thought you'd need something more … but maybe not."

"Something more?" I ask and force myself out of the chair, forcing myself to play his game if for no other reason than the fact that I can't do anything else. And my mother needs him. Fuck, I need him.

The fridge is small and the single bottle of white wine has been placed inside at an angle so that it fits neatly. "Thank you for chilling it …" I tell him and then spot a small plastic black bag on top of the dresser to the left. I recognize it as generic to liquor stores and inside of it I find a corkscrew and two plastic cups.

My fingers rest on both cups, my rational and logical side failing me. Silently, I hold up the cups, offering him one, but he shakes his head. The silence turns to a faint ringing in my ears that gets louder and louder. The images of today crash through me like a tidal wave as I open the bottle and pour the wine.

chapter eleven

Marcus

ONE CUP OF WINE AND HER RED EYES GLISTEN. IT'S A good distraction, asking her about Cody. She's more defensive than anything when it comes to him … when it comes to us.

Two cups and her stiff shoulders loosen while her answers start to come easier. Her reluctance falls just as she does, slowly falling to pieces as I feed her clues bit by bit.

He did something a long time ago and her mother put the pieces together. I'm not sure Delilah is following the little breadcrumbs I'm giving her. She'll blink one day and see it all. Tonight I think she's simply looking for a distraction.

Her mother wouldn't have been able to, if he hadn't started up again. If I hadn't helped her along. Not that I added that last little piece out loud for Delilah. She doesn't need to know. All she has to fully accept is that he had done something bad and that her mother didn't mean it. Just like the sweet alcohol, it offers her the smallest sips of peace.

"Don't cry," I say, consoling her as she sniffs again, closing her eyes and pretending like she isn't on the verge of breaking down. I've seen so many men and women respond to death. It's almost always the same. Delilah's different. I attribute that to her cases and how hard it tried to make her. Or rather, how hard she tried to make herself so she could continue. So she could make it all make sense.

We all have our limits, though.

"Ask me something else … something about us." Her dark chestnut gaze meets mine. Every time she looks at me, she centers. More than likely refusing to let go of this opportunity where she can use me. She could have so many questions answered, resolve so many of those cases that keep her up at night. And the riddles between myself and Cody would be revealed if only she asked the right questions. If only she could pull herself together. If only she could trust me enough.

We have time, little mouse. She'll get there.

She doesn't ask me any of that, though, as she grabs the bottle, eager to pour the last bits. "You watched me?" she asks with her back to me. The thin pajama pants hang loose on her hips and the burgundy tank top hugs her tempting curves.

"Yes."

"You stalked me?" she says and the empty bottle lands with a clink on the dresser. She sips her drink with her back to me.

"Yes."

"For years?"

I hesitate only a moment before saying, "Yes."

Finally, she soothes my anxiousness, turning around to face me and she leans against the dresser. She's gorgeous when she's full of accusations.

"Why?"

I can't help but smile at her. Years … she knows. But *how many years?* is the question she's still lacking.

I answer her the only way I know how. "If only I could tell you." Why do any of us torture ourselves with the things we can't have?

"Tell me something." For the first time, she gives me a demand and it makes me harder for her than I've ever been.

"And you'll tell me something in return?" There's only a slight movement from me in response to my eagerness. The tips of my fingers slip against the bedsheets. As if that would be enough to ground me ... as if it would hold me back.

"Of course," she says, whispering her answer and then biting down on her bottom lip. My cock stirs at the motion. I've never been a giving soul. There's always a selfish reason.

"You saw them for what they were." I speak without thinking.

"What do you mean?" Curiosity knits her brow.

"Just like the case last month ... Ross Brass." At the mention of his name, Delilah stops the cup midway to her lips. A coldness flickers in her gaze.

"It's not all black and white. It's covered in as much gray as it is blood. But once you see them for what they are, you don't let go."

Perhaps she'd rather I talk about anything other than herself because her mind wanders. I'm certain she thinks of her mother again. Or her father. It's given away by the drop of her gaze and the slower rate of her breathing.

"Do you want to know what I think?" I ask her and my throat is suddenly tight.

Confusion is apparent in her dark brown eyes and I'm certain she almost asks, *about what?*, but instead she only nods a yes. Maybe two cups have already been two too many.

"I think it will all be all right but it will take a few days and you'll be just as anxious every day. Each day more anxious than the last until they have another name. Someone else to blame for your father's death. I think that's what you'll need to move past the worry."

"It will be all right?" Skepticism laces her question. It's almost sarcastic.

"With the note I left, no one will want to pin it on your mother. They'll have someone else in mind."

"Who?" she asks in a single breath.

"Someone who deserves to die."

"You're an angel of death," she says as if it's fact and I can only laugh. "That's what they tell me."

My amusement is a short but deep rumble in my chest. Her hips sway slightly and I pat the bed next to me, getting her attention.

I wait for her as she walks slowly to the very end of the bed and sits. I'm well aware she can see me, really see me if she looked up. Her eyes would have adjusted to the dark by now. My pulse races and just as she's about to, just as her thick lashes raise, I tell her to go turn off the light first.

"Turn it off and come back." She hums and doesn't hesitate to rise from the bed, making a soft groan.

She can't see me yet. Not yet, not just yet. Panic flows through my veins as the floor creaks with her gentle movements and she turns off the sole light that was on in the bathroom.

"So you are an angel of death?" she asks as the light disappears with a soft click.

"I don't decide, though? Do I?" I say to her, bringing her attention back to the conversation as she comes back to me like the good girl she is.

"They're going to die, regardless. I simply pull strings so it flows easier. So they kill each other and the victims, the ones who would fall pray to them otherwise, are reduced. That's not so wrong, is it?"

Delilah's quiet, so silent that I hear the moment the plastic cup, nearly empty now, hits her bottom lip.

"Like your cases. The ones they tampered with and never

solved. They made that decision and it led to … whatever it is it leads to …" I debate confessing, but I can't help myself.

I can practically feel the way her pulse ramps up when I tell her, "I did you a favor, I closed them."

"This isn't the game we play," Delilah says, not asking about the cases I know she seeks answers to for refuge. I should have known better. She doesn't care about those cases right now. Not in the least. There's only one murder on her mind. "Did she do it because he hit her? Can you tell me that?" Back to her mother …

No. The answer is there on the tip of my tongue, but I can't bring myself to say it. Then I would have to tell her. And that's a depressing conversation for another day.

"If your mother had pressed charges, what do you think would have happened?"

"He wouldn't have been found guilty. He would have kept it quiet and they would have split." Tears muffle her words.

"Not to him … to her. What would have happened to her?" I have to remind the disappointment in me that she's too close to it and too uncertain of so many things. Too conflicted like Cody can be. It's not her fault that she didn't think of the other piece. No one ever thinks of the other one. The victim and what's left behind. As if a punishment makes those wrongs all right.

Her inhale is quicker, louder, but she remains silent.

"I don't want to talk about it." Finally. We agree on something tonight. The pieces are in motion, and there's nothing left to do but allow the dominoes to fall.

Before I can relish in leaving this conversation alone for the night, Delilah stands, readying herself to leave perhaps. But first she tosses the empty cup into the small bin by the desk. "Thank you for … covering for my mother."

"And for you," I remind her, suddenly feeling hotter than I'd like.

My fingers itch, eager to keep her here. Again, they skip across the sheet, this time with more desperation.

"I don't like seeing you like this," I say, barely getting out the words. Even though it's nearly pitch black and the sounds from beyond the door fill the silence with both the chirps of crickets and the rushing of cars passing along the road, all I can hear is my heart beating as she crosses her arms against her chest.

At the sight of her breasts rising, my cock stiffens.

"I owe you," she tells me, but she already owes me more than she could imagine.

"You do," I say, agreeing with her admission and my tone gives her pause.

The day she came into that barn is the day he stopped. Every monster has a boundary. Look at what good came from such an awful man. At first, my fascination was simply due to watching out for her. She was his keeper in a way and I had so much to learn from him.

But it grew to be more. I don't know how or why.

I had a chance to kill him years ago, and didn't. So many chances and at some point I had to admit, I allowed him to live because of her.

I settled on a threat instead. The fool should have never set out to pick up his old habit.

Rather than counting up her debt, I happily contribute to it and say, "I have something to help you sleep if you need it."

I can hear her swallow from all the way over here.

"It's called sweets."

"My father told me not to take candy from strangers—" she starts to say but then stops herself midword. With an instant pang of sadness and regret evident on her beautiful face.

With her head falling back, her bottom lip drops as her mouth opens and sorrow overwhelms her inhale. She's trying to stifle her cries.

"Come here," I say. It's a demand and I'm not sure how she'll take it, so I soften my next words as I add, "Let me make you feel better."

chapter twelve

IT'S NOT THE WINE. I CAN'T TELL YOU THE NUMBER OF DEFENDANTS I've seen in the courtroom who blamed their actions on alcohol. It's never the buzz of a night out that's to blame for what they've done. Never.

We do the things we want to do. It's that simple.

If it wasn't already planted in the back of our minds, the seeds of the action wouldn't exist.

So it's not the wine. As much as I'd like to believe it is. The sweet taste is still on my lips as I stare across the dark room at a man who terrifies yet excites me.

I could claim my actions before were due to curiosity. I could claim that I wanted information, not unlike an undercover detective. In fact, that excuse had lingered on the tip of my tongue ever since those first unforgivable thoughts entered my vivid imagination.

Marcus's large hand smooths the comforter beside him. My body is heavy and weak; every piece of me is practically lead, weighed down in this moment.

Hot, molten lead, to be more specific. Unable to keep its form and desperate for somewhere to go.

There's not a single soul I could have confided in. Not one … not even Cody.

No one but the man who beckons me to come lie with him. And if I'm honest with myself, it's something I've wanted since he first whispered my name.

Swallowing thickly, I make my way to him, letting the floor emphasize each of my steps with a creak. I don't bother with pretenses, so in that time, I lift the hem of my tank top over my head, uncovering my small breasts and the cool air instantly caresses my body.

I don't know how he'll react but I imagine this is what he's after, and with the weight of today still firmly weighing down on me, I want it too. I'm eager to forget it all and feel something else that is far more intoxicating to lure me into the depths of sleep.

A hiss of intake is followed by a groan of satisfaction from the man in the room, but I don't bother to look him in the eye. Leaning against the bed, I kick off the loose-fitting sweatpants, but leave on the one garment that will stay between us for the moment. With my clothes tossed carelessly on the floor of the cheap motel, I drag down the comforter that he just smoothed and crawl in.

It's not lost on me that I'm exposed, bared to a man who stays in the shadows and won't let me see him.

Something about that fact makes it even easier to do what I'm about to do next.

When I crawl on the bed, the springs give a slight protest with a soft squeak. My fingers dig into the mattress and I lean forward on my hands and knees at the top of the bed. My eyes are closed, my breathing even and I plant the barest of kisses on his hard jaw lined with stubble. He's rough against my gentleness, but something about the simple act, breaks down any wall of protest.

"Tell me it's going to be all right?" I whisper the plea, my forehead resting against his temple. If he were going to push me away, now would be the time and it's quite possibly something that will happen. An act that would destroy me.

But I would take it. I'd take it just as much as I'd take him laying me down on my stomach and fucking me raw on this bed. If he'll make everything right again, I'll let him do whatever he wants to me.

Time tortures me as I wait for what feels like forever for an answer. My eyes remain closed even when I feel him move, shifting next to me until his deft fingers slip down the curves of my side. With goosebumps following the trace of his fingertips, a shiver elicits the darkest of wants.

"It will be." His answer comes with a nip on my shoulder, a warning maybe. "You know I'm a bad man, don't you?" His warm breath trails down my shoulders like a silk sash falling from the finest of robes and all at once, he's no longer touching me.

My long lashes flutter open and I stare directly ahead at his throat. The cords in his neck tighten and the dark stubble begs me to brush the tip of my nose against it, just to feel how sharp it is. "I know exactly who you are," I whisper and although it feels true as each syllable slips out, so many questions in the back of my mind doubt my conviction.

His lips brush against mine and his smile plays against my parted lips. With the rustling of the sheets, his bottom teeth graze along my lower lip until he nips me.

The sound of shock and want mingle into a deadly concoction as I yelp, still on all fours, in only my panties. Still with my eyes closed.

His thumb brushes along my backside. "You left these on," he says and the click of the heat turning on does nothing to soothe my already heated skin.

Swallowing, I nod my head, expecting to feel him there, but

he must be leaning back. My core is hot and my nipples harden. Without his touch, I could be alone on the bed for all I know, but I haven't heard the bed signal his movements.

"A touch for a touch?" he asks, giving away his position which is only inches from me.

"Yes." The single word falls from my lips both light and heavy, with an eagerness and yet with apprehension.

His heat wraps around me as he leans in closer, the rough pad of his thumb tracing the curve of my breast and then the other. I whimper, my thighs tightening and my needs climbing higher.

"I have to warn you, Delilah," he whispers and the roughness of his stubble scrapes against the curve of my neck. It's then I can feel his bare skin against mine, my forearm pressed against his chest. Sweeping my hair to the side and exposing my back, he nips my neck and presses his hand against my upper back.

My head lowers in a bow, my ass still raised. "I'm going to take my time with you," he says and with the dizziness of a lust-filled cocktail flooding my veins I moan in response. My cheek brushes against his thigh. I'm not naïve. He's naked on the bed and his cock is near. I part my lips, willing and ready and lift my hips to accept him, but his hand bears down firmly against my shoulder blades, pushing me against the sheets.

The sound of him stroking himself is followed by the head of his cock being pressed against my lips.

"Lick it clean," he commands and my tongue darts out to taste the salty bit of precum that's waiting for me.

He strokes his cock again, his knuckles brushing against my skin.

"I'll have every bit of you," he says but it's almost as if it's a promise to himself. I take his words for what they are, a hell-bent eagerness for this man to consume me.

"Yes," I say and breathe out, feeling everything slip away. My sanity included.

It's not until he places his lips at the shell of my ear to tell me, "But you didn't beg," that I think it won't happen. He won't thrust himself inside of me and take what he wants.

I open my eyes only to stare at my own grip on the edge of the bed. The sound of his footsteps rounding the mattress is barely heard over my pounding heart.

"I told you that you'd beg for me, that you'd feel deprived without me inside of you," he says and my response is right there, so close and so wanting to be heard, but I can't speak.

"It'll be fun to play with you, though."

He keeps his promise, taking his time until I'm wrung out and begging. Even then … he still doesn't take me.

According to him, I didn't beg fast enough, and I don't crave him enough. Yet.

Even when I whimper that I need him, it's not enough.

chapter thirteen

THE ACHE BETWEEN MY THIGHS IS UNRELENTING. EVEN in the hard chair of the interrogation room, I can barely sit without feeling him. His fingers played with me, toying and testing. Leaving me satisfied, aching, but wanting more.

My cheeks are stained with a heat that would reveal a harlot to anyone who dared to pry. The sarcastic huff notes the ridiculousness of my thoughts. Given that I'm sitting across from a man who's attempting to pin a murder on me, my focus needs to be anywhere but on Marcus.

"My mother?" I ask Detective Skov. His dark brown eyes are just slightly lighter than his thick hair. It's grown out an inch at the top and not at all tamed. Along with his overgrown stubble, on the cusp of being a beard, the man looks like he doesn't give a damn about rules and regulations. I've given him my explanation more than a handful of times now. Each time he asks nearly the same questions.

What time was that? Did you hear anyone? Did you see any-thing else? Can you describe ... on and on. I know the tricks of the trade. He's looking for any chance to cast doubt on what I've said. To see if I'm lying.

"She's not coherent," he says and I exhale in frustration. I begged her this morning, telling her if she wanted to say some-thing, to just cry instead. It's better for her to appear unstable than to give them an alternative version of the story.

It's not lost on me that if she slips up, if she goes weak, I'm fucked.

They'll know I lied and charges will be pressed; I'll be dis-barred. It'll be the end for me.

"She wasn't coherent when I found her either," I tell Skov again. Two hours in and I'm only repeating myself now.

I can take it all day long. I don't know that the same can be said about my mother, though.

Glimpses of her disheveled state flicker in front of me and I pick under my nails rather than look back at the man I'm certain doesn't believe me. He knew my father and by association, my mother and me and my sister. Only by name, though.

"Is this a normal reaction for her?" he asks and I glare up at him.

"A normal reaction to finding her husband dead? My father," I say but my voice breaks and I force my eyes closed. "I'm sorry," I whisper and with both elbows on the table I hang my head in my hands. "I just ... I'm sorry," I say, apologizing again.

"For what?" he asks and if I wasn't truly destroyed from ev-erything that's happened, I would smile at his idiocy. My story is ironclad. It's all up to my mother.

"For my shortness," I tell him and take in a steadying breath. "I'm usually more ... Talkative and approachable and ... I'm usu-ally better." My voice cracks again as I speak and I shake my head. "I just don't understand or believe it. He can't be dead."

Believe your lies and everyone else will too. I'll never forget that phrase from Criminal Investigations 450 written on the chalkboard in a room full of expectant, soon-to-be lawyers. So long as they passed the bar.

"I should have …" I let the statement trail off and close my eyes. My mind drifts, wandering back to the front door of the home I grew up in. My throat's tight as I remember opening it, the creak and the ominous silence that greeted me.

"It was supposed to be a girls' night," I say and my words are etched in agony as I stare up at the detective and let the pain of it all be revealed in the statement. "That's what we should be doing right now. We should be out having fun while my father attends a conference."

"As far as you know, there isn't anyone who would want your father dead."

Just as I'm about to respond by bringing up his cases from years ago or disgruntled former business partners, the door opens and Skov's partner, Gallinger, comes in. The two are complete opposites. The clean-shaven, pristine cop is at complete odds with Skov's disheveled state.

Even his polite smile and nod, plus the way he whispers to Skov, appear to be in direct conflict with the man's appearance.

"How are you, Delilah?" Gallinger asks me, pulling out a chair and sitting across from me.

"It feels like everything is coming apart," I say, making the admission because it does. And it adds to the testimony.

"You have to know how this looks," Gallinger says while gesturing with his hand, sympathy in his gaze. Skov turns, still standing and paces behind him.

"I do. Trust me, I do," I tell him and my heart beats harder, wondering what change brought him in. Did my mother say anything? *Please, God, please, I will do anything.*

"We found a note at the crime scene, did my partner tell you that?"

A flicker of hope lights with me like the small flame of an ancient furnace. "He didn't, no."

I was beginning to think Marcus never left it. Or it simply wasn't found.

The small slip of paper flitters across the table and I make great effort to only touch the plastic edges of the evidence bag it resides inside.

Bad men die.

I don't have the ability to read past the first line. My breath is stolen from me as my blood runs cold.

It's Marcus's handwriting.

He didn't try to hide it. He's pinning it on himself.

"We're running forensics," Gallinger starts to say but my head spins and a ringing in my ears drowns out his voice.

I can't breathe. I can't focus as the man speaks. Leaning forward slightly, I manage to control my breaths. In and out, in and out.

"Are you—"

I cut off his question, but I can't complete the statement as I say, "I recognize …"

My throat is tight. With my eyes closed, all I can see are the glimpses of last night.

"Recognize what?"

He had to have known I would recognize it from the cases. Analysis will point them there. To my cases. The unsolved ones that the fucking reporter brought up only a month ago.

"I got my father killed," I blurt out and I don't know why it sounds so truthful to my ears.

My hands shake at the thought of this all leading to me.

Shoving them in my lap, I try to decipher Marcus's intent. Why lead them to himself? To cases I've worked on? Other than to keep me as a suspect or involved in some way.

"This is bad. I need …"

I can't think straight as my head swarms with the onslaught of coincidence.

1. I come into town.
2. The handwriting of the note matches my cold cases.
3. I kept my mother from coming in, who now isn't speaking.

The heat that runs along my skin is fire, but still I feel cold as ice.

"You can tell me whatever it is you need," Gallinger presses and I don't fail to notice that Skov has stopped pacing, watching me intently.

"I need Cody Walsh," I tell him and focus once again on breathing in and out. My palms press against the metal table just to feel something in this moment. "When you run forensics, you'll find they match cold cases. They're our cases from years ago. We suspected a serial killer named Marcus."

"You think he killed your father?"

"Or he's framing me." I whisper the fear at the same time a realization comes over me.

"According to the mortician, he was dead hours before you arrived," Skov says, piping up. "Gallinger filled me in a moment ago. If someone's trying to frame you—"

Gallinger cuts off Skov, saying, "Which is why it doesn't make sense that the killer waited hours after the murder before fleeing the scene when your mother says she found your father." He's quick to find a hole in the story.

I'm silent, processing the evidence they have.

The logical side of my brain pieces together my own defense first. Footage from the gas station, the toll pass stations on the highway … there's enough to keep me away from the time of death.

A sense of calm comes over me, but only for a moment.

"My mother isn't a killer. This signature—" I start to say, but stop myself. The expectant gazes of two men searching for more stare back at me.

All I have to do is be quiet. There isn't enough evidence to convict my mother or me but there's also evidence to the contrary. Evidence that points to a killer.

But there's one little statement I want to deliberately let slip. "You think he was going to kill my mother too? He was waiting for her and then I arrived? Or was he going to kill me?"

I've never been the best actress. I can put on a show for a courtroom, but tears? Real tears? Those are hard to come by under normal circumstances, let alone this.

"If he took off when you showed up …"

In this moment, though, it's easy to cry, mourning for my father and also shedding tears of relief for my mother. "I saved her from being killed?" I let the question fall in between us, my voice full of hope as I stare wide eyed across the table at the man who knows damn well I didn't do it. I'd bet my last dollar he's eager to get a taste of the cold cases instead of pinning my father's murder on a woman he's known for years.

With a tap on the steel table, the one detective leaves and then the other follows.

They make me wait for at least forty minutes; the only noise to keep me company is the click of the heater turning on and then back off.

All the while I pray my mother doesn't say anything. Not a word.

She promised. I told her this morning, it was all she needed to do to keep us safe.

With the fears of the unknown by my side, I startle when the metal door opens again. Raking his hand through his unruly hair, Skov tells me I can go. And that he's sorry for my loss.

It dawns on me that he's said it more than three times now and I wonder how close he was with my father. Not enough to ask, though. Not enough to create more dialogue than needed.

"My mother?" I ask him. "Is she okay?" The thudding in my chest is heavy and refuses to go unnoticed. I only hope I can silence it.

"She needs help," he says and his thick brow furrows.

"Is my sister here? She's waiting for her? I'm sure you know she's a—"

"Yes, we're aware and your sister is on her way." Skov's lips part to say something else, his hands on his hips and I can imagine the accusations. That I shouldn't have kept my mother away last night. That I should have known she needed help.

That I'm part of the problem.

The corners of my lips are weighted down like the lead in my chest keeping me where I am until he repeats that I'm free to go.

"Thank you." My whisper grants me a nod from the man and I mentally prepare to see my sister.

Remorse isn't the word I'm feeling. It's so much more than that.

I know what she walked into alone, dreading what she'd find.

People move about me in blurs of blue and white. The phone at the front desk never stops ringing. Somehow I manage to continue moving along, taking one step after another.

I speak at the appropriate times, thanking someone at the desk as I wait in the lobby.

Through the windows of the front doors, the parking lot is clearly in view. Several cop cars are lined up in front with an assortment of random cars on the left.

I can just imagine how the red and blue lights would have

hit the house late last night. How they would have shined bright against the brick. All the while, my sister was alone.

The doors open and the freezing cold air blows in. There's not a soul here I recognize.

I busy myself checking my phone. Texts from my sister, asking where I am and then others … all that would prove my sister didn't know where I was or why my mother and myself weren't there.

Texts from Cody. He was worried. It's only then that I realize he would have gotten the news that my father was shot dead and my mother and I were missing.

The streams of texts and messages flood my soul with guilt.

What the hell is wrong with me?

There aren't enough apologies in the world, but it's what I start with: *I'm so sorry. I'm okay, I swear, just shaken up.*

It's not a lie but it feels like it is. I don't know what I'll tell him when I see him. That's the worst part.

As I'm holding my phone, a new text comes in. This time from Marcus.

I want you to meet me at an old barn.
The red barn on Cannon Road.

I respond:
I know it. Why there?

My father used to meet his friends there to work on tractors and other machinery. It was a hobby of his. I don't have time to mourn the memories because two things happen at once.

My sister cries out, a purse dangling from the crook of her arm and her coat hanging from her shoulder as she runs toward me.

"Baby," my mother calls out behind me and the two pass just

to my left, hugging each other with tears streaking down their faces. I stand there alone, feeling my phone go off. Glancing down, I see it's both Marcus and Cody.

I can't even begin to think of a response to Cody. I'm depleted and I have a pile of lies to explain to him, none of which I want to … and a million apologies on top of that. I don't know what to say to him and that's become a staple in our relationship.

Again the doors open and all that hugs me in this moment is the chill of the autumn wind.

"Cady cat," I say and I don't know why the weakly spoken nickname comes out like that. I haven't called her that in years.

Slowly, her grip loosens on my mother and she peers at me, the kohl liner around her eyes making them look even larger than they are. She readjusts her black wool coat before pulling me into a firm hug.

My grip on her is tighter than I consciously allow. I can't let her go even if I wanted to.

"It's going to be okay," she tells me, but I'm not sure I believe it.

chapter fourteen

Marcus
Nineteen years ago

H E LOOKS JUST LIKE THE REST OF THEM. THERE'S nothing at all distinctive about his features. Maybe the reddened cheeks would set him apart if it were any other day. But with the festival, all the adults with beers in oversized plastic cups have red cheeks.

He smiles too, just like them. His isn't as white and polished, though. Years of smoking took its toll. Maybe his skin is slightly more yellow too, although it's hard to tell from this far back.

Slipping my hands into my jean pockets, I keep my distance, slipping down the cracked sidewalk between rows of people cheering on the green floats. My shoulder brushes against the brick wall and occasionally there's a bump from someone stepping back or trying to get around the crowd.

"Hey, watch it."

"Oh, I'm sorry, kid."

"Where's your mom?"

I ignore them all, keep my head down and smile. I've found if I just point ahead and keep walking, no one stops me. They don't bother to get a response before turning their back to me and carrying on.

It's warmer down here than it is at the barn. It took me three days to get here although it's only hours if you take the highway. I learned that from my last hitchhike.

From the barn and my safe place, all the way to a different small town I grew up in, is only three hours away. Three long hours down the highway carved into the mountains.

The next float strolls by and this time the man stops. He shouts something, cupping his hands around his mouth to call out across the street. His smile broadens and the cheers get louder as the music does. Everything is so damn loud, but it's silent just the same.

It doesn't matter; it doesn't mean anything.

For Harold it's just another reason to drink and then get in his car.

I wish I could steal his car from him when I'm done. That's a regret I have. But my teacher, the monster he is, would never do such a thing. He doesn't take trophies. That's a rule.

Even if I could steal the car and take it from him, it's not like I could drive it.

So for now, sneaking onto trains and in the back of trucks to get back home will have to do. But I'd be damned if I didn't admit the trunk would be a good place to sleep at night. A closed-off, locked space … I can only imagine.

A cool breeze blows by and I instinctively look for the stairways down to the stores. They block the wind too and when the stores are closed, bundling up in the corner and hiding behind a trash bag works quite well. They can't see me. So long as they can't see me, then everything is all right.

"You okay?" a woman asks as she stumbles into me, her sharp red nails digging into my shoulder as she braces herself against me. I get the idea that her instinct was to keep me upright, but she staggers in her high heels.

Her lashes are dark and long and there are little diamonds at the corners of her eyes. "Little dude, you shouldn't be out here all alone," she tells me and looks past me.

She seems like one of the good ones. One of the ones who need protecting. She's so much taller than me. Pretty bird. That's what the man would call her. But only once he was done with her.

"You lost?" she asks when I don't answer. I smile up at her, shaking my head and tell her I'm just going home. She smiles back. "Be careful, cutie."

The short interaction almost makes me lose him. I can't lose sight of him. Not today. Today is the day it has to happen. A numbness pricks along my skin as I follow Harold around the corner, quickening my steps and slipping through the crowd.

Harold disappears into a liquor store, one he's been in a number of times. I bide my time, finding a rock and carving something into the concrete. It won't last, just like the promise I make with the stone won't either.

Kids play with rocks outside of stores. No one looks twice.

With the parade, the noise and the crowds to slip back into, the timing is perfect for my first.

And Harold has to be the first.

Harold has a habit. It's a bad one that he's yet to learn from. He drinks, then gets into his '86 Ford and drives home. His brother, a senator, got him off this last time. The charges suddenly disappeared, as did his sobriety test results. The scandal was all over the news. And even though there isn't a damn thing distinctive about Harold, I knew him. I recognized him.

Because he's the man who took my parents away. He caused the accident; he set all of this into motion. He should be my first.

The moment I saw his picture in the crinkled newspaper that reeked of the coffee it was stained with, it all made sense.

It was meant to be this way.

He took my parents, and that led to everything. He started it all and who I was before will end with him. Only then can I truly be Marcus.

The bad guys always lose and he is a bad guy. Even if he smiles. Even if his brother is a senator. Even if tonight he decided to walk instead of getting into his car. His victims don't get to decide anything anymore.

If he hadn't done it again, if it hadn't been in the papers I scavenged while rummaging in the dumpsters that lined the alley hours away from here, it never would have occurred to me. I wouldn't have chosen him. But he did do it again and they let him go. They gave him another chance, but that's not fair when the man he killed didn't get another chance.

Harold is a bad man and his time is up.

A numbness pricks down my arm, my fingers twitching for the cheap blade I found last week. The very day my plan came together. It's funny how things all align when you have a plan. How the pieces fall into place and it's so much easier to sleep, to move forward.

His death is my purpose.

As we round the corner of the liquor store, the parade falls behind us. With a bottle wrapped in a brown paper bag, it seems he's given up on the beer and moved on to something harder. I've watched Harold for nearly a week and his routine is simple. He leaves his home around noon. He wears jeans stained with old paint. He goes to the bar down Fifth Street and when they kick him out, he goes to the liquor store he just came out of.

Then he goes back down to Fifth but he takes the alley. It's so he can piss on the wall or the cars in the parking lot behind the bar. He's only done it twice, but his rough laugh that echoes late at night indicates he truly enjoys it. It's just as much a part of his nightcap as the bottle of gin he's got gripped in his right hand.

I'm grateful he's gone down this way tonight. I don't know why he's already headed down the back path, given that he wasn't even at the bar for long today and left to see the parade. Old habits die hard, I suppose.

Back here it's quieter, but the music still filters through. I keep to the left, next to the trash cans and look down at the old stone that's unrepaired and the rubble of concrete that was used to fill the gaps years ago.

My heart races, moving so much faster than my footsteps in the worn sneakers that don't quite fit. Everything feels hot, even though I'm aware I'll be freezing tonight, wherever I lie down to rest. The blood rushes in my ears so loud I can barely hear him.

His jacket rustles when I tap his shoulder. I have to look up to do it, my neck craning because he's a larger man, rotund from drinking and not doing a damn thing else. When he turns I'm quick to hit him in his groin, catching him off guard to steal his wallet.

Chase me down the alley, my inner voice prays. My sneakers squeak as I run farther to the left, farther away from the couple kissing past the dumpsters at the start of the busy street.

So we can be alone.

"Little shit." His groan fills the smaller space, the alley that leads down to an old row of homes built for the steel mill. You can barely fit a bike through this alley. I remember when my brother did it, though.

With everything raging inside of me, I don't count on the tears or how my gaze becomes glossy at the memory.

Cody had me on the back of his bike, and he was able to ride down an alley just like this one. I remember how scared I was that he was going to hit the wall or that his handlebars would catch the side of a brick. I shouldn't be thinking of him right now. I lose myself, my focus, I lose everything remembering how I held on so tight to him. Stopping in my tracks, right in the middle, the man curses behind me and grabs my shoulder.

I don't even recall my hand wrapping around the blade, but when I strike him in the gut, once then twice, that's when I realize what I've done and that I'm still here. I'm not back with Cody, holding on to a small bag of candy.

I'm not there at all. I'm holding a bloody blade and looking up at a man who fails to say anything.

Harold looks older than the picture in the paper when I look up. His skin is a little more yellow too, and more wrinkled than the paper. The shock in his gaze was also absent then.

I hesitate for only a moment when his wide eyes look down at me. He stumbles back just slightly and I stand facing him in the narrow alley, his wallet in one hand and the blade in the other.

My heart is still racing, but he's more disoriented than I am. And I'm the one with the plan. He swallows thickly before calling out for help.

The man's on his ass, scooting backward. He's trying to get away, but what's done is done. There's sorrow and sympathy, but it's odd how it comes, how it's because it's like Cody's watching me. He wouldn't want this, but Cody's not here and he'll never know.

Everything speeds up then. I only hesitate because he's watching me. The moment Harold turns his head to look behind him, maybe to cry out for help again, I strike. Eating up the short distance between us with long strides and slicing his throat.

Once, twice, and a third time.

It gushes at first, hot and bubbly. It's different than what I've seen in the barn.

He clutches at his throat, trying to speak.

I don't tell him why. I wonder if when we die, we can still ponder things. I hope not. I want the things I think about to rest once I'm gone.

I watch him, and make sure he's gone. It doesn't take long. It's so much faster and simpler than I thought it would be.

A breeze goes through the alley and my face is cold. Streaks of what feels like ice make me shiver involuntarily until I brush away the tears. They're unexpected.

I clean off the knife on his shirt before dropping it down a sewer. The last act that involves Harold has to do with his wallet. I collect the cash and pocket it. Only forty-three dollars. Then I drop the wallet down the grates along the street too.

The white noise fades fast and I can hear the parade again, like nothing happened. Picking up a stick, I trail it along the mortar between the bricks of the building. Because that's what kids do, they like sticks and rocks and keeping to themselves.

I keep walking and I don't look back. Instead I think about Cody and how that was the only time we rode down that alley. How when we went down it, I couldn't wait to try on my own. I was going to have my own bike soon and I was going to do it too.

I don't hear anyone scream like I thought I would. Watching the parade from the end of the street where it's taped off I wait, but no one ever screams.

The sirens come and no one wants to part to let them through.

It's for the better outcome.

It's for all the pretty little birds.

chapter fifteen

I WAS NEVER ADVENTUROUS. I DIDN'T WANT TO GO PLAY outside. My father locked the door once after telling my sister and me to go on the front porch. He yelled through the closed door to go play and turned his back to us.

I suppose telling us we couldn't stay inside all day during summer got old, so he resorted to kicking us out. When the streetlights came on and dinner was on the table, we were finally allowed back in. But kids were supposed to be outside playing when the sun was out. Luckily, I almost always had a book to keep me occupied.

Inhaling the fresh smell of the forests to the left and the hints of hay from the field to the right, I don't know why I didn't play out here more. It's peaceful.

The field didn't scare me like it did my sister. She said she could get lost in the long rows of corn and that freaked her out.

She hated it out here. I remember her, so much taller than me, with her arms crossed over her chest in her favorite blue jean jacket. She'd rather lose at hide-and-seek than take one step into that cornfield. I don't know why it spooked her like it did, but I love it out here.

The red barn always looked beat down to me back then and the years haven't been kind to it now.

I wonder what Marcus knows. There's no such thing as coincidence when it comes to him. There's a reason he brought me back here to the place I know my father used to hide away in.

When my mother and he were fighting, he'd always take off to help Mr. Dave fix up the old machines. There's more than a time or two I can recall Mom hunched over the sink, gripping the counter and pretending not to cry when I stepped into the kitchen after hearing the argument from upstairs.

She'd wipe away the tears with her back to me, and dry her hands on the flannel towel that hung from the cabinet below.

"Clean yourself up. It's almost time for breakfast." It wasn't always breakfast she'd say; the meals were interchangeable and all corresponded to the time of day.

I can picture it so clearly, the same tearstained cheeks she had only yesterday with her hair up in a silk wrap and not a dress to be seen for days.

When they fought, the kitchen was her safe place. This barn was his.

"What does it mean to you?" Marcus's voice calls out and it scares me, causing me to stagger a step back. He's in jeans and a hoodie, maybe ten feet away under the shade of an old pine tree. Leaning against it, with his hands in his pockets, he looks relaxed which is at odds with everything I know about him.

"What does what mean? What does what mean to me?" I have to speak up a little louder than comfortable for him to hear me. The gray clouds part in the muted sky and as Marcus makes his way to me, I see his face easily enough.

Sucking in a breath, I turn to stare at the barn, pretending I didn't just see his features plain as day.

"Don't tell anyone you saw me," he commands although it sounds like a question. His charming smirk looks far too boyish on him. Maybe it's the pale blue eyes and faint wrinkles around them that give him his boy-next-door appeal. His dirty blond hair tousled by the wind makes him appear all soft, but his jaw is hard and his features severe the moment he tilts his head. "You understand that, don't you?"

More than anything, he looks just like Cody.

"You're his brother … you're Chris—"

"Don't," he says, cutting me off and I silence myself, chewing on the inside of my cheek. My pulse races and my heart hammers. They found dental records. The world thought him dead. My mind filters through the tragic tale. If he's Christopher, Cody's brother …

"I can see the wheels turning," Marcus says, coming up beside me. I stay facing the barn, wrapping my arms around myself as the wind blows.

"Is that right?" I ask him, peeking up but quickly looking away. He's leaner than Cody; I can't help but to compare every bit of him to his brother.

"Don't think about it."

"I'm not sure what you mean."

"Everything eludes you today …" Marcus says and disappointment is evident in his tone.

"What did you mean by your question?" I ask him. He stands beside me, his arm almost touching mine. He's taller than me but on the hill like we are, he's even taller and he practically towers over me.

Power radiates from him. Even the air seems to bend around him.

"This barn. What does it mean to you?" he asks and I shrug.

"It's an old place and … I used to come out here sometimes, but not a lot." I almost bring up my father, but I choke on his name.

"If they knocked it down, tore it to pieces?"

"It wouldn't matter to me," I tell him, and peek up questioningly. "Why would you think it would?"

"What about your family home? If they took it apart brick by brick?"

"You could take it … I'd still be okay." My mind spins with questions, wondering why he thought this barn would mean anything at all compared to my family house. Is it because of my father?

"Is there no place you thought of as home?" he asks me genuinely and when he does, his arm brushes against mine, offering the barest of warmth.

"That tree over there," I say, motioning toward an old oak tree near the center of the field. "That's the wishing tree."

"It grants wishes?" His smirk is heard just as it is easily seen. It warms me, though, something deep down I can't explain.

"When we were kids, some boy on the bus said you had to run through the field late at night and climb it to wish on the stars or else your wishes wouldn't come true."

"I never heard that one," Marcus says and my heart flickers.

"I think in most towns it's wishing on shooting stars." I turn away from him and stare at the auburn leaves, mixed with hues of gold as I add, "But here we had that tree."

"So if it were to be chopped down?" Marcus asks.

"I'd be all right. None of this …" I almost tell him it's not the place, it's the people. But I bite my tongue at the thought that he'd threaten to take them away.

"You'd break. At some point, we all break."

"I feel like I already have and it has nothing to do with where I grew up." I don't hide my vulnerability.

"It has everything to do with that, and trust me Delilah, you are far from broken yet."

There's an eerie air that surrounds us, almost feeling like a push and a pull at the same time. A warning and a promise.

"Is that why you wanted to meet?" I ask him. After last night, I don't know what to think.

"To ask you what a barn means to you?" he says and huffs a humorless laugh. "No, that's not why."

He doesn't offer any explanation and the wind blows gently between us. Moving the hair out of my face, I wait for him to say more, but he doesn't.

"Thank you for the note." Marcus is silent, staring off at the old tree. A crease is in the center of his forehead.

"It's your handwriting," I say, prompting him to say more.

"I'm aware."

"Well … how?" I can't get the question out; it feels very much like I'm stepping over his boundaries.

"That's not something for you to worry your pretty little head about." The mannerism in which he speaks sounds so much like Cody too. I haven't noticed it until now, maybe because he's never been this casual before. Or maybe it's because I can see his lips now. The same lips I've kissed.

"You and Cody?" I can't help myself as my heart breaks, splitting down the center. "Does he know?"

"I don't want him here." He clears his throat, hardening his voice and that depth of darkness comes back to his cadence as he adds, "I mean, I don't want to speak about him. Not here."

"I'm sorry I brought it up." A hint of fear simmers in my blood.

"I thought maybe it would help me, to see you here."

"Help with what?" I dare to ask.

I don't know why, but there's a deep-seated pain that rests in his gaze. I wish I could stop it, erase it from all existence. It doesn't belong there.

In a single blink it's gone, replaced by a narrow gaze and a teasing smirk. The air shimmers and I nearly second-guess what I saw. "There's no one here …" His voice is deep and seems to rumble from his chest. "I could do anything I want to you."

I know only days ago, the statement would elicit more fear than anything else. As he looks down at me, like a hunter at his prey, there isn't anything I feel other than want.

He makes me want more than I ever thought possible. It's all the teasing. It has to be the way he plays with me.

As if that is something that should turn me on. I'm a foolish girl and so very aware of it when I ask him, "And what is it that you want to do to me?"

Thump, thump, the thrumming in my veins provides such little heat compared to what I know he could give me. "It's more …" he starts but then huffs a laugh and asks a question instead. "Would you kiss me still?"

"What?" Nothing he says tonight makes any sense. Not with what I currently know.

"Now that you don't need me?"

Is that what caused the pain in his gaze? He's truly mad.

"Do you want to kiss me?" he asks bluntly as I stand there, feeling as if I'm nothing beneath him and wondering how he could see me as anything at all.

"Yes." I answer without thinking.

"How badly?"

My heart beats madly as I see the desperation in his cold eyes. On tiptoes, I kiss him. No thought at all, just a desire, a wish come true that didn't take crossing a barren field and climbing up an old tree. A real kiss between a man and a woman. It's tender, but quickly deepens. His hand splays against my back and braces me there.

Ever so slowly, I reach up, my hand resting on his collarbone and the other sneaking up.

It's over far too quickly at the sound of tires in the distance, just beyond the tree line where the backroad is and where my car is parked.

The gentle moment vanishes, and without a goodbye, Marcus leaves, stalking toward the barn. I'd follow, but my name is carried with the wind.

"Delilah," Cody's voice calls out followed by the sound of a car door shutting.

Fuck, fuck, fuck.

I'm sure he can tell something's off—I can see it in the way he strides to me, at first deliberate and then slowed. My breathing is erratic and my mind races not knowing how to pick up the pieces of where I left off with Cody Walsh.

So much has happened since I met him in a darling coffee shop with a soft goodbye kiss. Too much to explain and far too complicated.

"Delilah," he says and relief is evident in my name on his lips.

"Cody …I …" I struggle to put anything into words, pulling at my sleeve and meeting him halfway to where he is. The barn is at my right, the field at my back and in front of me, is a man who stares down with both worry and devotion.

"How did you know to find me here?" I ask rather than digging deep. I've just kissed his brother, a man who helped me help my mother get away with murder.

The confessions threaten to tumble out and smother me even in the fresh air.

"Your cell phone," Cody says and his expression wrinkles with questions of his own.

"Right, right," I say, turning away from him as the clouds

return and the gray sky morphs to dark shades of blue in the sky-line. It's darker sooner this time of year.

There's never been a time in my life where I caught sight of Cody and felt what I feel now. This feeling like I should be running and hiding from him is completely alien but still it seems like the right thing to do. The dread that seeps into my blood, weighing everything down like lead, keeps me planted right where I am.

"I'm sorry I didn't call and I didn't answer ..." I push out the apology, needing it to be heard in its sincerity. "You didn't deserve to worry."

"Don't be. I know why ..." He's calm, far too calm. As if he knows. My heart hammers and I wonder what information he's gathered.

There's a silence between us, and an uncomfortable prick at the back of my neck. I'm certain that somewhere, Marcus watches.

I want to tell him. When Cody looks at me like he is, with his hands slipping into his jean pockets, his Henley blowing slightly in the wind but still firm on his broad shoulders, I want to wrap my fingers in the light gray fabric and pull him closer. I want to confide in my friend and be held by my lover.

I don't deserve an ounce of that want. I've ruined it; I've sacrificed us ... even if he doesn't know.

"I'm sorry about your father," he finally speaks. Glancing behind him, for only a moment, I see my father standing there at the entrance to the barn, locking it and telling me this is no place for kids. To go away unless I want to work.

His voice is so clear in my memory. My eyes prick and that could be the wind, it could be the unforgiving breeze. But my throat getting tight isn't from the weather.

"Thank you," I say in a nearly inaudible whisper. "You followed me here to give me your condolences?"

"Don't do that," he says, scolding my sarcasm, but it's not in a superior way. There's only pain that lays in his words.

"I just … I'm not well right now," I say, giving him the honest answer. I don't want Marcus watching us. Not when Cody doesn't know it. Not when I just kissed him. "I'm not doing well."

"We need to talk about this."

"We don't, though," I say and shake my head in denial.

"They brought me on the case." His tone is firm when he answers.

And for a moment I pause.

"The case? My father's murder?" That's what he wants to talk about … not us? I deserve the pain that grips me and tears me into two. "I don't want to talk about this right now …"

"We can't wait on this, Delilah." Cody doesn't let up and I know just looking at him that he's not going to let me walk away and hide. He's not going to back off, not a single step. It's an indescribable pain, knowing that there is no way to go back and how badly I've hurt him and ruined us.

I don't want him to know. If I could keep it from him and let him down easy, it would be best, wouldn't it?

"There are questions …" he continues and I have to close my eyes, taking in a steadying breath. With everything between us, the tension, the disappointment … the last thing I want to think about is my father's death. A snide voice hisses, *it's murder* in the back of my mind. *Your father's murder, not death.*

"Can we talk about it another time?" I ask although I don't wait for a response and turn away from him, wanting to get to my car. With the sun hidden behind the clouds, the autumn turned brutal without any warning.

Cody's quick to grab my wrist. It's not so much that it hurts or that it jostles me. The firm grasp only keeps me from moving away, but it's the desperation in his touch that has my eyes pinned to his and my breath stolen.

My heart races.

"I fucked up, Delilah," he says just beneath his breath. His ever-confident tone is shaken and his gaze falls before mine. Glancing behind me, an act that sends a chill down my spine, knowing that Marcus could be and probably is watching.

My shoulders shudder with the cold breeze as I wrench my hand away, although my flats are firmly planted where they stand.

"I know he spoke to you," Cody whispers even though, to his knowledge, there's no one here to eavesdrop. The breeze blows through the tree leaves and another chill runs through me.

Ever the gentleman, Cody removes his jacket, but he doesn't lay it across my shoulders. Instead he offers it as if he's not sure that I'll take it.

In a formfitting Henley, snug on his shoulders, he looks back at me with a softness in his blue eyes. "Please, even if you're angry." My pulse weakens watching him struggle in front of me. His eyes are rimmed with red and the chill has bitten his cheeks, turning them a pink hue to match the tip of his nose.

Reaching out to grab it, I take a half step closer to him and slip his jacket around my shoulders, even if it is far too oversized for me. The warmth is immediate, blanketing me as if it's safe now. As If nothing can hurt me beneath the shield of this man.

With his hands in his jean pockets, Cody says, "I know he spoke to you and I've lied. I've kept things from you."

The world blurs behind him.

"There are so many reasons I can't—I couldn't." He's quick to correct himself but that mistake forces him to heave in a flustered breath.

"Just tell me the truth," I plead with him.

"That's what I want to do, Delilah." His eyes hold nothing but sincerity. "I want to tell you everything."

chapter sixteen

Marcus

Twelve years ago

SOME THINGS NEVER CHANGE. LIKE THE STREETLAMP ON Parkway Avenue coming on before the rest of the lights in the vicinity. Or the bench outside of the hardware store being fully occupied with high school kids. The roll of wheels from skateboards and the chatter bring back memories.

Back then, they were the big kids. Now I'm around their age, maybe older.

The keys clang in my hand as I twirl them around my fingers. The small shop area used to be bustling this late at night. I noticed the new mall down the highway coming in and wondered if it would affect the stores here.

Maybe some things do change.

I don't even know what I'm doing here.

Things are tedious upstate and I may have been a little reckless. While the heat dies down, it's best to get away. I could have gone anywhere, though. Nothing explains why I ended up here in the town I grew up in.

With a few hundred dollars in my pocket, and a car to stay in, I could go just about anywhere. So long as I don't get caught, I'm golden. The fake license, the fake storylines—it's all worked out well for me these last two years. It's easy to make necessary acquaintances when you know people. And more importantly, when they know your name.

It's best they don't see my face, though, or ever meet me in person. I'm far too young. I've had to kill too many men already for their arrogance and laughter when they see me. I can't risk a damaged reputation because some old fuck doesn't know what's good for him.

Like I said, it's tedious. And I needed to get away for a while.

The jingling stops, the clatter of skateboards hitting the sidewalk and the rev of engines at the streetlight behind me turning to white noise. None of it makes any noise at all when I stare straight ahead. Because I see them. Cody's still living with my uncle. A smirk kicks my lips up as I think, I might be as tall as him now.

They walk side by side, Cody right at Uncle Myron's height. Although it's obvious he's younger. He should be headed to college. I saw online and on social media. He got into a few good schools but he hasn't decided yet where he wants to go.

He's got a girlfriend too and a job at my uncle's friend's construction site.

He wants to be a cop, though. My brother ... a cop.

Shaking my head, I wave off the woman who stopped to ask if I'm all right. "Fine," I answer her and her brow wrinkles. Before I can head out, following down the path Cody and Uncle Myron just took, she asks me, "Are you a Walsh?"

I've practiced my expressions a million times. It's a way to keep people from knowing what you're thinking. Or vice versa to control a situation. Still, I feel my own expression fall.

Just like how the feeling of dread drops into the pit of my stomach.

I don't recognize her. Not in the least. The tight white curls that stop above her shoulders may have been dark brown locks long ago. I don't know who she is, but with that questioning look in her eyes, I can see that she remembers me.

"No ma'am," I say, putting on a slight Southern accent. "Have a good evening."

With the dull thud in my chest and the numbing tingling on my skin, I head off with my hands in my pockets and search out my brother. I only look back once and the woman's still standing there, a bag in one hand and a cane in the other. People move on, people stop talking, and people get forgotten.

Maybe it's selfish for me not to want to forget Cody, when I'm doing everything I can for everyone to forget who I used to be.

He has everything going for him. I've kept an eye out for years. It helps me sleep at night to just check in.

He doesn't need someone like me. He's going to be a cop, for fuck's sake. Melancholy drifts into the darkness of my mind when I turn the corner and no one's there. Hell, maybe one day he'll arrest me.

I wonder if he'd know it's me. I don't see how he would. I'm dead and long gone and he's the man everyone thought he'd become.

"Hey kid," I say, tilting my chin up at one of the smaller kids a good bit away from the others. In his striped shirt and baggy black pants with more pockets than anyone would know what to do with, he's trying to do some trick on a skateboard that looks far too big for him. "Want to earn a dollar?"

"Yeah," he says with his eyes wide.

"Would you go in there and get me a bag of jerky?" I ask him, digging out five dollars and handing it over.

"You just want me to buy you jerky?" he says, hesitantly staring at the money I'm holding out for him to take.

"It only costs a few bucks, bet it'll be a bit more than a dollar left over." His hazel eyes peer up at me and then shine with delight when I add, "And it's all yours."

"You got it, mister," he says, picking up the skateboard at the same time as he snatches the five.

It would be easy to just buy the damn thing myself, but this is how you meet people. It's how you build trust. And no one suspects kids. They don't know what's going on. They don't talk to people and if they do, they aren't taken seriously.

Maybe I shouldn't set myself up here, not when some woman I don't even know recognizes me.

I'm just … checking in and then I'll be gone.

Back to the barn where I belong.

chapter seventeen

Cody

Nine years ago

THIS TOWN IS HAUNTED. OR THERE'S SOMEONE following me. There isn't any other explanation for it.

At first I thought it was nerves from starting this job. Working murder cases and being called out to dead body after dead body would take a toll mentally on anyone.

But I keep seeing him. I swear I see the same man over and over again.

I swallow thickly, the folded note tucked safely in my hand as I sit at the busy bar. I used to think I saw him back home too. Every so often, a block or two behind me. More than once I've chased after a figure that ran when I called out his name.

The grief counselors said it was in my head. But to follow me here?

I'm either haunted by him, or he's here.

"Another?" the waitress asks and I nod my head, adding a *yes, please*. The first four beers should be enough. I'm already hearing his voice again and remembering the last time I said goodbye. It wasn't good enough.

The regret is what I need to let go of. That's what the therapist said, but if I let go of it, then I let go of him.

I could feel myself on the edge of crying. It wasn't fair he was going to live with our aunt and I was going to our Uncle Myron's. The lawyers didn't want us split up, but the judge said it was for the best. We were to stay with family and that meant we were going separate ways.

So when Christopher hugged me and he started crying like I wanted to, I had to be strong. Dad would have wanted me to. I made it quick and then I ripped him off of me, telling him I'd see him soon and to act right.

I've carried that guilt and regret with me for as long as I can remember. As I sit here in the bar, it overwhelms everything and that should be my cue to stop drinking, but the beers come easy and the memories … I don't want to let go of them.

"A love letter?" the waitress jokes, nodding her head at the note in my hand as the beer hits the bar top. I only huff a laugh and she gets the hint, taking off before I feel obligated to say anything more.

A small boy's laughter resonates in the back of my mind, complete with a picture of my little brother smiling as he makes fun of me: *a love letter.*

He wouldn't be a child any longer, though. And whoever wrote this, isn't my brother. The second part of that statement is the one I'm hung up on.

I was a little messy with this one but you'll help me, won't you?

I've done what I can to help you and I know you want to help me too.

Now's your chance. I've been looking forward to this. For so long. I miss you.

He didn't sign a name. The note is written in blue ink and the handwritten font itself is unique. All the letter *A*s are written two different ways. When I looked it up in the system, searching for a match so I could come up with a suspect list, I was shocked at the number of hits it got.

All over the tristate area and for all sorts of crime. From petty theft five years ago, to money laundering cases that led to murder and a wanted serial killer in this part of Pennsylvania. There was even a hit from an apology note dating back almost a decade ago. A brick was thrown into a small sandwich shop and food stolen. The apology note is what tipped me off. Christopher used to say sorry that way. *I know it was wrong and I'll make it right.*

He always said that right after he said he was sorry. Always. The deep-down gut feeling just won't let that go. The detectives working the case left a synopsis that sends a chill down my spine.

They suspected a young boy at first, or a very uneducated adult because of the grammar and spelling. As the crimes increased in intensity and number, they were able to narrow down the criminal profile. It was textbook how the crimes progressed.

Now he's a serial killer. And a shadow who's followed me for years.

The beer slips from my hand, luckily landing with a clank and then bottoming out on the tabletop. With a glance over my right shoulder, then the left, I pull my shit together.

My brother would have been that old then. My brother would fit a description of a young white male in his early twenties.

"I didn't tell anyone," I say then clear my throat, sitting at the very end of a bar in Delilah's hometown. "I was just starting, only a month in. And I thought ..." I pause to take in a deep breath, inhaling the scent of pale ales and IPAs from the draft the bartender pours. The mug is tilted and the foam spills over to the sound of another classic rock song coming on.

"At first I thought I … I didn't know what to think. It was a hunch and I thought maybe I just wanted him to be alive, you know?" The men in the back make a ruckus when someone hits the dartboard. We're surrounded by clatter and barflies, but I've never felt more alone.

Until Delilah leans forward, her hands wrapped around an untouched glass of white wine. She peeks up at me and then scoots closer, her right side brushing up against mine.

"You wanted him to be alive."

"It was more than that … the way he said things … they were different for me than they were for the other notes and they hit on memories.

"It was like he wanted me to know, but he never outright said it.

"I thought it was all in my head … that the suspect was a surrogate or worse, was playing me."

"I was there," Delilah whispers, his gaze turning to the sweet liquid in the wineglass. She runs her finger around the rim of it. "You never told me."

"I didn't tell anyone," I say and my excuse sounds just like what it is. An excuse. Her small hand is gentle as she rests it on my thigh and rubs back and forth in a soothing motion. Her lips part but she doesn't say anything. Neither of us does for a moment until she takes a sip of wine and then leans closer to me.

"You were hurting, you were scared and didn't know who you could trust or if what you were doing was the right thing." She adds to my excuses, my reasoning for going along with it back then.

"Maybe it worked like that at first. But then … he'd … he'd set people up to go down and give me leads on them."

"You worked together?" she asks and I nod. The truth is begging to be spoken aloud finally. All those cold cases. All those men who disappeared. I knew it was coming. I knew Marcus wanted to interfere and I let it happen.

Instead of bringing any of that to light, I lift my beer to my lips and take a swig.

"I should have told you." I nod my head, agreeing with myself. "We were partners."

"I could have told our superiors. It sounds crazy, Cody. You sound crazy even now when … when I believe you," Delilah says and glances at her wine, then back at me. Her plump lips are a dark shade of red that complements her warm umber skin.

It hurts to watch her, knowing she's conflicted and that she's hiding from me. She doesn't know I know. I can see how much it kills her. Every time she slips beside me, letting her gentle soul be seen, she pulls back, stares at her wine and the sadness overwhelms her.

It's not fair to her that it happened this way.

"I was afraid to trust him at first …" I trail off, remembering the instincts pulling me in all directions. She's got to be going through the same. I can be there for her, though.

An older man rises beside us, making his way to the back probably to relieve himself. With him gone, there's no one surrounding us. The place is only half-full and most of the people are at the other end of the bar where the flat screens are playing football.

"I know … I know he kissed you." I let the confession slip out without looking back at her. Even though I can feel her gaze pierce into me, begging me to look back at her, I continue, wanting to get it all out so we can start over. So we can start fresh now with no secrets or lies between us. "I know he traded … he plays games …" I suspected something was up when I started to receive fewer texts from him, but the ones from two days ago when she never texted and her father was found dead spelled out everything.

He was with her, protecting her and he didn't want me to worry.

It's like stepping into an ice bath remembering the message he sent. If I hadn't been stopped at that red light, I swear to God I would have crashed.

"That's why you backed away from me?" I ask her, finally taking a peek down at Delilah and finding those big brown eyes staring up at me. They're bathed in insecurity and begging for forgiveness.

Her lips are parted and her breathing is staggered.

"It's because he stepped in, not because of something I did?" Even as I speak the last part, I know that's not all true. It's because he told her first. I should have told her. The moment I wanted her in my bed every night. The moment he came into my place and scared her. I should have told her everything.

"Cody," she whispers, emotion drenching my name.

"I can deal with that. As long as you still want me," I admit to her and feel the ache of needing her, truly and deeply needing her to forgive me and care for me again. I waited so long to make a move and it's because of my brother. The way he spoke about her … I thought he wanted her and if I kissed her …

I thought he'd moved on and I thought wrong.

"Cody. I did more than kiss him," she says. Her confession is spoken in a tight voice and the nervous exhale that follows adds to her uneasy posture. She won't even look at me, staring across the bar at an empty seat instead.

He did more than kiss her? The betrayal and jealousy are felt instantly, deep and primal. Licking my bottom lip, I stare straight ahead and attempt to take another swig of beer, but I can't. I'd rather throw it at the back wall. Every muscle coils inside of me.

If he thinks I'll let him use her like he used me, he's dead fucking wrong. Brother or not, I'll kill him for bringing her into this. He said he was protecting her. That doesn't mean fucking her.

After a moment, I swallow thickly, take a drink and tell her, although I still stare at the back wall as I do, "If I had told you … you wouldn't have."

"You don't know that and this isn't your fault. I made that decision."

She doesn't know who she's dealing with. She doesn't know the lengths that Marcus is willing to go to. Every warning screams at the back of my throat, yet there's only ringing in my ears when I peer down at her.

"If you want me to go, I won't. I'm not going to just let you go either," I finally tell her and her reaction at my admission is everything. From the soft inhale and slight lean forward, to the way her hands seem to inch across her lap to get closer to me. I haven't lost her yet.

"I won't lose you," I tell her and I promise myself. My pulse picks up and the heat between us is coming back. "I don't know what would happen to me if I did."

chapter eighteen

Delilah

CADENCE'S PLACE IS SMALL, BUT PLENTY BIG ENOUGH for the three of us. She's got a corner lot for her condo and Mom's been on the porch outside almost all day. I keep checking on her and so does Cadence.

Clicking send on the email, my stomach sinks and the sip of coffee doesn't help the sickness that's settled there. Claire's agreed to let me stay here rather than come in for an immediate evaluation as the board demanded. I'm on leave and they can't mandate that I be brought in on a whim when I haven't been formally charged with anything.

I have two weeks and then I need to follow procedures. Starting with a psych evaluation.

Even Aaron, the secretary, sent an email asking if I was all right. I'm more than certain the office, and probably the whole courthouse, is buzzing with gossip of my father's death and my possible involvement given the note that was left.

Miller and Judge Malden also sent their condolences via

flowers to the office. Aaron provided me with pictures. The prick that travels along my arms as I close my laptop on the kitchen counter accompanies the questions. So many questions but the main one being, do they suspect I was involved?

Sometimes we let our minds get away from us, and I remind myself of that. There's no way they suspect me. My mother, though? It's almost always the partner when a husband or wife is murdered. Almost always.

"I swear, it never stops." My sister's already speaking, her voice coming into the kitchen before she's even down the stairs. Her heels click as she rounds the banister. "I'll only be gone for an hour, though," she tells me even though she's staring into her purse, digging for her keys most likely. She adds, "tops," and like I suspected, her keys dangle from her hands.

Her hair is perfection, with thick natural curls that shine down to her shoulder blades. A black pencil skirt and a cream blouse are classically professional, yet on her body they could look scandalous.

"They really called you in two days after?" I ask her and she lets out a sigh of frustration before slinging the black leather hobo bag onto her shoulder.

"It's not them, it's my patients."

Guilt rides down on me. "I'm the workaholic, not you. Maybe you would say I'm projecting because work is what I wish I were doing."

"No," she says and then leans forward, giving me a kiss on the cheek with both of her hands gripping my forearms. She leans back, still holding on to me as she adds, "I'd say you don't want to be left alone with Mom." Her diagnosis sinks that knife a little deeper. "And I don't blame you."

"Go analyze someone else's psyche," I say, batting her hands away, once again opening my laptop and taking a seat on one of only two barstools lined up at the end of her counter.

"Just … one hour," Cadence says and I wave her off, not bothering to look up and give her more reassurance. It's her house, her life. She's right, I don't want to be alone with my mother who looks like a shell of herself and is constantly crying or staring off at nothing. But I deserve just that.

The clicking of her heels is steady and determined, followed by the front door opening and closing. I can even hear her car turn on and then drive off. All the while I stare over my left shoulder, past the small living room with only a single sofa and one reading chair tucked into the corner. I have a direct line of sight out the glass doors to the patio and seated there, with the same mug she's had for hours, is my mother. The wicker furniture is comfortable enough, but I know the thin blanket my sister gave her can't be giving her much comfort since it lays on her lap and doesn't even cover her upper half.

Her nightgown is thin and she's got to be freezing, but the last three times we asked her to come in, she only shook her head and began crying again.

"I loved him. I loved him so much," she whispered the last time I went out there.

I wanted to talk to her, to try and process everything that's happened between the two of us, but she merely stared ahead blindly with a sad smile on her face, telling me she was counting all of her mistakes. She said she'll be out there for a while and not to mind her. With a small pat on my hand she looked me in the eye and added a *please* and another apology.

I debate on the likelihood that she'll come in if I go out there and ask her to again. It's slim to none, but I have to check on her.

Cadence still doesn't know it all. A single whispered conversation confirmed that our mother killed our father. My sister left, locked herself in the bathroom and then asked me for time. That was last night and this morning she's avoided any real conversation. We need to all sit down. The three of us know a secret no one else can ever know.

First, I need my mom to tell me what she's willing to let my sister know. It's obvious Cadence blames herself for something that she said triggered our mother. At least that's what she believes.

Whatever happens and whatever's spoken between us, I want the three of us to know we still have each other. Given the current state of each of us individually … I don't know how to make that happen.

All I know is that the police suspect someone else and have evidence that leads to that person.

You need to believe someone else did it. It's so much easier when someone else did it.

The consequences of delivering what feels like justice come with some sense of relief. A drunken attorney once told me that. I didn't think much of him back then, but oh how I wish those words were true right now and that I could, even for a split second, believe that someone other than my mother had done it. And that the police would find them, prosecute, and all would be right in the world. Save one more gravestone that shouldn't exist.

The morbid thought is interrupted by the buzzing of my phone, vibrating against the granite countertop. If it was anyone else, I'd just watch it ring and not answer.

But it's Cody. And after last night, the lone hour I gave him before coming back here to my sister's, I can't ignore him.

There's so much I need to tell him still. So much I want him to tell me.

"Cody?" I answer, holding my phone to my ear. I don't remember the last time I didn't answer on speaker. But with my mother in view, I don't want to risk her hearing any of this.

"How are you holding up?" His tone is caressing, and a bit of it soothes me, a bit reminds me that so much is hurting.

"Not the best, not the worst," I tell him and stand up from the stool, leaning against the counter and stretching my back a bit. "Slept like shit and feel even shittier now."

My voice is deadpan but when Cody huffs a gruff laugh, the semblance of a smile tilts up my lips for a moment.

"Did you talk to the DA?"

"Yeah, she said I need to come in for counseling when I get back." I'm not given a chance to wonder how or why Cody would know that as I straighten. He doesn't give me the chance to wonder.

"There are some concerning thoughts from the PD back home too."

"Thoughts? Do they have a lead?" My pulse races and it hurts, physically, to feel it pounding in my chest.

"Can we talk about it in person?" Cody asks and I glance over my shoulder to watch my mother, thinking only of her being here and how that could be problematic with Cody coming over, but she's gone.

"Hold on," I say without thinking into the phone, pushing back the stool. The sound of the legs scraping is so loud Cody can probably hear it on the other end.

"You all right?" he asks but I'm too focused on the wicker chair and the puddle of blanket that blows slightly in the wind.

Where did she go? With my brow pinched I open the sliding glass door and call out, the phone pressed to my shoulder so Cody can't hear. "Mom?" I look around, searching to the left and to the right, but she's nowhere in sight.

"You okay?" Cody asks, calling out my name on the other end.

"I don't know," I tell him as I pick up my pace to go inside and call up the stairs for my mother.

It's quiet. Too quiet and my damned heart starts racing again.

"What's going on?" Cody asks at the same time I feel someone or something behind me.

When I turn, I fully expect it to be Marcus.

I don't have enough time to tell Cody who it is as the scream is ripped out of my throat and a bag thrown over my head.

With the dizziness, the clatter of my phone hitting the floor and the wind knocked out of me, I swear I try, but then there's another bash to my head.

chapter nineteen

Marcus

There's always a calm before the storm. Some may think there's hope that it's over when the gray skies clear and the harsh wind silences its angry cries. I'm more than aware that hope is nowhere in sight and that the quiet moment is for readying, for preparing for the violence that's sure to come.

There's a reason I paired them together years ago. They were the only two people outside of the chaos who needed to stay there, in the blur on the edge.

She's only a little mouse, not even a pawn in the games. And yet … he couldn't hold on to her; he couldn't contain her. He couldn't keep her safe in his small, insignificant world.

My brother failed me. It's a betrayal of the worst kind. He's too careless, blinded by her and that's only going to cause more problems. I was too late, but he was supposed to be there with her. Cody was supposed to be watching her.

Without him, my pieces are limited and for the first time in years, I'm lacking. I'm behind. And it's all his fault.

"Tell me the moment you find her." My command is short, my tone even and just as placid as the autumn skies above me. The shades of red and orange bleed in my mind. Just as they did, one by one, massacred in the alley behind the abandoned warehouse, giving me every detail as I flayed the flesh from them. I had enough of them, watching the condo from their positions in windowless vans. So fucking obvious.

I slowly tortured one while the others watched.

Ask a simple question: *What car did they leave in?*

Get a simple answer: *A black Mercedes SUV.*

And ended his suffering with a gunshot to the back of his head.

Cody should be grateful for the use of the gun. It would have been better for me, for my sanity rather, to be a bit more harsh. But evidence will be on his side.

"Of course. Is there anything else?" The man I've hired who's on the other end of the line is a specialist of sorts. He acquires things … certain precious things.

I swallow thickly, breathing in deep to stay levelheaded. *Is there anything else other than her?*

Time changes so much. There's always been more, far more important things than the little mouse who set me on this course. But now?

How could there possibly be anything other than her?

A stirring in my gut travels up my throat at the thought of her no longer existing. At the vision of her laying in a pool of her own blood like I've seen so many times with people in their last moments.

A strangled muffle echoes from the small closet. A quick glance proves the blood has leaked through the gauze once again. The bastard bit off his tongue and tried to swallow it.

An honest effort at suicide if ever I saw one.

I couldn't kill all of them. After all, someone had to talk. And he will, with two hands that work just fine.

"Did you have something to say now?" I ask him, not bothering to hide my face. He will die the slowest and most painful death I can conjure for the last words he spoke to me:

You're no ghost. You're no grim reaper.

You're just a man about to have his heart ripped out.

Any of the myriad enemies I have could be behind this. But there's only one I can tie each of these pricks to. Only one who would go after her entire family.

There's a reason she's supposed to be mine.

Everyone will pay.

This world will burn if they hurt her.

chapter twenty

Cody

"Tell me again what happened," Skov asks me. Again. The fucker doesn't know when to give up.

"They were already dead," I tell him. My tone is menacing and I pray to God for more control than I currently have while staring at the half-wit across the steel table from me. Every so often his left eye twitches. The dumb fuck can't control himself or his nerves.

"You're wasting time looking in the wrong direction and meanwhile, she's gone!"

"This isn't the first time she's been hiding out—"

Rage is unbecoming. Marcus told me that once. He cautioned me to contain it, but the worst bits of it boil over as I listen to this incapable fool imply that Delilah, my Delilah, left of her own free will.

"She was taken." The back of my teeth grind all while the words spill out. "Someone went to her sister's home, and took her."

"And the men there when we arrived? Did someone else kill them too?

"You just happened to be at the scene, your girlfriend missing, men dead on site …" The dumb fuck who has it all wrong leans forward on the steel table, inching his face closer to mine.

The skin around my knuckles is tight as I clench my fist with the unbearable need to slam it into his smirk as he adds, "And you just happened to arrive after everything went down."

"There would be evidence," I grit out, although my vision blurs and I swear I see red. "Gunshot residue on my hands, perhaps, if I'd fired a fucking gun!" The words claw up my throat, each one raising the intensity as I stare him down. I stand up straight, throwing the metal chair back and listening to it clang as I scream at him. "Do your fucking job!"

The snide look on his face vanishes, fear flashing in his gaze as he backs away slowly. My shoulders hunch, my breathing coming and going as if I've just chased down the man responsible for all of this. Everything is tight and suffocating.

"I think it's best you calm down, Special Agent Walsh."

The statement isn't uttered with contempt, not with anything other than innate concern as he takes another step back.

Everything is so hot; I'm nothing but a caged animal in here. "I need to help find her." I barely get out the words before inhaling deep and slow. My head spins. "This can't be happening."

Where the fuck was he? Marcus killed them, but what about the woman he claims to love so much. Where the hell was he when she needed him?

With both hands behind my head, I turn my back to the interrogator. "I don't have time for this. I didn't do it and she's out there." The statement is simple and accurate.

"You just happened to get there … and Miss Jones? She was already gone?" He repeats the same question but without the doubt and thinly veiled sarcasm. As if he's only double-checking facts.

Lowering my arms and picking up the chair, I tell him, "We

were on the phone." The metal legs scratch against the floor as I put the chair back into place and take a seat. "She screamed, the phone dropped and I heard her screaming and then it was muffled and then ..."

Fuck, my hands tremble and I can't even look him in the eyes.

"A man's voice said something and then the line went out. I was close, but not close enough. The first thing I did was call in the disturbance."

Lie. The first thing I did was message Marcus. They have my phone. They'll have the number. *Fuck. Fuck. Fuck!*

He got there first and left a fucking mess for me to walk in on with cops trailing behind me.

"And when you got there, the suspects were exactly as they were when we found them?"

I can only nod. Nothing else is able to come out.

"It's one hell of a coincidence ..." Skov states, taking the seat across from me, leaning back casually.

"I'm aware," I say.

"You know we have to go through it all. Everything that was on you, your office, your records."

The filing cabinet flashes in front of my eyes. I nod then tell him, "I understand, but put men out there. Don't waste time." I plead with him instead of giving any thought to what's inside that filing cabinet in my office.

Please, for the love of God, don't look in the cabinet. It's locked. There's no reason to. Not unless they wanted to pin this on me. Not unless they tie the phone number I messaged to any other crimes.

Fuck, fuck. Doubt surrounds me and it's then that the interrogation door opens.

The other officer who took me in, I forget his name, strides in with heavy footsteps. His thin lips are pressed in a tight line and he flashes me a narrowed, untrusting gaze.

"I'm only going to ask you this once, and I expect full disclosure and honesty." The severity in his tone sends a prick of warning down my spine. "You only have one chance to keep your job, Special Agent Walsh. If there's even a possibility of that. How is the wanted criminal who goes by Marcus involved in all this? I want to know everything you know about him."

and i love you the most

W WINTERS

USA Today best-selling author, Willow Winters, brings you an all-consuming, sizzling romance featuring an epic antihero you won't soon forget.

Some love stories are a slow burn. Others are quick to ignite, scorching and branding your very soul before you've taken that first breath. You're never given a chance to run from it.

That's how I'd describe what happened to us.

Everything around me blurred and all that existed were his lips, his touch …

The chase and the heat between us became addictive.

Our nights together were a distraction, one we craved to the point of letting the world crumble around us.

We should have paid more attention; we should have known that it would come to this.

We both knew it couldn't last, but that didn't change what we desired most.

All we wanted was each other …

This is the final book in the This Love Hurts trilogy.

This Love Hurts and *But I Need You* must be read first.

dedication

To my readers who wonder,

"What happened to you that you write like this?"

I found others like me, and that was enough.

"It is sometimes an appropriate response to reality to go insane."

—Philip K. Dick

prologue

R UN. *JUST RUN.*

The trees over the fence are brutal as their bark scratches down my right forearm. Branches whip at my face and I nearly impale myself on the spiked iron rail at the top of the fence before releasing it and dropping down. The hot blood smeared across my skin is more than enough evidence that damage has been done, but I don't even flinch. Dried leaves lash out at me as I scramble through the brush, the twigs littering the ground crunching beneath my feet as I fall.

Oof. Biting down on my lip I silence the cry that threatens to be ripped from me on impact. With a racing heart and tears pricking at my eyes, I force myself to move. I can't look back and I can't stop.

Everything's on fire, every weak muscle inside of me screaming with agonizing pain. I imagine this is what it's like to die, and that very thought keeps me moving.

Run. Just run.

The cries from the new boy are still vivid in my mind. It was only moments ago and I swear they still echo in my ears. His shrill scream rings clearly in my head, tainted by my heavy breathing as I draw in a lungful of air that's far too cold.

He won't last. They'll be back.

He should have run like me. The thought stays trapped at the back of my clogged throat as my bare feet almost slip on the damp grass before crossing onto the hard mud along the brick wall of some apartment building. I unlocked it. I tried to grab him but he only cried, whimpering on the floor and refusing to move.

My heart races as I glance one way and then the other.

For the first time since I swung the shovel, I stop. I stop for only a second, and his cries mix with another small boy's wail.

Marcus. The burn of tears is unmistakable now as they streak down my face. His voice haunts me still. The way he cried but tried not to … I'll never forget it. I may be a child, but if I live through this, I know I'll never forget. Some memories are stained into who you are. The core of your soul is forever changed as a result.

My head is swarming with horrid memories and amid the nightmares is his smile, his consoling smile that everything would be all right. The images don't line up with the reality. His whispers that everything's going to be okay clash with the screams that prove it's not.

It's not all right. And it's because of me.

From somewhere deep within the weak voice whispers to run, but my small hand clings to the worn brick on the edge of the building I'm tucked behind. As if holding on to it will keep me from being seen. The tight grip doesn't allow me to escape. For a moment, I consider turning back and yelling at the boy I left behind. The door was unlocked and open. If he's still there …

They'll kill him too. They'll do so much worse than that.

A staggered breath doesn't fulfill any need for oxygen. The

memories suffocate me, knowing what they'll do if he doesn't run like I did. I can't move an inch in the freezing cold. The wind howls as I stare down a row of houses lining the quiet street.

In my mind, we were so far away from anyone who could help. But as I steady my breath, I see nothing but houses. I can't remember if we screamed for help, but I know we screamed in pain. If only I'd screamed louder. My chest is hollow and my head dizzy.

They were so close. So many people. Several cars are parked along the street.

One is missing a tire, and as I stare at it, my gaze is caught by two men perched on a stoop.

Like me, their hoodies practically swallow their lanky bodies, but the two men are tall and older. Just as I see them, they notice me. "Hey kid!" one calls out. He's got an unkempt beard streaked with enough white that I can see it from here, and a questioning gaze in his eyes.

Frozen and paralyzed, I don't speak until both of them stand. My mind struggles with the fact they're just on the other side of the street. They were so close. How could they have been so close?

"Are you all right?" The second man yells out the question before elbowing the other, and both of them start down the steps.

They're coming for me, but I don't know them. More importantly, they may have known. They could be lookouts for all I know.

"Kid, you okay? You need help?" they question, jogging across the street and heading right for me.

Some form of an answer begs to escape, but I can't respond. All I can think is that maybe they did hear, maybe they knew. Maybe they're going to send me back.

I can't think, I can't answer, I can't do anything but run.

I need to speak first, though. Just in case they're truly

unaware, they need to know about the other boy, but the words don't come. How can I speak the truth when it kills me even to think of what happened?

I think of Marcus and what he'd say. He'd be brave enough.

My jaw is sore when I yell out, "The yellow house! They're in the yellow house on the corner!"

It's enough, just run!

The voice isn't my own and I take off as the two older men, only feet away, exchange puzzled glances. The alleyway is narrow, far too narrow for them to follow me, but I dart through the darkness, my bare feet stumbling over broken bottles, trash and muck. I would run through the fires of hell to get away, to be far away from all this.

I can't bear the thought of being back there and telling them what happened.

Telling them what I did and what happened because of it.

Run. Just run.

I run as far as I can. I run to what I thought was his home. I was wrong.

I was wrong about entirely too much.

chapter one

Cody

"YOU'VE GOT TO BE FUCKING SHITTING ME," SKOV HISSES, slapping the papers off the steel table.

"That's what the lieutenant said." From where I sit in the steel chair, the shrug of Detective Gallinger's shoulders appears nonchalant. I know better.

I watch the two men argue in hushed tones, one standing in the hallway leading to the interrogation room and the former barely a foot inside. His white-knuckled grip on the door and bitter inflection have me on edge. Even if they're being forced to release me, Skov could pull some shit and keep me here. Trapped in this room, I'm useless. With every second that ticks by, all I can do is hope the door will burst open and someone will announce they've found Delilah. Half the time I imagine it, there's a sense of relief that follows. The other half of the time I've stared at the clock as these two cops drone on has led to me imagining they've found her lifeless body. All the while I did nothing to save her, because of them. My gaze narrows as I stare at the back of Skov's wrinkled button-down.

"It hasn't even been twenty-four hours yet." The statement comes out with a guttural groan from Detective Skov. He's a fucking idiot and so is his partner, Detective Gallinger, if either of them think I'm going to fall for this good cop, bad cop shtick. I'm an FBI agent, for fuck's sake.

There's only one piece of this act that's based on reality: Detective Skov wants me to go down for all of it. For every whisper of Marcus there's ever been. He's decided I am Marcus. That I created him and I've been the one responsible for the deeds attributed to Marcus. That part isn't entirely untrue. I'm responsible for more than anyone could possibly know. Even if they managed to find any evidence and could put the pieces together, there's so much that's gone unwritten. So many moments where I played a part in pawns being moved across the chessboard. The weight of that blame would have buried me alive over the past few hours if not for my constant monitoring of the clock while the names of men who could have possibly taken Delilah continued to pile up.

Skov's got a hunch I'm behind it all. He's made that more than clear. Even worse, he thinks Delilah's involved with Marcus's crimes. The dull pain in my chest aches from rage every time he speaks her name. He should be searching every inch of Cadence's place with a fine-tooth comb. Looking for any evidence in the woods behind her apartment complex. Checking for any signs of a struggle from her mother who was also taken.

Anything at all other than wasting his time interrogating me and throwing out every accusation he can. If anything happens to Delilah, I'll murder them myself. All of them. The men who took her and the detectives who kept me in this cage so I couldn't go after her.

Picking at the dry skin on my knuckles, the two go back and forth over whether or not I should be released. Whether or not they can hold me against the lieutenant's orders. Whether or not the case is about to "break wide open."

As if I can't hear them over the groan of the ancient heater tucked into the drop ceiling above.

All the while, my frustration and anger simmers. I've sat here far too long, answering questions from men who know far too little. The weight of my sins pressing against my chest is heavy as I breathe in as deeply as I can, yet what's happened still feels suffocating.

They took her. My trembling hands find their way back onto the steel table, the metal feeling like ice against my heated flesh. My throat is raw and hoarse from screaming at the men who appear hell-bent on ending my career. Hours of fighting them, and for what? For nothing. Time is slipping away and I can do nothing to save her while I'm trapped here.

They have the wrong man, the wrong theory ... and all I can do is bite my tongue and pray to both God and the devil that Marcus already has her. I hope he tracked down the men who dared to take her and skinned them alive. With the back of my teeth grinding against one another, I silently wish he saves one of them for me. There's a bit of comfort in the thought that she's with him, safe and unharmed. More than a bit. I'd sell my soul for that to be reality.

The interrogation room door creaks as it opens further, allowing light from the hallway to drift into the dimly lit room. The fluorescent light above me hums and flickers, and it's then I realize how tired and dry my eyes are.

The temperature in the room is cranked up too high, uncomfortably so. After being awake for nearly twenty hours with no rest, I know their intention was to exhaust me and keep pushing until I crack and give them what they're looking for—answers about Marcus. My eyes are dry, itching and burning. Adrenaline, however, still pumps in my veins, so much so the very thought of sleep is nauseating.

"I'm going after your badge." Detective Skov's voice is barely heard as the details of what happened before my arrest play back in my mind. The phone call when everything was all right and then her chilling scream before the clatter of the phone dropping. The line went dead after that. She was there, then she was gone.

The detective continues even in my silence. As I rise, the legs of the chair scrape against the floor carelessly. "That reporter was onto something," he starts, and I vaguely recall Jill Brown and her accusations. "And I don't care if I spend the rest of my career getting to the bottom of it."

"Can I go?"

Skov's dark gaze narrows with his jaw clenched tight. It's Gallinger who answers, "Yes."

Thud, thud, thud, my heart races, the adrenaline in my veins somehow increasing and forcing an anxiousness to overwhelm me. I need to find her.

"There's not enough evidence." Gallinger continues to talk although I'm barely listening as I gather my coat and walk out. His black boot finds the painted cream brick of the wall behind him as he leans against it. "If you have any intel," he says, raising his voice so I can hear more easily, as if I haven't been listening all the while like they intended, "you'll fill us in, won't you?" His thick eyebrows lift in question.

"I don't trust you, I don't like you, and I'm going to destroy you," the detective I've left behind mutters beneath his breath, but it's loud enough to be heard.

"Fuck both of you." My response is as dull as the fucks I give when it comes to these two. The glares from each of them burn into my skin as I walk as casually as I can down the hallway.

"This way, Agent—"

"I know where to go," I say, brushing aside the officer in charge of escorting me to the front to collect my belongings.

"This is the last time I let you walk out of here," the prick of a detective calls out after me. There's an audience of sorts at the end of the hallway: three officers, one with a cuffed man who appears homeless sitting on the bench against the back wall, and the other two pushing papers around.

Blinking away the pain in my sore eyes, I barely read that it's nine in the morning. Too many hours have already passed, and it'll take another twenty minutes to fill out paperwork and get the hell out of here.

The process is painfully slow, and the entire time my conscience is plagued by sounds of that phone call. One minute she was there, the next she was gone.

The bastards took their time. An hour of waiting, followed by the thirty minutes it took to hail a cab and be taken back to my car. All the while my mind was screaming. They know the same as I do: the first seventy-two hours are crucial. And yet they chose to spend the better part of the first twenty-four hours interrogating me.

Anger consumes me as I face the cold hard truth: either they don't believe she was taken, or they think I've murdered her.

There is no other explanation.

Glancing in the rearview mirror, the sight of my reddened gaze brings my fatigue front and center. I rub my eyes with the heel of my palms to no avail. I can't blink away the last day and a half, let alone the last two decades.

It's all my fault. With every slow blink, I picture Delilah and all the times we had where nothing else mattered. It all melted away when I was with her. She was an escape and I lost myself in her company. I think about the last time we were together, imagining the sight of her pouty lips with her top teeth digging into her bottom lip as she moaned. The feel of her silky ebony hair as her neck arched in ecstasy, allowing the stray strands to brush against my bare skin. With a deep inhale I let the memories take me away. Even something as simple as the smell of her caramel skin allowed me to slip away from the chaos and into her bed.

The honk of cars behind me is the only reason I come back to reality, forced to stare back at a now green light. Forced to move forward, but having no fucking clue where to go.

I need Marcus. For the first time in my life, I truly need him. This isn't a vendetta or vigilante mission. This isn't searching out justice when the system failed.

This is so much more. This is righting my wrong and saving an innocent before it's too late. I shouldn't have touched her and brought her into this. I should have known better.

The busy street blurs as I glance between my phone and the rearview again. My brow pinches and, shortly after, a prickling sensation travels from the base of my skull all the way down my spine.

A white sedan has trailed two cars behind me for miles now, even though the two vehicles between us have changed periodically. Whoever it is has kept their distance but followed ever since I left the station. I'm sure of it.

The clicks of my blinker resound like a ticking clock. Although I'm not certain what will greet me when the pendulum stops.

The car follows, not bothering to wait for more than ten seconds. It's definitely a tail. My right hand forms a fist, one that pounds once on the leather wheel in frustration. It's the fucking detectives. As if the situation couldn't get any worse. I can't make out the driver, but my gut tells me it's more than likely Skov.

Pressing the pedal down, I don't waste a moment, cutting off the car next to me and veering right across two lanes. The exit isn't for another two miles. I only take my eyes off the road, the speedometer revving, to ensure the white car gives chase.

Recklessly it does and the driver, wearing large sunglasses that cover most of his face, nearly crashes into a minivan that can't slow fast enough to accommodate. With the act comes a screech of tires. More horns blare. I'm sure he's aware his cover is blown, and he barely manages to squeeze into the rightmost lane.

I use the loss of momentum due to traffic and cut my wheel hard to the left, where the exit is only a block away. My phone on the passenger seat smashes into the dashboard, while whatever's behind me slams against the back of my seat.

Adrenaline pumps hard, so hard my throat feels tight with the pressure of my racing pulse. All I can hear is the blood rushing in my ears.

The driver of the black coupe I cut off lays on his horn and slams on his brakes, which gives me plenty of room to make it to the exit as I leave the tail behind, still caught between cars a lane over.

Rounding the bend of the exit, it takes longer than it should for the panic to subside. My eyes track every car that surrounds me on the interstate from the rearview.

It's only once I'm sure I've lost him that I start to doubt who was behind the wheel.

It could be the cops. Or it could be someone helping whoever took Delilah. Fear and anger swirl into a deadly concoction in the pit of my stomach.

Even minutes later, the dominant feeling that remains is still dread.

Twisting my sweaty palms around the steering wheel, I readjust my grip when I'm certain there's no one else following me.

Guilt and shame are next to greet me, slipping in as the trepidation wanes.

Marcus's words resonate in the darkness of my mind: *It's my fault.*

They took her when it was my watch. I should have been there. I shouldn't have given her space. I was supposed to protect her.

If I could go back, I never would have returned her kiss. I never would have given into temptation. I've been in too deep with Marcus for far too long to think it wasn't going to catch up with me. There's not a doubt in my mind that this is all related to someone I fucked over.

Not knowing who's following me, I come to the conclusion that I need to be careful with every step. I can't leave a trail for anyone to follow. I need to call Marcus, but certainly not with my cell which still lays on the floor of the passenger seat. My head shakes as I see the screen split in two with a jagged crack down the center.

It takes twenty minutes, heading in the opposite direction of the hotel room I was staying at when Delilah was taken, to reach a pay phone in a corner lot of a strip mall.

I know the number to call by heart. Marcus had a habit of changing the numbers he used, but he always went back to the first one we ever spoke on. For the first year the only ways we communicated were through letters and notes left at crime scenes. The year after is when he called me for the first time and I finally heard his voice. It broke me to hear the voice of my brother, grown into a man and disguising it on the other end. That was the year I met Delilah too. I suppose she's always been a part of it.

I stared at the phone, memorizing the number he called me from while his voice burned into my mind.

It killed me in my soul to know for certain what my brother had become. How could he have thought I wouldn't recognize his voice? His mannerisms and the way he paused between words were identical to the voice of a gleeful child. It's odd to realize how unique a person's speech is. For years I listened to a saved voicemail that was only fifty-three seconds long. It was a birthday message and the only recording I had of my little brother. None of the fine details and idiosyncrasies in his voice escaped me over time.

I dial the number now, each press on the small metal keypad chilling my middle finger as I do.

It rings and rings, seemingly in slow motion. The cars pass, and in the distance someone calls out to another person ahead of them. All of the noises distort around me before fading to white noise, but the harsh ring of the phone not being picked up is what stays with me. The click of an unanswered call carries a sense of finality and foreboding.

With a trembling hand, I dial the number again. Marcus has used it dozens of times with me over the years. He used to go back and forth between this one and new numbers. I wrote each one down every time he called, searching for a pattern and some way to find him. He always went back to this phone number. It's the only one he repeated.

Ring, ring, ring.

Nothing. Nothing at all.

I try again. And again there's nothing.

With a sinking feeling in my gut, I swallow thickly and call once more.

With thick clouds gathering above me, the gray soon blocks out the sun and the sky is shattered as lightning strikes, preceding the rumble of thunder in the distance.

Again … nothing.

Staring at the pay phone, I hesitate to leave it. If I could leave a message, I would. A plea for him to tell me she's all right. Even if he were to never let me see her again. Even if he never spoke to me again.

To simply know he has her would ease the sickening feeling that threatens to overwhelm me as I set the handset back where it belongs.

With my limbs heavy and the darkness coming, I head back to my car in time to hear my cell phone ring. Hope is an awful thing, and it's shattered as quickly as it came. It's only Evan, a member of my team.

Back when I had a team, that is. There's no doubt I'll be forced to take leave.

Another wave of guilt and shame makes my stomach drop as I realize that's more than likely why he's calling. He's giving me a heads-up.

The phone continues to ring in my hand and I let it.

I can't answer. What could I possibly say? What truth could I provide right now that wouldn't morph into yet another lie?

Only a moment after the vibration stops does another come, indicating a voicemail.

I can barely stand to look at it. Evan has been my right-hand man and the closest partner I've had on the team for years. He was practically my mentor. I've killed for him and he's done the same for me. Yet here I am, hiding and knowing damn well he'd never understand. There's no justification for bringing Delilah into this shit. Let alone what I've done with Marcus. There's no way to confide in him about Delilah without also confessing the truth about Marcus. The three of us are tied together, our histories unable to be separated.

Rolling down the window, the bitter wind strikes my face and I let it. The brutality is nothing compared to what I deserve. My only options are Marcus, who won't answer the damn phone, or lying to my partner. My eyes creep open slowly, the tiredness intensified by the chill in the air, yet all of it muted as I realize I can lie so well. All I truly need to tell Evan is what I heard on the other end of the line when Delilah was taken. I don't have to tell him everything. All I have to do is tell him I need help finding her.

If I had no other information, no other insight at all, what would I be able to tell him? What needs to be omitted?

The wheels turn and a sense of control takes over. For the first time since I've left that godforsaken interrogation room, a different sensation comes over me. Evan will believe me. He'll help me even in the face of knowing it would need to be kept quiet. At the very least, I can use him to find out any information that would possibly lead me to Delilah.

chapter two

Delilah

I DON'T KNOW HOW LONG I'VE SLEPT, BUT IT MUST BE twenty-four hours that have passed. At least a day, maybe two. The hopelessness is nothing compared to the terror every time I think I hear something. There's some kind of piping above this room. The sound of water rushes in and out occasionally. The cracked cement floor of this ten-by-ten-foot cell reeks of urine and it's stained with blood. The brick walls are old and crumbled in places where it appears that others have attempted to escape. Beneath one broken section, discolored with what I imagine is blood from the fingers of someone prying the stones apart with their bare hands, is yet another layer of brick.

Without a single window, I have no idea where I am or whether or not my screams can even be heard.

Pain strikes my body and spikes with every small movement, from my puffy and split lips that leave the tang of blood in my mouth every time I try to part it, to my ribs that I think are bruised or broken. If I breathe too deep … it's excruciating to the point that my body doubles over. It only makes the agony even worse.

The voices of victims have stayed with me, haunting me in the quiet hours that have passed. Their recollections of the madness and panic when they were taken and held in various prisons play over and over again.

Women who confessed their testimonies to me in between sobs with tears streaking down their faces, clinging to the truth they thought they'd die in those cells, whisper their stories to me here. Just as I did in my bed on so many late nights when I heard what they'd gone through, I cry for them and pretend I'm not crying for myself as well.

I've barely slept. Given how dry and sore my eyes are, I doubt I've blinked more than physically necessary since I woke up last. All I can do is stare at the steel door, dinged and battered with rust covering its surface. Unlike me, it belongs in this place.

If I could bear to sit up, I'd test the hinges and attempt to pry one out … *as if I could possibly budge the iron with just my hands* … I huff sarcastically at the thought, and the small movement causes me to wince with pain. As it is, I lie here on the cold hard ground, staring at the door and attempting to recollect what happened, trying to recall if there were any clues at all.

I have none, though. They were silent. They wore masks. Even when they stuck me in what I think was a van or a bus, something large enough for me to nearly stand in when I woke screaming, even then, they were silent. There was no radio, there was no indication of anything. With a bag over my head and my wrists bound as I was transported here, I have no evidence or inkling whatsoever of where I am.

Moreover, the list of those who'd want me dead or ransomed, or simply out of the picture has grown in my mind.

Men I've put in prison who may have been released.

Enemies of Special Agent Walsh … rivals of Marcus.

With the reports and articles released months ago that continued to spew lies about my intentions and abilities with the cold cases, even the mourning, innocent family and friends of victims may wish for my death if they believe Jill Brown and the accusations she threw at me.

When my memory isn't flooded with previous cases, and my mind isn't examining lists and motives, my subconscious drifts to a more peaceful place. To hope that two men will find me. Marcus and Cody.

Picking at a broken nail, emotions swim up my throat and I force them down with a harsh swallow. My tired eyes drift shut and I see the two of them. A warmth covers my chilled skin and, for a moment, I'm blanketed by the familiar, unmistakable scent of a certain man. His breath on my neck, his lips teasing mine as he lays me down in bed. Marcus's hand slips lower and he soothes the pain.

My eyes open slowly, the vision fading in front of me as I come to terms with reality.

Never once did I think of myself as a princess locked in a tower and waiting on her prince when I was younger. Never did I play the part of damsel in distress. This isn't a fairytale; my princes lie and cheat and kill. They hide in dark corners and play vicious games with violent men.

Sniffling, I wonder, what's the likelihood they'll come save me? What information could possibly lead them here? Is there any indication of who took me?

Given the time that's passed, my gut sinks and any sense of peace or hope is shattered. If they knew where I was, they would be here by now.

Assuming they had any intention of coming for me.

What keeps me from thinking the worst is that they're out there, somewhere beyond the confines of this cell where evidence can be found. I'm stuck in here without a single clue.

If I could have given Cody information in that split second I turned around, it would have been that the man was at least six feet, and tanned skin peeked out from the gap between the sleeves of the black sweater and gloves he wore. Not an inch of his face was recognizable, but dark eyes stared back at me from the slit in his mask. His expression was angry and unforgiving.

The only saving grace I have is that my face was covered as well, my vision obscured the entire time. That is the only piece of this puzzle that offers me any hint of reprieve. They didn't want me to see them, which means perhaps they'll let me live.

Fate laughs a wretched sound at the thought. The one thread of hope is instantly stripped away from me when a man I recognize all too well appears in the place of the steel door. It opens with a slow creak and as I heave in the air, two men, masked just the same as the one who first struck me, stand behind him.

"Miss Jones." Brass's cadence is sickeningly sweet. He greets me as if we're old friends. "It's been too long, don't you think?" He's the shortest of the three and unarmed, although the two men behind him who are broader and more muscular, each hold a rifle in their hands.

Hired help? My mind whirls with connections and associates. But names mix together and cases bleed into one another as exhaustion and fear work against me.

"Miss Jones?" he repeats and I force my tired eyes up to meet his icy gaze. Herman and Reynolds. The two names linked to Brass ring clearly in my head, and faces are paired with photos of the criminals who got off. The three of them worked together, laundering money and diving into deeper, more sordid crimes. That's what men do when they have wealth, they indulge in sin and those three together … bile threatens to climb up my throat. Herman's dead now. I'm fairly sure Marcus killed him because of the threatening note left for me at my office door; everything is circumstantial, though. Herman did have a team who worked with Reynolds. And Reynolds certainly worked with Brass. Does this all have to do with the note? Or with Herman's murder?

Brass's teeth are far too perfect, too even and white as he flashes me a crooked grin, the left side of his smile higher than the right. He huffs a laugh and half-heartedly looks behind him at the two men, who stay perfectly still and silent. I stare hard at the other two men, but I'm not certain one could be Reynolds. Perhaps these two are working for them, but their heights and silence don't match what I know of Reynolds, or at least what I can remember.

Cases flutter in my mind as Brass stalks toward me. The men stay where they are, and the door remains open. I suppose they're here for intimidation. Ross Brass always was a bit of a repulsive, slimy prick.

I'm not his usual victim. Brief images of the young girls he's responsible for the deaths of send a chill down my spine. I'm too old for his liking. So this is all about revenge, or maybe it's a threat.

Please, God, let this be a threat and only that.

"I said, hasn't it been too long?" Impatience lingers in his question.

"Not long enough," I manage to answer, ignoring the vicious pain that radiates up my neck and travels down my shoulders as I raise my head to meet his gaze. My own is as hard and cold as ice.

The humor and obvious satisfaction that graced his expression a moment ago falters slightly at my response.

"I had a number of names on the list of vile criminals who could have taken me, but to be honest, you kidnapping me … murdering me … whatever this is," I say, then half-heartedly attempt a nonchalant gesture. As I do, the back of my teeth slam shut and grind as I swallow down the nearly unbearable pain. I attempt a huff of laughter myself and add, "Well, I didn't even think you cared that much."

The anger that lights in the flecks of amber dotting his irises is exactly what I'm after. I need him off guard, I need him reckless so I can get any information at all from him. "What exactly is this?" I dare to question as his nostrils flare.

His posture stiffens as his hands slip into the pockets of his black suit pants. His white button-down is crisp, and his thin, black tie dangles in front of him as he paces along the wall opposite from me, seemingly checking every inch of my prison.

In some ways, his stature and clothing are out of place in this shithole. In other ways, though, a man like him belongs here. It's like a piece of him feels right at home and there's an air about him that confirms it.

"What is this?" he hisses, echoing my question and a chill runs down the length of my body when he smiles thinly and says, "It's called revenge. We had a deal."

"A deal?"

"Not with you," he adds and the coldness penetrates my skin, seeping down deep. If it isn't about me, then taking control of the situation is out of my reach.

"Then with who?" I manage to speak, although my question is shaky.

A snort of a laugh leaves him, and his right hand slips out of his pocket so he can run his thumb along the stubble covering his jaw. "I almost feel sorry for you."

"Why on earth would anyone feel sorry for me?" I respond morosely but as I do, the pain gets the best of me and whatever false armor I wore cracks around me. Even worse, Brass sees it.

With his back to me, Brass doesn't answer me as he signals for the two men to leave, but what he says next gives me one more piece of the puzzle before following behind them:

"He interfered and took what was rightfully mine, so I'm taking what's his."

chapter three

Cody

AS I LEAN FORWARD IN THE CHEAP CHAIR PLANTED IN THE corner, heat rolls down my shoulders. It's an anxiousness that doesn't quit and leads my foot to *tap, tap, tap* on the rug below. I've debated even being here in this hotel room. According to Evan, I've been told to go home and stay there. It's an unofficial house arrest from my superiors.

That's hours away from where Delilah was taken, though.

My home address is where the two detectives will go first if they find any evidence that can lead to yet another arrest. They've been informed of the decision to send me home and keep me off the case. Courtesy of Evan himself. With Skov hell-bent on pinning this all on me, I'm certain he'll demand he be the one to take me in. It'll give him some sick sense of satisfaction.

Clearing my throat, I force myself to lean back and then rub my sore eyes with the heel of my palms before checking my phone again. It's habitual. Between the articles I've flicked through on my laptop and the texts on my phone, I'm going crazy from the waiting

Evan still hasn't messaged since he told me he was looking into a lead and to stay here. Delilah stayed here before. Not this room, but here in this hotel.

I have to force myself to stop thinking of her. I covered every inch of her sister's place and left no stone unturned. I searched it up and down and found nothing.

Evan wouldn't give me all the details over the phone, and at first it pissed me off. Now it's left me with a churning feeling deep in the pit of my stomach. I'm not sure what he had a lead on or where it will take him, but he knows where I am. He knows, and now Marcus knows since I left him a message. Delilah's sister knows too as I reached out to her, telling her I'm an investigator on her sister's case, needing to get any information I could, but only reached a voicemail.

Every trail has led to a dead end.

What's to come is uncertain, and without control and without allies … without knowing Delilah is still alive, it feels as if death has its grip on my shoulders. Holding me down and forcing me to watch as the devil strips everything from me, claiming his pay for my sins.

Knock, knock, knock.

The thuds on the door aren't gentle or expected, and instinctively, my right hand jolts to my gun on the side table. Until I hear her voice.

"Special Agent Cody Walsh?" She knocks again. "Are you in there? Please! It's about my sister."

Delilah introduced me to her sister years ago, but it still takes me a moment to realize it's her sister. The rhythm and subtle inflections in her tone mimic Delilah's. The ache that travels through my chest is undeniable.

If only Delilah would knock on my door. If only it was all a misunderstanding.

I'm silent but swift as I rise, eager to find out if her

sister knows anything at all. I've read through the reports a dozen times. She gave her statement and, in those lines, she didn't know a damn thing that could help. If she does, she isn't aware of it. The details she doesn't think are important are the ones I'm after. The ones she didn't think were worth mentioning.

Her small hand is fisted and prepared for another rap against the door, her lips parted and ready to call out once again when I open the hotel door.

Her deep brown eyes widen at the sight of me, and her mouth slams shut. It's only then I realize I must appear disheveled at best. Unhinged at worst.

"I … I didn't mean to wake you."

You didn't. The answer stays glued to my tongue. I still haven't slept. It's going on thirty-six hours since Delilah was taken, and I'm still wearing the wrinkled trousers and the shirt I was in when I got the call.

Cadence's gaze travels lower, noting that I'm not in sleepwear.

Tightening her cream wool coat around her waist, she straightens her shoulders to state, although it's more of a plea, "I need to talk to you."

"Come in." My answer is raspy and I find myself clearing my throat as I open the door wider for her.

She's halfway into the room, staring between the bed and the chair in the corner when I start by saying, "I read your statement. Have you remembered anything since you gave it?"

I hesitate to do it, but I lock the door before offering her a weak smile. "I don't want to make you uncomfortable—"

"No, please." Inhaling deeply, she drops her coat to the middle of the bed and then takes a seat on the edge. "After what happened," she says and her voice drifts off, leaving the statement unfinished.

"Right." I give her a small nod and resume my place in

the corner chair, turning it to face her. "Have you remembered anything?"

"I came to ask you questions," Cadence blurts out, nearly interrupting my question, a hint of skepticism in her tone. After a second, she huffs a humorless laugh that doesn't reach her eyes. With a frown pulling down the corners of her lips, she wipes the edges of her eyes with the sleeve of her deep ruby designer sweater. "Sorry," she says. "I just … I have questions."

Staring back at Delilah's sister, seeing every resemblance I can find in the woman across the room, I offer her another smile, although this one is weaker. "You remind me of her."

Cadence's smile is tight but genuine, and dampened by the pain in her eyes. "So you remember me, don't you?"

With a nod, I answer, "I do. Cadence Jones, Delilah's sister. We met years ago."

"I know you were seeing her." Her statement catches me off guard.

"I didn't know she told anyone."

"It was all over the papers," she confesses. "I read about your so-called affair. Pair that with her limited free time … well I assumed she'd met someone."

I can only nod, remembering the beginning of … whatever we were. With a tight throat, sadness rocks through me.

"So I have questions."

"Of course you do," I respond lowly.

"And I'm sure you know … statistically speaking, when someone is in a relationship and taken or—"

"I know the partner is the first suspect. Lover or husband." My tone turns colder as Marcus comes to mind. Clearing my throat again, I lean forward and reach for the tumbler on the table, only to find the whiskey's been drained from it. "I love her and I'm going to find her," I say with every intention of upholding my vow until I glance down, from Cadence's hopeful gaze, to the laptop screen that's turned black.

Hopelessness is a traitor. "Would you like anything to drink?"

Cadence only shakes her head, not a hair out of place in her bun as she does so. It's at odds with her face, completely devoid of makeup other than traces of mascara around her eyes, which only adds to the darkness beneath them.

"It's the second day." Her voice cracks and it resonates in my chest. "Please tell me you know something." Her plea morphs into a whisper, the almost palpable sadness overwhelming it.

The only words I have for her are, "I'm sorry," but I refuse to say them. It's what I've told the loved ones of bodies I've found, all the men, women and children who weren't found alive. I can't do that to Delilah. I won't utter a statement that echoes defeat.

"We're going to find her."

"I was hoping you would tell me it wasn't real." Cadence's expression crumples. "After my mother's body—" Her statement is left unfinished, but I know what she's referring to. The news covered it and Evan sent me the report. Her death was quick.

"I'm sorry about your mother," I say, offering my condolences, wishing I'd spoken them sooner.

Her eyes glaze over and her shoulders hunch forward as she stifles a sob. "I'm sorry." Her apology is barely heard as she reaches into her purse, pulling out tissues.

If I could comfort her, I would, but I don't want to approach her. I've never been the best at soothing someone else's pain. My uncle made a point to tell me that fact frequently.

"Let me get you a bottle of water," I offer and stand, making my way to the room's small fridge and pulling out one of three that remain. The whiskey on the laminate desk stares at me, the amber liquid sloshing as I close the fridge door.

"Thank you." Her voice is weak, so much smaller than it was a moment ago.

She's still sipping on it when I've retaken my seat.

"What questions do you have?" I ask her to move this along.

"Do you know who took her?"

"No."

"What can you tell me?" My chest aches as she searches for any information at all.

"I wish I could give you answers. But I called you for them because I don't have any."

With trembling hands, her gaze moves to her lap and it's quiet for far too long. More than a moment passes with Cadence visibly distraught and neither of us having any new information for the other.

Just when I think she'll stand to leave, she leans forward with a look of uncertainty on her face. "There's something I have to tell you." Her tone is deadly serious. "I couldn't tell the cops."

"You can tell me anything." Although it's the truth, the statement comes out too eagerly and she hesitates, but gives in. More than likely due to having no other options.

"There is no man who killed my father. My mother killed him. So it couldn't have been Marcus or whoever the police are claiming killed him."

I already know. Delilah didn't tell me, but Marcus did in so many words.

Debating whether or not I should feign ignorance doesn't last long. Instead I lie. "I know. She told me."

Shock lights her eyes and I can see it from across the room. "Did she tell you why?"

"No." I haven't the faintest idea why her mother did what she did. All Marcus hinted at was that it was deserved.

"My father wasn't a good man."

"Good men and bad men, it's not quite as well defined of a line as I once thought it was."

"What do you know about my father? Because there's no gray about it. Only black and white."

"Only what Delilah told me."

She huffs sarcastically. "He was her hero, so I'm sure she didn't tell you the truth."

"And what's the truth?"

"He was a liar." She's quick to answer. "I knew him to be a liar and a thief at times. I knew him to be … cruel."

As I turn to glance at the clock, Cadence sees and her strength leaves her.

"Delilah never knew, but our mother had just cause for what she did as far as I'm concerned."

"Delilah never knew what?"

"She never knew what kind of man he was." She swallows thickly, the sound eating up the silence. "It's strange how she doesn't remember. How he was her hero, yet he was my villain, all in the same scene."

"He hurt her?" I surmise. "He hurt your mother?" She only nods in answer and reaches again for the bottle of water.

"Did he ever hurt you?"

"Not directly, but that doesn't mean it didn't hurt me."

"Whoever has your sister … I don't think it has anything to do with your father or your mother," I tell her honestly.

"I know … but why would anyone go after her? Is it the threat? This Marcus?" She doesn't contain the exasperation clearly getting the best of her. She needs answers, but don't we all? "Brass or whoever it was who left that note in her office? Who? Who!"

It takes great effort to keep my expression unmoving as she lists suspects and tells me her theories.

Neither of us make any progress. We can't help each other, and that truth is evident to both of us before the hour is through.

"I came to tell you I don't think it's Marcus and to look somewhere else. The cops think it's Marcus, which is ridiculous."

"What do you mean? Who told you that?"

"That detective with the beard … Skov. I told him Marcus doesn't exist, it's just a name used as a cover," she says incredulously and I can't fix my expression fast enough. With a tilt of her head, I can tell she knows that I know something about Marcus.

I want to tell her; I want to confess everything. If for no other reason than to rid myself of the burden of these sins and lies. They've piled up and now they're drowning me.

I still don't know who has Delilah. I don't know how to get her back. But I know it's because of myself and Marcus. It's because I couldn't walk away from her.

Because I brought her into something that was slowly killing me.

"What do you know? She told me Marcus wasn't real. I asked her, and she told me it was just a name whispered by liars to hide evidence."

"When was that?" I can't help but to question, and her gaze narrows.

"Years ago. I told the cops there's someone else behind those murders. It isn't one man, and Delilah told me that years ago."

"I don't know about that." I decide right then to hide behind lies. She can't be brought into this.

"What do you know?" she asks with a look of ridicule.

"Nothing, but you need to stop this. You need to stay away and let us do our job."

Shaking her head, she stands abruptly, anger taking over. "I can't—"

"You need to stay far away," I say, cutting her off, striding to the door of the hotel in an instant and opening the door as wide as it'll go.

"I mean it, Cadence." I warn her like I should have warned her sister, regret lacing each word, "Stay far away."

chapter four

Marcus
Fifteen years ago
Six years after abduction

THEY'RE ALL PAWNS.

I trace over the words at the top of the page in my notebook: *They're all pawns. Writing down three more names to the list on the rightmost side of the yellowed pad with deep strokes of the blue ink pen, I pause to look at the tally.*

There are three columns and over fifty names total. Three different groups of men, but all of them responsible for atrocities in the name of unity and solidarity. Everywhere I've gone there are always dogs like the ones I trailed today. Men, and even women, who go along with the men in power and do their bidding without question. It doesn't take much to get them to move. A nod, a promise of ambition, and the desire for one man to have something done.

He never says how. The men in charge never give those details, and that's why I've deemed the ones on the lists under the underlined names dogs. They're owned by the men in charge, happily wagging their tails and barking orders to others as if they have any status in the pack at all. Snarling and backing the weaker ones into corners, they're as moldable as they are feral.

The three kingpins, including Talvery, a crime family boss in this area, can't be bent or broken. But the men beneath them could easily be swayed. Or put in a ring and made to fight one another.

I haven't decided which is best yet. All I know is that there are plenty of pawns to play with. Plenty of them to start the game and deliver justice piece by piece.

The snap of a twig beneath heavy feet rips my gaze from the three names I've added. The graveyard is a scenery of grays and greens. The stones and the oak trees and the grass, long overdue for a cut, nearly hide the one I've been waiting for.

His name is inconsequential. What matters is the fact that his sister was a bird.

Another twig cracks under his weight as he comes into view. All of the burial plots surrounding where he stands are covered with time. The one at his feet, however, is marked by fresh blades of grass and overturned dirt.

A month has passed, but spring has only just begun. I don't think he's noticed me, and I stay quiet, merely observing him as I have for months. All I've done is watched. If Mr. Jones taught me anything at all, it's to take it all in, every detail, and to learn the habits of whoever it is that's selected. Mr. Jones chooses victims. I don't lower myself to his level, and I promised myself I never would. I don't think I'll be seeing much of him anymore. Not after I left him the note. I've never seen so much damage caused by a simple letter.

Smiling at the thought, I close my notebook and take in the boy I've been waiting for.

Charlie, the thin boy in worn jeans and a dark hoodie stares straight ahead, seemingly at nothing. He still hasn't dropped the flowers he brought. He does this when he works the day shift at the garage. The sun setting is the only reason he leaves. One might say he's guilt ridden and for good reason.

He sits feet from me, but still fails to realize he's not alone, at a grave with an inscription that reads:

When you are not fed love on a silver spoon, you learn to lick it off knives. ~ Lauren Eden

Although, that's not the woman's name carved on the tombstone.

"You okay?" I speak up without walking toward him, still leaning against the tree. After an initial shudder of shock, with his grip tight around the bouquet, Charlie's gaze meets mine. It's easy to tell I scared him at first. He's been afraid ever since they killed her.

"Yeah, just … Yeah, I'm fine," he says, then offers me a tight smile and finishes the thought. "Just leaving flowers."

"For who?" I play up my youth. I know I look younger than I am. Poor nutrition will do that.

"My sister."

All men are fueled by motives, by desires. Revenge is a deep-seated motive. We all have it buried inside of us. Including a high school boy, burdened by his mother's poor choices and his sister's death.

"What happened to her?" I chance a couple steps closer, eyeing the grave as if I haven't seen it a dozen times before.

A gust of wind blows by, followed by silence. In the last few weeks, Charlie's told four people what happened. He broke down at his workplace, the garage. He's been slipping away and devolving. I nearly second-guess my decision to approach him today, the two-month anniversary of her death, and the two-week anniversary of the man who killed her getting off scot-free.

But then he answers, "She got involved with the wrong kind of people."

"The wrong kind of people?" I know damn well who his sister was and the relationships he's referring to. Knowledge is the only path that will save the damned.

"Yeah ... they weren't good guys." He swallows thickly and his reddened cheeks burn brighter as he closes his eyes and allows the wind to batter him. "She said she was seeing ... someone." He shakes his head, huffing out a humorless breath and says, "Sorry, kid. I didn't mean to—"

"My mother says it's best to talk if you can," I lie. I barely think of my mother anymore. Or my father. "So if you want to talk, I can listen," I say, taking a seat on the stump of a tree closer to him but still at a distance. The stump isn't a product of a saw. It wasn't cut down; the bark is torn and the rings rough and jagged beneath my ass from where a storm long ago brought down the old tree.

"What are you, like ... eleven?"

"Fifteen," I tell him and smile. Charlie, the brother of Elizabeth Riggins, is almost twenty. He stayed in his hometown of Fallbrook to be close to his mother, and I imagine her hands dig deep in his pockets with that very hug he offers her each time she gives him a sob story. A broken home and a drug addiction aren't uncommon around here. It's a prime location for dogs to run free.

"So she fell in love with the wrong guy? It's like Romeo and Juliet." I speak nonsense, now seated lower than him so he's forced to look down at me. Pulling an apple from my jacket pocket, I bite into it watching as he shakes his head yet again.

Charlie Riggins will think me a young fool, but I know him for what he is. A young man at the precipice of who he'll become. He's mourning and barely holding back a smoldering fire that burns within.

"Romeo he was not, kid."

I smile every time they call me kid. They always do that. Children aren't threatening and they don't understand. That's their first mistake.

"He was a bad man," Charlie comments with his gaze settling on the cuts in the stone. His fingers trace over the quote. I'd planned on asking him what it meant, but silence holds back my swallow, the fresh apple tasting like the corrupt fruit it is instead.

Bad men always lose. A voice I only hear at night whispers that fact to me.

"So what are you going to do about it?" I ask Charlie, nearly choking as I swallow.

"Do about what?" he says with all sincerity.

"About the man who killed your sister?"

"I don't know that he killed her." The hair on the back of my neck stands on end; I didn't expect him to lie to me. He knows he killed her. Even if he doesn't have the proof I have, he knows.

"You blame him, though?"

"Yeah … he took her—it doesn't matter." He stops himself from saying more, not wanting to tell me she was last seen getting into the car with him. Plenty of witnesses saw them fighting, although they don't know what they were fighting over. It's the same thing it always is. Money.

Finley stole from his boss and she saw the money, took it and spent it. Addiction will make you do stupid things. Finley killed her to save his own ass with the boss.

He's a dog and I have a plan for him. A plan that involves Charlie.

"There's a guy I've heard of. His name is Marcus." I tell him the story I've developed and worked out over the last few months. "I think he knows a lot of bad guys, and I think he wants them dead."

"Dead?" Charlie sounds shocked I'd use that word. Although I can feel his gaze on me, I don't look back up at him.

"He said they deserve to die," I say before taking another bite of the apple, although this time, it tastes sweeter.

"Oh yeah?"

He doesn't take me seriously. They never do.

"Yeah, he killed a bunch of Talvery's guys last week."

That gets Charlie's attention. The atmosphere turns darker as the sun falls behind the tree line. Soon it will be nearly pitch black under this canopy. I don't have much time left to convince him.

"I've heard if you pray at the graveyard, he hears. That's why I'm here. I wanted to pray."

Goosebumps and the chills that come with my story are an added blessing. The wind whips by and Charlie slips his hands into his hoodie's pockets, still refusing to take his concerned eyes off of me. I can practically see the wheels spin in his head as he contemplates Finley's death. Praying for a justice that he knows damn well he'll never get otherwise.

"What are you praying for?" he asks me and I finally meet his gaze when I answer, "That the men who hurt us get what they have coming to them."

The coldness swirls around me and another minute passes, the night sky getting darker. Charlie arches his neck, looking up at the canopy of leaves as if asking them a question.

"What's your name, kid?"

"Marcus says I shouldn't tell strangers my name," I'm quick to respond, and I can tell he doesn't like that answer.

With his head tilted he questions, "You know this Marcus well?"

"I've spoken to him once."

"How'd you do that? Praying and waiting for an answer?"

"Why? Do you want me to give him a message? The last guy did. I don't mind being the pigeon. Birds are good, he says. It's the dogs that are bad."

Present time

It surprises me how many times I've overheard conversations discussing the difference between light and dark. It's written in poetry and plays. It's presented as if it's fact. As if truth can't be seen in shadows. As if clarity does not shine on the depths of sin within each of us. There is no forgiveness that comes simply because the sun has risen. It is not so easy, nor so simple.

The only difference between light and dark is what our eyes have adjusted to. What we choose to see and believe. The reality is that nothing changes solely because of the amount of light we let in. Anger has always continued to rise anew regardless of every time a person smiles and states some charming line about the sun always coming out after rain, or sings a lyric describing making it through the night.

I've often thought I hold that opinion because of the cells we were kept in. We could never tell if it was night or day. There was constant little light in an ever-present darkness. Even in the barn, the day would blur with the night because I often couldn't sleep through either.

Perhaps the sentiment is more closely related to the quiet. If only people knew that. It's not the difference between what you can see. These concepts of good and evil, right and wrong have far more to do with what we hear, what we think, and what takes over our minds.

In the night, the burdens of our pasts berate us and remind us they exist without the noise and calamity of the daily ins and outs of society that distract us. The nights are quiet. When you choose a life like I have, all that surrounds me is silence and everything inside of me screams. It's a constant, just as it was in the cell.

Those thoughts that gather in the darkness for others are a constant for me.

All of the sins I've committed, the games I've played and the chess pieces I've skittered across the board only to have them fall … the voices in my mind mull over each decision constantly.

Countless days have passed where I've wondered if I'd made a mistake. If the men I pit against one another deserved the fate I played a part in delivering.

Men have died and I've gambled on their lives in order to serve a different, greater purpose.

They've all been pawns and nothing more. The question of whether or not I'd made a mistake was easily answered with a name of a victim. Often dozens of them. All the little birds I couldn't save and occasionally, a bird I was able to help flee.

For every man whose downfall I played a part in, there was always a list of names to justify their deaths. The innocent and the undeserving. Each and every time.

As I step out of my car, there's only one name that echoes in my mind now: Delilah Jones. Her name is in response to my own and what justice I deserve. I cannot live if she does not make it out alive.

There's not a thing in this world I've held more conviction toward than that simple fact.

I played with her life and for that, she may already be dead.

With the bitter wind battering my back, I stare up at the row of doors to these run-down hotel rooms. Delilah's sister pulls the coat tighter around herself and offers me a polite nod, as strangers often do. In my jeans and navy cotton sweater, with a phone held up to my ear, I'm sure she doesn't think anything of me standing outside the building, leaning against the fence. I'm just a man on a phone call going about my business.

Cadence doesn't know I was waiting for her to leave.

It's easy to return it as she smiles tightly and goes about her way to where she parked her car. I'm certain she feels the sting of the conversation she's just had with my brother as she picks up her pace. It's obvious she's been crying with her red-rimmed eyes and dark circles beneath them. She's a wreck not knowing where Delilah is and what's happened to her. Aren't we all?

There's a pain that resonates through me when I watch her wipe under her eyes with a steadying intake. One I haven't felt in so long. A pain that mixed with the smell of dampened straw as I lay freezing cold praying for either death or for the boy's scream to go away. I thought that pain had all but vanished, but the wound's reopened, rawer and more ragged than I remember.

Listening to the click of her heels fading in the distance as she goes, I recall Cadence's conversation with Cody. Not a damn bit of it was useful. It's unusual that the calls and meetings I listen to deliver next to nothing for me. Hours and hours I've listened to men debate and make decisions they have no right to establish.

This is the first time though I sat with bated breath, listening through the small camera embedded in Cody's briefcase, praying for some detail I've missed to unveil itself. Some bread crumb that would lead me back to Delilah. My throat is tight as the car door to her sister's vehicle opens and closes with a thud in the distance.

The only thing I've learned is that Cody sees people differently than I do. I once thought we saw the world the same way. A piece of me had come to the conclusion that we had a common understanding and mutual feelings about the world around us. For the longest time, that shared understanding offered me peace. A small bit of it, but knowing Cody and I felt the same way … it kept me from breaking. He was like me. I was the constant internal screaming others fear at night, and he was the distraction and morals they feel comfortable focusing on in the day. We needed each other. It all made so much sense to me. It was perfection.

When it comes to Delilah, it's apparent we don't feel the same.

Cadence doesn't remind me at all of her sister. He's wrong about that, and the simple fact he commented that Cadence reminds him of Delilah is enraging.

There's nothing similar between them. Every nuance and detail, from their outward appearance to their character and their motivations, is strikingly different. The contrast couldn't be clearer. Perhaps they both heal others with acts of service, but one offers justice and the other a shoulder to cry on. Two very different things. I'm not interested in pacifying one's fears and past. The only thing I find similar is a slight accent that's worn off on our Delilah, but it was present years ago. She doesn't have it any longer; it fell from her lips long ago and never returned.

With a heavy inhale, the piercing cold fills my lungs and I take the steps two at a time. With every move forward, I go over the information I have regarding Delilah's abduction.

There was an organized team—quick, so more than likely experienced. The van was nondescript. The men who stole her from us were highly motivated. Which means the abduction wasn't solely for money. They weren't simply paid off; it's personal. Each and every one of them refused to spill a detail, sacrificing themselves rather than providing me with information. I offered mercy, but not a single one took up the offer.

All I needed was a name. Only one question needed to be answered: Who has Delilah Jones? A cold sweat spreads across the back of my neck as the reality taunts me once again. I've failed her.

Knock, knock, knock. Each pound of my fist is deliberate. In the past I've left a note behind for Walsh. I've never stayed. There isn't anything that could have come from us seeing eye to eye like this. It was only ever a message I wanted to deliver to my brother.

This message, however, he deserves to receive in person and with full clarity.

With my jaw firmly clenched and the sound of the lock unclicking, I wait for the door to open, but it doesn't.

It takes me a moment to realize he must've seen me in the peephole and decided to unlock the door and wait.

How long has it been since that very thought didn't spike fear through me? The last thing I've ever wanted is to be seen.

Turning the knob slowly, I gently push the door open to find the daylight scattered in stripes from the blinds and laying across my brother's figure. Motionless on the couch, he stares up at me. The sight of him disgusts me to the point that I nearly snarl.

In nothing but dark gray sweatpants, he's planted himself in the corner chair, a bottle of whiskey on the table and the glass in his hand.

He's nothing if not the image of a man who's given up. The shadow of stubble on his jaw nearly matches the darkness under his blue gaze.

"Contacts?" he questions with a horrid half smile that's undoubtedly forced. I take my time walking in and closing the door behind me. An air of despair lingers around my brother, the stench of it repugnant.

He's given up on her. He believes her to be dead. The realization only spikes my anger that much more. "So a beard and contacts is what you do to go unrecognized," he comments as I take a seat across from him. I can imagine a different world, one where I looked just like him. Pathetic and distraught, and not at all ashamed to show it. I've never been so grateful to be the opposite of my brother. To be the one taken and shown what the real world was like.

He was the good and I was the bad, but together, we made the world a better place. Or so I thought.

"I had one of them," I say, commenting on the purpose of bothering to come here. "One of the men who took her." My throat goes tight and the air leaves my lungs in the single word *her*. I'll be damned if it doesn't hurt to speak of the recent events.

"And?" Hope drenches the single word and the leather chair groans as he leans forward in anticipation. I've no doubt he assumes I have the information we need. "What did he say?" he questions further, suddenly eager. Maybe he hasn't given up. I'm not sure why, but it makes the pain strike my chest violently. My back remains to him as I stare out of the window of this shitty cheap hotel room, knowing she stood in a room like this only days ago. Only sunsets ago she was here, and she was well. Maybe distraught and confused, but she was safe from what ails us.

With my head hanging lower, I stalk toward the end of the room and stare at the small fridge, envisioning the one in Cody's loft instead. She closed her eyes for me and we shared our first kiss in that kitchen. I can still feel the warmth of her against my embrace.

Without an answer from me, my brother rises, his voice raised as he practically yells, "What did he say?"

"Nothing," I answer coldly, my mind refusing to move from where I know she once was. She was there for the taking, and I didn't do what I should have. I left her in the safety and comfort of my brother. I failed her, thinking that what they had would be better for her than what I could offer her. If only I could go back.

"Nothing?" The word sounds incredulous from my brother's mouth.

It only sends the irritation to skitter across my expression and the thoughts of what once was possible vanish. She's gone and I'm not the only one to blame.

My hand clenches at my side, so tight the skin turns white against my knuckles. With my eyes narrowed I confess, "He had a seizure before I could finish my interrogation."

Light dims from my brother's gaze, the anger he felt a moment ago vanishes and the same dejected look he wore when I first came in reigns once again.

The ice in the tumbler clinks as he falls back in his seat. He doesn't bother to wipe the spilled alcohol from his hand as he runs it down his face.

He's exhausted, as am I. But he's given in and that's unacceptable. He's not the half of me I used to know.

"This is your fault." I spit the accusation at him. His gaze is nothing but daggers as he raises it to me. Venom lays between us, and the tension thickens from its bite.

"My fault?" He practically sneers the question.

"I should have known better than to leave her." I hesitate to say it, the words breaking something deep down inside of me and spilling a darkness I haven't let myself feel before. Jealousy mixes with the rage and disappointment as I add, "I should have known better than to leave her with you."

Cody's mouth parts, his bottom lip quivering with anger, but it's just as quickly shut, snapping and offering me nothing but silence. Turning his head to stare straight ahead, his eyes focused on the sofa as if someone lays there across from him, his eyes gloss over and he murmurs, "Fuck you." He doesn't move his gaze as he picks up the tumbler once again.

I can imagine what he sees, what holds his attention. The memories of her, lying on his sofa. He took her there once. All I did was watch as he held her.

I could have been the one to have her.

Instead neither of us do.

I'm reminded of my mantra and the reason why I left her with him. *Bad men always lose.* I was always going to lose her. It seemed justified to let him have her.

But he's just as corrupt as I am. They all are. The ones who find sanctuary in the day and the righteousness. All of us are bad men. It's just to what degree we share that piece of us.

This isn't how I pictured the reunion with my brother. My hands aren't wrapped around his throat, squeezing the life from him as he begs for mercy. He doesn't blame me as I imagined either.

A part of me knew he wouldn't beg, but I expected hatred in the same dose as I feel toward him. Some part of me still capable of feeling guilt and remorse is aware that he must blame me.

Perhaps it's because I feel it too. Whoever took her ... there's a very strong chance that it's because of one of us.

Just as the words I repeated over and over on the drive here are tasted on my lips, the accusations and spiteful truths, I'm silenced by his phone.

He's faster than I am, reaching for it as if doing so is enough to save her.

My pulse races as he furiously types back. I could look to see who it is and what was sent; instead I wait, unable to move. It's the fear, I know it is, that keeps me from breathing. It paralyzes me. Either it's something that will help find her, or it's nothing.

I would rather live in this moment of hope, but isn't that what fear is. You must be consumed with fear, to have even a glimmer of hope. It's been so long since I've felt such things pierce their talons through my flesh and bones.

"There's movement on Ross Brass."

It's an odd thing, hope. It flickers and leaves me with distrust.

Before I dare to question, Cody adds, "He's sending the information now." My brother anxiously taps his thumb against the side of his cell phone. He sways for a moment and at first I think it's the alcohol, but then I realize the fool hasn't slept in the least. I've lived off short hours scattered through the hours since I was eight years old, since I was trapped in that cell.

Instead of questioning his current sanity, I ask the more important question, "Who sent it? Is Brass the one who has her?" His name is one of several I'd put on my list of suspects. As far as I knew, though, he hadn't used his phones or credit cards. He has no associates in the vicinity. Facial recognition from the precinct hadn't pinned him or anyone else from my list in a ten-mile radius from Cadence's place.

Angered that he has a lead, our only lead, and I didn't know it first, I press for more. "Who's giving you this intel?"

My question brings his gaze to mine. "Evan, a member of my team. We've been keeping an eye on him since the threatening note that was left at her place." Herman's face shows clearly in my memory. Narrowing down a fine line of men, all threaded together with blue ink that connects their violent acts and greed, names appear in my mind. Lists of names. So many of them, but at the very top are Brass, Reynolds … and Talvery. The crime boss who relies on Reynolds for the laundering. The one who's unknowingly funded and backed the series of depraved transgressions. I fixate on a series of potential events, each one falling like dominoes. I move pieces and play out the game, but I can't focus. With every thump of my heart, her gorgeous face, her warm touch, and her perfect lips interrupt my thoughts.

Walsh and his partner type away. Messages coming and going as I wait, allowing myself to remember, allowing a warmth of memory to keep the hope burning inside. It's weakness, but that's exactly what she is to me.

"His movement puts him an hour away." Cody speaks up as he reads through whatever it is that Evan Aldaine sent him. "It's not his stomping ground."

"An hour in which direction?" I ask. "Which town?"

"Two towns over from her sister's. Saint Peters."

"Where was he seen?"

"Not him, an associate who was involved with the abductions before. He was at a liquor store when facial recognition got him. He used a pay phone around the back, and that number sent a message to an old device known to be used by Brass."

"She's only an hour away," I say, breathing out deep at the realization. Even if she's gone, she's close. "I need to find her."

Again the names and associations tally in my mind, I scour my thoughts and memories, but I need time and access to my information. Anxiousness scurries across my skin in a cold sweat. Time is ticking and time has never been an ally.

"When was—" I start to say, but he cuts me off before I can finish.

"Video surveillance from two hours ago." Two hours … so much could have happened between then and now.

"So we have a name," I say and swallow thickly, trying not to think of what he's done to her. What *they've* done to her. If

Brass has her … it's revenge or silencing. Fuck. Fuck! Herman's death and all that blood is on my hands. There's not a doubt in my mind that Brass isn't aware I'm the one who killed him all because of that note. Because I reacted without thinking. He dared to threaten her, and I simply knocked his piece over on the board. I didn't think of the moves that would follow.

It's my fault. A chill runs down my back, but Cody continues. His heavy gaze blinking furiously as he rubs his eyes.

"That's all we have for now. Aldaine is looking into any addresses that any associates of Brass have in a twenty-mile radius of that liquor store." Cody leans forward, engrossed in the messages and reaching into his briefcase for the laptop.

A numbness pricks at my fingertips. It's because of me. My decision. I can barely swallow since my throat is so dry.

Another list of names comes to mind. Too many of them. The number of associates for Brass and Herman, and Talvery if he's also involved … too many. "It will take hours." I'm not even aware I've spoken out loud until Cody responds.

"It's too long. Too many hours have passed already."

"We'll find them." Cody's confident in my moment of hopelessness and despair.

Whoever it is … I will give them anything, kill anyone. I'll hand over myself in exchange. We just need to find her.

chapter five

Delilah

I'M GOING TO DIE HERE.

After everything that's happened, this is how I'll spend my last breaths. It's hard to wrap my head around that fact, but for the last sleepless hours, it's all I've done. I've mourned the dreams I won't see come true. I've cried for my sister who's so very alone now, worried about both my mother and myself.

More than anything, I've pictured the two men I gave myself to last. My heart aches for what they'll go through. I've seen it before, written on the faces of loved ones. It's a pain that's undeniable when the uncertainty vanishes and the truth that their loved ones are dead can't be combated with hope. Especially for men like them. Heroes … or … whatever they truly are. Men of justice and power.

Even though I don't know what they think of my relationship with the other, I hope they both know I've loved them in the way that I'm able. Each of them. A hot tear slips down my cheek to my lips where the salt gathers and seeps into a cut there. Saying goodbye is what hurts the most. It's the last goodbye and I can't even do it with a kiss. I imagine it again and again, and each time the agony cuts deeper into my soul.

Evaluating the past is easier than thinking of what's to come. So many faces flash before my eyes. I don't remember all of their names, but their faces have never left me. As I roll over on the cold hard ground, staring up at the bright light they turned on full blast and left on, I allow myself to think I've made a difference.

For grieving families and poor souls who would have fallen victim to murderers, kidnappers and rapists I helped put behind bars. I've certainly made a difference in a few short years, but it's so very small compared to what I'd hoped.

One life changed is significant, I remind myself. Not a single thought, though, is enough to soothe the truth that brings me lower and lower: I'm going to die here. My hands tremble and I shove them under my legs, attempting to swallow although my throat is dry.

I don't want to die. My chest heaves in a breath as I tumble down a dark hole of despair.

"I'm not ready to die. I could have done so much more," I whisper in a croaked voice and just like the last few times my thoughts wandered to what could have been, Marcus's face returns. His heady scent surrounds me, paired with the chill that's ever present whenever I think of him. Who would have thought the cold would be so comforting. If he could meet me there in my death, I'd accept it. I'll go willingly, if only he'll meet me there. My hand finds my cheek where he last held it and I imagine my hand is over his. I close my eyes, and I swear I can feel his lips against mine.

Creak, thump. The heavy door opens abruptly and the harsh sound rips through my thoughts. Swallowing down every emotion other than hate, I stare up at the hardened gaze from Brass. My body's stiff and anger flows through my veins, keeping my tired body from sagging.

"Brass," I say and his name is nearly a hiss from my lips. Contempt lengthens the single syllable. At first it's hard to see through my blurred vision, but as I steady my breathing, the red light that appears in his hand becomes more clear.

It also explains why his gaze isn't on me. It's on a tiny screen from a silver and black video camera.

Thump, thump, thump, my heart gallops away.

He's videotaping.

"I'm going to need you to do me a favor, Miss Jones," he says as fear creeps into the back of my mind.

Even though my stiff body turns cold from head to toe, I do everything I can not to show the terror that runs rampant at the thoughts of what he could possibly want to record.

As he steps in, so does another man. Slender in build, slightly taller. All in black and he wears a mask still. I'd feel a glimmer of hope at the sight of his mask if it weren't for the camera. It's not that he doesn't want me to see him; he doesn't want whoever is going to view this video to see who he is.

"My mother?" I ask him, needing an answer to one of the prevailing questions that have haunted me while he's been gone.

Brass tsks as the second man shuts the heavy door. I can't help but to watch as it closes completely with a heavy click and the slim light from the hall fades to nothing. Then there's another turn of a lock. Someone must've locked it from the outside. Or it's automatic when the door shuts.

"I'm so sorry to inform you, but," Brass begins and then takes a deep inhale as if it pains him to tell me, "your mother didn't make it."

My throat seems to close on its own. As if I'm choking, but there's nothing except for air present. The trembling that runs through my body is involuntary.

"Liar." I speak the single word while attempting to hold back the shock and grief. I prepared myself for that reality. I knew it was likely, but still I prayed ... Prayers have come easy while I've been caged by these four walls.

"We couldn't have any witnesses," he says and shrugs carelessly, although the thin, wicked smile stays put. "Your sister is lucky she—"

"Leave her alone." My statement was meant to hold a threat, but with the sorrow still wracking through my body, I'm only begging him.

"This is good, but this is not what the video is for, Delilah." Brass speaks clearly, not troubled at all as I heave in the wretched stench of the room.

My mother's dead. With my head spinning and my emotions swarming through me, Brass approaches far too quickly, reaching down with his left hand, the camera firmly in his right. His fist grips my hair close to my scalp and my neck snaps back as he forces me to stare up at him. The time is ticking away as I gasp and scream into the camera with its steady red light.

"We're making a family video, Delilah," Brass says. "I need you to tell Marcus that he wasn't supposed to intervene."

Marcus. His name alone is chilling. I'm struck from hearing it. What does he know of Marcus? My Marcus.

Another second passes, and it's too much time for Brass's liking. With a nod to the masked man, he releases me. Falling to my palms harshly, I barely catch myself, struggling with the pain from before as a fresh burst of agony rips through me. The masked man struck me so hard on my cheek, my head whips to the right, blinding my vision and I'm knocked onto my back.

It happened so fast, I can barely grasp what happened.

Marcus. What does he have to do with Brass?

"He took what was mine. He intervened and broke our deal." Brass's anger shines through as he answers the unspoken question. My chest rises and falls faster and faster as I listen to him, slowly piecing it all together. "Herman was essential and Marcus knew that."

Marcus did kill him. He killed him for me, and now …

Crack! I scream out as my body doubles over and I clutch at my stomach. I didn't even see the kick coming. The pain radiates through me and I find myself huddled in as small of a figure as I can. It doesn't help me, though. Even as the cry is still tearing through me, the masked man fists my hair at the nape of my neck, pulling me up and forcing my bruised body to unfold as I stand.

"Now, Delilah, you need to tell Marcus not to intervene. Do you understand?"

Fresh tears leak from the corners of my eyes and I stare ahead at Brass. He's a man of confidence and so certain that he has the upper hand. I don't know what Marcus has done, but I know if I do what he says, Brass could kill me. He feels he needs me now. That in some way, I'm a piece, a pawn, in their game.

Even as my lips quake, I press them firmly together, barely able to shake my head from the grip the man still has on me. He yanks at me savagely, forcing a scream from me and shoving my body against the wall of brick.

"Say it!" Brass screams, eating up the distance between us. "Say it!" His scream is so loud and so close, it vibrates my chest, making it ache and the fear of what's next suffocates me.

Between every command is a beating. Merciless and unrelenting. I would stay silent if I could, but whimpers and screams are as constant as the commands.

"Tell him we had a deal."

Blood coats my mouth.

"Tell him it's his fault."

Betrayal and hurt are the only thoughts that distract from the pain.

Brass's next confession would hit me harder, if I hadn't already suspected it. "Did you think the evidence disappeared on its own?" Brass licks his lips, getting so close to me that I can smell the stale coffee on his breath. "Marcus is the one who let me out.

He's the one who tainted the evidence. We had a deal," he says, emphasizing the last part with his brow creased. "He did this to you. You should loathe him."

Wincing, I expect another strike. Instead I'm released, watching Brass's back as he paces to the other side of the room.

"Say it." This time when he speaks, his voice is calm, gentle even. "Tell Marcus this is because of him."

I'm given a small moment to consider it all. Every moment that led to this before I respond, knowing I can't give him what he wants, regardless of my own conclusions.

"Our actions are our own." It's a truth I've said countless times before. It's been followed by folders being slapped down on a steel table as I pulled the truth from criminals who committed atrocious deeds, but followed up confessions with *buts* and the names of others they blamed.

A huff that's half disbelief and half disgust is blown from Brass as he rounds me. His boots slap on the broken concrete ominously, but not a single piece of me stirs. I accept it. I will take what's to come now without hope of something more.

"I'm going to die here," I whisper out loud. At first it's as if Brass doesn't hear what I said, but slowly it dawns on him and a thin smile curls his lips up in the most sickening way.

"Yes, yes you are. And you deserve it."

chapter six

Marcus

I HAVE TO FORCE MYSELF TO WATCH. EVERY WHIMPER THAT'S uttered from her lips, the quick and stuttered intakes of her breath, and the cries of pain she can't hold back no matter how hard she tries—all of it shreds me.

I tell myself not to look away, and it takes everything in me to stand perfectly still as I do. The projection screen fills the back wall of the hotel room. When the screen pauses, her eyes scrunched and her head ripped back by a man in a mask, I realize my blunt nails have dug into my skin to the point of drawing blood.

"The cell consists of four walls that have deteriorated. One of Brass's men was spotted in Saint Peters, and another has family only a mile away …" Riggins has a habit of thinking out loud. Once a young man hell-bent on justice, he grew to play a part of my Army. I was young and reckless when I had him kill his sister's ex. It was easy to do. I simply gave a boy a gun at the perfect time. That time happened to be right when his sister's ex was walking to his car parked in the back of an alley after his shift had ended.

He would get away with it easily. I forgot, though … I forgot that killing someone, being the reason they've died, changes a man.

He was an innocent who tried to kill himself after he'd taken justice into his own hands. The attempt left a hole in his head, a scar on his face and turned him into a man who had no purpose. I needed to take care of him after destroying the life he once had. So I gave him a place in a world he could never leave. Charlie Riggins and so many others are my Army, and this is all they know.

The blue dry erase marker he's holding screeches as he sketches a triangle on the whiteboard. The computer screen he resides in doesn't have a camera on my end. I'm able to see him and anyone else I deem fit to be a part of this planning. For now, though, it's just us. "The map has three points and somewhere within this region, there's a bunker or a basement … something that's been added to over time, it looks like."

Riggins comments, "The additional stone appears to be the same as before. Could be historical."

"It could be the stone from a masonry." The thought leaves me, spoken aloud but not with conscious consent. My focus is solely on Delilah and the pain that etches across her face when Brass tells her that it's because of me he was released.

That's the moment she broke down. That pain that touched every inch of her being is felt inside me as well. Regret consumes me and I'd let it devour me if I didn't know she's still alive.

I can still save her and then I'll explain. I needed him for one more play. He was a pawn, but I made the mistake of not realizing she'd entered the game.

"Masonry … one of …" The sound of papers rustling comes through the speakers on the laptop as Riggins searches for something. The wheels to his desk chair roll him smoothly across the screen to a computer station. The rapid tapping of keys brings down the video of Delilah and replaces it with files upon files as Riggins searches for the connection.

My head hangs low and I can barely swallow the guilt that's thick on the back of my tongue.

"Someone's father or uncle. I remember seeing one of his associates has a masonry."

There's the connection. Reynolds and Brass are in this together and they'll die together.

"Bring up the video again." I give him the command but Riggins continues to guess, putting the pieces together the best way he knows how. I need to see her face. I need to see her again.

"Where did I see it ..." he muses as I struggle to keep myself upright. "The factory maybe? And he's using the same three men who were in on the abduction of the girls." My frustration can't be seen as I lean against the desk to remain vertical. I let a man go who had three men in his back pocket with evidence to pin the case on. Three pedophiles and a partner who would back him financially, every step of the way.

"Could be ... if I recall, he specialized in headstones."

"They will all die," I whisper, my eyes barely parted, same as my lips, as I stare down where my hand grabs the edge of the cheap dresser.

"Yes. Reynolds. His in-laws own a masonry and at least two properties in the designated area."

A sense of control comes flooding back knowing we have addresses. "What are they?"

"One's a piece of land that looks to be about twenty acres in the middle of nowhere. The other is a morgue."

"Rewind it again," I say, standing upright to speak firmly. "Send the two addresses and rewind it one last time."

"Sir, we need to scan the vicinities—"

"Send me both addresses." My tone is sharp with the request and in return there's silence.

"Marcus said—" The fool still believes I'm only second-in-command to the enigma named Marcus. Riggins spends his days like any other coder for a private security firm hired out by the government. When I tell him Marcus is calling on him, he answers immediately. After all, he owes Marcus everything and Marcus has never told a soul what he did. He took the blame for the murder. He paid the hospital bills. Marcus took care of everything for Riggins. In return, he's asked for so very little.

The screen in front of me is stagnant as Riggins continues to resist. I'm only vaguely aware I'm on edge and not the calm mouthpiece I typically play.

Clearing my throat and ignoring the heat that surges through my body, I take control as I should … As Marcus's second-in-command.

"I'm aware that Marcus wants every bit of information."

"That's what I'm here for, and you're rushing this." Riggins's tone holds a warning. "What we don't know is what will bury us. We don't move until we know." His dark gaze peers into the camera, staring at no one although I stare back. "You're the one who told me that. I gather everything we need. You execute the mission, picking the players we need. It's always worked that way. We shouldn't rush this."

I confess what I shouldn't. "We don't have time." The incessant ticking of the clock has tortured me every moment she's been gone. What am I supposed to do? Sleep, knowing she's being tortured? Eat, not knowing if she's starving to death?

"There is no reason to rush …" Riggins's words are slow, his expression suspicious. He's a fool. He's a damned fool. There's never been a moment in our collaboration where he's questioned me. He's been eager to have his rightful place delving into the darkness and aiding however he can. I was prepared at any point to kill him. He was going to die before I stepped in. Marcus saved his life, even if he's never realized I am Marcus.

"Sir … I think you may be overreacting. Are you …" His swallow is audible. I can practically see the wheels turning. "I think you may be …"

"May be what? Distracted? Emotionally invested?" *As if I didn't already know.*

"There are two addresses. If you go to the first, and you're wrong, they could know we were there. They could prepare for us, and then what?"

"My contact and I will split the locations."

"We don't have men here. It will only be you."

His uncertainty and hesitation are infuriating. "Send me the addresses."

"You're not telling me something," he says, coming closer to the truth. "Does Marcus know?"

A sarcastic laugh leaves me in mourning. I risk confiding in him the longer this goes on.

"If she was yours," I nearly whisper, "if she was yours, would you wait any longer?"

Riggins's expression adjusts as the realization hits him. "This isn't about Brass and the cases." A sad smile picks up one side of my lips.

"No. It's not."

"Does Marcus know?" he questions again and I nod like a fool as if he can see me.

"Marcus is aware."

"Yes."

"I thought it was …" he trails off and clears his throat. "Never mind."

"Tell me what you thought."

"You've slipped recently … you haven't been focused, and I thought Marcus would notice and maybe he has … maybe …"

Tension rolls down my shoulders as heat burns its way through me, threatening and igniting a less forgiving side of me. "What do you intend to do about me slipping?"

With a click on the keyboard, Delilah's brought back in front of me.

"You should have told me, so I could step in." His voice is apologetic and I have to bite back my retort. He couldn't do an ounce of what I do. He's a hacker; he's a thief when needed, but he's not a murderer. He's not manipulative and decisive. There isn't a single other person who could take my place … other than perhaps Walsh. Or so I once thought. He's the only man I considered being in a partnership with. Charlie and the Army of men I've gathered, men who owe me and owe it to themselves to join this fight are only pieces of the puzzle. They don't see the big picture. Not like Walsh and I did.

I stare at the paused image, her lovely face contorted with agony. Her caramel skin dirtied from both dry and fresh blood, and those amber eyes reflecting nothing but betrayal and sorrow.

The heavy thudding of my heart accompanies the film as it rewinds in front of me.

"I'll watch again while you send the addresses to both me and my contact, Walsh."

"Yes, sir," he answers dutifully.

It doesn't go unnoticed that, for a moment, I lost his unwavering support. For a moment there was a question and a hesitation. And more importantly, that one of my men knew I'd been distracted. If he noticed, there's not a doubt someone else has the same suspicions. That uncertainty adds to the fear that threatens to bury me alive.

chapter seven

Delilah

Senior year of high school

I HEAR MY MOTHER BEFORE I SEE HER. MY GAZE SLIPS FROM *my makeshift ponytail in my hand, to her reflection in my vanity mirror. With a laundry basket balanced on her hip, she shakes her head at the sight of me. "You're not going to the semifinals with that hair."*

"It needs to be simple," I say in protest and look over my shoulder. My mom's happy today. Lighter than she's been recently. I think driving Cadence back to Auntie Susan's so she's closer to the winter gymnastics camp she goes to every year after holiday break upset my mom. It's like her mind's been occupied recently, and a dark cloud has been hanging over her head.

"It needs to be polished," she responds, taking the hairbrush from my hand and I have to bite my tongue. She's not wrong, and I've never been good at doing my hair like Cadence is.

"If your sister was here—" I can already hear her telling me how she'd have done my hair up like she has for these student government competitions the last two years.

"Then I could wear that blue jacket she had," I say, cutting off my mom and smirk at the thought. If having my sister at home was good for one thing, it was her closet.

My mother huffs and a smile forms on her face. I watch her as she brushes out my hair and makes it more presentable than I ever could.

"We should have gone to get our hair done yesterday," she comments, almost to herself I think, and her voice is forlorn. I almost tell her that I reminded her in the morning, but I keep my lips shut tight. She's having a good day, and I'm not going to ruin it.

"I'll do your hair and you bring home the trophy. How about that?" she says and smiles, pulling the hair tight with the band.

"It's not a trophy, it's a plaque and if we go to finals, a scholarship." I can't help the pride in my voice, but the nervousness shuffles its way through me too. The judges are heads of various university departments. I can't mess this up. My portfolio needs more accolades, and a scholarship couldn't hurt either.

"You're going to be so much more than I ever could." My mother's musing breaks the silence. "I just know it."

"Mom, it's just a competition," I tell her, trying to downplay it. Dad said it's important, though. My extracurricular activities matter and first impressions last forever. Again, anxiousness wracks through me.

"I know, baby. I know." Her tone is … upsetting. I can't shake this uneasiness as I watch my mother. She's so close to me, but I've never felt so distanced from her.

"Are you all right?"

"Just thinking about things, baby girl. Don't pay any attention to your mother." She puts the brush down on my vanity opting for a comb instead, and a jar of pomade.

"You're going to make this world a better place," she tells me.

"As if I need more pressure." I don't hide the sarcasm in my response. "You know you could still do something about making the world a better place."

"I already did. I had you and your sister."

The creak of the front door opening travels all the way up the stairs to my bedroom.

My mother peers at the open door, and I watch her smile fade and her movements falter.

"Dad's home early. Maybe he can come." I can't help but smile at that thought. He'll see me in action. My mother's smile reappears, mirroring my own but she doesn't answer me.

I can't die here. Not like this. Not yet.

Even though my body aches with every small movement, I push myself up onto my hands and knees. My palms press against the cracked cement floor as my body arches involuntarily from the pain of laying still for hours with so many cuts and bruises. I don't know how long it's been, only that it's been far too many hours of feeling hopeless and beat down.

There aren't any cameras in here that I can tell. The four walls of old brick could tell endless stories I'm sure, but unless I'm blind to them, there isn't a record of what's happened here apart from the camera Brass brought in. My eyes strain as I inspect each crevice again. Some stones are damp, others stained from water or blood or something else entirely, I'm not certain. Crawling and then slowly standing, I test any crack that may be weak from decay and time. Everything aches, but the pain doesn't affect me like it did before. It simply is.

I spend my time testing every weak spot, searching for any out. Nothing gives, though. The door is next. It's a foolish thought, but I test the doorknob. It's iron and the handle is antiquated. If I gave a damn about history beyond legal cases and precedents, maybe I'd know more about this location and what it was possibly used for, but I haven't a clue. In my wildest guess I imagine the Civil War and bunkers where men hid or held prisoners. The thought has occurred to me more than once: How many people have died here?

I question if I should risk screaming for help, but I'm certain I'm being held underground. Given the damp smell and the layers of stone and dirt, I would be surprised if I wasn't hidden away beneath some rotten barn or perhaps it's only a small door, hidden in brush that would reveal a stairway and lead down to this dungeon.

I test the hinges on the door, praying they haven't been kept in good condition. They match the knob, so I imagine they're original. And just like the knob that's unmoving, so are the hinges.

Losing the last piece of hope and purpose, my arm drops heavily to my side.

I have no way out, no weapon. My mind races with all of the stories I've been told, the horrible nightmares that came true.

"There's always a way." I whisper the sentiment. I'm slow as I sit cross-legged facing the door. Someone will come through that door. That person, although a villain on the surface, will be my saving grace. He'll open the door and prove it can be done; he'll bring a weapon … which I could take from him. Something, some shred of hope will be delivered with the creak of the door.

It's a soothing thought as I lay my head back against the hard brick and ignore the screams of pain from every inch of my body. My head is dizzy, my throat dry. I'm starving and I have no idea how long it's been since I was taken.

I told myself I wouldn't cry anymore, but damn if the tears don't spill easily while I wait for whatever it is to come.

chapter eight

Marcus

THREE DAYS TOTAL HAVE GONE BY SINCE SHE'S BEEN taken.

Two hours have passed since the video was first sent via a link to an old burner phone that Charlie Riggins discovered. Without him, it would have taken far too many hours for me to discover the video had been sent. It was sent along with a threat but no demands: *You killed mine, I'll slowly kill yours and there's not a damn thing you can do about it.* Brass gets off on pain. He wants to torture me and he'll use her to do it.

I gave him no response. No threat, no reaction whatsoever. Anything I give him will only fuel his desire to get back at me by hurting her. What I want, though, is to slowly choke the life from him. To watch terror fill his eyes as I squeeze until the pumping of blood halts and his lank body goes limp. My fingers twitch at the possibility.

There are some men who are fueled by wealth and power, others by delivering consequences. Brass and I share this one thing in common: we're both men who fit into the latter category.

Too much time has passed and we have two locations. The addresses stare back at me like the wires to a bomb, one red and one black.

Riggins is right. If we go to the wrong location, we'll tip Brass off and he could flee before we get there. We could split up, but then we're even more outmanned and outgunned.

Fuck! There's no easy choice and we have to make a decision. Risk going to the wrong location and losing the element of surprise, or split up and risk being overrun. I slam my fist down on the cheap nightstand, and the particleboard splinters beneath the impact at the same time that my phone goes off.

I already know it's Walsh, asking me a question I don't have an answer to: *Which address do we take?*

Each second that ticks down on the clock is torturous as I scan the video for any other clues and come up empty. Delilah's cries for help drown me in those moments. She wouldn't need to cry out if I'd been there. If I'd protected her.

Once I decided I wanted her, I should have stolen her away.

I shouldn't have trusted my brother. I should never have let him lay a hand on her. She was always mine to have. And I belonged to her.

I haven't slept, I haven't eaten. I'm a shell of a man without her.

Staring at the phone, at Walsh's question I already knew was coming, I picture the two wires yet again. I can't risk the wrong choice, not when her life's on the line. There's never been a moment since I made the decision to be the person I am where I've felt such despair and uncertainty.

A moment passes without a response from me and Walsh calls, the phone ringing in my hand. Swallowing thickly, I answer it.

I don't know what to say, so I don't say a damn thing.

"You there?" he asks and at that I respond, "Yeah. I'm here."

"My partner is on his way. We can take the farthest address. Backup has been called. They'll be coming in from the south, so taking the northernmost option will cover our asses if she's at the south location. We'll call it in and they'll be there quicker than we can get there."

The very thought of men I don't know getting to Delilah first, risking they aren't corrupt and needing to have faith that they'll be able to save her ... I can't and won't risk it. I can't risk her simply being passed into the hands of another enemy.

"If you're going north, I'll take the south address."

"What? No, we can't split up."

"We can and we have to," I say, staring at the map Riggins laid out. He goes north while I take the south location. It's on us to save her. Not a man I don't know. She is everything to me, and who are they? They're no one I know or trust.

"I'm calling it in," he says, practically screaming on the end of the line as he stresses, "we need backup."

"I'm not waiting," I tell him.

"If they see you there—" The resentment that's lain dormant surfaces.

"I don't care." We cut both wires. That's my decision. It has to be done.

"Marcus. Don't be stupid. We need more men." My brother already sounds weak and defeated; I hate him for it. Almost as much as I hate the fact that Delilah loved him first.

"We don't have time!" How does he not get it? Brass only had her beaten the first time. The man is an amoral sadist with no boundaries he won't cross. Every minute is risking her. Risking further pain and suffering inflicted upon her and for what? For a better chance and better odds? I will save her. And my brother better be man enough to do the same. "Leave now. We don't have any more time to waste."

"Marcus … Brother, please, don't do this." The sound of Cody swallowing is audible, fear and pain choking him. Was he always this weak? Or is he only weak for her? The question stirs up a pain we don't have time for. Hanging up, I leave the conversation where it is. He goes to the north address and I take the south.

Cody

Fucking hell. Marcus is going to ruin everything.

His impatience is unprecedented. "Pick up the fucking phone!" I scream into the line before pressing end and wishing I could slam it down to get out some of this anger. Tension rolls through my body, knowing I'm potentially headed to a hostage situation with only a pistol, no vest and Evan may or may not be there when I arrive. It's fucked.

With a long exhale, I try to calm myself as I take the next exit and find myself driving down a tunnel of overgrown trees. The canopy of branches above me simulate night on the dirt road lane although the sun hasn't quite set. I'm close to her and that's what matters.

Marcus will get her if she's there. He will. A part of me brings back childhood memories and times when we both thought superheroes existed. Back when we used to play Batman and Robin, when all was right in the world. Even then, my younger brother never did like playing the sidekick. He'd take off without me and do the things that frightened me without thinking twice. That's the man he is and I remind myself of that. I have Evan and the two of us have taken down far more dangerous targets. Backup is coming. If nothing else, we'll hold them off.

It'll work. It has to work. Marcus isn't wrong, we're coming up on seventy-two hours, Brass has to know he's shown his hand and we'll be coming for him. The stakes are higher now and time isn't on our side.

In a single text, Evan is informed and without hesitation, he agrees to meet me there.

It's strange that I would go back that far in my memory for such comfort, given the horrible deeds my brother has committed on his own for a decade now. He's murdered and slaughtered, he's wreaked havoc without thinking twice and all on his own.

He's never needed backup, he's never even needed me. If she's there, he'll kill them all and save her. And if she's not, then that's exactly what I'll do.

I'll kill them all. I'll hunt them down one by one until I have her safe in my arms.

My sweet Delilah; I'll save her.

One of the two of us will have her soon.

Marcus

The drive is silent and far too long. Even with the window down and the bitter cold air whipping across my face, I feel every second slipping by and it exacerbates my suffering. There are two of us and only one of us will find her. One of us will come face-to-face with Brass and have the pleasure of killing the fucker. My hands twist on the steering wheel, my thumbs running along the smooth surface of the leather. Death is not justice for men like him.

Taming the wild beast inside of me, I'm less concerned with him than I would be if she wasn't there. He is nothing and no one compared to her, and he has no idea of the depths I'd go to simply to know she's safe and out of harm's way.

I'm not certain if the locations Riggins sent are bomb

shelters or something else, but Riggins sent the satellite images last taken from over a year ago. His search was unable to find more current intel. Assuming nothing's changed, there are doors that lead to underground tunnels hidden behind some brush. The radar showed several tunnels and each could have its own exit passage. It's a maze at best. A trap at worst. My phone hasn't stopped alerting me since I put the car in drive.

I don't answer; I won't negotiate with Cody. Even if we are outnumbered and outgunned, there is no excuse for failure. We have the element of surprise and the need to win. One on three or one on ten, it wouldn't matter. There's not an army that exists who could keep me from her.

If, however, we show our hand, arriving at the wrong location and tipping off Brass through security breaches, then there's no one to stop them from taking her somewhere else. Meaning it could be days or weeks before we have a chance to save her … or never. He could kill her and walk away. We'd never have a chance to save her.

My throat is tight and my vision blurred as I hit the gas harder, revving the engine and tearing down an old dirt road. It takes another ten minutes before I have to slow and park alongside a thick row of pine trees. Beyond that is a small shed, decayed and rotted from years of unuse. I follow the map Riggins sent me, noting how the calls have stopped altogether.

Walsh must be there now.

Both of us at each location simultaneously.

Good, is my first thought, but then the anxiousness eats me alive as I take each step carefully, searching out the grouping of three trees that signal the location of the opening Riggins said was best. What if Walsh got there, and what if he doesn't have the same fight?

What if the worst of both outcomes has come true? The overgrown weeds hide the panel well, so well that I already know this entrance hasn't been used for at least a year. Tearing through it, I rip the door open, the rusty lock breaking easily.

The knowledge that it was far too easy makes one thing known—I cut the wrong wire. Even with that hopelessness washing over me, I continue the motions, wishing I'd listened and done what Walsh asked.

I contemplate messaging him, but I can't waste the time. It takes me five minutes to carefully make my way down the first passage. It's musty, dark and the light switches don't work. The wiring must be outdated and it's obvious no one's been down here for years.

Fuck!

My heavy breathing is the only thing that breaks up the silence as I make my way down the second passage, knowing damn well I sent Walsh to the other location and that's where she is.

She isn't here. I made the wrong choice. A cold sweat breaks out along my skin and I feel sick to my stomach.

There's no one here to fight, and I may have lost her forever.

chapter nine

Cody

EVERYTHING FEELS HEAVY TO THE POINT THAT I'M reminded of both my immense exhaustion and the spot in my chest that pains with every small movement. The anxiousness running through every inch of me is so overwhelming, I nearly miss Evan's vehicle. It's tucked away behind the overgrown brush, camouflaged in varying shades of dark moss.

I barely glanced at the map Marcus sent, but I fucking hope we're close.

My keys jingle as I slam on the brakes to pull up close behind him, shaking off the fear of failure as I park. I'm quick to shut off the car and slam the door as I leave it; all the while my pulse thrums heavily and every movement appears to be automatic. Like I'm not the one doing it. It feels like I've lost control of my body, although I'm aware what's happening around me.

The truck rocks as I leave it there, meeting Evan halfway from his car to mine.

"Four men," he starts. The friend I've deceived thinks this is about a case that's gone wrong. The bit I fed him about a man who wants revenge is true enough, but he can't find out the details. My head's dizzy as I lean against the back of my pickup and look up at Evan, not sure how this will end for either of us. I'm vaguely aware at some point from this moment forward, Marcus and him may meet. That can't happen. I'm backed into a corner with no way out and everywhere I look, someone close to me is going to be hurt.

The deep bags under Evan's eyes match mine and I have to remember there's a chance this all goes according to plan. "It's just over there," he says and points, and it's then I see the binoculars hanging around his neck. "What have you got on you?" he asks and my response is a reflex, just like everything else.

"Just my Glock."

With a nod, he motions to the back of his sedan and I follow him, grabbing another handheld and a few magazines.

"I'll go in first and you cover me." I give the command, my jaw tense and the thrill of the hunt mixing into a deadly concoction with the fear that's consumed me. A darkness falls over my gaze as I stare off into the distance and Evan goes over the plan. If this were just like any other takedown, there'd be a hint of a smile on my expression.

But it's her. At that thought, the wind feels knocked out of me yet again. Evan's hand slaps down on my shoulder as if he can sense the change. "We'll be in and out, and she'll be all right," he says, his calm voice even and consoling. His brow rises as he waits for me to agree, staring back and not showing an ounce of nervousness. "She'll be in your arms in minutes and in your bed later tonight," he says, then lets out a huff of a laugh and it forces me to smile.

"Yeah." I nod and pretend it's all going to be all right.

The clouds ahead wash the entire sky in gray. The sun's

setting soon and the dim lighting is on our side, but not so much that I'm certain we'll make it to the entrance without being seen.

"I'll go first," I say and nod, staring at the open field. I point to the trees where I can vaguely see a mound of dirt that stands out as if it doesn't belong. Before I can even question if he sees it too, Evan's already nodding his head.

"You'll need these," Evan adds, slipping a bolt cutter into my hands. "Anything else you can think of?" Without hesitation, I shift the cold metal tool into the back of the holster at my waist.

One deep breath and heat licks across my skin. Another and I silently give the motion, then the order to follow.

My pace is steady and my motions as stealthy as they can be. I creep down to the field and hurry along the edge in the shadows until I come to the end of it. Pausing and waiting for Evan, I scan the perimeter, listening to the wildlife in the distance. It's a challenge, though, to hear a damn thing with the blood rushing in my ears.

A quick nod and another signal, then I sprint out to the mound, not covered by a damn thing and knowing full well Evan may cry out and bullets could fly.

Not a single noise ricochets in the air. Nothing at all as I remove the dried and dead brush, seeing the shiny metal lock and the two-by-two-foot panel that covers the opening. It's not dusty or covered in cobwebs, and that's a damn good sign they're still here.

My muscles are tensed and coiled as I hunch down and break the lock with the bolt cutters. A single groan leaves me, the sound carrying through the night along with the sharp crack of broken metal. My heart hammers as I wait a second and then another before pulling the metal loose and dropping it to the dirt with a soft thud. Standing higher, I motion over my shoulder, making eye contact with Evan and keeping a lookout over the horizon as he runs toward me.

Cold sweat lingers on my skin as he comes up behind me and I open the panel, my gun drawn and ready for anything, but all that awaits is a tight stairwell, aged and weathered from decades of uncontrolled heat and humidity.

I head down first and drop to my ass at the sound of a ping as a bullet whips by and ricochets off the rusted metal wall.

Fuck!

Bang, bang, another gun fires and I push myself against the wall, firing back before I can even look.

Evan calls down as I search in the darkness and spot a man running around the right side of a dark and chilled tunnel.

He's dressed all in black but his figure is easy to make out as he takes off and I instinctively chase after him.

I can't lose him. He may be the only one who came looking with a sensor or security alarm of some sort alerting him. If we can get the rest of them by surprise, that's far more appealing than allowing this fucker to give them a heads-up.

"FBI," Evan calls out and I grit my teeth. There's not a word or warning that comes from me as I lift my gun and fire.

My first shot strikes his shoulder and as he falls forward, the man screaming, another person behind him stares back wide eyed from the other end of the dingy hall.

His expression is full of shock and I fire again, the handgun's grip sending a jolt to my palms as I pull the trigger again and again. Before the second man has a chance to react, I've shot him in the chest twice and the first man is silenced with another shot in his back.

"Walsh." Evan's voice comes from behind me and isn't the usual tone. There's a skepticism and I'm certain it's because I haven't followed protocol. I turn to face him, half-ashamed about my next move, half-eager to get it over with.

"Was he even armed?" he questions and I let my expression mirror his as it morphs from hardened determination to a look of disbelief. As he walks ahead of me to examine their bodies, I strike Evan in the back of the head, just behind his ear. The blow lands with a thud and a crack.

"Sorry," I mutter beneath my breath as he sinks to the ground. I catch him, the gun still hot in my hand and lower him down. It'll hurt like a bitch when he wakes up but he'll be fine in a day or two.

There were four perps on site; now there are two, and Marcus will be here once he realizes she's not there at the south location. Guilt seeps into my blood at the sight of Evan's limp body, but I can't have him witnessing what I'm about to do. There is no protocol to be followed, no honor in my actions when it comes to saving Delilah and delivering consequences to each and every one of these pricks who helped kidnap and terrorize her. I can't have Evan questioning, hesitating, or worse, trying to stop me. None of these men can be taken alive.

Evan's morals don't align with what must be done.

A door shutting catches my attention, lifting my head as I hear a familiar voice call out. It's unmistakably Ross Brass, and my gaze narrows as I stalk down the tunnel.

He yells for Mitchel, and as he does I gently kick the limp body, stalking past it and the pool of blood that's gathered around his chest, soaking into the concrete floor.

"Mitchel!" he cries out again, his voice louder, and the adrenaline pumping in my veins pushes me forward. The layout of the tunnels is clear in my mind, and a plan forms but vanishes instantly when a second voice answers as I get to the *T* intersection at the end of the hall.

"There's been a breach," states a deep voice to my left. All the while I'm very aware of how Brass is positioned on my right. One man on either side of me, and only feet away judging by how loud their voices are.

"Fuck," Brass spits out. "Grab her," he practically hisses as the figure on my left suddenly appears in front of me, his gun aimed at me just as mine is aimed at him. He's tall, wearing all black and moves like he's ex-military—obviously trained for this kind of situation.

Just as I pull my trigger, two shots are fired from behind. *Fuck!* It could be backup, it could be Marcus. It could be someone aiming for me and now I'm surrounded. I don't have time to think. All I can do is fire away.

Bang! The man in front of me gets a shot off but he misses, the bullet passing to the right of me although it grazes my shoulder. A hiss is elicited from the burning contact, but I barely have time to feel a damn thing. Ignoring the pain, I fire again, landing a shot dead center in the man's forehead, and pivoting to shoot Brass in his back as the fucker tries to run down the hall. I should assume he's armed, but it doesn't appear that he is. His shoes slap against the concrete, once then twice as I pull the trigger again and again. A guttural cry falls on deaf ears.

I hadn't noticed my erratic breathing until I turn to face the dark figure behind me along the wall. Marcus. Relief is instant as I heave in a gulp of air. His sharp eyes meet mine and it's only then I'm able to take stock of what happened.

They're dead. It's over. But where is Delilah?

"How many?" Marcus questions and relief washes through me.

"That's all four," I answer him, searching down each hall for any sign of life, or any clues as to where she is.

He stalks toward me, slowly coming into view, asking, "Where is she?"

"I don't know." Heat races through my blood, mixed with fear at the thought that she's hidden and we'll never be able to find her.

"Delilah!" Marcus screams and it's the first time I've ever heard his voice so clearly. The first time fear has ever appeared in it. The same goes for desperation.

"Delilah," he cries out again and, in the distance, her voice is heard.

I shouldn't feel any bit of envy or the pang of regret, but my motions falter hearing her distressed voice, crying out for my brother.

He takes off toward her voice as I find a ring of keys in Brass's pocket. I nearly call out to him, but I don't. The words are swallowed back down in the darkness as I realize I want to be the one to unlock it.

Before I can fully stand, the clatter of men and the warning of "FBI, we're coming in," calls out from behind me. Marcus's sharp gaze meets mine from a distance and I toss the keys to him, calling over my shoulder and waiting for the silhouettes to appear.

"Down here!" My eyes drop to Evan's body and I yell, "Man down! Man down!" Footsteps and clicks of weapons being readied echo down the chamber.

"It's clear," I call out and then glance back down the hall. One man stays behind with Evan while another eats up the distance in long strides, his gun still drawn but held close by his hip. Two more follow him, each on high alert. "I believe she's down here," I say and motion with my chin in the direction Marcus took, before looking back over my shoulder to hear one of the men by Evan call for a medic. "I think I heard her down the right tunnel."

"Where's your radio?" the guy closest to me asks, his brow pinched. I hesitate to answer.

"I lost it … I … forgot it."

Shaking his head slightly, I ignore the questions that cloud his eyes. The ones I'll have to face about the lack of following protocol.

"This way." I give him the command but about halfway down the hall, I already know what I'll find. The door is open, the light shining a stripe across the freezing cold tunnel and it's far too quiet.

Opening the door wider, it creaks an eerie sound.

"She's not here," he tells me, and then calls out orders. The sound of the radio, followed by droning voices giving commands, all fades to white noise.

He took her.

As the men gather and split off to head down different tunnels, I already know they'll be long gone before the search is done. It all feels unreal as I pull out my phone, ignoring the orders of men superior to me.

It only takes ten minutes before the place is cleared. Five after that for my phone to ping while I'm fielding questions and watching my partner slowly being brought back to consciousness. It all blurs to nothing, the motions not determined by my conscience.

I stare down at my text: *Where are you?*

But more importantly, his response: *Nowhere you'll find us.*

"You weren't supposed to be there. What part of 'go home' didn't you understand?" my boss hisses on the other end of the phone. "How did you even get this information? It's not in our system."

I can barely pay attention to him as I meet Evan's gaze while his head is being bandaged at the back of the ambulance. The look in his eyes is telling.

"Skov is asking questions and I have to go into the precinct. I don't know what to tell them, Walsh. What did you get yourself into?"

I opt to hang up the phone rather than answer. The reality of it all slowly chills me to the marrow of my bones.

The look of contempt on Evan's face gives away everything he's thinking when I walk over to apologize. Although I still can't tell him everything. There's no way I ever could.

I don't have to guess what he'll say when I finally make my way to him, every consequence berating me one by one. "You need to tell me the truth, or I will tell them what happened."

chapter
ten

Marcus

S HE SLEPT THE ENTIRE THREE-HOUR DRIVE BACK HOME. I didn't look back, I didn't listen to anything but the steady sound of her breathing and the hum of the engine.

With her in and out of consciousness, I cared for her how I've cared for myself too many damn times over the years. The makeshift ER in the basement is constantly restocked. These walls could tell endless stories about the faint scars of bullet wounds and broken bones that were mended in this room.

Riggins sent the doc, the only one I've ever trusted, who assured me none of her ribs were broken. The bruises that wrap along her torso send even more fury through me that Brass was given death so easily. I wish I'd been the one to take his life.

More than anything, she needed sleep. For fourteen hours, I watched her do nothing but rest while IVs gave her fluids and pain meds. She's badly beaten, but she's not broken. Not according to the doctor, but there's a different kind of brokenness that can go unseen.

A dark bruise rimmed with blue lines her jaw, trailing down her throat and it matches the other ones all over her body. I'm careful, with the sun setting on the second day, as I carry her to my bedroom, letting her rest in a more comfortable place. Slowly stripping away the dirty clothes reveals inch after inch of bruised flesh. Her perfectly caramel skin is tainted with shades of purple.

A whimper slips from her as her neck arches and pain strikes across her face when I pull the last piece, her bra, down her body. "I'm sorry," I whisper with every ounce of sincerity and I toss the bloodstained garment to the pile on the floor.

She's still in need of a deep sleep, but her eyes part just slightly and then she blinks, widening them and taking in a sudden breath.

"It's me," I say, then raise my hands in the air palms out to her. "It's just me, little mouse." I add every bit of comfort I can to my voice as she takes in the room, propped up on her palms with her slim body showing the sharp peaks of her collarbones. Every time I notice another detail of her abuse, anger rises from a simmer to a boil.

Swallowing thickly, I wait for her to look back at me, for her frightened gaze to see me before I tell her, "It's only me, little mouse. I've got you."

"Marcus." She whispers my name and the dried cut on her lip cracks open. She winces and I leave her only to get Vaseline from the nightstand. The drawer opening and closing is the only sound filling the room as I carefully dab the balm on her lip.

She watches me and lets me care for her; all the while she's silent. There's a look in her amber eyes I've yet to see from her. I'm careful as I lift her in my arms. Her own wrap around my neck and I savor the feel of her hit skin against mine.

"Can you stand?"

She hums a quiet confirmation and I set her down on her bare feet toward the back of the shower. I haven't thought much of my home with its dated bones and barren features, but as I turn the white porcelain knob I consider explaining that it's safe. It may appear empty and abandoned, but this home is safe. Not a soul is around us for miles and the moment they cross that boundary, I know and the house goes into lockdown mode.

The hot water sprays down, just missing her bare legs as she presses herself against the wall.

It steams quickly and I can barely look at her, her nakedness against the white tile only serving to highlight every beating she took. Sickness stirs in my gut as I reach under the sink for a bar of soap. I lather the bar under the spray, noting she'll need the medical kit when she's done.

As I list in my mind everything else that she'll need, she reaches for the soap, taking it from me and turning away slightly.

"I can help," I say and she shakes her head at the offer, not looking me in the eye with her lips thinned and a grim look on her battered face.

I struggle to respond other than gathering a fresh towel and shirt from the cellar laundry. I waste no time, not sure what Delilah is thinking and with a million confessions warring to be spoken first.

As I lay the towel and shirt down on the sink for her when she's out, I don't hesitate to tell her the thought I've had for days now.

"I'll never forgive myself for letting this happen to you."

"You can't control what happens to me," she says and it's the first sentiment she's spoken clearly. Even over the steady stream of the water, I hear her clearly.

My lungs stop, my breath halting. There's an air about her that's unforgiving.

Control is all I have to offer her. I'm damn well aware of that just as much as she is. My gaze stays on the side of her face that's turned to me. It's unmarred and equally unemotional.

It's quiet for a long time as a new tension settles between us. I'm reminded of what Brass told her—the truth about my involvement in his case being dismissed. An ounce of suspicion or perhaps hatred has come between us; unanswered questions and accusations unvoiced.

"I said I won't forgive myself and I meant it." There's a coldness in my tone this time, a seriousness that's been absent since she's woken, but it doesn't faze her, although she turns from facing the faucet to look me in the eyes.

The hot room heats even further as the steam billows out past the simple clear curtain that barely covers half the space.

Without another word, she carries on washing her skin, stiffening when the soap glides over the worst of the bruises.

"You're angry with me," I start and heave in a breath, prepared to let her take it all out on me, but she cuts off my next statement with a simple no. She doesn't even bother to look back at me as fresh tears stream down her cheeks. It's the first time she lets the water hit her face and I'm all too aware it's so I don't see her crying.

"I didn't sleep while you were gone," I tell her. "I did everything I could to get to you as quickly as I could." The excuses crowd themselves at the back of my throat just as my hands ball at my sides into fists. Her stern look breaks down into agony at my words.

My poor little mouse. I've seen this look before. The pain, abandonment, the hate and denial. It fucking kills me to see her like this. Shut off to the world. I know it all too well. It's a look I've worn for years, but it's not for her.

Not for my Delilah.

"If I were to tell you that the idea of you falling asleep at night, not having the same confidence, the same fight, the same love and devotion you had before I came into your life …"

"Stop it," she commands me and then both of her hands

cover her face. The sob is barely heard but her shoulders quake with it.

Daring to continue, I watch every nuance of her response as I tell her, "If a night passes where you don't have those pieces of what make you the woman I fell for … I would never forgive myself. If I were to say such a statement to you," I pause and swallow thickly before continuing, "would you try to let me in right now?"

"Please, I am not okay right now," she tells me, lowering her hands and staring straight ahead.

"I know. And I hate myself for it. I won't forgive myself—"

"Forgiveness." She bites out the word as if she hates it. "I'm certain you have many other things you don't forgive yourself for. Why should I be any different?"

Her question is a sharp knife to my heart.

"This is about—"

She doesn't give me time to finish before the accusation leaves her bruised lips. "You let him go."

"He was a pawn."

"He killed those kids."

"I know."

"You of all people," she starts but then stops, her nose scrunching as her body trembles. She reaches out quickly for the faucet and nearly topples over. I have to catch her and as much as she'd like to push me away, she doesn't have the strength. With the water spraying down my left side, soaking into my shirt and splashing across my face, I steady her and then turn off the water. She's lost weight, and this close to her, the darkness under her eyes is pitch black. Three days she stayed in a cell alone, beaten and left with nothing but the knowledge that she was there because of me.

"I'm sorry," I tell her. "I'm so fucking sorry."

"Why?" she questions in a pained whisper as more tears gather in her eyes. "Why did you do it?"

"Because there was someone else who needed to die. Because

I thought I could play God." I answer her honestly as she falls into my arms, her wet hair soaking my shoulder.

It's been a long time since regret overcame every emotion I held. In this moment, it's all I can feel other than agonizing pain. "If I tell you I was wrong, if I tell you I would take it back, would you even believe me?"

She doesn't hesitate to answer yes, which offers me a slight sense of relief. I accept it greedily, I take the glimmer of hope that she'll forgive me and I gently pat her down, dressing her in a white T-shirt of mine when I'm done and bring her back to the bed.

Before she can drift off, I make her a bowl of soup. She's only able to drink the broth, but it's something and she doesn't throw up from it.

With my back against the headboard, I rest next to her as she slips in and out of a light sleep. My head lays against the end of the iron rail and I stare up at the simple ceiling fan as it rotates. Her small hand, with cuts across her knuckles and her nails bitten back, lays across my chest. She placed it there the last time she woke, cuddling closer to me. It's a small reprieve from my ruminating.

Why did I do it?

Because I wanted to play God and I forgot … gods aren't allowed to fall in love. I've never felt so weak as I do now. There's not a damn thing I want other than to feel her forgiveness slip into the cracks of my brokenness.

Carefully, I lay my hand on top of hers, just to make sure she's still here, still holding me, still alive and willing to lie here beside me.

The small movement and gentle touch rouse her and I instantly regret it. Selfish. I'll never not be selfish for her. "Sorry," I whisper and bring my arm around her small body as she huddles even closer to me. Every hour that's passed has allowed a bit of her wall to break. I pray time is on my side.

Her shoulders lift and the bed groans as she adjusts herself. I barely breathe until she settles even closer to me and rests her head on my chest, allowing me to press my arm against her back and lay my hand on the dip of her waist.

I'll stay beside her for as long as she needs, mending every cut, tending to her every need until she's healed. I'll make damn sure there's not a single scar left on her soft skin when all is said and done. Not a memory of what they did to her will stay behind. Only this. The two of us, the way it should be. I close my eyes, comforted by the thought, but it doesn't last for long when she stirs.

"Why are you the way you are?" She whispers her question carefully and as I peer down at her, her lashes flutter and she stares straight ahead. Her thumb brushes gently along my side, making soothing circles.

"I found others like me, and that was enough." My memory drifts to what feels like a different lifetime. A small boy staring across a cell not unlike the one Delilah was just in. If she weren't settled across my chest, resting on top of me, I'd give in to the urge to move, to get up and do and think of anything else.

"I need more than that. I need you to tell me something. I need to know something about why you are the way you are."

"We can talk about anything else."

"Tell me … tell me, Marcus." My name sounds foreign on her lips. There's a hesitation, a tone she hasn't taken before.

Sucking in a deep breath, I swallow the lump in my throat. I hear his voice again as the back of my eyes prick.

"You already know, don't you?"

"You haven't told me," she whispers.

"You know I was taken, when I was a child. It happened so

fast." My body's stiff but I heave in a deep breath, readjusting on the bed. "I was walking by myself to my aunt's house. She wasn't used to having kids. One minute there wasn't a worry in the world other than getting home before the streetlights turned on, and the next …"

It's been a long time since I thought of that night, of the moments before I wound up in that cell. Delilah doesn't push for me to continue, but when I peer down at her, her gaze is fixed on the mirror, staring intently at our reflection in it.

"They kept us in a basement that was sectioned into cells. Four men."

"Us?" she questions.

"You've read the reports."

"They say you died," she whispers.

"Forensics weren't quite the same then," I admit, although my voice is tight.

"That doesn't explain why …" she doesn't finish. It doesn't explain why I fled, why I didn't go back to my aunt's. Why I couldn't bear to trust or talk to anyone.

For a moment I contemplate telling her about her father, but it's far too risky when she's in a state like this and, more importantly, there's another person I've never spoken about. Another soul who I failed and I'll never forgive myself for that.

"There was a boy with me. He was younger and he was," I stop to suck in a deep breath, steadying myself as I remember the details of what he looked like. "He had large eyes, the kind that are meant to tell stories," I explain. "He was my friend," I tell her. "For weeks we were in there and we had each other. Then one day they came."

I remember the sound of the gate opening, the loud creaking and how it startled me awake. "We slept together and when they came it woke us up, huddled in the farthest corner of the room."

"They took him?" she guesses and as I shake my head, I

realize there are tears running down my face. "They grabbed me, but I got away and I went back to the corner." My words are careful as they come out one by one, afraid of being spoken, but more afraid of not getting out the reason why my soul is black. "I shoved him out of it," I say and my bottom lip quivers.

"We could see what they did on the other side of the hall. In the other cell where they kept all—" I can't finish and instead I remember how I shoved him out of the way to scurry to the corner. "I pushed him aside and he was closer to them."

"They came for me, and I sacrificed the younger, weaker boy to live a little longer.

"I watched, forced myself to watch when I realized what I'd done. I'll never not hear his screams. He tried not to. He stared back at me and I know he didn't hold it against me, but they took their time and eventually both of us were crying. I swear I tried to convince them to stop and to take me. I begged them.

"They ignored me. They didn't stop until they were done. Raped him, abused him and after hours, killed him. All the while I watched and screamed for them to take me instead. That's the measure of who we are as people, isn't it? Our humanity. When it comes down to it, we'll sacrifice the ones we love just to stay alive."

"You were a child." Delilah's words are meant to console me as she lifts her chin, staring up at me, but I can't look back down at her. Not when there's more to say. To get out of me. I've never told a soul, but I'll give her my darkest secret. She can be a safe place for me and I'll be one for her.

"I was able to fight back. I didn't. I didn't fight and—" I almost say his name. It was so close to being spoken. "I didn't fight and he died because of it. Because of me. The next time they came, I fought and I got away. I killed two of them.

"I could have done it before, I could have fought and saved him. Instead I saved myself and this is what I'm left with.

Memories of him trying to hold back the pain while they brutal-ized him. He held it back for me."

"His name was Marcus, wasn't it?"

There is no answer for her. Not one that I can give right now.

I couldn't be who I was anymore. Not knowing what I'd done. I couldn't be …

"I couldn't forgive myself for that. Everything I've done since then, I did for him. I did it because I was able to do something to stop the pain and injustice around me." My lungs still and refuse to fill as Delilah's lips part and stay that way, her next words un-spoken and her bottom lip trembling. "But you …"

The words are caught in my hoarse throat, making it feel as if there's a swelling that will surely suffocate me. A heat wraps itself around me, drowning me with an anxiousness I haven't felt in so long. It last held onto me, dragging me down to the depths of hell, when I ran as fast as I could. When my legs gave out and I had nowhere to hide.

It holds me captive now as she stares back at me, her amber gaze glistening with unshed tears to match the streaks of those that have already run down her bruised and broken cheeks.

"Christo—"

"Don't call me that!" I don't mean to lash out at her, but I do. I haven't gone by that name in over a decade.

It takes every ounce of my being to pry myself away from her gaze and leave at once. Forcing my limbs to move and ignoring Delilah as she calls out the name of the boy I allowed to be killed in my place.

The boy who comforted me when he needed it himself.

The boy who reminds me always, that the bad men always lose.

She cries out for him, for Marcus. Not Christopher, even though that's the name she knows I had back then. That's the name of a coward who chose not to fight. We could both be here if I'd had fought. If I hadn't tried to hide myself in a damp corner of a dingy cell.

I should have known better. I wish I could go back. I wish I could take it all back.

With the thud of my bare feet on the wooden floor, I ignore the tears running down my face as I leave her in the bedroom, locking the door behind me in case she gets the urge to follow, and take refuge in the empty room down the hall. I bury myself in the corner of a darkened room, huddled like I was in my most shameful moment and close my eyes. Wishing I could just go back and make it right. Wishing I'd died instead.

Marcus is the one who was supposed to live. Not me.

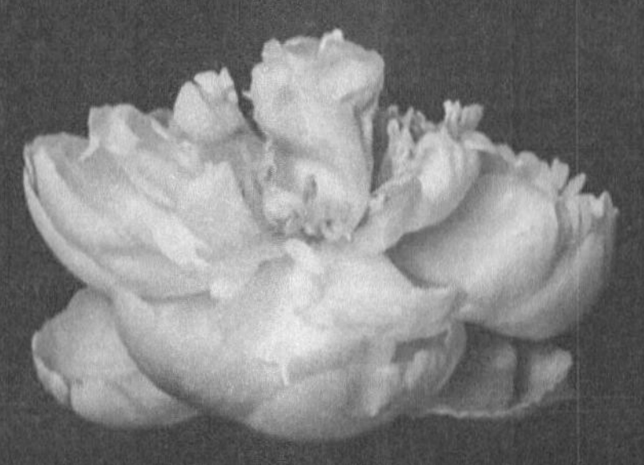

chapter eleven

Marcus

"THE COPS ARE CLOSE."

Riggins's message on my phone causes every hair on the back of my neck to stand on end as I slice a peach, the blade of the knife traveling along the rough pit.

He continues as I watch on the monitor of the open laptop sitting on the worn laminate counter. "With Marcus the lead suspect in Mr. Jones's murder, they're digging into all the cold cases and overturned cases Delilah and Walsh have worked on over the years. Some of these cases are far too close."

I nearly question Riggins, *which cases?* But there's no point.

"We need to pin this on someone and make sure they stop digging. Pin every case Marcus has been involved in on Delilah's father?"

"Marcus could be a disgruntled partner," Riggins suggests and every piece falls into place. It's the perfect plan to wrap up every loose end and fuck over those who have it coming to them.

"I know who can take the fall for it. I'll send you the steps."

Riggins asks a question he never has before: *How are you?*

Staring at him in the monitor, I know he's looking aimlessly into a lens I know doesn't show him a damn thing but a black screen.

"There are loose ends that need to be tied off. Let's focus on that." My tone isn't cold but regardless, Riggins's expression is less than pleasant. It appears he's reluctant to nod in agreement but he does.

Not wasting any time, I focus on the bastards who dared get between myself and Delilah and tell him, "All of Herman's team needs to be executed."

For the second time in the past few days, my ever-faithful companion objects. "Sir, if he's gone, then the connection to Talvery—"

"Do it." I leave no room for negotiation and reaffirm my position of superiority. "Someone else will fill the void and we'll nurture that connection. The next meet for Talvery's gun pickup is next week, isn't it?"

Although I already know the answer, Riggins confirms it and judging by his tone, he can guess what I have planned. "Send Herman's crew to the same location. Let them clash over it."

Ripping the two halves of the ripe peach apart, I take my time slicing the delicate flesh, remembering how it all piled together. Every failure, every error I made that caused harm to bystanders like Riggins. I was able to help Charlie and bring him in close, but others felt the collateral damage of plays like the one I'm about to make. Mass murders of rivals meeting on trading grounds. There's a reason I have a reputation, and it's because I determine who lives and dies. There are so many bystanders, though: loved ones of those who will be taken from them forever and, like in this case, the unknowing individuals who do my bidding. The ones who were in the wrong place at the wrong time.

These are sacrifices that must be made, though. One beast

will kill the other and if it's Herman's crew who survives, I'll find another way to end them. Either way, their days are numbered simply because they worked for the men who hurt Delilah. They'll all be buried ten feet deep before the winter is done with us.

"I am begging you to reconsider. They have ties that—"

"Every last one of them will die. Either by the supplier's crew or Talvery will end them when he discovers the mix-up."

"This doesn't solve the problem with the cops and—" Riggins's concern and hurried pleas are exasperating.

"I'll take care of pinning all that on someone who the cops already suspect. It will clean up this mess."

"Someone they already suspect?" he questions.

"You don't need to concern yourself with it. I'll send it all over by the end of the day." I'm deliberately short with him, but before he ends the call, I add, "Thank you."

It's easy to see the small bit of gratitude in the slight lift of his smirk. "Any time, sir. Is there anything else?"

"You're certain it was only Brass and Herman who took her. No one else helped?" I ask again. It must be the third time I've asked in the past twenty-four hours. I'll question it a million times looking for someone to punish whenever I'm reminded of what happened to Delilah.

"It's confirmed. Yes. Only those who are dead, and those we're going to send to their execution."

"Very well," I comment and then end the call.

I finish preparing Delilah's breakfast and when I bring it to her, she's quiet but receptive. Silence is draped between us. After setting the plate down next to her, I sit on the other end of the bed, taking small pieces of the cut peach from her plate and watching her.

The questions are simple, both of our tones feigning a casualness that I sure as fuck don't feel: How do you feel? Did you sleep all right?

My skin blazes with both embarrassment from my confession last night and the vulnerability in this moment. I don't miss that when I look up at her, she steers her gaze in another direction and I'm doing the same.

She doesn't dare bring up what happened, but she certainly looks at me differently. It brings her touch back to me, though, the longing in her eyes and the absence of every defense she threw at me yesterday.

It's difficult to forgive an all-powerful god—or a devil, for that matter. It's far easier to have compassion for a mere mortal. For a damaged fuck like me.

Our fingers brush against one another when we both reach for a slice of fruit. Her simper is rewarded with a pleasant rumble I can't control. It comes from deep in my chest where it's still warm and safe for her. The insecurity of where we are now is irrelevant. It's like a dark room meant for safekeeping. A hiding place, perhaps.

I wonder if she has a place like that, somewhere inside of her, where she could store all of my secrets, all the hideousness and memories I wish I could walk away from and the stories I'd rather rewrite altogether. But in that same place, a little fire sparks when her hand brushes mine and she sees me smile. I wonder if that place exists for everyone, or if it's just something I have for her.

I'll hide all her secrets away in that safe place. For her and only her.

With those thoughts in mind, I take advantage of the easiness, leaning across the bed and carefully running my pointer under her chin to direct her lips to mine. She obeys without objection, her thick lashes falling as her eyes close. The kiss is gentle and I'm careful of the cut still on her lip, although it's healed slightly. The bruise on her jaw is still there as well. I'm cautious with every small touch, but not nearly in the same way I have been before.

With the warmth still lingering, I lean back, letting her chin go and watch as she opens her eyes and peers up at me with those gorgeous hues of amber. There's a fire there, one I recognize and thank fuck it's there at all. She knows my demons and my sins, but she also knows my pain and that's quite a different burden to carry.

chapter twelve

Delilah

I DON'T RECOGNIZE THE PERSON I AM OR THE EMOTIONS THAT whirl inside of me, sinking to the pit of my stomach. I don't know what I dream of, but I know what I remember when I wake: the door to the cell opening, that click resonating, and then there he is.

Christopher Walsh, my dark knight, the grim reaper, standing in the dimly lit hall one moment, then his arms wrapped around me the next. He engulfs me, kissing my hair and telling me I'm safe, telling me they're all dead and they'll never hurt me again.

It's a moment of true terror, and then just as quickly, a moment filled with relief and love and a debt I can never repay. It's impossible to describe the crash of reality when I wake up, and he's hovering over me. Like if he dares to look away, I'd be lost to him forever.

The intensity of it all is at war with everything that's been embedded into my mind for days.

The simple fact that I was taken because of Marcus, is at war with the desperate need to lie in his embrace forever.

The battle is over with the whisper of a name each time: Christopher.

I can forgive Christopher easily. It's Marcus I have contempt for. Staring at my hero's sleeping form, I debate on doing something the logical side of me screams is mad. Still, the intention consumes me.

He has very few things in this old home. It must be from the '50s, a cookie-cutter cottage without any noteworthy or distinctive architectural details. It's lacking in maintenance as well as furniture. It's exactly the type of home I imagine the grim reaper would live in. A barren, cold and empty house. Last night when he left, I'm not proud to admit that I searched for a weapon.

I've seen grown men, victims of abuse, break down telling their stories. Only one I spoke with was ever violent, and shortly after he killed himself. Last night, Christopher reacted just as that man had. There's a sense of denial to it all, a fear of facing that reality before a quick draw of a curtain hides it all away and a different personality comes out to play. That's all it is, though, it's only a show.

He locked me in this room, and the same fear that washed over me watching a young man attack a social worker who was sitting next to me, hit me at full force. Mental illness comes in many shades. Christopher needs help. He's not well and that's a certainty.

I'm not well either, nor in a position to help him.

Still, last night I searched for a gun and instead I found cuffs. Maybe I am truly going mad, because as the soft sounds of Christopher's steady breathing comfort me, all I can think is that if I could cuff him to this iron headboard, I could talk to him. I could get through to him, I could rip back the curtain and help him in a way he so desperately needs.

For the last hour, it's all that's gone through my mind. The plan screams at me, begging me to do it. To slip the metal around his wrists and secure the other end to the iron rail.

I wouldn't dare broach the conversation with him unhinged. If he's secure, though, if he can't react and he's forced to listen, I think I could get through to him.

I could call him Christopher without him shutting me out, without him running away.

A deep sleep has taken him and all I've done is stare at his handsome form, noting how he appears so different. There's not an ounce of a threat and only a man lies in front of me. There's no sorrow, no pain. Not a hint of his troubles. If only I could see him like this when he's awake … if only I could see him smile.

With that thought in mind, I sneak out from under the covers, ever so slowly so I don't disturb him.

The floor groans, loudly snitching out my intention, but Christopher sleeps soundly. When I open the drawer, my back stiffens from the loud protest, but still, he sleeps.

I only second-guess myself for a moment, a very short one with the cuffs in my hand. He has at least four sets in that drawer and I have two, one in each hand.

I could cuff his wrists with one set each, and then quickly cuff the other ends to the iron rail.

The vision makes my heart race. I'm certain he would lash out if I don't do it quick enough. I nearly turn back, but a voice inside my head whispers, *Isn't that what he's doing already? He needs this.*

Without thinking twice, I don't attempt any careful steps. I'm not quiet in the least, and I'm not even gentle as I climb on the bed, linking one wrist and attaching it to the post before he's woken.

His wide eyes strike through me and force a yelp from my tight throat as I secure the other around his wrist successfully, but it's not attached to the bed. Falling backward I scream out, landing on my ass as Christopher rises, ripping his hand away, the iron and steel clashing.

"What the fuck are you doing?" he practically growls.

Anger and contempt stare back at me, followed by betrayal. My heart races with the fear, but watching him tug against the iron in an attempt to free himself calms me.

My caged beast is just that, caged.

"Cuff it to the headboard," I say, managing to get out the command in a calm voice, but it's so soft, he doesn't hear.

"What did you just say?" A threat laces his question. "What the hell are you doing, little mouse?" Rage seems to simmer around his shoulders. The moonlight shines in, creating shadows across his broad shoulders and sharp cheekbones. If we didn't have the history we do, I'd be terrified. As it is, I feel nothing but relief.

"Cuff the other end to the headboard." I give him the command and slowly stand. Only wearing a T-shirt of his, I rise and stand a few feet from him.

"You're going to run or y—"

"No." I don't wait for him to finish. "I'm not running." A deep crease settles between his brow and I'm thankful to see the anger wane.

"What are you doing, Delilah?" His question is still harsh and lowly spoken, but at least the fear is gone. That's what it was, not anger. It was fear.

It's been fear all along, hasn't it?

"I'm forcing you to stay with me tonight," I answer him and my fingers play at the hem of his shirt.

"You don't need cuffs for that," he counters. Instead of responding, I slip the shirt up my body and drop it to the floor, feeling my hair cascade down my bare back.

"Cuff," I say, whispering the single word. Vulnerability and a hint of fear that this won't work make themselves known, but mostly desire takes over. The heat in his eyes intensifies as his gaze travels the length of my body.

A moment passes and all I can hear is my breathing pick up. He seems to question me, glancing between the cuff and then my naked body.

"You better not lie to me," he warns and I offer him a sad smile.

"No lies."

When the cuff clinks and locks around the headboard, I tell him to lie down.

"Since when do you give the commands?" he asks, but does as I say. Positioning himself on the bed in a sitting position, he then slowly lowers himself so he's lying down.

"Lower still, so your arms are—"

"No," he cuts me off and there's a hint of defensiveness. It doesn't escape me that he could cover himself in a way as he is now. Although his hands are cuffed, he could easily kick out or fight in some capacity.

I could fight him on this, but I don't. I don't want to fight him at all and he's already given me what I asked.

I'm silent as I climb onto the bed, and each time I look up at him, he's staring at me with an intensity that's indescribable. It's like the prey daring the hunter. Power and lust are a deadly cocktail and they're all I can taste as I crawl toward him and tug his pants down his body. He helps me, lifting his hips, but both of us stay silent. The heater kicks on and the cuffs clank against the iron; other than that, it's only the blood rushing in my ears that I can hear.

His cock is already stiff, standing upright and waiting for me. My heart hammers as I wrap my hand around his length. With my eyes on his, I press my lips to his head and lick the bead of precum. I hadn't planned this, but I can't deny that it eases the tension. More than anything, I want him.

With my tongue starting at the bottom of his shaft, I lick up to his head, loving the rough hum of satisfaction he gives me. Holding him steady at his base, I swallow him down as much as I can while pressing him to the back of my throat and moaning.

"Fuck." Christopher murmurs the sexiest groan I've ever heard, his heels digging into the bed and his hips thrusting up.

The cuffs clink as he pulls against them again and they get my attention. I'm already hot, desire and the slight chill in the air pebbling my nipples. Without hesitation, I spread my legs and climb on top of him, sitting around his hips. I don't dare push him inside me, though, not yet.

"I told you, you would beg me," Christopher states, his lips staying parted with his heavy breathing matching my own. "I didn't expect you to steal that pleasure from me."

"I could still beg you," I answer and then drop a kiss onto his chest. My hair falls around my shoulders, landing on his broad chest as I plant kisses there and trail up to his neck. My clit presses against his pubic hair and the sensation overrides my common sense. As the heat builds inside of me, I rock against him, taking pleasure in the small motions, kissing and sucking up his neck, the rough stubble leaving small scratches behind, but I don't care.

When my lips meet his, he leans forward to deepen our kiss, his tongue pressing against my seam until I grant him entry. Although I'm on top, although he's the one bound, the kiss is very much led by him, possessive and demanding.

And I love it.

It takes everything I have in me to break it, letting my forehead rest on his as I whisper against his lips, "You lied to me."

I'm all too aware that his body has stiffened and I know his eyes are open with his lashes brushing against my face, but I keep mine closed.

"I didn't," he says and his response is whispered against my throat.

My swallow is audible, the fear of confrontation rising, when I answer him, "You told me your name was Marcus."

A prickling sensation travels down my body, as cold as ice and I don't dare move, much less open my eyes as he sits up higher, jostling my body as he does.

"I am many things, but I'm not a liar. You knew me as Marcus and that's who I am."

Slowly I open my eyes, kissing his lips that don't move.

"Tell me what your name is." I give the command, but I'm begging him and he knows it.

"Stop it." His own inhale stutters and my heart breaks for him.

"Please," I beg.

There's a heat and intensity between us that is raw and fragile, so easily broken but that's why it's so precious.

"Your name is Christopher."

"Stop it." His whisper is just as much a plea as my own and tears gather in my eyes as I confess, "And I love you. I love you and I'm so sorry for what happened to you."

"Don't say that name ever again," he warns me, but he doesn't move. He could buck me off, he could push me to the side with his body. He could fight back still, but he doesn't. He doesn't move in the least.

Not until I remind him, "You're the one who's cuffed, Christopher."

In a swift movement, he whips his body around, his arms crossing above my head as I'm thrown under him with a loud yelp.

Naked and caged beneath him, I nearly kick out, my legs drawing forward, but I spread them instead so I don't hurt him. With his hips between my thighs, my back pushed into the mattress, his rigid cock presses against my heat.

The shadows dance along his strong body as he hovers over me.

"Stop it," he warns and I shake my head, even now as I've lost my position that only held a semblance of power.

"I love you, Christopher."

There is anger and pain etched into the chiseled features of his face as I lie there under him, daring to reach up and cup his chin. Although he stares down at me, giving commands and taking away my power, it doesn't stop me from kissing him and he kisses me back. At first he merely molds his lips to mine, and then soon he's kissing me deep, feverishly taking from me.

Reaching lower, I guide him inside of me and then kiss his throat. I tilt my hips up as he thrusts his down, stilling inside of me when I gasp.

His girth stretches me to the slight point of pain, but the pleasure is so overwhelming the pain doesn't matter. It only adds to my desire for more.

He's still cuffed and it makes it harder for him until I slip under him, down the bed and let his forearms rest beside me.

The moment I kiss him and tell him I love him again, he fucks me ruthlessly. It's a punishing fuck and I bury my screams in the crook of his neck, the smothering heat and overwhelming pleasure rocking through my body.

chapter thirteen

Cody

"WHERE IS SHE?"

"I don't know," I say and my answer is riddled with the irritated energy I've had all night with him.

"You mean to tell me—"

"That I arrived. I heard her. I had to defend myself and by the time you got there, my partner was unconscious and she was gone. Yes," I snidely hiss the last word, my hackles raising as my palms dig into the steel table I lean across. "Yes, Detective Skov, that's what I'm telling you and I fucking hate you for it." I let it all out, the pain and frustration and disgust at how she slipped through my fingers and … how my brother stole her from me. "I loathe your sorry ass, and I hope you go to bed every goddamn night knowing she's still missing because of you."

His dark eyes narrow into thin slits as he bites back for me to watch it.

"Fuck you," I bellow from deep in my chest. The only thing

that keeps me from striking out at him, is the very firm fact that every bit of what I've told to him, I've condemned myself for as well. "I fucking hate you and the fact that you let her get away."

"Let her? Did she just up and walk away then?"

"Fuck you," I manage to repeat as I fall back into the metal chair.

"Did she run away from you?" Anger blisters from every part of me as my fist clenches in response. The door to the room that's become my second fucking home slams open.

"Enough," Skov's partner, Gallinger, barks. His slim frame appears even lankier with a cleanly shaven jaw. He slaps a folder down, this one thin and pulls back the other chair to take a seat facing me across the table. Skov is silent, but his shoulders tense. Whatever Gallinger has, it pisses Skov off which should give me comfort, but not a damn thing can soothe the pain that's run through me since I searched that cell and saw she was gone.

She left with him. I went through hell to get to her, and I didn't even get to see her to know she's safe.

"What do you know of Delilah's father?"

My gaze rises slowly to his. "Never met him."

"What about the cases he worked on," he says, then shifts his weight from left to right. It's a nervous energy I haven't seen from Gallinger yet.

"What about his cases?" I question and then shake my head. "He hadn't been on a case in … decades."

Silence sits between us.

"He was murdered," the detective starts and I keep my expression as neutral as possible. I can't give a damn thing away. Aiding and abetting is not on the list of crimes I intend to go down for.

"The evidence points to a partner."

"A partner?"

The folder opens slowly, at the same time that Skov

uncrosses his arms. Pictures appear of a young woman in black and white, and then another.

"A partner who had an appetite for young women and then went younger."

"Brass and Jones?" I'm flabbergasted.

"It explains a number of things but more than that, there was evidence found in Brass's home. Trinkets and keepsakes of the women. Things related to other cases."

"What does that have to do with Delilah's father?"

"He kept photographs. We suspected him …" Gallinger trails off as he shares a glance with Skov. "But not to this extent, and there was no evidence of a partner."

"You're shitting me," I say, feeling my shoulders stiffen. "There's no way her father—"

"He was nearly disbarred several times over the years for a series of claims. The women dropped the charges, but a pattern is a pattern and the timeline makes sense.

"We'll ask again, what do you know of Delilah's father?"

"Not a damn thing," I reply without hesitation. I'm struck by disbelief, so much so, it takes me longer than it should to add, "I don't have anything to say. So either let me go, or I want my lawyer."

The air turns colder as the two men sit back in their seats.

"If you've got your suspects—" I start to say but Skov interrupts.

"They're both dead and your girlfriend is still missing. It's convenient, don't you think?"

Leaning forward, I keep the threat in my voice thinly veiled as the command is murmured darkly, "Keep her out of this." My heart hammers and I can't breathe until the chill settles between us.

"You're free to go, Special Agent Walsh … from this interrogation, although I've heard your superiors are wanting explanations. Apparently there are some things that don't add up in your story."

"What about Delilah?" My throat is tight. I'll be damned if I let them stop looking for her. Marcus is a selfish prick and I don't trust him to give her back. I don't trust him at all anymore. I don't trust anyone.

"Her sister heard from her. She's no longer a missing person."

My eyes widen and I stare between the two of them as Gallinger closes the folder.

"You look shocked, Special Agent Walsh." Skov is nearly cocky with his comment.

Biting my tongue, I let the fact that she's safe outweigh the hurt of knowing my phone hasn't gone off. She didn't reach out to me. Neither of them did.

"You're lucky Evan Aldaine doesn't remember what happened to him," Skov says as he rises from his seat, indicating this interrogation is over.

"How's that?" I question, not bothering to look up at him as a prick travels down the nape of my neck. I stay in my seat although the two men are standing and the door to the interrogation room remains wide open.

"My guess is that you went in to save her from shit you caused. He went with you as your backup but you couldn't let him see whatever it was you did."

The shit I caused … his assumption hits far too close to home.

"Maybe it's because you went in with the intent to kill those perps," he says and shrugs, in the nonchalant way that he has to make it seem as if the most horrid things don't concern him, "I can't blame you for that." Sucking air between his teeth, he adds, "I'd have killed them too.

"But my guess is that she didn't want you to save her, did she?" His question gets a huff from me as I stare straight ahead, ignoring both of their gazes that penetrate the most vulnerable parts of who I am. "She ran away, didn't she? She knew this all happened because of you."

"If it happened because of me, then how is it that her father was involved with Brass and coincidentally died just a week ago?" I dare to question him, finally meeting his gaze.

"Why don't you tell me?" he prods, lifting a brow.

It's easy enough to smirk at him and respond, "Why don't you go fuck yourself?"

"The only reason I'm not worried about your ex, and I'm taking a leap there, I know. I just assume she's your ex now …" his comment is meant to get to me, and it fucking does but I do my best not to show it, "… is because you aren't yelling at us to find her. You know damn well she left you."

Insecurity grips me at the back of my neck.

"You're free to go, Walsh. If you have any information for us … be sure to drop by." Skov's condescension is laid on thick.

Gathering my things, I head out, hating this place. Hating every fucking thing. Shrugging my leather jacket on, I turn right to head to the parking lot and get the hell out of here. With my phone in my hand, I nearly miss Evan standing to the right of the building, a cigarette in his hand, the end of it glowing bright burgundy and smoke billowing from his mouth.

Fuck.

"Evan." Shame keeps me from holding his gaze. Fog forms in front of my face. The temperature is only going to drop further tonight with the storm coming in. Rain washed away the snow, but what comes tonight will stick.

"I thought about calling and leaving this in a message, but then I thought maybe I could tell if you're lying to me better in person." Evan's statement is a slap to my face and I deserve it.

He doesn't owe me a damn thing after what I did to him. If I'd failed and that fucker killed me … he'd have killed Evan next.

"I'm sorry." I say words that I know don't fix a damn thing.

Blowing out the smoke, he drops his cigarette to the pavement, stubbing it out with the heel of his sneaker.

"You need to go into the office—don't tell them anything other than you want to resign." There's not an ounce of emotion in his tone, only an order spoken dispassionately.

"What?"

His gaze narrows for a moment, but then it's gone. There's no animosity, only certainty that stares back at me. "It is what it is, Walsh. You stepped out of line. We've known for … how long now?"

"I don't know what—"

It's surprising how grateful I am that he silences my lies. "If you don't resign, they'll keep looking into it. From what I can tell, you brought that lawyer into it. You want her to go down too? End it."

"I'm sorry."

"You used me. For a woman." Contempt finally shows up to the conversation.

At least I have the balls to own up to that. "I did."

"Don't ever come to me for anything again." He holds my gaze as he adds, "You're dead to me."

My throat is tight with remorse. "Evan, I—" The knowledge that I betrayed him in the most heinous of ways keeps me from continuing.

"What is it, Walsh? Spit it out."

"I fucked up and if I could go back, I'd change it."

"Was it worth it?"

I hesitate, letting the question sink in. Which part? All the way back to the beginning? *Was it worth it?* Were all the lies and deceit, all the murders and corruption worth having my brother in my life? Was it worth it to deliver justice to those who would have gotten away with creating more pain and misfortune than they already had? Was it worth it to fall in love with a woman who could never love me back? Was it worth it?

I can't answer the question. The silence lasts too long between us. A look of disbelief accompanies a huff of disgust from Evan as he looks past me, shaking his head.

"Don't call me again." Before I can respond he adds, giving me nothing but his back as he walks away, "I told our boss to expect your letter of resignation on Monday."

chapter fourteen

Marcus

WITH HER IN THE BATHROOM, I'M QUICK TO SIT UP on my knees, press my shoulder against the headboard, and push on the top rail. It's old and the metal gives against my strength. Gritting my teeth, I have to heave my weight against it once more to slip the thin cuffs up the column.

I'm quiet while I consider my next steps. Silently stalking to the dresser, I take a moment to unlock the cuffs from my wrists and the other ends that were attached to the iron rail.

She is strong; she is determined. And that does nothing but make me hard for her. However, I have my limits and my little mouse is going to learn she can't take advantage of me in any capacity and get away with it. With the cuffs free I make my way back to the bed, right where I was. The water at the sink turns off as I slip the two cuffs around the pole that isn't attached to the broken rail. This one won't give like the other did, not with Delilah's small frame.

Lying down with my hands above my head, I wait for her. I'll wait as long as I have to in order to get her in my place instead.

Christopher. She dared bring up that name. The only thing that keeps me sane is her desire to love me with her words and her body. When she leaves the bathroom in all her nakedness with the pads of her feet against the bare floor, I focus on that. On her desire to use that strength she has, to try to heal me. To love me.

I'm already hard again for her and filled with the thrill of teaching her a lesson.

There's not a bit of her that has any suspicion as she lies down right where she was before, content on falling back to sleep, I imagine. With her head on the pillow, her body close to mine and one hand on my chest, I know it's going to be difficult to get both of her wrists cuffed to the bed. I decide I'll take them one by one. The first is the crucial one. If I can get one with hardly any fight from her, I can force the other. My heart pounds in my chest. She brought this upon herself. And I love it.

I love that she has fight in her.

Making my moves as quick as I can, I snatch her hand from my chest and pull it to the cuff. It slips around her wrist as her eyes go wide.

She struggles with a yelp and a violent push against my chest, but I'm faster. I'm stronger, and it's easy to pin her down and close the cuffs around her wrist.

"No!" she finally yells out.

"Oh no, little mouse, you started this game."

Her body writhes against mine, her gasps undeniably filled with fear. The cuffs click as I link them together, placing her thin frame where she held me captive. The heat of her body is addictive, her curves against mine everything I've dreamed of for years. As my fingers trail down her soft skin, and the goosebumps travel along with my touch, she begs me to stop.

To stop.

My body's still pressed against her as tremors run through her. For a moment, I worry I've hurt her; I lift my weight and account for every bruise. Even still she violently pulls away from the cuffs, with motions that do nothing but dig the metal deeper into her wrists. A moment passes, followed by another before I realize what the two of us were thinking are two very different things.

Her amber eyes don't peer into mine with pupils dilated from desire. Instead they're closed tight with fear etched onto her features. I hate myself.

A sudden gasp warns me of the silent sob that threatens to spill from the only lips I've ever craved to kiss. With the tips of my fingers just slightly brushing up her tank top, I wait for her to calm down. I let a moment pass as the seconds tick by, praying she'll come to her senses.

But I'm the one who's confronted by the hard reality with every breath that passes and the panic not leaving her stiff body. She's terrified of me.

"I would never hurt you," I murmur and I'm not sure she heard me as tears leak from the corner of her eyes and her face presses against the pillow, refusing to meet my gaze. Clearing my throat, I tell her again, clearer and louder, "I'm not going to hurt you."

My timbre trembles toward the end of my statement and that's when I truly realize the damage of this raw moment between us. Both of us bared, and both of us scarred.

"You think I'd hurt you?" My tone is wounded.

Delilah's inhale is stuttered with tears caught in her thick lashes. Bruises still linger along her cheek and down her jaw. I'm gentle as I cup her face, mindful of the pain she's in. I swear I can feel it, I can feel her pain, and I haven't the faintest idea if she can feel mine.

My gentle touch only elicits a harsh whimper from her. With my throat tight and the haze of what I thought was between us subsiding, I lean back, listening to the bed groan as I put more distance between us.

Instantly her nipples harden, the cool air replacing my warmth and I climb off the bed, placing the comforter over her body. With her wrists bound to the headboard, just as she'd cuffed me, I wait for her to look at me. Her lips are cracked and her eyes puffy. Her body badly beaten and weakened. Yet she's still perfect to me.

When her sobs cease and she dares to peek up at me, I repeat the sentiment, "I would never hurt you."

Shame seems to wash over her, but she doesn't respond. She doesn't tell me that she knows I wouldn't. It's a sharp knife to my heart realizing that she doesn't know that truth. How could she not know?

"I thought you loved me," I tell her and instantly feel foolish at the confession. Maybe it was something else. *Pity.* It's been so long since I've fallen victim to that emotion. She didn't love me, it was only pity.

"I do." My gaze whips up from my battered hands to hers. The room is dark, the blinds and curtains still closed tight. It's so quiet I can hear her swallow. "I do love you," she admits, and I swear my heart pumps once, sending the warm blood where it's meant to go, but it's far too slow to keep the organ beating. There's too much pain that floods the space.

"You thought I was going to hurt you," I say, stepping back and the floorboard creaks beneath my weight. That's when I realize I've never allowed anyone in here. There isn't a soul who's entered my home since the day I claimed it.

Yet I brought her in here, because, for some absurd reason, I thought she belonged here. It didn't occur to me that perhaps I shouldn't have brought her here. Not until this moment, as she stares back at me. Her eyes are filled with a knowing look as she whispers, "Yes, you scare me."

The confession forces me to turn my back to her, my palms keeping me steady and upright as I flatten them against the top of the dresser. The old wood feels cold beneath my skin, but it holds me up as I let it sink in.

"Christopher," she calls out and instinctually I condemn the name with a threatening tone as I tell her, "Don't say that name again." The murmur awards me a sharp intake from behind me. Yet again, since I've taken control, I hate myself.

Loving her has proven that in spades. The more I love her, the more I hate myself. Every event leading up to this moment swarms me. Regret lingers on all of them.

I question everything. Even the moments in the barn, when I let her father live because he truly loved her. How … wrong. How fucked up! Anger simmers along my skin and I rip away the thin T-shirt. My blunt nails drag across the back of my shoulders and up the nape of my neck.

"You scare me, but I love you."

"Don't lie to me," I bite out, leaning forward on the dresser and slowly opening my eyes to see my reflection as I add, "I don't deserve that." The moment the statement is spoken, I deny it; I deserve everything she throws at me. I don't hold any right to anything from her. Certainly not her honesty when I've kept so much from her for years. Sorrow and regret chill my skin, to my flesh, down to the marrow of my bones.

She murmurs, "You can love someone while fearing them."

"No, you can't." It hurts to admit that, especially to her. To the only person I know I've truly loved since I was a child. Maybe I'm broken inside, so badly broken that I can't recognize what true love is. I only imagined it.

No, that's not true. Denying the question in my head, I know damn well I love her. I have loved her for as long as I can remember now. Hanging my head, I mutter, more to myself than to her, "The only fear that's to be had when you love someone is the fear of losing them."

I don't even know she's heard me until she answers, her voice strong enough to force me to look back at her, "You're wrong. There are so many different kinds of love."

"I only know one." I stare back at her, my gaze lingering on every inch of her skin until I make my way to the pain in her eyes. This is my fault. It's time that I pay for it.

"I wish I weren't afraid of you," she confesses, her voice distorted by raw pain.

"That makes two of us, little mouse." It takes a deep inhale before I can get the rest out. "I'm sorry I brought you into this." My voice shakes as I say words that sound like goodbye. My sweet Delilah rages against the cuffs for the first time, the metal clanking against the iron frame as she attempts to pull herself upright, but it's no use. She's not getting out of there, not until Walsh comes to get her.

"I never should have come near you." I utter the confession as Delilah shakes her head, her wild eyes refuting it.

"No," she exclaims. "Stop talking, stop it!"

"I'll leave you alone. I won't hurt you again." I speak aloud what I know to be right, even as my vision blurs and my chest seems to hollow with agony.

"Marcus, I'll call you Marcus!" she screams over top of my apology. "Please don't leave me!" she cries out, fresh tears spilling. "Please, Marcus, please," she begs me, her body arching in protest.

I am a weak man as my grip tightens on the doorframe, so close to leaving her like I know I should. "Please, Marcus, please! Don't leave me!

"Walsh will come for you."

"Please! I want you! Please!"

She wants me. I let the soothing balm of her words calm a piece inside of me that longs for her affection. I know it's only because of the predicament she's in. Cuffed to a bed in a broken-down house, all alone and in the dark, she'd seek comfort from anyone. But still I hesitate to leave.

"Don't leave me," she whimpers, her head hanging low and her words weakened by defeat.

"I told you, little mouse," I say and look back to see her, really see her and what I've done to her. "We all break."

She screams out as I close the door behind me, striding as far away from her as I can to dim her cries. It won't take her long to quiet, I'm sure.

I don't give myself time to think; I text Walsh my address without allowing another moment to pass for me to reconsider, to hold onto hope that I'm wrong.

I watch the clock, knowing he's nearly an hour away.

Curiosity gets the better of me when her cries turn silent. I have to know she's all right more than anything else. She couldn't possibly hurt herself, but still, I have to be sure.

Although her shoulders rise and fall with deep, unsteady breaths, her eyes stay closed as the door creeps open.

The comforter's slipped down her body and I use that as an excuse to bring it up around her shoulders. She's still as I do, but I know she's awake when she slightly leans into my touch. She keeps her lips pressed tight as her bottom lip trembles. The plea is so close to being spoken.

Slowly, I lie down behind her. And when I do, an inhale of relief greets me, her lips parting and her body slightly gravitating toward mine, her back to my front.

It reminds me of the night I first lay with her, when I told her to close her eyes.

If only we had the luxury of living our entire lives like that, in blissful ignorance.

It's selfish to lie down with her. Everything about her calms me. With my eyes closed, I breathe her in, knowing it'll be the last time. I wish that the memory of this moment would comfort me, but given how I have to be careful of her bruises and that I'm the one who made her cry last, this moment will only serve as a reminder to why I should stay far away.

We breathe in unison and it's her steady breaths that calm mine. When I kiss the curve of her neck, she whispers that she loves me, and I believe her, I really do.

So much so, that it lulls me to sleep beside her.

It's not until the door creaks open and my brother stares back at me, that I wake up, my eyes tired and full of shame.

"I didn't mean to be here," I confess to him as his eyes widen with unspoken questions. I do my best not to wake her as I creep out of bed and turn away from him. His weight shifts at the door, causing the floorboards to creak.

"Just get her to her sister."

Cody nods in agreement and I walk past him, neither of us saying another word as I leave him to save her from this nightmare in a way I never can escape.

chapter fifteen

Delilah

"I'M BEGGING YOU." MY SISTER'S VOICE IS STRAINED AS I sit in her office. The faint bruise on my left arm is barely there anymore. I've traced it idly this past week. It's the last remaining reminder of what happened. Physically speaking, that is.

"Cody begged you, and now I'm begging." The mention of Cody's name does something to me. There's a place inside my chest that's felt empty for days. I can barely look at him. I know he wants me still, and he blames himself when he shouldn't. I told him he shouldn't. My sister told him to give me time. But time isn't going to change any of this.

Her voice is thick with embitterment when she says, "For Christ's sake, do you want me to get down on my knees?"

"Is this because I asked to meet you here instead of your apartment?" I know damn well she's not pushing the issue just because I don't want to go back to her apartment. Still, it's a defense. The reason she wants me to go into therapy is multifaceted but she understands I didn't want to go back to her place, and have this conversation in the place I was abducted.

I'll be fine if I never go back there again.

My sister starts in again. "You didn't go to mom's funeral. You aren't sleeping."

"And how would you know that?" I question snidely, even though she's right.

"You look like hell, Delilah." I scoff at her comment. "And you should," she stresses, almost as if an apology.

"You went through hell, so it makes sense that you'd look like it."

"Well, thanks for that," I say and pull my purse into my lap, sitting stiffly on a very comfortable sofa draped in deep blue velvet. The clock above my sister's desk ticks away as she sighs, both frustrated and saddened. "You need to talk to someone. It doesn't have to be me."

Playing with the thin necklace that drapes across my décolleté, I do my best to consider what she's asking me to do. She wants me to tell all my secrets to someone like her. A man or a woman who supposedly won't judge me, yet they'll have the option to give me pills if they deem them fit.

Isn't that a part of judgment? Sighing to myself, I ask her, "Do you really think it's going to help me?"

I know what would help me, but he's not answering me. I have no way to see him, no way to make any of this better.

"I'm seeing someone," my sister says and leans forward, "after mom …" She leaves the word *dying* unspoken, leaning back in her seat. The leather groans as she continues, "And what happened with our father."

I can't bear the mention of our father. Staring past my sister's cream blouse, I focus on the textured wallpaper that lines her office. It's a simple damask pattern in a pale blue and cream colorway.

"Don't bring up Dad, please." Cadence's shoulders sag slightly, her brow raising in condolence. I didn't realize how much she loathed him until I saw her reaction to the news that our father was a serial killer.

Beyond a moment of surprise, she believed every word to be true without hesitation.

I still don't know what I believe.

He took the fall for all those murders. Some of those murders, though, really were his handiwork. Without a doubt, I know he must've killed them. I remember the names of some of those women. They news was peppered with them when I was younger. A series of young girls going missing, each time happening closer to home, and a public outcry for their bodies to be found.

I remember the way my mother stared at the television, demanding my sister and I never stay out late and always check in even though we were so much younger than the victims. There's no way she knew my father committed those murders. At least not then, but somehow, I think she found out. Or maybe she only suspected.

I wish she were alive so I could ask her. I wish I knew what she was thinking and why she stayed with him if she thought he'd killed them.

"You know he did it, don't you?" My sister's question brings me back to the here and now, and the faint memories of childhood vanish. "Did you read the articles?"

"I read them," I lie.

"The parts about you aren't true."

"I know," I say to go along with her although I imagine some parts are true; not in black and white, but they're true in the gray areas. Maybe because I know the truth and I'm holding it in. Therefore, whatever comes out is most certainly a lie.

"There's no evidence that you were involved. They can't pin a thing on you. It's all—"

"Circumstantial," I say, finishing the sentence for her. "I know," I repeat, my voice quieter and the fight in her eyes draining.

"It's not okay that anyone thinks you were a part of any of this."

The steady ticking of the clock passes between us before my sister starts up again, saying, "You're not okay."

"I know."

"What if …" she starts with a hint of optimism and leaves her place in the wingback chair across from me to round her desk. The drawer opens and closes quickly enough, and she presents me with a pale blue journal.

"What if you put whatever you're feeling in this?"

"You therapists and your journals." It has the softest leather cover, but it feels like betrayal in my palms.

"I'll feel better if you'll tell me you'll at least try," she says, attempting a compromise. Her tone is telling, as if she's certain this is the solution. "If things get bad or start to slip even the slightest … will you come talk to me?"

"So you can be my shrink?" My response is both dismissive and playful. "I thought you got a promotion and you won't have time for patients?"

Her smile makes me smile. It's humble and small, but I know this is a big deal for Cadence. "The Rockford Center won't be open for another month. So I can't start my position there just yet, but it'll be nice to be in a brand-new facility and with patients who …"

She trails off and the smile fades. My sister is a hero in so many ways. In ways I could never be. Christopher's face flashes before my eyes and I nearly lose it on the spot. It takes everything in me to hide the swell of emotions.

"Well, you know." She sucks in a breath and relaxes her posture then asks, "What's going on with you and Cody? Have you talked to him at least?"

I struggle to answer her honestly, so I deflect, although I'm sure she's well aware that's what I'm doing. "I don't have time to think about my sex life right now, not with the board meeting coming up." Another lie. So many damn lies.

The truth about Cody is that it all makes me feel like I've lost my mind.

Love and hate are both insane.

If they were products of a sane mind, the two emotions would be logical and controllable. God knows they aren't.

chapter sixteen

Marcus

I'VE WRITTEN SO MANY NOTES WITH DEEP STROKES THAT left the paper embossed with names. Too many to know for certain, but at least thousands of letters and hundreds of names. This one is so very different from all the others.

At the top of the page, the blue ink barely touched the notepad. Featherlight script trails down the page, each letter carefully placed. It's not a warning or a message, but a question that I'm not sure she'll answer.

Maybe I'm selfish, but I had to ask her, even if I don't know how she'll respond to it.

Even worse, I'm not sure how to sign it. I don't know which name should appear at the bottom. Which man she'd be willing to meet one last time at the barn where all this began.

Christopher or Marcus. The pen hangs in the air just like the question, and it feels as if my life hovers with them.

It started at the old barn that served as my refuge and then became the hell that raised me … and it should end there. I'm willing to close this chapter, I'm willing to never write another name down for as long as I live, so long as she'll listen to me. So long as she believes me. I've never wanted anyone to see me and to know my story, the way I crave for her to know every detail. Swallowing thickly, I sign the note and drag air into my lungs. Listening to the crackle of wood splintering and smoldering in the fireplace, I turn to watch the embers burn bright.

This place holds secrets in every corner, moments where I devised plans and sought evidence of justice in the keepsakes I've taken. Although I've parted with a number of them now, all in efforts to put blame elsewhere.

Whether or not Delilah meets me, I'll leave this place and never return. Walsh will wander here, I know he will. He's come many a time in search of me. He's the only one I've met here. He must know it means something to me. After all, I brought the love of our lives here, I mended her here and lay beside her without worry. He will come back. He'll find the note I left for him. Riggins is expecting his call if ever my brother needs anything. I'll leave it all to him.

The knowledge that this address was once the home of a family I sought justice for has escaped him for years. I had to buy it and live here just so I could sleep after I slaughtered the men who took their daughter and ripped their family apart. After ending their lives, I stole every penny they had and took on their wealth and names for years. Even the deed to this place bears the name of a man who's long dead but according to records, resides elsewhere and the place is thought to be empty, waiting for him when he returns.

I imagine one day I'll forget this address, but I'll always remember her name. For so long, it's the names of the victims that I used to justify what I'd done. I murdered, I stole, I manipulated situations to wreak havoc and send bad men to war against one another. And all of it was justified if I could name their victims.

It's her name, Delilah Jones, that prompts me leaving this place forever.

I simply can't go back. Not after what's happened.

The only other thing I regret is bringing my brother into this. He could have had a different life; instead I led him into the nightmare with me. Delilah and Cody will forever be the names that counter the one I took, Marcus.

I can't do this any longer, but I don't know how my brother will recover. I don't know where any of us will go from here. Which is why I have to meet her one more time.

Crossing out the name at the bottom of the note, I write another there instead.

Maybe she'll realize I'm trying. If that doesn't prove to her that I am willing to do anything to keep her close, I don't know what will.

chapter seventeen

Delilah

All I can think as his silhouette comes into view, is whether I'll have the strength to call him Christopher and what he'll do if that name slips from my lips.

He isn't the man in a dark alley they call the grim reaper. He isn't a supervillain with inhuman strength. He's not a demon or the devil. He's a man who was hurt, cut deep and never able to heal. So he bled all over the world, letting all those who he felt wronged him drown in it.

Christopher is a broken man and that scares me, because I don't know how he'll ever heal, but my inner voice screams to help him. Because I irrevocably love him.

"I haven't been able to sleep," I say, ignoring the heavy thoughts when I've made my way to the large oak tree just beyond the barn. The field is barren and recently harvested. In the distance, a sliver of silver stains the background, snow that's yet to melt from the storm this past week. It's cold and lonely and in the dead of winter, there's not a soul out here on the edge of this Podunk town.

The bitter bite in the air has turned the tip of Christopher's charming nose and his high cheekbones a shade of pale pink. Even his chiseled jaw holds a hue of rose. With a black wool coat and dark blue jeans, a hint of stubble on his face and freshly cut hair, he could pretend to be a CEO or businessman and I'd fall for it. Those baby blue eyes of his could fool the best of the world into believing whatever he said.

"You look beautiful, though," he murmurs and eats up the small distance between us with quick strides. I swear I feel warmer just looking at him, even if he is feet away. "Even if you are tired," he adds and then swallows thickly. The nervous energy pricking between us is almost palpable.

I nearly call him by name, telling him I can't do this. Instead I rip my gaze from his, ignoring the stampeding in my chest to search along the tree line for anyone who could be watching. In this position out in the open, we're exposed. Anyone and every-one could see us, if only they knew where to look or bothered to be here. But we're all alone and why would anyone bother to look for us?

I'm of no consequence and my father will forever carry the moniker of serial killer for crimes I know Christopher has committed.

With that thought in my mind, I focus on the building be-hind Christopher. The run-down barn my father bought years ago is decrepit and in disarray. He didn't keep up with it in the de-cades since I've left home, that much is obvious.

I tell myself the only reason I came is to forgive Christopher for pinning all those murders on my father. To acknowledge that he saved me and to thank him ... To kiss him one more time. To end a business deal of sorts that we made in a cheap hotel room weeks ago when he told me I would beg for him. He wasn't wrong, but there's no need for such a deal to exist anymore.

The very thought makes my heart ache with longing. Maybe

I should confess to him that I don't know what I'll become, but a part of me longs to be with him. That a small voice whispers wherever he would take me, I'd feel at home. Whatever I'd be beside him, I'd feel is right.

He clears his throat and my attention is brought back to him. To his handsome face and the obvious tension between us. It blisters as if we're surrounded by fire, when in reality it's the chill of winter that batters us.

"I don't know how to start," he admits and takes a heavy inhale.

Shoving my hands into my pockets, I clear my throat too and stare down at my feet. I've worn my best pair of heels even though I knew we were meeting at the old farm by my family house. I'd be lying to myself if I said the dress beneath my double-breasted trench coat wasn't picked out just for him, along with the lacy lingerie.

I even chose the dark red shade because I know the color complements and suits my caramel skin. I wear it on every first date, and yet I chose to wear it this evening. As the sun sets, leaving us little light, and the cold surrounds us, daring me to expose the deep-V of my bra. As if I would.

Embarrassment rises inside of me. "Whatever you have to say," I tell him, "just say it."

There's a pain that flashes across his face, and I have to admit, I feel it deep in the marrow of my bones as well.

It must mean something, I tell myself, when you can't stand to say that final goodbye. He takes another step forward, and before I can deny him or even think twice, he leans forward, closing his eyes and I close mine too, my entire being relaxing from the gentle kiss. My coat rustles as I reach out to him, letting the cold hit my hands as I splay them against his chest, wishing we were anywhere else.

The kiss surprises me, as does my reaction to it. These last few nights I've dreamed of him, but it's only this side I can accept. The other things … what he's done and why he's done them, they still scare me. They terrify me. The version of him now, lures me to sleep. The other half of him is what wakes me in the middle of the night with violent screams chasing my breath.

"This is for you." Christopher's words are whispered, his lips pressing against mine just slightly until he pulls back, making me lean forward and subconsciously I rise onto my tiptoes, needing more and unable to break the kiss.

He does end it, though, leaving me longing and my heart pounding in my chest. A fear slips into my blood, raging as my pulse quickens. There's something here between us, some sense of pain that threatens to drown me if ever I didn't have this man.

Before I can bear to speak the thought in my mind, that this moment isn't a goodbye, that the kiss he just placed on my lips wasn't the last we'll share, Christopher pulls out a small box.

It's simple by design and plastic. He doesn't hesitate to pull back the lid and apart from a silver hinge, the only thing in the box is a small red button.

"What is it?"

"It breaks me every time I come here and I didn't know why … I didn't know why I couldn't stand to be here and how I questioned everything when I thought about this barn."

"This barn?" A deep crease settles between my brow as my mind races for an explanation as if I should already know what Christopher means.

"I learned from your father. I came here, lived here and I watched everything he did." The confession wreaks havoc on my consciousness, on the memories I have of my father. No. I'm quick to deny it all. He's lying.

"Christopher," I say and his name is a warning, one that pulls me from the shock of his confession. "I know my father … he … I don't know what he did but …" My head shakes on its own, the small child inside of me screaming that whatever the man in front of me is about to say, it's not true.

It doesn't take more than a second to pass, before I know that it is true, though. He wouldn't lie to me. Christopher wouldn't fill my head with a tale that could destroy me. Not if he could help it.

He's silent and it's then I notice the small box trembles in his hand. Tears gloss over and the vision of him, the man in the shadows, the man who's done so much wrong in this world, it blurs.

"I want to share it with you," he whispers. Swiping quickly under my eyes, I pull myself together, standing straighter and steadying my breath. "I have to. I have to tell someone." His swallow is audible and there's a vulnerability in his eyes, one that shines in his sharp blue eyes, begging not to be denied.

"I'm here," I answer him in a ragged whisper, still coping with my own truth and realizations, straightening my shoulders and praying that if nothing else, a confession will heal a small piece of him. I'm desperate for that mending to take place. More than my own sanity, I crave for him to be well.

"It's going to take more than one conversation, I'm afraid," he tells me, leaving the question hanging there and before I can ask it, he gives it life. "I need time and I want it with you. I need to," he pauses and stares past me, and then glances over his shoulder at the barn. "I need to acknowledge what happened."

"What happened?" I dare to ask him and instead of answering, he brings the plastic box up higher and asks me, "Will you destroy it? Would you destroy the barn because I wanted it to end?"

My eyes widen with the question and I take a half step back. "It's a bomb?" I breathe out at the realization, letting him hear my fear.

"It's an ending," he offers me, his voice strained. "Would you let it end if it meant that tomorrow I would seek you out? Every day after, I would go where you went and tell you every secret and every confession. I would give you everything if you would let me. But would you end this piece so I never had to see it again? So I could let it rest?"

There's nothing but agony in his question, a strength that's undeniable, but it's crippled by pain. "Please," he adds, "would you do it for me?"

The need to put an end to his pain is greater than any fear. I didn't recognize it as a truth until my hand reached out, my fingers covering the back of his hand and my thumb pressing on the button without a word spoken. There's a soft click as the button is pressed, my inhale nearly a gasp. As he steps forward, a hand wrapping around my back, I wish I could watch as the sight unfolded.

The bang of an explosion that rips a shocked, sharp breath from me. The base of the building giving out and the clatter of what nearly sounds like thunder surrounding us. It's a violent moment, destruction claiming the building and the warmth of fire felt far too soon as it engulfs the building.

But as it is, I can't pull my eyes away from his hungry gaze. As the building collapses and flames rage in the distance, only a few hundred feet away, I'm held captive by Christopher and the intense pull and spark between us.

He's the one to break it. To let the box fall to the ground as the burning rubble collapses in the distance. He's the one to grip my hips and pull me closer so he can crash his lips against mine. His touch is possessive and just as hot and smoldering as the fire.

I'm the one to take it further, though, slipping my hands through his coat and up his shirt, desperate for my skin to be against his. He follows suit, pulling my coat open and dropping his lips lower, trailing down my throat and along my collarbone.

"I need you," he groans against my skin and I've never been so thankful to hear those words.

It's a storm of chaos as he drops me to the ground. The desire is at odds with every move he makes. Hovering over me, caging me in, yet savoring our deepened kiss with the low groans of a satisfied man. Carefully lifting my coat, he only uncovers what he needs to gain access, slowly slipping my underwear down and all the while his gaze stays on mine, waiting for my reaction.

"Please," I beg him in a whisper, such a soft sound compared to the chaos just beyond us, but if feels as if I screamed the plea. It's the only sound that matters. Lowering his lips to the crook of my neck, he runs my arousal over my clit in steady circles before moving his fingers lower and teasing me.

Pleasure ripples through my body, forcing me to arch my back. The heat wars against the bitter cold in the air. As I moan my pleasure, Christopher silences me with a kiss. This one is different from all the others—gentle, caressing yet possessive. As he pulls away, I stare into his piercing gaze and then my lips part in a silent scream. He enters me in a swift stroke, completely and fully, his own lips parting and a deep rumble of lust leaving his throat.

It's painful, thrilling and gratifying all at once. The heat takes over every inch of me as he moves. His thrusts are forceful, but each time he kisses me, peppering them on my skin with a delicacy that doesn't match his motions, I need more. It's sweet, agonizing torture as he pushes the impending threat of my orgasm higher and higher.

We're both out of breath when he finds his release, my nails scratching down his back as I cry out his name.

Smoke billows steadily from the rubble of the barn, and the scent is carried along gusts of wind. The chill returns faster than I thought it would, but then again I've never been a few hundred yards from a raging fire of destruction.

"You meant it didn't you, when you said you'd come find me? That you'd stay with me?" I know he didn't say those exact words; *stay* was never spoken from his lips, but that's what I want from him. I don't want him to leave because I'm afraid he won't come back. Selfishly, I would sleep better if I knew he was beside me. I would sleep so deeply feeling him lay next to me.

"I think you need time to decide what you want."

"And if I want you to stay?"

"If you want me to stay, I'll stay."

"I want to leave this place. I want—"

"Give it time. You need to know so much more than you do. The only thing I ask is that you don't tell anyone who I am."

I almost tell him I'd never tell anyone he was Marcus, but he continues and what he says feels like a knife to the heart.

"I'm not ready to be Christopher. If you have to tell my name to someone, I'd rather be anyone else ... I'd rather be Cody. Please," he whispers, "don't tell them what really happened. I'd rather be Cody and if you could lie for me, I'll tell you everything, give you everything and be whoever you need me to be. I'm just not ready to be Christopher again."

My tears slip down my cheeks silently as I watch him staring at the flames subsiding in the distance. "Please promise me, Delilah. You can call me Christopher, but don't tell anyone. Please. I'd rather be anyone else to all of them."

I try to hide the pain in my voice as I whisper, "I promise" and wipe away the tears, as if they were never there.

chapter eighteen

Delilah

HOW MANY TIMES THIS WEEK WILL I UTTER THE WORDS "I love you," and yet it feels like I'm saying goodbye?

"Please tell me what happens," my sister urges me and my throat feels tight as I stand outside the mahogany wood doors with the phone pressed to my ear. The foreboding doors extend from floor to ceiling in the hall.

It's not these exact doors that I laid eyes on when I first experienced the awe of what was just behind them. The courtroom and the men who brought justice to those who desperately needed it. But they're all the same, aren't they? All these doors.

When I was a child, they intimidated me, as did the men who sat beside my father on the other side of them. Now, though, they're only doors I don't wish to ever step through again. They hold no meaning any longer.

"Did you hear me, Delilah?" My sister's voice brings me back to the present.

"Hmm?"

"Tell me what happens."

My answer is far too even, far too calm for the lie it is when I say, "Of course I will."

I could already tell her the outcome, though. I won't fight it. The accusations aren't true, but I won't fight them. With what little I have left, there's not an ounce of me that gives a damn to fight the charges brought against me.

Ending the call with an honest *I love you*, I pocket my phone and face the board that will address the charges and my standing in this courtroom.

Their voices drone on with their stern expression reflecting revulsion or concern as my gaze travels down each of the faces I recognize so well. Men and women I strived to earn a position beside.

It feels like that was a lifetime ago.

"Miss Jones, you realize that we are discussing disbarment?"

"I do."

"Do you have anything at all that you'd like to say?"

"It was an honor," I say and my tone is respectable, but there's not a bit of fight in it. All that I was is no longer recognizable in the echoing chamber of this room. "It was an honor to prosecute alongside you all."

"Do you not deny the unethical nature of your recent actions and the speculation of criminal activity?" The question comes out incredulously.

"You didn't do this." My friend, boss, and mentor's eyes are wide as she makes the statement. Her expression is one of complete shock.

"I urge you to reconsider—" Another member of the board who appears more confused than anything attempts to bring order to the room as murmurs erupt.

"It is her mental health," Claire pipes up again. She isn't wrong, but I'm not willing to go back to the reality I once held so close to my heart.

Malden rebuts Claire's assertion, saying, "There is no evidence to support that and you do not speak on her behalf."

"Delilah, say something," Claire's command is more of a plea. Her ever-imposing features are distraught. "You did not do what you are being accused of," she speaks clearly and her tone is far more stable than it was a moment ago, but the crease in her brow and sorrow in her eyes tell me she's anything other than balanced. She's on edge. They all are.

The five of them stare back at me from where they sit and I feel nothing. I represented them and this court. I failed them. If nothing else, I can admit to that.

The tension in the room is all for them. I feel nothing.

"I am content with the board's decision that I am not fit to practice law." I practiced that statement this morning. I practiced speaking it calmly and clearly. It is my decision and it is best that I never hold any power of convincing others what is right and what is wrong again. "I am not fit for it."

"For the moment—" Claire emphasizes with a pleading tone as she stands to her feet. The words aren't meant for me. Her palms are on the large conference table as she leans over. "She cannot be held to the standards of the court when her mental state is in question."

"Without any evidence from Miss Jones to support your statement that she isn't mentally well, or any—"

"We have not even done an investigation!" Claire's voice rises and all four men stare down the table at her. She's losing it, her emotions getting the best of her. I wish she wouldn't fight for me.

There's a moment of deadened silence. It seems to dawn on her that it's four against one. There's a part of me that feels guilty, but if she knew the truth, she wouldn't take my side in this. She'd join those four men and take their judgment in stride.

"The charges brought against her are severe and there does not appear to be any defense other than your claims that she is not well, Miss Eastings." The argument progresses. Four against one until Claire heaves in a steadying breath and adjusts her blouse before taking her seat once again. She's worn the look of defeat many times, but never did it age her like it does now.

I wish I could tell her I was sorry. If I could lie in this moment, I'd thank her and apologize for not fighting by her side as she speaks up for me. The reverence and compassion are still met with gratitude just the same, but I cannot lie. I'm not sorry to allow this to happen. I'm not sorry to be silent now and accept their judgment. I never want to cross beyond doors like ones behind me after I leave today. Never again.

Her passion should be saved for someone else. Someone who needs a voice to fight for them. Someone who's gone through hell and once they've reached the end of it, they remain surrounded by a fire that holds them hostage until someone stronger can put it out.

Those people exist. The devil staying by their side to torment them with the memories of what injustice has been done to them. They surround us every day, hiding their pain and carrying on as if they're like us, but they aren't. The pain consumes them and they're the ones she should save her passion for. Not me.

I knew what I was doing, and I walked into that purgatory after a flame that singed my mind. The devil still walks beside me, but I choose him for comfort.

"The complicit nature of your actions regarding your father's death and potential crimes surrounding it and many others that have been recently opened with new information previously held in, not only your father's possession, but openly in your family home ..."

There are over fifty cases that he refers to. Fifty names that are now etched in stone lying in quiet graveyards.

This bar cannot be tainted with someone who worked so closely with so much injustice.

"This information that's been brought to our attention and the formal complaint brought against you … it's," he says, then with an audible exhale, Malden finishes, "it's alarming to say the least."

"What you do today could affect your ability to defend your-self in these cases, Delilah," Claire pleads with me once more, her eyes glossy and the corners of her thinning lips turned down.

"I didn't—" I nearly defend myself, I nearly explain to her simply because she's more than a boss and a friend, she's someone who will need answers. It's who she is; I should know because it's who I used to be.

My shoulders rise as my lungs fill with a steadying breath. "I make no statement. I will not participate in the investigation and I have no desire to refute any complaints that have been brought forward."

"Miss Jones, you have to know," David Perry speaks. He's an-other lawyer, older, the same age my father would be.

"I accept whatever decision the board makes."

"She is not well," Claire says once again, although she doesn't rise from her seat and her fingers lace together in front of her.

All I can think, as the discussion continues without my voice being needed, is that I loved this. I loved all of this for so long. It's yet another love that has turned to goodbye.

With their voices muted and my vision blurring, the crack of wood split with the hiss of a fire envelops me. The flames rage in the back of my mind, wild and untamed. A piece of my sanity whispers, it's unethical as well. My passion is buried with the soot of what happened in the last months. My fervor is no longer log-ical, it is not black and white and line by line of precedence and rules. The burning need for justice is still there, not even buried beneath the surface, I feel it still and I doubt that will ever change.

Regardless of what these men and woman say today or tomorrow, I am not fit any longer, but not for any reason they could possibly imagine.

Maybe if they knew our story, all of it from every one of us, they'd realize I should have never been in a courtroom. I wasn't meant for a life of what is right and wrong. My life was meant for one moment, one travesty that created a ripple of transgressions.

chapter nineteen

Cody

I
T'S NOT THE WORST THING IN THE WORLD, I THINK TO myself.

As if resigning is what's on my mind. As if that's what has me staring forward at a battered dartboard across the bar. The lively room is at odds with every emotion that's dim and muted inside of me. This constant loss that seems to only hollow out more and more of me as the days wear on.

I have nothing left. That's all I can think. Every piece of my world crumbled so quickly and without any chance at all of me stopping the wreckage. It was foolish for me to think I had any control at all or that I could keep up with the lies and sins.

With every tick of the clock, I accept my role and how I set the pieces into motion. I let each cog of the wheel turn, only watching as the time passed and the inevitable occurred.

There's a rousing cheer from my left, a group of men happily clinking their bottles together in celebration of whatever just played on the televisions that line that wall.

At one point, I would pretend to share their sentiment, for no other reason than to blend in so I could continue to hide my secrets in plain sight.

Now, though, I seem to prefer fading. It feels … justified to say the least.

Ghosts of a glass filled with white wine and an easy laugh sit at the end of the bar where I first laid eyes on Delilah. I knew then the person I was and still, I tainted her. I remember how she twirled a curl of her hair between her fingers that night years ago. I remember how she glanced at me. I remember thinking I could never give in. And yet … I did. Now all I have left are memories that never should have been.

Even as another patron takes the seat next to mine, a beer in both hands, one for him and one for the woman beside him, all I think about is her.

The scent of white wine and florals that drifted from her when we sat across from one another at a high-top table like this. The night she first kissed me will haunt me forever.

For what it did to her and the series of events that followed, I can't bring myself to feel anything but a deluge of regret.

"There you are." Delilah's voice is amiable, which doesn't fit right on her. Even the grace of a gentle smile in greeting only adds to the loneliness.

With her small hand raised, the bartender recognizes her and brings over a glass. All the while we wait in silence and I drink her in.

"How are you?" I ask the simple question and I never realized how much it means to me. To go days without knowing and suffering in each moment that I question it, it truly carries the weight of the world in three small words that are so commonly spoken without regard.

"I'm not okay," she admits, a sadness seemingly lifting up the corners of her lips before she takes a sip of the sweet wine. Her dark red lipstick leaves an imprint on the clear glass.

"Is there anything I can do?" I ask, wishing I could go back and fix it all. But just like shards of a broken mirror, it'll never be the same again even if I could mend all the pieces and make it seemingly whole once more.

She only shakes her head slightly and then her amber eyes meet mine. "How are you?"

"I've been better," I answer although I hold so much back. How is it that even after all of this, I still can't give her the honesty that begs to be spoken?

"I'm sorry," she whispers and retreats to her wine, admitting, "I wish I knew how to make it better, but I don't."

"You're with him?" I have to ask. I have to know for sure. Seeing him in bed with her ... I can't wrap my mind around it. How I could love someone so deeply, yet hold back because someone else needs her love more. It's as if I'm wrapped in barbed wire and I don't know how it happened or how to escape, but either way, I simply stay as still as I can so the razors don't cut any deeper.

"I was," she answers and both of us watch her thin fingers glide down the stem of the glass. "I was with him yesterday," she tells me.

"You love him?"

With her hair pulled away from her face, styled in a high bun and her sheer black blouse hanging delicately off her shoulders, she can't hide her expression. It's one that clearly displays sorrow. Not for herself; the melancholy is saved for me.

"I do," she answers simply and then takes in an uneasy breath, pushing her half glass of wine away from her. "I didn't mean for any of this—"

"I know," I say, cutting her off and turning my body to face the bar so I can stare straight ahead at the worn wooden dartboard once again. "I didn't mean for it to happen either."

Even as I feel her slipping away, I haven't a clue what to say to her. Everything that comes to mind would only make things worse, it would only tangle the wire that much tighter around my throat. I have to say something, though.

"You know, even if I'm not with you, even if you never kiss me again, I'll still love you." The feeling of loss coats my confession. "You know that, don't you?"

"Funny." She manages a sad smile that doesn't reach her eyes. "I was about to say the same to you, but it sounded too much like goodbye."

"I never did like goodbyes," I comment if for no other reason than to end it, but she doesn't let it go.

"You'll let me go? You'll be all right if I'm with him? You won't hate me?"

"I promise. I'll be all right. I'll let you go." With a nod, she accepts my answer and the air is different between us.

"Another drink?" I ask even though hers isn't gone yet.

She only nods, her eyes turning glossy. "Another drink."

chapter twenty

Delilah

A HOT SHOWER CAN WASH AWAY A WORLD OF HURT. Something about the cleansing heat lies to the mind and whispers that it's all gone, it's all going to be all right and that the filth and dirt that wish to linger won't come back tomorrow.

Even with my eyes wide open staring at the tile in my shower, I listen to the promises and let myself believe it's all behind us now.

Taking my time, I dry myself without a hurry to do a damn thing. I let my lush curls create a halo around my face and accept myself for all that I've become.

When I step out of the bathroom and the red dials of the clock blink in the telling fashion that the power's been tripped, I feel the pull of a soft smile.

I don't think of my gun; there isn't an ounce of fear that runs through me. Instead there's a warmth of knowing. Maybe it's because I feel his presence already. The air is different—easier, calmer and more peaceful. As if he alone is my fate and what makes it all make sense.

There is no thinking, no torture, no pain. Only him and I.

"Have you thought about it?" he asks me and I hum an answer as I open the top drawer in search of something to wear. With the towel still wrapped around me, I settle on a simple black satin camisole and matching boy shorts.

"Have I thought about what?" I question back without even seeing Christopher yet. The towel drops around my feet in a heap with a soft thud and when I look up Christopher's waiting for me, stalking toward me.

He takes his time to place a palm on the dresser on either side of me, essentially caging me in. "You know what," he answers and places a small kiss on my bare shoulder before pushing off and taking his place on the end of the bed.

One thing I've noticed in the past few days is how he doesn't stay still for long until I lie down with him. Then it's as if we could remain together forever.

"I was thinking of something," he says, letting the previous conversation go for a moment. As I slip on the cami, I keep my eyes on him.

"What's that?"

Falling back onto the bed, he watches the fan spin above it as he tells me, "I remembered this plate. You know the switch plates for light switches in children's rooms?"

"The wall plate?"

"Yeah," he answers and I still don't know where he's going with this.

"Yeah, I know them."

"I don't remember much about my parents, or my aunt really. But I remembered last night that I had a wall plate of this cartoon character in my bedroom when I was a kid, and I think it was at my aunt's house too."

"A wall plate … what made you think of that?"

"I was just wondering what my parents would think. And I remember they loved me. They loved me so much they screwed a cheap switch plate on the wall with some cartoon dog on it. I barely remember living with my aunt, but I think she took the switch plate and put it up too."

I'm careful with my words. I've never talked to Christopher about his family. With Cody I only ever spoke about his uncle and even those conversations were short. He's not well and the last Cody spoke of him, he'd forgotten who Cody was. "You've been thinking about your childhood?"

"I was wondering why … you know … why it happened and if there was any sign that I would be like this before I was taken."

"And?" I prod him for more after a long moment of quiet.

"And all I remember is how much I loved that stupid wall plate and that my mother was the last one to kiss me good night and turn off the light. I remember watching her do it."

"I don't think I had a wall plate that I remember, but I had wallpaper of pink polka dots, just a few inches off from the ceiling."

"Sounds like a nightmare," he comments and I let out a small huff of a laugh.

"Do you want to keep talking about it?" I ask him, reaching for my face cream, but hesitating to open it. I made a deal with myself. If he talks, I'll take it. If he doesn't, then I'll talk. I'll learn his secrets, and he'll learn mine.

"I want to know if you'll come with me? For a short while?"

"Where are you going?"

"Somewhere away from here. Away from what I'm used to. Some place that doesn't have memories hiding in every corner. Would that be all right? I … I can't stay here any longer. Not when everything looks so different but I can't be anything other than what I've been."

I'm not sure how my sister will feel if I leave again. Biting the inside of my cheek, I don't comment on that or acknowledge my thoughts of his brother.

Instead I reach for a small plastic bag on my dresser. "I bought something today," I tell him and that gets his attention.

"You want to open it or should I just show you?" I ask him and he stands slowly, taking his time as his eyes narrow suspiciously.

"Show me," he commands and makes his way back to me. The bit of curiosity that adds to his charm vanishes when I pull the cuffs from the bag. They're simple metal, just like the ones he has.

The tension thickens, and his swallow is audible. "For you or for me?" It's a serious question and I knew his reaction might not be one of an eager man.

"For me. For you to cuff me to the bed and for me to—"

"I don't need that, Delilah."

"I do, though," I stress. "I can admit it and I need you to know that." Any indication that he'll refuse leaves us. "I need this and I need you to do it." I've dreamed about being cuffed underneath him, I've felt that fear and then a mix of desire. "I mean it. I want this."

"You want me to cuff you to the bed?" he questions with his chest pressed against my shoulders. He destroys the distance between us until my bare back all the way down to the swell of my ass is pressed against him. "And then what?" he asks, fully giving in to my wish.

"Whatever you want," I whisper, meeting his sharp heated gaze in the mirror of my dresser. His head falls forward, his lips brushing against the shell of my ear. As he plants a soft kiss there, I add, "You can do what you want to me."

He groans in the crook of my neck and the vibrations travel from his warm breath there all the way down to the most forbidden places.

"I accept your gift of cuffs then," he says, lifting his gaze to meet mine in the mirror and we share a devilish simper between us. I can get lost in him and he can get lost in me. Together we'll heal each other. That's the only hope I'm holding on to. Everything else can fade away and burn for all I care.

Well, almost everything else. We still have our family.

"Have you thought about my question?"

"If I'm willing to go with you?"

"If you don't come with me, I don't know that I can leave. I don't know what will happen to you. I wouldn't be able to live with myself not knowing."

"How long will we be gone?"

"Not long. We'll keep your place; we'll visit. I never could go long without seeing my brother."

"Do you think he'll stay?" I ask him in all seriousness.

"I don't know, I haven't heard from him."

"You reached out?"

"I did. I apologized." The ever-present knife in my chest twists at the knowledge that Cody didn't respond to Christopher. One day I hope the two of them will be all right. One day they'll work together and be side by side.

"I'm sorry."

He kisses my cheek quickly and then stands up straight behind me, his fingers trailing down my arm ever so gently. "It's not your fault," he tells me but that doesn't mean I can't be sorry.

I know his secrets. I know his pain. Even if I've never felt it like he has on his skin, I feel it in my soul. It's etched in the crevices of my bones.

He doesn't have to whisper them. They're written in his piercing eyes, the shards of light blue reflecting the agony of years of pain.

"I see you for who you are. And I love you. You love me?"

"Of course I do. I've always loved you."

chapter twenty-one

Delilah

Ten months later

HIS GAZE IS SHARP; HE HAS THE MOST PIERCING BLUE eyes I've ever seen. As I freeze where I'm standing in the middle of the aisle, the faint noise of dull music mixed with the sound of carts rolling by fades into the background. It all blurs together in aisle four of the grocery store as my grip on the loaf of bread I'm holding turns so clammy that the plastic slips.

The pitter-patter of my racing heart and my blood rushing in my ears is all I can hear.

Nothing else matters. I can feel his eyes on me. Every time I blink, I see them, surrounded by shadows.

I take my time, placing the items from my cart back on the shelves with trembling fingers. There are only four things seeing as how I just got here, a bag of rice being the first item to go back on the bottom shelf before I slowly and meticulously roll my cart to the end of the only aisle I've been down.

It's chilling, the fear that rolls down my spine knowing he's watching me. Feeling him again. *Is it fear, though?* My heart beats wildly in response to the question, fighting and railing against the decision to act calm. I can't let anyone know. I just need to get out of here … So we can be alone.

My heart isn't afraid, not like my logical side is. When the shadow is just barely seen, tall and foreboding, my stomach drops and my heart flips with recognition. It's an undeniable feeling when you miss someone you know you shouldn't. I try to focus on the sound of wheels squeaking against the linoleum floor and the noisy clang of metal from carts being lined up in order to help ground me.

"Do you need any help?" The question comes from a young man in a red vest that barely hides the nondescript black logo on his white shirt beneath it. I recognize him; I've seen him a number of times in this grocery store. I'm certain he's rung me up a handful of times since I returned here a month ago.

How did I think I could move back, even if the house is on the outskirts in the middle of nowhere, and *he* wouldn't find me? How could I be so foolish to think he wouldn't come for me?

A sinking feeling in my chest moves my hand there, and the paper list in my hand crinkles as I do. I'd forgotten all about it and as I gaze down at the blurred pen lines and wrinkled paper, I do my best to school my expression.

"Oh, no," I say and my throat is too tight as I speak. I close my eyes, forcing a simple smile to my lips and clear my throat. "I just realized something," I answer, finally looking the young man in his deep brown eyes. "I have a call in ten minutes and I'm going to take it in my car then come back," I lie, that smile staying in place although everything in my body wants me to run. Run from here, get far away from other people.

The young man, who looks like he's college age or maybe younger, offers me a friendly smile in return. "Understood," he says with a nod and returns to lining up stacks of carts with the one I've just brought back up front.

Even now, as I take each deliberate step through the glass double doors that slide open automatically as I approach and feel the cool breeze of early spring against my heated face, I try to rid myself of the memories that flash before my eyes.

The bar. The drinks. The feel of a chilled glass of white wine mixed with the scent of whiskey from the man next to me. The court cases and late nights spent getting lost in bed with a man I knew I shouldn't be with. The flirtation, rules being broken.

My heels click as I remember losing my law license, as every dreadful moment returns with the stain of blood. So much blood. Acts of passion that couldn't be taken back. The pain that's already present mingles with so much more.

Wrapping my arms around myself, I attempt to protect my body from the wind but it's useless. The weather isn't what batters me.

The remembrance of his lips on mine and the searing heat of his light touch, force a gasp from me. It's a short one full of longing, knowing those moments are now nothing more than lost ghosts of the person I was. Of the people we were before it all went to hell.

All of the memories are a cocktail that infuses into my conscious thoughts as I listen to my keys clink while I unlock the door to my sedan with a low beep that fills the practically vacant lot. From the time I entered the grocery store to now, a mere fifteen minutes at that, the sun has decided to set, casting a shade of red across the dark tree line of thick forest beyond the store parking lot and stealing the light that was here only a moment ago.

The leather seat groans and the door shuts with a loud thud. All I can do is sit here, my purse now on the console. My keys in my right hand, resting against my lap with the metal digging into my palm since I'm gripping them so tight. My breathing comes in faster and faster although I'm doing everything in my power to stay calm. *He'll be here soon.*

When I hear the click of the back door opening, the one behind my seat, I close my eyes. He didn't make me wait long.

He enters the car accompanied by a chill from the evening wind and the car rocks gently until he's seated behind me and the door is shut. His scent fills my lungs first and as it does, I remember that I've been told that smell is the sense that holds the most memory. Maybe I read it somewhere, but I've never known something to be truer than that fact is now.

When I open my eyes, his chilling gaze is on mine in the rearview mirror and my treacherous heart chokes me in an attempt to escape. It hovers at the base of my throat, pounding viciously in protest.

I did always love him. There wasn't a moment that I didn't love him.

He knows that. He has to know that I still love him; we just simply couldn't be together. We decided. We decided together.

"You said you'd let me go," I whisper, speaking over my strangled breaths.

My gaze never leaves his, even as tears prick my eyes. Not until he answers me.

"I changed my mind."

"You don't get to do that, Cody," I say and my cadence is melancholier than I'd hoped it would come out.

Life is unfair. It's uncertain and torturous. It takes and gives without remorse. I'm grateful for what I have with Christopher, but damn does it hurt to see Cody as he is. Left wanting and alone. He doesn't deserve that, but I can't give him what he deserves. Not when I love someone else the way I do.

If I can't give him my whole heart, he deserves to have someone else's.

I can easily give Christopher everything; it feels as if it's always been his to have. That is life and that is love. I accept it now, the simplicity yet the sheer magnitude of it. Because I only have one life and one love. What choice do I have, other than to give in to it?

"You haven't called," I say, daring to peek around my shoulder and look him in the eye. "I thought you might, but you haven't called once."

His jaw clenches once as he swallows thickly. "I didn't know what to say … I still don't. All I know is that I wanted to see you."

Shock runs through my body at the sound of the passenger door opening and Christopher climbing in. My body's paralyzed for a moment, although my heart races recklessly. Against the stillness of everything else, the vulnerable organ rages to be heard.

The leather seat groans as Christopher takes his seat beside me, and the chill of the wind is ended with the thud of the car door closing.

For a moment, there's only silence.

"Christo—"

"I've missed you," Christopher speaks before I can finish. With a pinch in my brow, I confuse his statement as being directed at me at first, but his gaze, a gaze that matches his brother's, is focused on the rearview mirror.

"You didn't call." His statement is more of an accusation compared to the manner in which I said it.

"You didn't call either," Cody responds with more nonchalance than I could have imagined. It's surreal being in one space with the both of them. I dream of it often. Of each of us well in all ways and able to be in one space together. Two brothers separated, both put through a different kind of hell. One more so than the other, far too early in life.

But don't they both deserve a happy ending? Wouldn't it be better for them to be together again? To lean on one another?

Easing back into my seat, I turn easily, my hand gripping the warm leather where the heater blows and I stare back at Cody to explain. "I thought you might need some space and time, so I didn't …" I can't finish the thought. Tears prick my eyes and my voice is tight as I practically beg him, "You could always come with us." It's both an offer of peace and an offer for happiness.

"It's not—"

"And watch you and him?" Cody's voice cracks, and his gaze shifts from me to his brother. "Watch you love her like I should have?"

Christopher is silent as the tension thickens in the small space.

"Cody," I say and my voice is pleading. "You know it could never work between us. Not after everything."

Hanging his head slightly, Cody's strong grip finds his chin as his gaze finds the back of my car seat.

"I didn't think it would end like this." Christopher's voice is low and apologetic. "When I," he pauses to clear his throat and the man I know to be weak in ways most won't admit, confesses something out loud that he's only whispered to me late at night when he thinks I'm sleeping. "When I put you two together, I thought you would take care of her. Look after her. I thought you needed each other."

"You didn't think I'd fall for her?" The allegation is clear in Cody's voice and Christopher's response doesn't come with hesitation.

"I didn't think about love at all." The declaration comes with distaste and then his voice lowers when he adds, "I knew nothing of it."

It's quiet again for a long moment, a moment in which I can barely breathe as I look between the two broken men. One with fresh wounds still bleeding, and the other with deep scars that will never fully go away.

"I missed you too … both of you." Cody reaches for the handle of the car the moment the last word is spoken.

"Wait," Christopher yells out, far too loud in the cabin of the car, but it keeps Cody from leaving, although he's already pulled the handle and the hiss of the wind can be heard. "You should call. Soon. If you need me, you should call or write."

Cody nods and I find my goodbye trapped at the back of my throat, tears pricking as the three words beg to be spoken. *I love you.*

I still love him, but it's not my love he needs.

"We'll speak soon," is all Cody says before leaving us alone in the car. All I can do is watch his back in the side mirror as he walks away.

I don't even realize I'm crying until Christopher brushes away the tears. It's then that I recognize the hot sensation and the taste of salt.

I lose myself to the sorrow of loss, even as Christopher holds me, as he shushes me, his arm rubbing against my hair. My strong, broken man attempts to rock me and I let him, until he whispers, "I will never keep you from anything. You can always leave. I know—"

"Don't you dare," I reprimand him, not an ounce of me calm and my breathing coming out erratically. "I would never, and you better never leave me either."

I would die a lonely death if ever he left my side. Whether my lungs still moved and my heart still beat, a piece of me would crumble to ash.

"As if I could ever leave you. Little mouse, you are my only obsession."

Grabbing his hand in mine, I pull it in close to my chest and rest my head beneath his chin. "I love you," I whisper against his chest, breathing in his masculine scent that lures me to bed every night and listening to the steady beat of his heart he once denied.

"I love you."

chapter
twenty-two

Marcus

Her fingers slip between mine, delicate and warm against the scars of my past and the roughness of callous acts that will stay with me forever.

"I already miss him," Delilah says to me. Her gaze stays fixed ahead with the admission, past the streetlights and vacant sidewalks of this Podunk town.

"You miss everyone," I say, offering her a truth. She hasn't seen her sister and stopped speaking to her altogether when Cadence begged her to go to therapy. I think one day she'll cave to it. I think it would help her more than anything and if my information serves me right, there may be information to gather at that Rockford Center that her sister works at. All in due time, though. Right now it's only the two of us and we can take as much time as we need.

Her long lashes flutter and her beautiful amber gaze meets mine for the first time since we drove out of that parking lot. "I know you mean that I miss my sister."

A short, low grunt vibrates up my throat in confirmation.

"She just doesn't understand." Her words hold both disappointment and heartache. "None of them do."

I nod in agreement. We've had this conversation more than once. It's not their fault that they don't understand. How could they?

"I wish you'd smile," I whisper to her, bringing her hand she placed in mine to my lips. With a single kiss of her knuckles, warmth floods my chest. She smiles. A beautiful smile that belongs there on her pouty lips. I'm not sure when the cracked pieces slipped into place seemingly effortlessly, but it's the smile I could have focused on. The bits of happy before the nightmare sets in.

I want it. Cravings for more of it tempt me every day.

"I'll smile when you smile, Christopher," she answers me, the simper still playing along kissable lips.

My name felt like a curse for so long, burdened by the weight of a past that sat on my shoulders, dictating my thoughts in dark whispers of remembrance. When she says it, though, with that pained voice, it echoes forgiveness and so much more than that.

It's like a second chance. If I can only live up to what lies between the two of us, everything else drowns itself in a haze of dark fog when she says my name.

"I love it when you smile too, you know?" Delilah adds, slowing down at a red light and leaning back in her seat. Her small hand rests against her cheek as she closes her eyes. I imagine she sees him there, my brother.

"He wasn't smiling," I comment beneath my breath and it's my turn to stare past the solid red light although no cars pass in front of us. The dread of knowing his pain overwhelms me. To love someone so desperately, but let her slip through fingers that cannot contain her.

"He'll smile again." Her confidence comes with a pat of her hand over mine. Squeezing my fingers, she adds, "I have faith."

I've wondered if I'd stolen this beautiful little mouse from him. If something about me tainted her. But then I remember everything. Every piece of this puzzle that built the picture of us. I don't feel guilty for taking her. I'm sorry I didn't claim her as my own long ago.

She was always meant for me. Nothing else resonates with my intuition. There is no rhyme or reason to life, nothing fate could ensure that makes logical sense as to how I else would end up in bed with Delilah every night. My thumb resting against her bottom lip before kissing her every night so she may sleep deeply and dream of sweeter things than I have to offer.

She was meant for me, and I was meant for her. Life isn't fair like that, but I happily accept its offer.

In return, she has all of me. I have a beautiful woman's forgiveness, her love and her life. I'll keep it safe, forevermore.

"I love you," I admit to her again. She says it far more than I do. "I love you more than anything." If it weren't the truth, I wouldn't be here with her. Starting over, spending a quiet life together with only us. She knows that.

Bad men always lose and I lost myself to her. It's a fair trade and one I'd make ten times over.

"And I love you the most," she tells me. I know that it's true. It might hurt her, maybe even both of us, but I need her and she loves me the most.

Cody
Weeks later …

It's far too quiet to keep the thoughts away. The memories come and go as easily as the breeze whipping across my face in the pitch-black night. There isn't a star in sight, nothing but the faint lights from

Jackson Street peeking through the thicket of pine trees lining the empty playground. The muted creak of the swings blowing in the wind is my only companion.

Unless I count the moments that flicker in my mind. Every single time I could have made a different choice. Every moment I questioned myself.

Every kiss from Delilah and even before that. Her accidental, delicate touches that sent blazes of heat through me when I first I met her. The stolen glances and tension I ignored for too long. Regret balances in front of me, dancing from the children's playthings as if it knew all along I'd end up here: alone and hating my silence.

If I could go back … The thought lingers but doesn't complete itself. I'm not sure where I'd go back to. Which moment I regret the most. Back to the very beginning I suppose, to the moment my brother and I were separated. Maybe to the night my parents left our home for the last time before the accident.

With a shaky breath, my lungs fill with a bitter chill that freezes every inch of me. The moment my eyes close, the faint click of incoming footsteps has every nerve ending on high alert. Someone's coming, judging by the feminine thud of heels against the lightly dusted sidewalk. The snow won't stick, but the moments will. Memories never leave us. They're what make us who we are.

With my head back, I take a deeper breath, waiting for whoever it is to walk on by and keep going. To ignore me and leave me to this misery I've created for myself.

But the heels stop directly in front of me as the hammer of a gun is cocked. The sound echoes loudly in my mind.

"You're Marcus," a woman's voice says, although it sounds like she isn't confident in that accusation. Slowly, my eyes open to see a pale blue trench coat hanging from a brunette's slim frame. Her eyes reflect the colors of the forest, a stunning hazel, but more than that, terror.

My leather coat rustles as I lean forward, ignoring the pistol pointed at my head only two feet from me.

I could easily throw her to the ground before that trigger would be pulled. I could disarm her. I could do anything at all but sit here in silence, waiting to see what she'll do.

When she clears her throat, the uncertainty comes in thicker. Her voice wavers as she repeats, "You're Marcus."

I simply stare back at her in silence. No one knows who Marcus is. Not a soul. I found the note Christopher left for me. I've exchanged a few messages with his contact Riggins. But as far as anyone knows, Marcus died and was buried with Herman, plus Delilah's father.

"I know you are," she adds, refuting my unspoken thoughts. "You're Marcus and I need your help." Swallowing thickly, her fear permeates the air around her and her hand holding the gun trembles.

"You need my help?" I question her, feeling a heat ignite in my blood, the chill I've felt in the days past slipping away.

"Yes. Please," she begs and then she shudders. "My name is Evalina Talvery." Her confession sends a prick down my neck. The wife to the head of one of the most violent crime families that's ever lived. I know all about the Talverys and their dealings. I know her husband and I've even heard of her daughter and the rumors about her. "I need help. You can help me," she whispers the last words and they're barely heard before being carried off in the chill of the night.

"Please. I know you're Marcus, I saw you," she says, accusing me yet again.

I could so easily help her in the way I've been trained by the FBI, taking her in and providing protection. But it only takes one look at this woman, hardened by what she's seen, and I'm certain she'd never have gone to Cody Walsh. No, no.

"Please. I have a daughter, Aria." Her bottom lip wavers,

but the glare in her eyes betrays the sadness she wishes to portray. "You have to help me. Please, help me. I can give you information."

Christopher said if I needed anything, he'd come back and help. He promised he would in that note he left. He can show me how it's done.

Leaning back, I stare at the end of the pistol and speak words maybe I knew one day I'd admit, "Yes, I am Marcus."

The This Love Hurts trilogy is, in timeline, the first trilogy set in the Merciless World. If you haven't read Aria Talvery's story, daughter of the most violent crime family in Fallbrook, start with **Merciless** today and fall madly in love with Carter Cross. There are many players in this world, and so much more to come.

There is more to this story and to others in the Merciless World. Up next is **Love the Way You Kiss Me**. Prepare to be wrecked in the best of ways by this intense and heated romance. Available for preorder now.

Declan Cross's series starts this fall. Preorder **Tease Me Once** now. For a look at the entire Merciless World, all sixteen novels so far, turn the page and enjoy binge-reading.

The Merciless World has consumed me, and I will continue to write in it for as long as the stories continue.

about the
author

Thank you so much for reading my romances. I'm just a stay at home mom and avid reader turned author and I couldn't be happier.

I hope you love my books as much as I do!

More by Willow Winters
www.willowwinterswrites.com/books